Call of Cthulhu® Fiction

THE SPIRALING WORM

Man Versus the Cthulhu Mythos

by
David Conyers & John Sunseri

Introduced by C.J. Henderson
Cover Art by David Lee Ingersoll
Layout ands cover design by Charlie Krank

A Chaosium Book
2007

D1528346

CHAOSIUM
INC.

ACKNOWLEDGMENTS

"Made of Meat" by David Conyers originally appeared in *Temple of Dagon* (2005) http://www.templeofdagon.com. This story has been revised and expanded in this edition.

"Impossible Object" by David Conyers originally appeared in *Dreaming in R'lyeh* Issue 2 (Night Platform Press, 2005).

"False Containment" by David Conyers originally appeared in *Horrors Beyond* (Elder Signs Press, 2005).

All other stories are original to this volume.

Special thanks to Tim Curran for his permission to make reference to Kharkhov Station and the events of from his novel *Hive* (Elder Signs Press, Inc. 2005).

This book is printed on 100% acid-free paper.

FIRST EDITION

10 9 8 7 6 5 4 3 2 1

Chaosium Publication 6040. Published in 2007.

ISBN 1-56882-212-X

Printed in Canada.

CONTENTS

"Man's best possession is a sympathetic wife."

—*Euripides*

This volume is gratefully dedicated to our beautiful, long-suffering wives
Suzanne and Elizabeth, for their understanding and their patience.
Without you, we are nothing.

INTRODUCTION

C.J. Henderson

You know, no one ever reads these things, not even the authors of the books in which they appear, so I'm thinking, what the hell, why not get something off my chest about these two guys. What's it going to hurt — right?

David Conyers and John Sunseri — these two; man, I'm telling you . . . where do I even start to explain how I feel about this pair? Now understand, I don't know exactly what made you buy this book. Maybe it was the fact you're a big H.P. Lovecraft fan, and have to have every mythosian book that comes along. No harm in that — after all, there's a lot of us around here in that boat. Maybe you've been seeing their names in this or that of the better anthologies a lot lately, or some of the finer horror magazines. Perhaps some relative who never knows what to buy for you saw the cover of this particular tome and said to themselves, "I don't know anything about this stuff, but that should be perfect for you know who." Possibly it was even just a whim purchase.

Who knows? What's important is that you bought it. You bought this book, and not one of mine. Who cares if you own everything I ever wrote. It's the principle of the thing. You could have bought one of my novels for someone else. But no — you had to throw your hard earned money at these rabid hounds. And why? I mean, what do you get when you read Sunseri and Conyers? Not some Lovecraft pastiche; that's for sure.

Oh yeah, the monsters are there. I'll give you that. Their work is stuffed full of critters, all shapes and sizes. And the mood, the weight of a dark and indifferent cosmos, well good lord, that just spills all over you. Get into one of their stories and you're fairly dripping in atmosphere from the first few paragraphs on. And, if you're not some idiot speed reader, just grabbing a couple of words a line and not really there for the feel of what you're reading, I mean, if you're someone who actually devours every single word — who wants the experience of each phrase to be like that of a good bourbon, something that needs to be taken in measured sips to really be appreciated — then you understand that these sons of bitches know how to throw out a mood that ensnares.

But let me tell you right now, they don't do it in the way Lovecraft did it. No, sir. Not at all. These guys, they have the nerve to think that humanity has broadened its consciousness since his day. Back when H.P.'s way of thinking was so revolutionary that he literally tore the doors off the horror genre, creating an entirely new brand of scares, one so deeply rooted in both science and psychology that it would render all the world's previous ideas of what terrified quaint and passé, well all right, it was okay to be bowled over by an ending where a guy threw up his hands and swooned, crying out;

"The horror, the horror."

But nowadays, as the real world has caught up to the ol' gent and his writings, having ushered in such modern innovations as serial killers and concentration camps, kiddie porn and nuclear bombs, even Lovecraft would step it up a notch. Don't forget, he knew human beings were adaptive. Remember, even he had Henry Armitage kick some mythosian ass after only a few stories. He knew damn well the next step was for humanity to expand its consciousness and to stand up for itself or die trying.

But, because of some of the Derlethian minds that followed him, the mythos now has a fine and long lasting tradition of standing still as if nothing has changed. You know as well as I do, when it comes to Lovecraft, the experts are in lock-step agreement, thou shalt not innovate. Even after such experimental horror enthusiasts as Hitler and Mao, Stalin, Amin, Pol Pot, and the such — amateurs but visionaries who slaughtered their own populations, murdering tens of millions — tried to show the world how to embrace the nothingness of existence were themselves beaten back for their efforts by those dull but well-meaning types who feel you can stand up to horrors beyond your comprehension, still the traditionalists steadied the rudder and calmed the waters, decreeing that all should stay the same.

And that's where I came in. Hell, as my fuzzy and highly prejudiced mind remembers it, I arrived on the scene and single-handedly made it fashionable for human types, ordinary mortals, to stand up to the terrors of the mythos. With nothing more than both contempt for my betters and Lovecraft's blessing from beyond the grave, I swept in like a cleansing northern wind and gave a chill notice that the old days were . . . well, the old days, I guess.

And what is my reward? Do they throw garlands, adorn my sweating brow with scented oils? Do they scatter roses and gold dust before my horse's feet? They do not. And yes, I don't have a horse, but that's not the point. The point is, all the world has done is send guys like Conyers and Sunseri after me to do just what I do, and to — gasp — yes, this is the hardest part of the insult for me to bear, to try and do it better.

What nerve. What gall. Did they ask permission? Did they contact my people? No. I mean, well, I have as many people as I do horses, but again, that's besides the point. These two upstarts just sit down and start knocking out these tremendous tales . . . it's upsetting, that's what it is. I mean, I have to labor like Sisyphus to come up with stories as good as these, and they just pluck them out of the air like a stage magician summoning up another rabbit. Some days, I'm telling you, it just doesn't pay to get out of bed.

But, it does pay off handsomely to read the work of both these fine gentlemen. All kidding aside, if you actually were foolish enough to start with my nonsense here, instead of diving right into the treasures that await you beyond, well I do thank you for the kindness, and to prove I mean it, I will start wrapping this up directly.

As if you needed me to tell you, Sunseri and Conyers are two of the best writers working in the mythos today, and most likely tomorrow as well. Their understanding of what it takes to bring this time honored body of work into the modern age of double-dealing governments, triple agents, terrorists, political ambition and all the rest of the mind-boiling horror we blithely call the evening news puts them ahead of dozens of what some might mistakenly call their 'colleagues'. Like Lovecraft, they bring the most modern theoretical science of the day to their work with the casualness of a Rubens' brushstroke. Also like the ol' gent, they do it their way, and could care bloody little for the thoughts of the rabble.

As one of the rabble's leading citizens, however, I'd just like to say that even as I stand here with pitchfork in hand, I'm thinking we have better castles to storm than theirs this blustery evening. In fact, I'm thinking if you were smart, you'd curl up with a good book.

You wouldn't happen to have one lying about — would you?

C.J. Henderson
New York City, 2006

MADE OF MEAT

David Conyers

I

"Y ou'll be there won't you . . . ready to save me?" The Cambodian officer's voice was distorted. Peel wondered if this was entirely to do with the poor transmission echoing through the short range radio. The British spy, James Figgs, casually leaned on the jeep next to Peel, his legs wet and filthy to the knees where his tropical boots had splashed the jungle mud. He just shrugged to say, *how the hell should I know?*

Peel spoke into the radio void, aware that anyone could be listening, but doing so anyway because no other choice presented itself. "We'll be there, Deka, at the rendezvous just as we said we would." That was as much as he would say. Peel was not going to risk reminding again the local officer where the rendezvous was, not over an open channel. He just had to assume the crazed man remembered. "You still there, Lieutenant? You read me?"

"Sure," the crackling voice spluttered, "but you've . . . saved me?"

"You did bring the package?" Figgs interrupted.

More crackle, interference which Peel was sure had nothing to do with the jungle canopy, or the bats soaring through the late afternoon skies, but the Cambodian Army's attempts at radio jamming.

"Yeah . . . got your . . . package."

"Good. Then we'll see you soon, Lieutenant."

Peel cut the connection. Just because they couldn't see the enemy didn't mean they were here alone. Both men knew that Cambodian soldiers were prowling the rainforest, searching for their traitorous officer. Peel's eavesdropping on the local military channels earlier this morning confirmed that the Cambodian army desperately wanted Deka back, preferably in one piece so he could be interrogated.

Whatever secret Deka carried, Peel had no doubt the Cambodians would kill to protect it. So there was no comfort in waiting, exposed in the foliage, knowing that even now they might be in the crosshairs of a sniper rifle.

All they could do was wait, to see who turned up.

Peel checked his 9mm Glock automatic. He'd cleaned and oiled it only last night, but re-examined it again because he expected to use it, knowing that gunfire was never pleasant. Damn his superiors back in Sydney, denying him permission to bring heavy armaments on such a delicate extraction. London had done the same to Figgs, although their agent seemed better informed than he was. At least that was Peel's assumption, based purely on the Englishman's casual attitude.

"You've never dealt with the Tcho-Tcho, have you Peel?"

"I read your report." Peel was about to say that he had been assigned to this region one year ago, to teach the Malaysians counter-terrorism strategies, and so knew the lay of the land as well as the Brit did, for Figgs' specialty was Southeast Asia. But that was long before Peel had heard of the Tcho-Tcho, a Montagnard hill tribe whose men filed their teeth, raped their own women and performed the most unusual and painful body mutilations ever witnessed, and all with smiles on their faces. "I know what to look for."

"Yeah, reading is one thing Peel, but you don't become a soldier by reading books, just as you don't get to know the Tcho-Tcho, not until you have to negotiate with the sick bastards face to face." He held up his gun to show how this was best achieved.

In his heart Peel knew the MI6 officer was right. During the Vietnam War the CIA had trained the Tcho-Tcho as mercenaries. For all their efforts and good intentions the Tcho-Tcho proved to be overly sadistic. They also practiced the worst of all social crimes, cannibalism, eating their own people and American soldiers as readily as they'd turn a knife and fork upon the enemy. No wonder the Americans ditched them as soon as this little-known quirk went public.

That was the past. In today's world where everyone feared terrorism, old allegiances were quickly abandoned and new ones formed. The Tcho-Tcho were back in favor again, especially now when they had something to sell to both Peel's and Figgs' respective governments; a weapon, a new development in biological warfare. Peel had felt sick in the stomach when he saw a photograph of the volunteer doctor in the report, and the thing growing on him. Deka said it was the milk of Shub-Niggurath, whatever that meant.

"You think it was a good idea, sending Deka in?" Peel asked to fill the silence. "He was a Cambodian, and the Tcho-Tcho . . . they were never going to trust him."

The other man shrugged. "Well, it's too late, and he's away from them now, so to worry at this juncture would be a waste of time. Relax, Peel. In an hour this will all be over and then you and I can go back to drinking beer in Singapore."

A noise.

Both men turned toward the dark trees, drawing their weapons. A chomping startled them, movement in the jungle, a man sprinting quickly, breaking the undergrowth, alerting all to his approach. They suspected Deka, but neither Peel nor Figgs would take any chances, and so hid behind the trunks of palms. A mile down the road there were rice fields and Buddhist temples, where normal Cambodians lived and worked their daily routines. Here in the thick tropical forests where everything was closed in and dark, Peel felt vulnerable. This was Tcho-Tcho territory.

Both men had been in the business of spying long enough to know when to hold their fire, so when Deka stepped out onto the muddy road, they quickly holstered their weapons.

Figgs scoffed, "You took your time . . ." then his voice flattened before halting altogether. His eyes had just seen something his mind had problems describing.

Peel saw it too. He'd read classified files on Deka, and had met the man once, three weeks ago at a bar in Singapore. Back then Deka had been laughing and joking about Australian backpacker girls and how friendly they were. Today he was so nervous he was almost white, and so he should be. It would be scary enough to be a defecting lieutenant fleeing the Cambodian Army, but he was also fleeing the murderous Tcho-Tcho. Deka's price for a new life in London was the secret of the Tcho-Tcho's new biological weaponry, that something the cannibals were growing in the hills. He'd been asked to bring a sample with him, but neither Figgs nor Peel had expected Deka to infect himself to smuggle it out.

"What is it?" Deka asked. Peel and Figgs were nothing but wide eyes and open mouths. "What are you looking at?"

Figgs pointed first, at the man's left arm. Peel wondered why Deka hadn't collapsed from shock, and why he wasn't fainting himself.

Lieutenant Deka had been carrying a plastic bag, the kind supplied by supermarkets the world over, presumably carrying a sample of whatever bio-weapon the Tcho-Tcho were cultivating. Black, ropy vines — they looked more like the tentacles of a squid — had grown out of the bag and wrapped themselves around

Deka's arm. Many of the tendrils had burrowed into his flesh. Around these wounds his skin had deformed into lumps the texture of porridge. Some of those lumps had broken open, infected sores from which more tentacles grew. They were seeking more of the human body to infest.

Presumably for the first time, Deka became aware of his infection and promptly screamed. This surprised neither Peel nor Figgs, although they became alarmed at the noise he was making. Peel felt sick, smelt the putrid scent oozing from the infections, fearful that the smell itself might be enough to affect him, even at this distance.

"You've got to save me!" Deka pleaded, holding his arm as far away from his body as possible, as if this would help him. "You promised that you would."

It was Figgs who found the nerve to answer. "Relax, Deka, that's what we said we'd do. Didn't we?"

"Get rid of it, get rid of it now!" He screamed, his cursing language switched to Cambodian slang which Peel could barely follow, a bellowed cry that would carry far, alerting their enemies.

"Relax man. We can't help you until you relax. Walk over to the jeep now." Figgs spoke quietly and calmly, surprising Peel that he could. "We've got an antidote around the back. That will fix you up in no time."

For a second Deka looked grateful, faintly believing that he might just be saved from whatever alien monstrosity had hold of him.

Peel didn't believe a word of it, so he was disturbingly relieved when Figgs put two bullets in the back of Lieutenant Deka's head. The noise was loud, but no louder than the quickly silenced screams.

Reluctantly Peel sighed with relief. Figgs must have figured that if the local army had been watching they would have shown themselves by now. It seemed he figured right.

With unblinking eyes Peel gazed upon the fallen man. So this was the biological weapon they'd been sent to collect. Now that he'd seen the weapon in action, he wanted no part of it. The officer's shattered skull, the blood and dispersed gray matter that had once been a brain didn't even register with Peel. It was the infected hand, still twitching, still crawling through the mud exploring its surroundings by touch alone, that made him retch at his morning breakfast of cheap noodles.

Figgs responded differently, laughed, giggled hysterically. "I told you, Peel. You don't know the Tcho-Tcho until you have to deal with them face to face. You, you just got the next best thing."

The British agent wasted no time returning to their vehicle, opened the trunk at which he'd lied about a waiting antidote, and removed a canister of liquid nitrogen. The frozen contents were poured over the still twitching arm. It took several minutes for the alien growth to finally stop moving. Figgs seemed more concerned about not getting any on his feet.

"There are two metal boxes in the back, Peel — biohazard samplers. You want to get them out for me?"

Still stunned, Peel did not question what he was being asked to do. By the time he found the boxes, Figgs had slipped on thick gloves to insulate against frostbite. With a bolt cutter he snipped away two of the rigid tentacles and two of Deka's infected fingers. Then he used the cutters as prongs to place two of each portion into separate samplers. Insulation would keep them frozen, at least for a couple of hours. Long enough to get them secured in the diplomatic bags out of this country.

"One for Australia, and one for Queen and Country."

In the end both had got what they had come for, so why did Peel feel cold inside?

"You should thank me, Peel, that we even let you in on this little operation."

"Really, Figgs? You honestly think our respective governments will know what to do with these?" Peel knew without reason or logic that the samples were still dangerous despite their frozen condition. He'd already seen what they had done to Deka, and wasn't that warning enough?

"What they always do, Peel. Send them to laboratories on some remote island that the public can't reach, or deep inside an old coalmine that's been locked up for decades. To study, to understand, and ultimately to determine how our respective governments can transform alien life into a weapon. So don't balk, Peel, and don't pretend that our governments are any nicer than the Tcho-Tcho. We just have the decency to get licenses and legislation first before we pull our dirty tricks."

Peel said nothing. He wanted to walk away in disgust, to deny he had ever been involved, but the mess had already been made.

Because he needed to do something, he found the jeep's spare jerry can, poured the entire contents over the corpse. It was still bleeding black tar instead of blood, and smelt like an old tannery.

"I wouldn't bother. It's not like that stuff doesn't grow everywhere in this jungle."

Peel didn't care. He needed to purify himself as much as he needed to abolish this contagion. When he splashed the last of the industrial hydrocarbons he said, "You ready to go?"

Figgs nodded mockingly to the affirmative.

Minutes later as the Englishman pounded their vehicle down the muddy road, Peel seated next to him turned and aimed his Glock at the corpse, firing, igniting a gigantic fireball of fury.

Neither spoke until they were back amongst the rice fields and temples, where peasant farmers tended their crops and at last these sights brought comfort in their familiarity. Out here, the Cambodian army would be hard pressed to discretely assassinate them. But why bother, if Figgs was right, there were plenty more samples of the Tcho-Tcho bio-weaponry back there waiting for the picking, enough for everybody.

"You didn't come for Deka, did you? That was never your plan?"

"No, Peel, I did not."

Peel snorted a laugh, a chuckle loaded with loathing. "We promised him that we'd save him."

Figgs laughed harder, "But we did save him Peel. Ask yourself, would you want to go on living with something like that growing inside you?"

Peel didn't respond. He'd answered his own question already.

II

Seagulls picked at the discarded food littered on the North Sydney beach. Cold today, no one had ventured onto the sand, leaving the scavenging sea birds with few choices. What meager shreds they did scrounge were old and stale, just like the wearied man watching them.

Tired, his mind was lost in the rhythms of the pounding waves, and so he didn't notice that he was being observed by an army officer, the only other man by the sea on this cold winter's day.

"You like the ocean, Mr. Grogan?" asked Major Peel. The officer had worn his uniform out of respect, complemented by a freshly shaved face and scalp. Now he regretted his choice, for his head was chilled by the cool salty breeze.

"Call me a bloody sergeant, will you? Nobody else does these days." He threw bread to the squabbling gulls.

Peel wondered if Grogan ever missed walking along the beach. But this was a stupid question. Of course Grogan would miss many things. Anyone with both legs amputated above the knees most certainly would. "And to answer your question, young man: no, not really. I used to, when I didn't see seagulls with sharp teeth attacking me."

"Sharp teeth?"

"Oh yeah, they say it is all in my mind. But I've been on so much medication for so long — twenty different pills five times a day — I just don't know what's real anymore. Still, they say I'm calmer now. I suppose it keeps them happy."

"I'm sorry to hear that," Peel made sure he sounded sincere, but smiled to himself nonetheless. The battle-scarred veteran was obviously starved for conversation, so Peel let him rattle on.

"Yeah, well, war sucks."

The officer pulled up a chair, sat down uninvited. "My name is Major Harrison Peel, from the Department of Defense." This wasn't a complete lie, but it would serve today's purposes. "Do you mind if I ask a few questions?"

"You already have." The old man threw more bread. A fight broke as the scavengers exploded in a fury of white feathers.

Determined, Peel placed his briefcase on the table. He was planning to show Grogan the file he'd brought from the archives, but the wild and whistling Pacific winds prevented that. He couldn't risk the papers blowing into the ocean.

"You're in intelligence aren't you?"

Peel smiled, "Kind of."

"The Vietnam War's over, Major, it finished thirty years ago. What else do you spooks still think I've got to tell?"

Cocking an eyebrow the Major continued, "Sure, the Vietnam War is over." He paused to create drama, gazing at the stumps wrapped in a blanket, and wondered if the Sergeant still felt the cold in toes that were no longer real. "It's the other war I'm talking about."

Grogan looked at Peel for the first time, shock barely hidden in his weathered face, "*Which* war would that be?"

"Cambodia, Eastern Highlands, August Eighteen 1968?"

Just as quickly Grogan looked away, his pale liver-spotted skin lost more color than Peel would have thought possible. "Oh. That war."

Peel nodded. "You do know what I mean then, don't you?"

Grogan vainly attempted to lure a seagull closer, holding out a strip of bread in his bony fingers. "They never come too close, no matter how many times I tell them I'm safe, that I won't hurt them. But they stay away, because they know I could turn on them at any moment, slaughter them. It would be so easy to wring their scrawny little necks and not care about it afterwards. You know what I'm saying?"

Peel nodded; even though he was not sure exactly what the old man was alluding to, he had his suspicions. After all, it was why he had come today.

"It's the same with them young man, and you obviously know what I'm talking about there?"

Peel said nothing, certain that Grogan wanted to say more.

"When I first saw you, Major, I thought you were different from the other soldiers who occasionally visit me. Those military men come only on the very rare occasions, to reminisce. You don't reminisce. You only say what you have to. You know like I know."

It took Peel a moment to answer, because he didn't like that the old man was right. "What makes you say that?"

"It's that look in your eyes, like you understand everything I've said and don't dismiss me as an insane crank. Plus you look scared, just like me. Not scared of something you can see, like the kind of scared you get facing the end of a gun barrel in an enemy combatant's hand. That's an easy scared, you can understand that. No, you're scared of what you don't know, what you can't see. You're scared like these seagulls."

It was Peel's turn to shudder, for the old veteran's experiences reminded him of his own encounters. His personal turning point; his first understanding of the unseen worlds of horror, was that day in the Cambodian jungle with Figgs. "Well, Sergeant, I've only just returned from Southeast Asia myself. Cambodia to be precise, working hard against a new threat. I know you've heard of the Tcho-Tcho?"

Grogan didn't say anything, but he didn't have to for Peel to sense the old man understood well enough.

"What about Shub-Niggurath?"

Finally Grogan nodded. "Okay, but don't rattle on so much. Just speaking their names can be dangerous enough."

Peel leaned forward, looked into Grogan's sick yellow eyes. "You know why I came here today, Sergeant?"

"I haven't got the foggiest."

"I'm sure you do. You see, I'd really like you to tell me what happened, all those years ago."

The sergeant shuddered, "Why?"

"Because they're back, Grogan. The Tcho-Tcho, and we know you saw something that day. Something that didn't make it into the report the Americans gave us."

Grogan stifled a sob, hid his face in his hands.

"They know we're there," explained Peel, "we're hunting them. Trouble is, they know all our intelligence and we don't know how. They're learning our language and our codes at phenomenal speeds, and they're uncanny at guessing our movements almost all of the time. I think you know why this is happening. I think you can help, help me to stop more good Aussie men dying at their hands."

The Sergeant spat yellow phlegm. A seagull investigated, sensibly decided not to eat it. "You've read the report then," said the old man, "the one I'm sure you've got in that briefcase." He stifled another sob. "So why should I be forced to relive that experience again? It was horrible enough recounting it the first time, and the second, and third, knowing that no one believed me anyway."

Peel leaned forward, his face red with anger. "Because you're *not* the report, Grogan; you were there. Just like I'm there now, and I want the best bloody intelligence you can give me. Otherwise one day soon we could end up as bunk mates in this old home, and I don't want that."

The Sergeant took a moment to chew his lips, consider his options. "It's back, you say?"

"It, Grogan?"

At last the old man held Peel's stare, "You really want to know?"

Peel said nothing. He'd already answered that question a half dozen times.

The seagulls had also decided. They didn't wish to be a part of any of this and had flown off.

III

TOP SECRET
INTERNAL REPORT, COPY 3 OF 5
10 July, 2004

SUBJECT: Statement by Sergeant James Donald Grogan, as recorded by Major Harrison Peel, Special Projects, on the 8 July 2004.

Transcript from the Audio Recording
Addendum to the 1968 Report

I was with the Australian military in Vietnam, assigned to a 'special' outfit and flown into Saigon in 1968. Our base was Nui Dat in Phuoc Tuy Province. Three months we waited for action, bored but also dreading the time when we'd have to fight. That's because we'd all too often witnessed the victims of landmines and bullet wounds, and that was enough to scare even the most hardened of us. But our role here was inevitable, for we were soldiers here to fight, and we saw our first and only action on August Eighteen 1968.

Although we didn't know it at the time, our mission was top secret, one that the Yanks pulled together. Of course they decided to use us as diversionary troops while their soldiers completed the real mission, or so we thought. We were helicoptered into Cambodia two years before we were officially at war with that country. Not that we could tell the difference between Khmer Rouge and the Vietcong, they were all Charlie to us. We were there to kill, that seemed simple enough.

Of course the mission was a disaster right from the start. But it wasn't the VC or the Khmer this time, that day Charlie was the Tcho-Tcho. Savage little cannibals who did worse things than shoot you or take your legs off with a tripwire tied to a claymore mine.

They knew we were coming, those Tcho bastards. They were waiting for us; ambushed us while we were wading ass-deep in a bloody rice field. Well it was certainly very bloody a short time later. They massacred us quickly as it would take you to piss your pants when you're really scared.

When all the shooting stopped, and I really had pissed my pants, I came round thinking I should be dead, but I wasn't. I remember something hitting me in the head, but to this day don't know what. But whatever knocked me out cold, it saved my life. Unconscious, to the Tcho I was just another dead body. I was half submerged in the muddy water, buried under three fallen mates, all bloody, broken and smelling of guts and shit. But my mates true to their word — even though they were dead — hid me from the Tcho soldiers. I was lucky all right, I thought, but I also knew a poor bugger like me, his luck never lasts.

Somehow I retained sense enough not to move, still amazed that I'd survived, and terrified that I might not get out alive and in one piece. Then I heard them, the Tcho-Tcho, talking softly in their strange chattering high-pitched voices. Naturally I had no idea what they were saying. And then I heard this strong American accent. I looked, stupidly moved my head, but thankfully no one saw. There he was, one of the Tcho-Tchos, speaking the Texan drawl! Black leathery skin, loincloth and penis-sheath, oh, and a M16 slung over his shoulder thanks to Uncle Sam. It looked so odd, like a dream, him talking like a Yank and looking like that, like seeing President Nixon's voice coming out of Marilyn Monroe's mouth.

The Tcho officer was telling someone to get up. I risked moving my head again, this time slightly and slowly until I saw young Corporal Stewart Monk, lying in the mud where he'd fallen. Another Tcho soldier, directed by his command officer, was prodding Monk with a machete. Monk was sobbing and I knew why. You might think he was lucky to be alive, but he probably didn't think so, and neither did I. We'd all heard tales of what the Vietcong did to prisoners, but we all knew that what the Tcho did was far worse.

Tortures included staking you in the mud then placing yellow snails on your bare flesh, specially bred to eat away your skin while laying their eggs in your wounds. Other tricks, they'd hang you up from your feet then cut away bits of your flesh, one piece at a time, slowly eating these bits while you were still alive. Eating your own flesh in front of you and laughing. No one ever hoped to get taken prisoner by the Tcho-Tcho.

Anyway they pulled Monk to his feet, bound his wrists in wire until they bled, and pushed him on, forcing him to march with them.

The whole time I just lay there. If I moved they'd see that I was no corpse and I'd be their prisoner too, good to no one and even more shit scared than I was now. But lying there wasn't easy. You see, I kept catching glimpses of what the other Tcho soldiers were up to, cutting off the hands, arms, feet and legs of my fellow soldiers, carrying the meat away with them as food. It was all I could do not to scream and run, hoping that they would not cut from me, hoping that my dead mates were more than enough.

I don't know how long I lay like this, hours probably, but it felt like days, and the weight of the corpses on top of me grew heavy. Thank god the Tcho bastards eventually left without touching me, and marched on. I risked sitting up.

The battlefield was the worst kind of carnage. The smell was putrid, one I can't even describe even though I've smelt it in my head every day since. The muddy waters washed with so much red it was the only color I could see. Bodies were everywhere, and only a few fallen Tcho-Tcho amongst their number. All our guns and ammunition were gone, except one automatic I found still gripped in the hands of my Lieutenant, half his face missing where machinegun fire had torn apart his skull. He didn't need it.

Not knowing where I was, or how to get out (I still had no idea I was in Cambodia) I decided to follow the Tcho soldiers, discrete like, see if I could save Monk, and if not that, at least put him out of his misery before he was tortured.

Trailing them was a breeze. I was without a pack, so marching seemed easy now, and it was simple to remain unheard. They chattered and talked so much in their high-pitched voices I could have followed them in the dark. But I don't think they expected to be followed, not this far into their own territory.

But as I followed I became more and more uncomfortable, and I didn't know why. There were no rice fields out here, no pig farms, and no Buddhist shrines or those primitive villages you normally see in the Golden Triangle. Perhaps it was that huge yellow snail I almost stepped on that first unsettled me, or the roots of a tree that I swore shrank away as I approached. I swear at one point I thought an eye opened in one overhanging branch. It took a while, but I realized this was no jungle that I'd ever seen or read about, its black sticky ichors all over my boots. I should have run, and if I had, I'd still have legs today I'm sure. But you stick with your mates, look after them whatever happens, and that's what I did.

Finally the trail ended, and I saw the scariest slight I'll ever see. This was a Tcho-Tcho village, but the huts and campfires weren't what scared me. It was what the village was built around, a huge, pulsating tree that petrified me.

The stench hit me first, horrific, like those rafflesia flowers that smell like rotting meat to attract flies, but so much worse, and sweet. The tree, well it wouldn't fit in one of those Yankee air hangars it was so huge. Its branches were white and stringy, reminding me of body parts preserved too long in jars of formaldehyde. Its highest branches hung over the Tcho village like some kind of roof, and it was dripping black syrup that burnt like acid wherever it splashed. The Tcho seemed to know how to avoid this, and didn't seem to mind the obvious danger. But you're probably guessing this tree wasn't natural, could never be. You're right, and I was starting to understand all the mutations in all the animals and plants around this place.

I should have run, like I said. But somehow I was drawn to this monstrosity. I saw Monk then, on his knees with an M16 at his head. The Tcho officer who'd spoken English was talking to him again, all American-like, telling him he'd be one with Shub-Niggurath soon, the Mother of Speaking Children. That it wouldn't matter that he refused to talk, or couldn't remember details beyond his name, rank and serial number.

I thought about shooting Monk there and then, and then legging it. Trouble was I was too far distant to mark him with my pistol. If I got any closer I'd be spotted, and I couldn't risk that. So I waited, biding my time.

I didn't have to wait long. Descending from the white canopy appeared what I can only describe as a gigantic tadpole with its tail fused to the canopy. The end was a milky translucent skin over a black core. It fell upon Monk, absorbing him, eating him I thought. I think it was at this moment that I vomited.

When I looked back, whatever it was, it hadn't killed Monk, because I'd hoped it would do my job for me. Instead I saw Monk inside it now, thrashing and fighting, unable to escape his translucent prison. He was in agony, I was sure of that, as the pod raised itself back into the canopy.

But if you think things couldn't get any worse, well they did. The milky prison seemed to squeeze itself, and white droplets fell from the tadpole onto the English-speaking Tcho, now standing directly underneath. And then that same Tcho started talking Aussie-like, telling all his tribesmen of our mission as if they were Monk's words he was using, revealing our objectives, names and ranks of the unit, where we were based, who our commanding officers were, everything.

It was that moment that I ran. Not because I saw how the Tcho-Tcho were learning about us so quickly, not because I'd just seen poor Monk consumed by this monstrous tree, but because I'd just noticed that he wasn't the only prisoner in a pod. I'd looked up you see, between the branches, in the canopy and I saw them all, hundreds of the milky cells, and most of them encasing struggling humans.

I ran for as long as I can remember, then nothing. Somehow I'd ended up in a U.S. MASH camp. The field surgeons told me I'd stepped on a mine and blown off both my legs above the knees. All I could think about was how lucky it was that I wasn't poor old Monk right now, lucky that I'd only lost two legs.

Only later, when the drugs had been eased back and the depression set in, American military intelligence officers found me. But they didn't ask a lot of questions as I expected, they only wanted to know one thing: where the Tcho's tree could be found. Apparently their troops had failed to find this place, their target, while us Aussies had been nothing more than a diversion.

I'm fairly certain they bombed the tree later, napalm or fuel air explosives probably. I don't think they wanted me out alive either and able to talk, because that afternoon I spotted a body bag with my name on it! Luckily an Australian journalist interviewed me. The next day my name and my story were in the newspaper. They had to release me then, if they didn't want an international incident on their hands.

It was only after I was discharged that I discovered that my country had given up finding me, for the Yanks had reported that as far as the official mission reports were concerned, I was classified as missing in action, probably dead. I think those boys in MI would have liked it to stay that way.

After that I was flown home and ended up here, in this home for disabled veterans, no good to anyone. I've never left this place since, not once. Don't want to, because I know what lies out there. The nurses are nice, when they've got time for you. Now all I do is feed the seagulls, read trashy novels, watch game shows and wait to die, hoping that my fears won't join me when they finally lay me in the grave.

Hoping that one day my delusions end and I stop seeing seagulls with sharp teeth.

 END REPORT

IV

The march into the Eastern Highlands had not been without risk. Mosquitoes attacked relentlessly, sweat chaffed, and howling monkeys announced their presence everywhere they turned. But this was nothing. They were in enemy territory now, and Peel knew they had to get it right. The intelligence he had recovered from the old man in Sydney checked out. At last, the mystery might be resolved.

Their cover was as western tourists, with nothing identifying them as agents of the Australia government. The sniper who joined Peel had no name. So Peel called him Sergeant Joe, which was as fictional as his call sign. Peel didn't reveal his real name either, because if one were caught then they couldn't betray the other.

Despite their arsenal of weapons they weren't here to kill anyone, just laser-sight a target so a ballistic missile fired from the naval ship *Ballarat*, on maneuvers in the Gulf of Thailand, could find its way.

The Tcho-Tcho controlled this jungle. This was their land. Peel and Joe avoided the Montagnard villages just to be sure, knowing that many were home to the cannibals, or if not, willing to report the movements of two foreigners to the Tcho-Tcho, purely because they feared the repercussions if they did not. Out of sight, Peel and Joe slept in the jungles, ate only their issued rations, left no litter, and proceeded very, very slowly.

They found the alien tree after five days of searching.

Sergeant Joe wanted to get closer, to be sure. Peel outranked him and declined. He'd read all the reports, including those from as far back as 1968, plus American intel files that had come his way via various global contacts, and Figgs' latest memo confirming that the biological weapon secured from Deka had originated from the same tree.

When the valley shuddered, as if the tree had shaken itself like a dog thrashing its wet coat, they knew they were close enough. They knew that it would be suicide to get any closer.

"Are you sighted?" Peel asked.

The young sniper nodded, trembling now that they'd seen the whole jungle come alive and move, not like a plant in a strong wind, but like a wild angry animal. Who could blame him? Peel was terrified himself.

He called in the missile strike. The exorbitant bribes paid to the Cambodian government not to report this military action on a terrorist heartland had been far more expensive than the hardware expended.

Only when the jungle was a burning inferno did the two men walk back into Laos, thankful that they had not been seen. Thankful that they had not fallen prey to the Tcho-Tcho.

V

The membrane split, milky liquid gushed and the naked shape of an ill-formed man spewed into green pools of fetid rice fields. He breathed, sucking air into lungs that had known only viscous liquids for so long. Arms and legs again under his own control, he stood, witnessed the carnage around him, and dripped milky black fluids from his sheen.

The air was alive with heat and flames. Smoke made breathing difficult. When he could finally smell again, the scent of charred Tcho-Tcho assailed his nostrils.

More explosions, more flame. He fled into the jungle, away from the destruction. He knew he'd been freed, but he wasn't waiting inside the inferno to find out why.

As he fled, he noticed he wasn't the only survivor of this carnage. Other prisoners were dropping from the canopy, exploding out from their fallen pseudopods as they shattered on the black earth. Some of the men and women were quickly consumed in flames. Others so ill-formed they could no longer walk, because they barely resembled human beings. A few mustered their strength and courage, running from this site of destruction.

He ran for hours, perhaps days. At some point he was no longer under a green canopy, and found himself standing on the edge of a remote Montagnard village. The barefooted dirty children shied away, mangy dogs ran from him, old men pretended he was invisible, and none dared look him in the eye. When he spoke they pretended not to understand, despite the dozens of languages he barked their way.

He walked through the village unmolested, up a muddy road, realized that he was still nude and that he didn't care. For some reason he felt powerful, as if he could smite anyone. Once he'd been made of meat, but not any more. Now he was something more durable, something far more ancient.

He had no idea where he was headed, why his feet kept walking for him, or who he was. Then the answer came to him, in the form of a diminutive stranger.

This old wizened dwarf just stepped into his path, refusing to move. No one had done that before. None had challenged him in this way. Intrigued, the naked man decided to hear out the dwarf's offer before he destroyed him.

The dwarf's skin was black, lined like old parchment. His legs little more than bony twigs, and his teeth were sharpened points stained red. He wore a faded Nike jacket and a loincloth. In one hand he carried a staff with a wooden knot at the head, the sign of a Tcho-Tcho priest.

"Welcome Mother of the Speaking Children," spoke the shaman. "You have saved us once again."

He was speaking in the Tcho-Tcho tongue, and the naked man knew he should have been surprised that he understood him so perfectly, but he was not.

Bowing slightly, the shaman led him off the road, down a trail to a field of coriander, and stood him next to a large tree on the edge of dense rainforest. A few minutes passed without either man speaking, until the naked man realized he could no longer move his legs.

He stood like that for many days, growing and changing, becoming more and more rigid with each passing moment.

But he was never alone — the Tcho-Tcho young and old alike came to him. They watched him grow, worshipped him as they should. In a few years his branches were tall, and his roots went deep. Pseudopods were developing fast, and soon he would be ready to absorb more of his former kind, again stealing, sharing and imparting the stolen knowledge to his devoted flock.

In time all that had once been Corporal Monk was forgotten and changed, not that it mattered. Humans were nothing. Yet everything about Monk would live on, forever, inside the ever-growing tree.

He was, after all, as old as the universe itself.

TO WHAT GREEN ALTAR

John Sunseri

Siberia: Thousand Stars Mining Camp lat N61 long 101

"You think we finally found gold?" asked Piotr, lighting a cigarette.

"Found something," said Lyov, leaning back on the bench with his eyes closed. "The sandniggers up at the surveyor's shack have been shitting themselves with excitement all day."

Piotr looked around nervously, making sure the old man's words hadn't been overheard by the wrong people. He saw no Arabs among the throng of Russians crammed into the hall. "You shouldn't refer to our bosses like that, Lyov."

"What are they going to do, boychik?" asked the old miner, opening his eyes. "Send us to fucking Siberia?"

Piotr snorted — Siberia was all around them, cold and merciless. "They could fire you, old man, and then you'd be back on the train to whatever little shit village you came from."

"Such an attitude!" said Lyov, smiling. "You talk this way to a hero of the Great Patriotic War?"

"You're not that old, Lyov," said Piotr, blowing out acrid smoke and shaking his head. "Might as well say you were there at the Winter Revolution."

"No, I missed that one," smiled Lyov. "But I fought in Afghanistan, fought against vicious little cocksuckers that look a lot like our current masters. I'll do their digging, but if you want me to be polite and deferential to them, you can kiss me right on my hairy ass. They've bought a miner, not a lickspittle."

"So you don't think the morning team struck gold, then?" said Piotr, changing the subject to something less inflammatory.

"It's the wrong kind of earth," said the old miner. "I'm not saying they couldn't have found a seam, but I would think it unlikely."

"But the Company assured us!"

"The Company has no miners — that's why they hired *us*. Maybe one of their satellites found something that looked interesting, or maybe the chief shareholders have too much money and not enough brains. It's not just me, boy — the other experienced men down in the holes all agree that this is a bad spot for digging."

"But they found something," said Piotr, echoing Lyov's earlier words.

"Maybe it's oil," said Lyov. "Maybe they're running out down in the Middle East and want another source."

"Where are they?" asked Piotr, looking around, inhaling the harsh home-rolled tobacco smoke. "They said for everyone to meet in the conference hall, and we're all here, yet no bosses?"

Indeed, the room was packed to the walls with the miners and other laborers that had been working the deep shafts for the last three months, and the murmur of curious conversation hummed around them like electricity. Cigarette smoke hung heavy in the air, but no one complained — though it reeked like scorched rubber, it was still more pleasant than the stink of thirty seldom-washed bodies.

"And where is the morning team?" asked Piotr, offering the old man one of his cigarettes. Lyov took it, tapped one end on the table before him, pulled out a Zippo and lit the thing before he answered.

"Sequestered in the surveying shack," he said, inhaling deeply. "They've been having a debriefing all morning."

"Curious," said Piotr. "I wonder — what the hell did they find down there?"

"We'll know soon enough," said Lyov, hearing a noise up front and looking through the crush of men toward the front doors. They swung open, letting in a frigid blast of winter air along with another cluster of men — the morning team, all eight of them, stumbling forward as the Arabs prodded them into the hall. They looked stunned, dazed . . . and the foremen, wearing their traditional red-and-white *shumaggs* held in place with the black *ogals*, lined up in the open doorway.

They held Kalashnikovs.

There were gasps, shouts, querulous voices raised in outrage and shock.

And then there was the roar of automatic weapons as the Arabs opened fire.

"What the fuck?" yelled Piotr, rising to his feet, his cigarette falling to the planked floor. "What are they doing?"

Lyov instantly dropped to the ground and swept his right leg out, hitting the younger man behind the knees and sending him crashing to the boards. Piotr whoofed as he hit, and then Lyov had his neck caught in one heavily-muscled arm, restraining him.

"Shut up, boy," he hissed. "We won't have much time — get to the back door, but stay low. If your ass is sticking up, it'll get shot off."

"What's going on?" strangled Piotr. "Why are they shooting at us?"

"You could stand up and ask them," said Lyov grimly, "but I wouldn't recommend it. Now move!"

They did. Before them, men rushed at the front doors trying to overpower the knot that was calmly, systematically sending hot death into them, but Piotr and Lyov crawled under the table and snaked along the floor toward the back doors, where the camp kitchen was. Around them, screams echoed from the dying and whangs of ricochets as bullets whizzed through the air, and now they could smell the metallic tang of blood as it spurted from a hundred wounds, the reek of smoke from guns and burning clothes, but they made it unseen to the wooden door. Lyov looked back for a second, nodded as he saw that Piotr had followed, and reached up for the knob.

It opened, and another Arab, the one named Hassan, stood behind it, short-barreled Uzi cradled in his arms. He looked at them, gave them a sad smile, and said "In'shallah"

"Fuck you," croaked Lyov, and tried to struggle to his feet.

A quick burst of bullets sent him thudding back to the ground. Piotr looked at the old miner, his head a smashed, bleeding turnip, then looked up at the man with the gun.

The black barrel, staring at him like an eye, was the last thing he saw.

And then, a roar like thunder.

Vauxhall, London: MI6 Offices

"I'm Figgs," said the man behind the desk.

"Dixon," said the NSA agent. He didn't rise to offer his hand, nor did Figgs seem to expect it.

"Welcome to England, Mr. Dixon," said Figgs. "Is this your first visit?"

"I'm sure that info's in your files, Mr. Figgs," said Dixon pleasantly. "You do have a file on me, don't you?"

"Says you were here for a while during the summer of your junior year at University," smiled Figgs. "Flew into Heathrow and out of Glasgow. Pleasure trip?"

"A girl," said Dixon. "She went to SIU with me, invited me to come visit for two months. I stayed for one."

"So, that'd be a *no* on the pleasure, hmm?"

"Why am I here?" asked the American. "Why the face-to-face?"

"What did your superiors tell you?" asked Figgs, leaning back.

"They told me that you'd tell me what's going on."

"We needed some of your satellite time," said Figgs. "As a trade-off, your government made us promise to involve them in anything we have going on in the area. So we're partners for the duration."

"What area?" asked Dixon, leaning forward.

"Siberia," said Figgs. "Or, to be more precise, an area near the Tunguska River."

"Oh?" said Dixon. "What's there?"

"You ever hear of the Tunguska Event?" asked Figgs. Dixon was getting a bit tired of having his questions answered with other questions, but he supposed he understood — had they been meeting in his offices in Fort Meade, Maryland, he'd probably be playing the same game of feint-and-futz.

"1909, was it?" asked Dixon.

"1908, actually," said Figgs, but there was a faint bit of respect in his tone as he corrected his counterpart. "You a student of history?"

"There was an episode of *The X-Files* once," said Dixon. "Good show — you ever watch it?"

Figgs looked at him and smiled. "I believe we may get along, you and I. What can you tell me about the Event?"

"There was an explosion," said Dixon, straining his memory. "Destroyed a lot of trees. People think it was a meteor—"

"There was no impact crater," interjected Figgs.

"—or UFO's," finished Dixon. "The television show leaned toward the aliens."

"And what do you think?" asked Figgs. "What, in 1908, could have caused an explosion that devastated over two thousand square kilometers of land, destroyed 60 million trees, and left no natural explanations?"

"I tend to agree with William of Occam," said Dixon. "The simplest answer is usually the correct one. It was a meteor that broke up before impact, but caused a fireball above the forest."

"The scientists of the time would have disagreed with you," smiled Figgs.

"It was a hundred years ago," said Dixon. "Science back then wasn't as sophisticated as it is now. Who knows what they missed?"

Figgs looked at the American for a moment without speaking, as if considering how much to share with him. Finally, though, he shook his head. "I'm supposed to cooperate with you, but I'm not sure what to tell you."

"Tell me about the satellite time you folks bought," suggested Dixon. "What did you see at Tunguska?"

"A mining operation," said Figgs. "Brand-new, well-financed, state-of-the-art equipment."

"The Russians looking for gold or oil?" asked Dixon.

"It's not the Russians," Figgs responded. "They've got mining interests all over Siberia, of course, but they also lease out their land to other countries for exploration and exploitation — so long as the price is right."

"Who'd be stupid enough to take that deal?" asked Dixon, amused. "Put together an expedition, dig up some nuggets, and have the Russian government swoop down under the aegis of national security, take away your claim?"

"You'd be surprised," said Figgs. "Japan's got a lot of interests in Siberia right now — if you live on tiny islands and you lack resources, Siberia's like one big grocery store. And, hell, the Russians need the money."

"So this camp you're interested in — is it the Japanese?"

"It's the Saudis," said Figgs. "We've been doing a little digging, our lot, and it took us a long time to find out exactly who owned the place, but it turns out to be your mates down in the Gulf."

"So it's oil they're looking for, then?" asked Dixon casually, but a flare of interest rose in his gut.

"We don't know," said Figgs, frowning. "Whatever it was, though, that they were looking for, they've packed up and left in the last few days. Which would be an odd thing to do if you'd found oil."

"What do you mean, 'packed up and left'?" asked Dixon.

"I mean the camp's deserted now," said the British agent. "There was a monstrous fire three days ago, took out all the buildings, and now there's nothing but a black patch on the satellite images. Everyone's gone."

"So what's your interest?" asked Dixon. "Some industrial accident?"

"Ah," said Figgs, "but was it an accident? We've got some nice snaps — your satellites are very good, by the way — of maybe a dozen men wearing those Arabian headscarves loading up their trucks and driving away. But there were at least fifty men at the site, and most of them didn't make it onto the trucks."

"So what are you saying?"

"There's also a spot on the pictures that looks like something I've seen before," said Figgs grimly. "It looks like a mass grave."

"Hmm," said Dixon, shaking his head. "A big fire, a lot of deaths."

"The grave was dug before the fire started," said Figgs.

Dixon stared at him for a moment or two, then raised his eyebrows. "So?" he said. "A horrible thing, but why is Her Majesty's Government interested?"

"You say you watched *The X-Files*?" asked Figgs. "Good — maybe you'll believe some of the things I'm going to tell you now."

Siberia: Ruins of the Thousand Stars Mining Camp

"Jesus, it's cold," complained Dixon.

"What, it's warm back in Maryland right now?" asked Figgs, his lips curled into a smile. He looked menacing in his snow goggles and parka, like some alien bug. Dixon supposed he looked the same way, and he wondered what some reindeer herder would make of the two of them, standing in the Siberian snow like invaders from another world.

"There are degrees of cold," said Dixon. "I don't mind a little snow on the streets, but this is fucking ridiculous."

"I'm a Southeast Asia expert myself," said Figgs. "I don't much enjoy this either, but we've got to take a look."

"So you really, truly believe in this whole thing?" asked Dixon as they trudged through the three-foot-tall drifts, fought against the wind that lacerated them like flying knives, stumbled over hidden rocks and tree roots. "This K . . . Kth. . . ."

"Cthugha," supplied Figgs helpfully, his voice feeble in the wind. "And I can't say for sure that I believe it — but these Arab fellows sure did. And whatever they were doing here is all predicated on that belief."

"How did you come across this place, Figgs?" asked Dixon. "How did you spooks in London know where to look?"

"I believe that falls under the 'need-to-know' category, my Yankee friend," said Figgs, and Dixon could imagine the smile under the hood and goggles. "Kind of like your sources for WMD in Iraq."

"Touché," said Dixon, dodging as a branch above him dislodged its cargo of snow. They'd had a miserable trip thus far — Figgs and his organization had secured them temporary (and completely fictitious) documents so they could join a Finnish/Russian oil exploration crew in the heart of Siberia, and they'd had to do a little midnight requisitioning to snag the two Bombardier-Nordtrac snowmobiles they'd used for the seventy-kilometer trek through the wintry wilderness.

They had to be back in the next four days, or their field agent back at the camp wouldn't be able to continue covering for them.

"Look ahead of us," said Figgs, stopping. "Tell me what you see."

Snow, was the word that leapt to Dixon's lips, but it remained unspoken. Instead, he peered forward. They were on the edge of a clearing, and he could see what he assumed were stumps sticking up, though they were covered with a white carpet like the rest of the landscape.

"Mineshaft," the NSA agent said finally. "In the side of the hill, there."

"Spot on," agreed the Englishman. "Looks like they caved it in, though, doesn't it?"

There was a dark scar in the hillside, only spottily covered with snow, and even from their hundred-meter distance Dixon could see that there had been an opening and that it had been somehow induced to collapse in on itself — frost-dusted boulders sat implacable and immovable in a wall of scree and dirt, and even the whipping wind seemed to break on the mass of rock.

"I hope we're not looking for anything there," said Dixon, panting as his body sucked in oxygen, taking advantage of the brief rest. "I didn't bring a shovel."

"Whatever was in there is long gone," said Figgs absently. "They were just covering their tracks. Come on, then, mate — we've got a ways to go before we hit the camp."

Wisdom of the Stars Forward Assault Headquarters:
Somewhere in Europe

"It was there, then," breathed the tall man, caressing his ebon hands slowly across the carved wood of the chest. "We were successful."

"As predicted," said Hassan Abdel-Rahman. He was exhausted — his stint in the cold country of Russia, his subsequent flight through the bulk of Europe and the burden of carrying this treasure, this miracle in a cedar chest that lay on the table before him, had worn on him more than he would have thought possible. Even now, at this exultant moment, he found himself fighting a yawn, but suppressed it in deference to (and not a little terror of) his *imam*. "The infidels dug hard, once we crossed their palms with gold."

"That gold — you got it back, did you not?" smiled the cloaked figure. Hassan caught a glimpse of white teeth in the cavernous darkness beneath the hood, and nodded.

"We did, Master," he said. "And all traces of our presence were obliterated."

"Oh, I doubt that," said the priest. "Sooner or later, the Russians will come looking for their men. Sooner or later, the world will find the footprints of the Kingdom in Tartar territory."

"Forgive me for my presumption, *sayyid*," said Hassan, looking down at the chest, wishing his master would just open it and get the whole rigmarole over with. "But if the world wishes to discover our tracks, then it had best do it sooner rather than later."

The priest threw back his head and roared laughter, and for the briefest moment Hassan caught a glimpse of his *imam's* head beneath the hood — the bald, pale skin tight against the skull, the desiccated veins flat and lifeless, the pits where eyes had once been — but then the *sayyid* lowered his head and again spoke from shadows.

"Indeed, my most faithful and honest son," he said, his voice low and throaty. "Indeed. Now, let me see what you have brought me."

And with a whiff of cedar and snow, the lid opened.

Siberia: Thousand Stars Mining Camp, 2 Days Later

"Is this what we're looking for?" asked Dixon, fingers held against his nostrils. It had been several days, and the temperature hadn't risen above freezing in that span, but the stench from the grave still smacked him like a two-by-four.

"No," said Figgs shortly, looking around. "We knew the grave was here. We're looking for traces of whatever these blokes were digging for."

They'd been through the blackened ruins of the mess hall, the charred bones of the former barracks, and they'd found another mineshaft crumpled in on itself, discovered enough bloodstains and spent bullets to give them a good idea of what kind of violence had taken place here, but nothing that hinted at the Saudis' objectives in the first place.

"Well, shit," sighed Dixon. "You know what that means."

"What?" asked Figgs, turning to look at his partner. "We go home empty-handed?"

"No," said Dixon. "We've got to dig these dead fuckers up and go through their wallets."

Figgs looked at the American for a long couple of seconds, his eyes invisible through the opacity of the goggles he wore, then barked a cough of laughter that clouded in the gelid air. "You kidding me?" he asked. "An NSA agent willing to get his hands dirty on behalf of Her Majesty's government?"

"You come down to it," said Dixon, "and I'm a cop. A good one. I don't like mysteries, I don't like not knowing what's happened here, and you learn early on in this business that the best stuff is always found under a ton of garbage and slime and shit in some dumpster in south Chicago. The good cops go digging."

"Well," said Figgs, smiling, "let's find ourselves a couple of usable shovels."

❆   ❆   ❆

Later, Dixon would be able to nearly convince himself that what happened had had a logical explanation. Some scientific reason that he just didn't understand, perhaps because he'd barely managed to get through his physics classes at Southern Illinois, perhaps because he'd never had the temper, patience or ordered mind for the physical disciplines, perhaps because he and Figgs had been hallucinating.

But he never asked Figgs about it later.

And he never asked any of the NSA science geeks for their opinion, either.

They'd spent two laborious, tortuous hours chipping through the frozen ground of the mass grave, and had uncovered six bodies to that point, none of them possessing anything remotely worth their labor, all of them twisted and broken and sporting frozen blooms of blood around their bullet wounds. Dixon had found the next one, the seventh, his shovel snapping three of the cadaver's fingers off at the first joint inadvertently, and the American had dry-heaved for what seemed like the twentieth time and began scraping away the slushy mud around the man's face and arms.

There had to be some explanation, of course, some biological excuse.

Because while Dixon was sluicing the frozen dirt away from the dead man with his shovel and Figgs was working on his own corpse ten feet away, the laws of nature, for whatever perverse reason, decided to fuck with the American agent.

The cadaver's face, a foot from Dixon, twitched as if it were actually feeling the sub-zero air.

Dixon started, taking a half-step back.

And the dead miner's eyes shot open.

"Jesus!" said Dixon, his heart racing.

"*Cthhhuuuu. . .*" wheezed the body, foul, miasmic air hissing from its blue lips, one arm cracking free of the frigid dirt, a paper gripped tightly in its bone-white fingers, those shriveled, staring eyes bulging in the parchment face. "*CthuuUUU!*"

Dixon, working on some atavistic reflex, grabbed the paper and jerked back.

And the frozen body instantly burst into flames.

London, United Kingdom

"So that's it?" asked the voice on the other end of the satellite line. "A scrap of paper in a dead Russian's pocket?"

"Wars have hinged on scraps of paper," said Dixon, sipping from his glass of bitter. He and Figgs had made it back to the rendezvous point in time for the pickup and he now sat in a little pub near Whitehall waiting for his erstwhile partner to meet him and chatting with Dixon's's immediate superior on a line so heavily encrypted that God Himself couldn't crack it. "You'll get that translation for me?"

"I've got our language experts on the way in right now," said Plenary. "What do you think of this whole business, Dixon?"

"I don't know what to think," said the agent, looking thoughtfully into the glass at the dark amber beer. "But I'm worried. The Saudis set up a multi-million-dollar camp, then burned it down as soon as they found what they wanted. I know they've got money coming out their asses, but that's still a major expenditure on their part, and I'm wondering what kind of value received would explain it."

"They're our allies, Dixon," said Plenary.

"Yes, sir," said Dixon. "Why don't you call them up, sir, and ask them what's going on?"

"Yeah," said Plenary. "Good idea. I'll do that right after Hell freezes over. You say you're meeting again with Figgs?"

"He just showed up," said Dixon, noticing the MI6 man coming through the door of the pub, letting in some horizontal rain with him.

"Pick his brain, Dixon," said Plenary. "He's a major player, and anything he gives you demands attention."

"Got it, sir. I'll see you tomorrow."

"Come straight from Dulles," said Plenary, and hung up.

"Having a nice conversation?" asked Figgs, sliding down onto the chair opposite Dixon. "Maybe found a lady friend for a later assignation?"

"The boss," said Dixon, waving at the barmaid. "He wants me to pick your brain."

Figgs snorted. "My brain is still thawing out, mate. It may be weeks before I get feeling back in my fingers."

"How'd the translation go?" asked the American.

"You don't want to wait for your chaps to provide one?" asked Figgs, smiling. "I saw you making a copy of the paper."

"I imagine you're not going to lie to me," said Dixon. "What are you drinking?"

Figgs looked up at the woman and said "Pint of lager, if you please." She nodded, smiled at the men, and returned to the bar to relay the order.

"First of all," said Figgs, returning his gaze to his counterpart, "that paper was old."

"It looked it," said Dixon, remembering pulling it out of the dead miner's hand, seeing it crumple and crack as he drew it from the suddenly scorching flesh and shook the snow and grave dirt from it. "Any idea how old?"

"The lab boys are working on it," said Figgs, "but probably about a hundred years, give or take."

"Figures," said Dixon. "So, spill. What'd it say?"

"Roughly translated, it appears to be some kind of magic spell," said Figgs, reaching for a packet of potato chips Dixon had open on the table before him. "You mind? I didn't get a chance for supper."

Dixon waved his assent, then shook his head. "Magic," he said. "Cthugha."

"Yes indeed," said Figgs. "Just like I told you. Some elemental god of fire able to destroy vast stretches of land just by his summoning. You still not believe in this shite?"

Dixon chose not to answer. He'd been badly shaken by the spontaneous combustion of the corpse they'd dug up (and *don't forget* that he was trying to talk, urged his brain. *Don't forget* that, *as if you ever could. . .*), and switched instead to sane, rational business.

"So the Arabs didn't get the spell?" asked Dixon.

"Oh, I imagine they already had the spell," said Figgs, nodding as the barmaid reappeared with a pint glass full of bright yellow beer, waiting for her to leave before he resumed talking. "But this is the first time I've seen the thing, and guess what?"

"What?" asked Dixon, wondering if he was insane for even considering this cockamamie story.

"According to the spell, you also need a trigger," said Figgs, sipping his lager. "Something that you bury beneath the summoning point, something that will call this ancient god to whatever spot you decide. And thus utterly destroy said spot."

"A trigger," said Dixon.

"An amulet," said Figgs. "Something in a box that a poor Russian dug up. There was a tattered scrap of paper attached to the box, and he absent-mindedly put it in his pocket while he tried to open the thing . . . but he couldn't. So he brought it up to the surface, to a foremen."

"You're speculating now," said Dixon.

"I'm good at it," said Figgs.

"Go on," said the NSA agent.

"And at that point, the Saudis were done," said Figgs. "They locked up the men, machine-gunned them, and loaded up their god-summoning trigger. Then they left."

"Where'd they go?" asked Dixon, his mouth dry in spite of the cool beer.

"That's the question, isn't it?" asked Figgs, leaning back in his chair. "If I had to guess, I might say London. Or

Washington. Maybe New York or Los Angeles. Or, hell, Tel Aviv."

"Christ," said Dixon. "This shit isn't real, is it?"

"Hard to say," responded Figgs, taking another drink. "But remember the Tunguska Event, remember what happened there, and remember that the Arabs did find something buried in the exact spot they thought they would."

"So what's the next step?" asked Dixon.

"No next step for you, my friend," said the MI6 man. "Your job is done, you can fly home tomorrow and report, and we'll deal with it from here on out."

"My ass," said Dixon. "If there's even a remote chance this . . . this rigmarole is for real, I'm in this until the end."

"I'm afraid not," said Figgs, and now his voice was cold. "You came along on our little trip to Siberia, you found the paper, you have a copy of it at home, and you know about as much as we do. I'd say we paid for your satellite images tenfold."

"You bastard," said Dixon, but there was no heat in his words. He'd be talking exactly the same way, had their positions been reversed. "You're cutting me out?"

"We're not friends, mate," said Figgs, looking straight at him. "I'm the Queen's man, you're the President's. Amicable though the relations are between our countries, we'd be bloody insane to trust you with everything we know or suspect. And that includes the present situation. So go home, make your report, and let our superiors argue the whole thing out. I've given you more, probably, than you deserve already."

"If I hadn't been there, would you have dug up that grave?" asked Dixon, sliding his beer aside, putting his hands flat on the table.

Figgs considered the question for a long moment, then gave the briefest ghost of a smile.

"What'd you call yourself?" he asked. "'A good cop'?"

Dixon nodded.

"I wouldn't have thought of digging up those poor bastards," Figgs said. "Kudos to you, and my personal thanks. But that only buys you what you've got so far. Nothing else."

"I appreciate the hospitality," said Dixon, standing up. "And the field trip."

"My pleasure," said Figgs, perhaps a bit regretfully, raising his glass. "Have a safe flight home."

Somewhere in Europe

The truck rumbled through the darkness, through the hills, and Hassan finally gave up trying to sleep. He had gotten but the barest modicum of rest since digging up the treasure in the accursed freezing forests of Russia, and he suspected that it was the pulse of the amulet itself, the ancient breath and dark energies of the thing that were keeping him from the repose he needed.

The imam was in back with the chest, not so much guarding it as learning it. Six of Hassan's best men back there too, holding their weapons, sitting with their backs against the jostling metal of the truck's wall, ready for death or glory, but uneasily aware that, no matter how much they believed in the rightness of their mission, no matter how glorious would be the endgame of this decisive gambit, the burning sky destroying the very heart of the infidel, still the unburied talisman and the deathless once-man that caressed and cooed to it were unsettling in the extreme. Hassan could see the scene in his mind's eye, the dark bed of the Mercedes truck, the dim glow of the interior lights, and the tall, cadaverous robed figure bent like some eldritch spider over the cedar chest and its contents. He shuddered, his tired body jerking with some atavistic fear.

"Are you well, sayyid?" asked the driver, taking his eyes from the road for a half-second, sensing Hassan's discomfort.

"I am as Allah wills me to be," said Hassan, shifting to find a more comfortable position. "How much longer, friend?"

"Twelve hours," said the driver.

"Ahh," sighed Hassan. Twelve hours to reach their destination. It would be bright, then, the early morning sun shining down on the infidel land. And then, shortly after, it would be even brighter as the ancient avatar of Allah was summoned back into the physical world.

As Hassan imagined it, imagined the blast as the Cthugha-thing appeared in the sky, burning the very oxygen of the air, knowing that he would die in that moment, but hoping that he would see and remember the sight in Paradise so that his eternity would be filled with the joy of knowing he had helped obliterate the stronghold of the enemy . . . he heard sirens behind them.

Instantly the driver blenched and reached down for his sidearm, wedged between the truck's seats.

"No," said Hassan, sitting up straight and alert, his soldier's senses come to full life. "No, my friend. We are protected by God. Pull over."

"But, sayyid," started the driver, sweat glistening on his brow as the red-and-blue lights began behind them, reflected in the rear-view and side mirrors, filling the cab with swirling color. "Our mission!"

"Will continue," said Hassan, reaching out his left hand to gently pluck the driver's off the handgun. "Our imam will see to it."

And, indeed, in the back of the truck the holy man had raised his head at the sound of the police siren. Around him, the six men of the guard chattered excitedly and readied their weapons, but the old man ignored them.

Beneath the blackness of the cowl, through the darkness that clung to the imam like a clutching hand, the rictus white of his smile shone, the sunken cavities of his eyes flickered with anticipation. "Ahhh . . ." he breathed, his long, bony fingers slowly caressing the fragrant wood of the box, the ancient symbols already filling what remained of his mind, urging him to give voice to them, to release them again upon a world so long silent of them.

"*Fthagn*," the imam began. "*Cthugha krrugh d'nyeh fthagn, Cthugha ser'rev ïa ïa ïa. . . .*"

And in the night sky above them, a pinprick appeared.

Heathrow Airport
London, England

Dixon sipped his coffee while tapping keys on his laptop, wondering why the Brits, so good with beer and tea, couldn't make a decent cup of joe. He also listened with half an ear for news about his flight while he was writing and reading, but the peculiar speech patterns of the announcers coming over the airport's speakers made that a difficult task — it was as if the mandarins of Heathrow had decided, in their infinite wisdom, to put only those men and women with the heaviest and most unintelligible of Welsh accents on their loudspeakers. "Flight 92G to Chkk, haaa-cmm laittt, djoo baggage claim ninety-loopty", the most recent one had said, and Dixon had mentally shrugged and taken another swig of the dark dishwater the barman had given him. If his flight was late, he'd find out soon enough.

Ahh, he thought, watching as the little roll of paper in his built-in printer started moving. The translation.

It had taken them long enough — and he'd wondered, as the hours had rolled along and as he'd packed for his trip home, if he'd been deemed unworthy to share in the treasure he'd found for his masters. But it seemed as though all was forgiven, for here, on his encrypted printing device, was the transcription of the scrap of paper he'd taken from the dead (burning) Russian in that soupy mess of frozen earth and stiff bodies he and Figgs had excavated.

He tore the translation from his computer and started reading, and then the printer kicked on again, and he raised mildly startled eyes to it as another narrow band of paper began to emerge. *It'll say* this message will self-destruct in six seconds, *and then I'll have to deal with the airport cops when it bursts into flame,* he thought, smiling. He glanced over the paper already in his hand, noting the incantations and descriptions spelled out therein, wondering what the poor person back in Fort Meade had made of this gobbledygook while he was translating it, and noticing that whoever it was had spelled the fire god's name as Kathooga.

And now the second printout was done, and Dixon pulled it out and scanned it.

> *Dixon*, it began. *Your masters have convinced mine that you should have a bit more information than I gave you, so here's the document that started this whole dog's breakfast. I'm sure I need not remind you that the paper is confidential and eyes only, so don't leave it lying on a plane seat in Washington, there's a good chap.*

It was signed by Figgs. Dixon smiled, mentally congratulating Plenary, and pleased that he'd been kept in the loop, and began to read.

The communiqué had been intercepted by some British cell-phone eavesdropping program that wasn't supposed to exist, and had been a conversation between a known al-Qaeda operative in Leeds and some unnamed man in Saudi Arabia the spy called '*Imam*'. The conversation seemed innocuous enough to Dixon as he read the translation, but he came to full alert at the end.

> Imam: "And how progresses the project up north?"
>
> Spy: "Very well. The site manager expects to report good news any day now. However, there have been problems."
>
> Imam: "What problems?" *{spoken very sharply}*

Spy: "The Tunguska is frozen, and there are delays delivering some of the equipment."

Imam: "No names!" *{spoken in a hiss}* "Fool! Do you think there are no ears in the world to hear you?"

Spy: "Understood, Imam, but I believe that we are safe — the British have not the technology to listen in on cellular calls."

Imam: "I don't worry about the British. There are other forces in the game that you know not of, forces that would not look kindly on what we attempt to do, forces that would protect the accursed, unholy city of the damned that we will destroy when Cthugha is again summoned."

And after that, the conversation ended quickly, with nothing else of importance having been said. Dixon read it again, and then a third time, trying to make sense of it all. He also wondered why he was flying home when there was so much he could be doing here in Europe to get to the bottom of this strange situation — his cop training, his cop instincts cried out for him to get back out on the street, start ringing doorbells and collecting evidence.

But Plenary wanted him home, and Figgs had made it clear that it wasn't his business anymore, so Dixon would be a good soldier and march onto the 757 as ordered.

He sighed, finished his coffee and looked around for the waiter so he could order another cup. As he did, he noticed the television set over the bar and the CNN reporter speaking earnestly and silently — and behind him, a scene out of the *Inferno*.

"Excuse me," he said, standing and moving to the bar, papers in hand. "But could you possibly turn up the volume on that?"

"No problem," said the barman, reaching up and adjusting the controls on the front of the television. "Happened down in Italy early this morning — horrible thing."

"Authorities are at a loss to explain exactly what happened here," said the talking head, looking grave and serious, an expression newsmen learned in the cradle. "There was some kind of explosion and it completely devastated several kilometers of road and forest. The highway ministry has set up detours so that travelers can get from Tolmezzo to Udine, with no indication as to when the road may re-open, though rumors say that a hazardous material investigation team is en route from Rome as we speak."

"What the hell happened?" asked Dixon.

The barman shrugged. "Buncha communists down there," he said. "Probably messing around with bombs. Or maybe it was the Mafia."

"The Mafia blew up a highway in the Dolomites?" asked Dixon, eyes glued to the screen as the camera panned across the black, blasted landscape of melted scree and splintered mountain trees flindered to charcoal bits.

"Probably some judge driving by on his way to court," said the barman, grabbing a couple of pint glasses from the shelf and starting to pour beer into them. "Haven't you ever seen *The Godfather*? Great movie, mate."

"'Accursed, unholy city of the damned,'" whispered Dixon. "Oh, Jesus."

"What was that?" asked the barman, turning back over his shoulder with a quizzical expression on his face.

"I need a phone," said Dixon urgently.

"This is Figgs," came the voice on the other end of the line.

"What happened in Italy?" Dixon demanded.

"The Renaissance," said Figgs promptly. "Alberti, Da Vinci, the Florentine Enlightenment — what a time that must have been!"

"Goddammit," said Dixon, "they're heading for—"

"Vatican City," finished Figgs. "Sounds that way to me, too. Lucky for us, no?"

"What do you mean, 'lucky'?" asked Dixon, stretching over the bar so that he could keep the phone to his ear — the cord wasn't long enough for him to stand comfortably.

"I mean, we don't have to worry about Cthugha appearing in the sky over Piccadilly Circus or the Washington Mall, do we?"

"No," said Dixon, as calmly as he could. "All we have to worry about is the Vatican going up in a firestorm, and then a billion Catholics around the world looking for someone to blame."

"Agreed," said Figgs. "We're not going to let that happen. I just got off the phone with the boss, and he's calling the PM, and the PM's going to get hold of the Premier."

"And how about you?" asked Dixon.

"You're at Heathrow, aren't you?" asked the MI6 man.

"I am."

"I'll meet you in five minutes in Terminal One," said Figgs. "Go to the last gate — I'll radio ahead that you're coming."

Vatican City
Papal Apartments

"What do you make of this message?" asked the Pope.

"It is somewhat difficult to believe," responded Cardinal Di Vittorio.

The pontiff smiled. "Some there are who would say that about God, Ricardo."

"Are we to trust the English, then?" asked the Cardinal, frowning. "A group of Muslims coming here to destroy the city by calling forth some demon from the flames of Hell?"

"A group of *Arabs*, Ricardo," said the Pope gently. "Muslims — true Muslims — would not dabble in such things. And, yes, I find that I do trust the information from the British."

"Has God told you to do so?" asked the Cardinal, curiosity tinged with awe in his voice.

"No," said the old man shortly, closing his eyes and reaching for the plain wooden crucifix on the ornate table next to his bed. "No, my friend, I am not receiving any divine revelations right now. I am remembering things I have read, books in the *Biblioteca Apostolica* — and books in the more secret archives here. Have you ever heard of a book called the *Necronomicon?*"

"It doesn't exist," said the Cardinal, eyes narrowing.

The Pope nodded, though his expression was enigmatic. "And a good thing, too. Such a book, if it existed, might be filled with incantations and directions for summoning such demons." He sighed. "We must make preparations. Summon for me Captain am Rhyn and Cardinal Bruno, if you would."

The head of the Swiss Guard and the head of the Inquisition. Cardinal di Vittorio gave a small shudder, then turned and hurried on his errand.

He hadn't believed the message when he had received it. He was starting to change his mind.

Airspace over central France

"Thanks again for the ride," said Dixon, leaning forward and looking out the windows of the chopper as it roared southeast over the crags and valleys of Auvergne, heading for an eventual quick refueling stop in Marseille before heading over the Alps and down the Italian boot.

"We're seeing Europe, you and I," smiled Figgs, reaching past one of the soldiers seated next to him, opening a small weapons locker. "Can you fire a gun?"

"That's not in your files?" asked Dixon, turning his head back toward his counterpart.

"You finished the FBI course at Quantico," said Figgs. "But you weren't anything special."

"Twenty-ninth out of thirty-seven," said Dixon. "Good enough to put a hole in someone, not good enough to pick exactly where."

"That's fine," said Figgs, withdrawing an evil-looking handgun, briefly inspecting it, then reaching over to hand it to the NSA agent. Dixon looked down, saw an FN P90 and smiled.

"You use Belgian guns?" asked Dixon.

"We'd use American, but they keep going off half-cocked," responded the British agent.

"Tell me again what to expect when we get there," said Dixon. "Will the Vatican cooperate with us?"

"Not really," said Figgs. "They thanked us cordially for the information, they're grudgingly allowing us down there to observe, but they obviously don't want us underfoot. And the Italian government won't mess with Vatican City, so we're on our own. Do you think your lot will be able to get us more access than we have now?"

"I doubt it," said Dixon gloomily. "And we had a chance to elect a Catholic President last time around, too."

"Maybe you should have that Kennedy bloke in Massachusetts call ahead for us," suggested Figgs, leaning back and closing his eyes.

Dixon snorted. "So why are they allowing us down there at all?"

"You're forgetting, mate," said Figgs, eyes still closed. "We've got a copy of the spell, don't we? And the Pope doesn't."

Outside Montecelio, Italy

Hassan checked his weapon for the tenth time since they'd stopped, saw that it was still working perfectly, and set it down beside him on a crate. They were in a barn, the truck looming motionless in the middle of the vast space and his men going over and over their preparations for the upcoming ritual. All of them were antsy, eager to get going, and there was an undercurrent of electricity about them, a web of nervous energy readying itself to burst coming from each of the men.

They had seen miracles, and they all knew Paradise was very close.

Hassan forced himself to close his eyes and tried to relax a bit. But when he did, the memories exploded in his head.

The Italian policeman getting out of his car and cautiously moving forward along the side of the truck, Hassan watching him in the side view mirror, hoping the driver would remain calm.

The policeman stopping, hearing or sensing something in the sky above him.

A roar like doomsday, and the dark sky suddenly rolling in flames, the cop falling backward, mouth open, screaming as his hair ignited, his clothes burned, Hassan opening the door and looking out, looking up at the roiling, churning mass of reds and oranges and yellows pulsing above them in a spectacular cloud of nuclear chaos, lines of fire shooting down like arrows into the policeman, his eyes boiling in their sockets, his testicles exploding like chestnuts, the meat melting on his bones.

The imam striding around the side of the truck, the amulet in his hands held high to the sky, chanting the ancient, non-human words, guiding the child of Cthugha, forcing it to blast the unfortunate Italian into atoms, keeping their own truck free of flames, free of the infernal heat that even now hammered the surrounding area like floodwaters gulfing over a broken dam, the trees going up like kindling, the grass flash-fried into soot, rocks exploding and even the ground-soil burning, burning like paper, smoke oily and black making pitch of the false day, plunging the world into eldritch night.

And then the imam finishing the spell, squeezing his spider-hands around the talisman, forcing the flame-beast to close in on itself, to compress, to force itself smaller and smaller, roaring its hatred, its defiance, finally its sheer rage as it shrank, shrank, now ten meters across, now five, now one.

And then a pinprick again. And then only night and smoke.

"Are you ready, my child?" came the imam's voice.

Hassan opened his eyes, saw the gaunt figure above him, wreathed in shadows, teeth shining in the gloom of the barn. He sensed all his soldiers around him, guns gripped in their hands, ready to follow their master on to death and glory, sensed their terror, their exhilaration. And he had a quick sense, a fleeting flicker of thought that died almost as it was born in his brain, an unholy, faithless, damnable notion . . . *what if we are wrong? Wrong about everything? Would Allah want this to happen? Are we martyrs, or monsters?*

But it only lasted the briefest split of a second, and then he stood, staring straight at his leader.

"Let us go, sayyid."

Vatican City

"I do not have much time, my friends," said the Swiss Guardsman in heavily accented English.

Dixon didn't think the guy meant it when he said 'friends' but supposed diplomacy was important.

"Then let's not argue," said Figgs. "My men, Mr. Dixon and I will come along with your group but won't interfere unless you want us for backup."

"Impossible," said the Vatican soldier. "You are, of course, welcome to stay here in the command center."

If you want access to the paper I have in my pocket," said Figgs, "you'll let us come with you. You said you don't have much time, and I agree with you — the terrorists are probably in the city already. Every second we waste here is another second they could be planting their bomb and getting ready to knock down the Sistine Chapel."

The Swiss winced, but held steady. "Impossible," he repeated. "I am to cooperate with you within reason, but what you request is simply impossible. We will be going into places that are barred to all but a few men."

"The catacombs," said Figgs. "Jesus — the Pope knows what's going on, doesn't he?"

Dixon shook his head as he saw the man's face freeze up at Figgs' casual blasphemy, and hurried to intervene.

"We want to help," he said, boring his eyes into the soldier's. "We won't get in your way. We're all trained soldiers. We won't desecrate anything. The fact that you know our quarry will be underground suggests that you know how important this mission is, and so do we. Please, Captain — let us come with you."

The man thought about it for a long second, then shook his head with finality. "I cannot," he said. "But I beg you — let me take that paper to His Holiness."

"No dice, asshole," said Figgs. "C'mon, mate, let's go find us some Arabs."

"No," said the Swiss Guardsman coldly. "You will stay here."

Suddenly, the men under Figgs' command had their weapons out and aimed. It was like a magic trick, Dixon thought — one second they were all at rest, listening respectfully as their commander argued with the Vatican soldier, and the next they looked like the extras in a Chuck Norris movie, bristling with guns and attitude.

A second later, the other Swiss Guards in the room had their guns out, and they were in the middle of a Sergio Leone movie.

"Shit," said Dixon, shaking his head in frustration.

"Looks like we've got us an international incident, here," said Figgs, smiling. "If we survive the next few hours, we're all of us going to be on CNN."

"We will survive the next few hours," came a voice from the door. Dixon turned and saw a tall, imposing priest — no, a cardinal — standing there looking mildly amused.

"Your Excellency," said am Rhyn, standing at attention. "You should not be here."

"Neither should you," said the cardinal. "And, especially, neither should either of you" — this to Figgs and Dixon.

"Yeah, I know," said Figgs. "There's a new episode of *Coupling* on the telly tonight, and here I am in the land of dead languages and funny hats."

"I've seen your Beefeaters," said the priest dryly. "You win the funny hat battle."

Figgs smiled. "So you're the tiebreaker, apparently," he said. "What do you say?"

"You can go with the Guard," said Bruno. "And with His Holiness' compliments. He knows you've come a long way and done the Church a great service."

"Thank you," said Dixon.

"'Bout bloody time," said Figgs. "Where are we going?"

"I'll need that manuscript of yours," said the cardinal, extending his hand. The man exuded confidence, power, charm.

"I'll read you anything you want," said Figgs, "but this isn't leaving my hand. Capisce?"

Bruno grinned. "Absolutely. Tell me then, how is the spell supposed to be triggered?"

"You need to be underground — but you knew that already. The next step is . . ." began Figgs, and they all started moving as he talked.

The Catacombs Beneath Vatican City

Hassan held a flashlight in one hand, his gun in the other, and as they moved as silently as they could through the infidel ossuary he kept forcing himself to look away from the jumbles of bones that were shoved up against the walls in every tunnel they moved through.

These weren't the caves they allowed the tourists into, the St. Callixtus network with its neat burial niches. These were older, deeper, and Hassan wondered how his imam had known of their existence, let alone the secret entrance he had led them to in the woods on one of the hills outside Rome.

But the imam knew many, many things that were supposed lost in the whorls and maelstroms of time; he had known about the trigger buried deep in the Siberian earth, had found the spell of summoning in a book discovered in a tomb near Riyadh, a book only the holy man was allowed to touch, though Hassan had once seen it — a book bound in human skin, the words *al-Azif* scrolled on its cover in blood-red pigment, and even that brief glance had caused Hassan a fortnight's worth of nightmares.

So here they were, moving deeper and deeper into the earth, and now the very walls bled water, glistening droplets of mineral-heavy condensation glowing like sickly jewels in the beam from the torch.

The imam moved ahead of the rest of them, scuttling through the darkness as though born to it, like the white rats that rustled in the invisible distance or the bloated bats that hung drowsy and diseased on the high ceilings above — the holy man moved surely, securely through the dark tunnels, never missing a step or hesitating at the many junctions. Hassan and the rest of the men were hard-pressed to keep up with him, lighted though their way was.

After what seemed like hours, long hours moving ever downward, ever deeper into the guts of the rock, and through stretches of miles of bone-lined passageways, bones enough to make a mighty army, Hassan heard his master stop, twenty feet ahead, and sigh.

"Is there trouble?" he whispered, his finger tightening on the trigger of the Uzi.

"We have arrived," said the imam.

Hassan slowly resumed moving, and his men with him. As he inched forward, the tunnel widened, the ceiling growing up away from the floor, and ten more paces brought him to the end of the tunnel and the yawning mouth of a cavern.

More than a cavern. A *grotto*, huge as the Colosseum, stretching out into vast spaces even the powerful beam of the Maglite couldn't reach. The bones of the unnamed, unmoored multitudes spilled out into the tremendous emptiness and made a carpet of white, jagged spikes that blanketed the rock like ash and cinder from a great conflagration, and the air was cold and moved in sudden jags and blasts as the wind moaned in the black, deep vacuum.

Hassan fought to remain firm, steadfast, but felt his knees buckle slightly as he gazed out into the eternal blackness before him, heard the currents of air moaning like monstrous insanities all around him, felt the presence, the sickly electric current of the amulet and its skeletal keeper intensify, as if it had come home. Sweat beaded on his cold flesh. He struggled to keep his breath even.

"It is here," whispered the holy man, his fingers caressing the box, his eyeless sockets staring straight up at the great vault of the invisible roof. "The deeper we go, the more room Cthugha has to enter our plane. And this place, this accursed sepulcher of the febrile, weakling Jerusalemites, is very, very deep."

"Praise Allah," said Hassan finally.

The imam turned to him, the tall man's expression unreadable, his posture taut with repressed excitement. For seconds, he didn't respond.

"Praise Allah indeed," he said finally, and then "*Cthulhu fthagn.*"

"What does that mean?" asked Hassan.

"It means 'all glory to our Lord'," said the imam, smiling hugely in the dark. "For whom we will open the way."

And they moved deeper into the pit of bones and screams.

❋   ❋   ❋

"You know where the hell we are?" asked Dixon conversation-ally of the soldier next to him. The man turned, glared for a second, hefted his Beretta Browning significantly and turned back to the tunnel.

"Yeah, me neither," said Figgs from his other side. They were near the end of the little procession, with the SAS men Figgs had brought, but with the night-vision goggles and the infrared beams the Swiss Guard were using, they could see everything surprisingly clearly, though it all looked monochro-matic and two-dimensional, and sometimes the American had to catch himself from stumbling on the loose scree or the occa-sional bone lying in their path. "But Captain am Rhyn seems to have some insider information, because we're making a beeline for somewhere."

"The two of you shut up, now," came the cardinal's voice from behind them. "We near our destination, and noise travels far in the caverns."

"Who are all of these poor bastards?" asked Figgs quietly, reaching out with a booted foot and kicking an ancient tibia back against the wall.

"That is a story for another time," whispered Bruno. "If we come back alive, I may tell you. But for now, *hush*."

So they did.

They moved slowly, cautiously through the darkness, guns ready, unaware that the Arabs had beaten them by a matter of ten minutes to the holy grotto of the black winds and multi-tudinous bones.

The ritual was already underway.

Caverna d'Ognissanti:
three hundred feet beneath the Basilica of St. Peter's

"Fthagn Cthugha krrugh d'nyeh khrach rho're!"

The words were mostly the same, but there were subtle differences this time, and Hassan knew that this was because the imam was summoning the actual being of Cthugha rather than one of its small, weak children. One of those children had been enough to destroy twenty kilometers of mountainous land in the Dolomites.

And they were deeper now. Much, much deeper.

The holy man produced candles and positioned them around their makeshift altar, stuck randomly into piles of twisted, broken human bones, and though it had seemed impossible that such small flames would remain lit with the winds roaring around them, they had — and now, with every word the imam chanted, the flames leapt and grew stronger, as if eager for the culmination of the spell.

Hassan's men grew more and more ecstatic as well. They stood in a loose circle around the priest and his altar, eyes wide like excited children, watching as the man chanted and waved his bony arms in sinuous sigils through the air.

Hassan felt the tug, the excitement, the urgency rippling through the bone-strewn cavern, but he resisted it. That worm of disquiet in his guts was still there, still gnawing at him like the ghost of Hamlet's father.

He'd long ago made peace with the fact that he must, to protect Islam, sometimes kill innocents. Those miners up in Russia had not been bad men, and some of them had even been fellow believers from Kazakhstan, and yet he and his team had systematically murdered them and bulldozed them into a pit in the ground. Hassan could accept those actions because they led to a great prize for Islam, a wondrous victory.

And yet, and yet he was beginning, now at this late date, to wonder about the imam. That man is not really a man at all, is he? his mind whispered. The imam could quote the Koran exactly, was conversant in every aspect of the one true religion, had easily gained the confidence of not only the establishment in Riyadh, but also the Royal Family itself.

And now Hassan found himself wondering if the imam was Muslim at all. The blank stare a few minutes ago, before the holy man had finally said 'Praise Allah'. The strange, choking, alien words spitting from the man's lips like chunks of sharp, hot iron as he worked his invocation above his altar. Most of all, that child of Cthugha the man had summoned in the mountains, that hideous, testicle-tightening chaos that burned like nuclear fire and tried to fight its way into the world, blasting everything into atoms.

Was that an aspect of Allah?

Would they be rewarded with Paradise for their actions?

What was he doing down here?

And then, before the questions could torment Hassan further, he got hit with a bullet.

"Looks like we got four of them," said am Rhyn, crouching down behind a two-meter tall pile of jumbled bones, peering through his night-vision scope. "Good thing they had those candles going down there."

Dixon watched from his own spot, pistol useless in his hand at this distance, watched as the other Arabs dove for cover and raised their automatic weapons. He winced, knowing what was going to happen next.

Whang came a ricochet from a few feet ahead of him as a bullet struck the rock floor of the cavern, and then the roar of gunfire as the sound finally caught up with the lead. The Swiss guard riflemen had scoped and sighted on five targets in the enemy group, and had hit four with one synchronized attack.

Somehow, though, they'd missed the easy shot. The tall, spidery-looking imam still stood over his little table, still waved his arms in the darkness. As Dixon peered through his own night-vision glasses, looking at the strange figure all limned in ghostly green — everything was green in the enhanced lenses, green bones glowing dimly, green men scuttling around down there, trying to find cover from the invisible rifle fire, green flames dancing in the windy air — the figure seemed to stare back right at him.

"To what green altar, O mysterious priest," whispered Dixon.

"Keats," said Figgs next to him. "That bloody 'Grecian Urn' poem we all had to memorize in public school."

"We missed the primary target," said Dixon, listening as the men around him began firing again, hearing a sudden scream from below as another Saudi was hit, ducking as more ricochets whined from the rock and bone nearby.

"He keeps standing straight up like that," responded Figgs, staring intently through his goggles, "we won't miss him for long."

"At least this should interrupt his spell," said Dixon, lowering his own binoculars so as to blink his eyes a bit.

"*Ïa ïa ïa, Cthugha!*" roared the imam as the incantation came to its end. Italian and English rifle bullets whizzed around him, all of them missing him by inches.

A pinprick of light appeared far above in the chill air.

And then reality exploded.

"What the *fuck?*" roared Figgs, leaping to his feet, flinging the night-vision scope from him like it was radioactive.

Dixon fell back as the light appeared in the vault of the cavern, appeared and multiplied and roiled out into the world, and even as he squinched his eyes as far shut as they would go against the blinding light, the new sun that twisted and flamed in the false sky, still he screamed as the pain of such luminosity hit him.

He bowed his head, shaking it against the pain, and fought to his knees, then his feet, hearing the roar of Cthugha as it forced itself into the world, a roar that sounded like discordant, atonal piping amplified to airplane-engine decibels, and it took Dixon long seconds before he was able to open his eyes again.

When he did, he saw men writing around him, men claw-
ing at their own eyes and mewling like whipped cats.

They were all looking through their magnification glasses when
that light appeared, Dixon suddenly realized. All were blind. All
but him.

The imam exulted, tossed his head so that his hood fell
against his back, exposed himself to the ancient god above him.
His pale, taut skin blistered against his skull, blackened and
shriveled away, and he raised his arms to the heavens, the
amulet clenched tightly in one bony fist.

"Yes, my lord," he whispered, desiccated lips withering on
his teeth, flesh melting away from his bones as his true form
began to appear. "Enter. Enter and destroy!"

And the rent in reality grew bigger.

Dixon forgot caution and common sense and let instinct
take over.

Not animal instinct, which screamed at him to run from
this madness, to get out of the cavern while he still could, but
some other instinct, some atavistic terror and repulsion and
hatred that lingered in racial memory, urging him to destroy
the alien, to fight with bone and blood and courage against the
insane, chaotic powers that so often tried to invade our world
of sanity and physics and safety.

He sprinted forward through the burning bones, slavering
to kill.

The imam opened his palm to the raging fire above him,
revealed the talisman.

"The fingerbone of John the Baptist," he shouted through
skeletal teeth, through ropes of wriggling muscle that
gleamed redly as they formed on his face, through sudden
fangs. "Long lost, long hidden from the world, now let it be
the gate for the Elder Gods to annihilate this whole planet,
this whole universe!"

"Fuck you," said Dixon.

The imam whirled, more human flesh sloughing off him at the sudden motion, more alien sinew and gristle forming, and saw the NSA agent sliding to a stop in the clearing, gun raised.

The monstrosity snarled and whipped his other hand forward, toward the American intruder.

And a line of fire blasted down from the boiling sun.

Dixon fired one hasty shot, missing, and dove to the ground just as the plasmic blast splashed into the rock where he had stood, spattering blobs of liquid stone around like water in a frying pan, and the man screamed as a bit of the lava hit him in the calf, burning instantly through his jeans and into his flesh. He nearly dropped the gun, but instead fought through the haze of agony, the blinding light above him, and squinted for another shot.

The imam — what had been the imam — stepped toward the fallen man and gestured again.

Dixon got off another shot and saw a hunk of the creature's arm explode in a mist of green and red ichor, and then he rolled again, his leg screaming in inchoate agony, just as another thunderbolt of fire splashed into the ground next to him.

"You will be the sacrifice," whispered the beast. He had been planning to use the Arabs for the blood he would need to complete the ritual, but this pitiful man would do just as well, if not better.

As the new shimmering flesh began to fill in the hole in his arm, he reached forward one final time . . .

And Hassan finally managed to struggle to a sitting position, the blood oozing from the bullet wound in his stomach, finally got the Uzi aimed.

And the imam jerked and jolted as the stream of bullets riddled his back, tried to spin around, danced as more and more lead filled his burning body, more and more flesh absorbed the punishing blows of the bullets, and he screamed a crescendo of rage and anger like a galaxy dying.

Dixon took careful aim as the thing spun away from him, tried to forget the fire that even now crept toward him as it burned the forest of bones, tried to forget that he'd finished twenty-ninth in his class at Quantico, and fired.

And the fingerbone of St. John the Baptist shattered in the monster's claws.

The imam released the fragments and turned one last time to look at Dixon, the thing's body jerking and fighting against the river of bullets that the Arab pulsed into it, and Dixon thought he might go insane just by looking into those flat sockets, those bony caves in which green fire danced like leprous vortices.

But then their light faded.

And then Hassan used every bit of strength he had left to raise the Uzi a few crucial inches.

The imam's head exploded.

Dixon looked over at him, at the Arab who had finally let the gun drop, who had finally given up struggling against the hole in his body, the killing metal that even now spilled poison into his bloodstream.

"In'shallah," he whispered, a slight frown on his face, as if he were worried, and then he died as well.

And Dixon looked up, looked at the roiling, burning mass of nuclear fire churning above him, spitting out tentacles of deadly flame like solar flares, beginning to rise up in the huge vaulted cavern toward the arching roof, toward the rock that separated it from Vatican city, and that rock began to melt, to form runnels of magma as it dripped down onto the floor far below, igniting piles of bones instantly.

Dixon had no idea what to do now. He'd destroyed the amulet, hadn't he? The summoner was dead, right? What more could he do? He sat down on the hot stone of the cavern floor, next to the dead man and the dead monster, and decided there was nothing to do. Nothing at all. Except, maybe, bear witness to the end of the Earth.

And then he heard the noise, the noise of chanting.

Rome, Italy

"Sorry I wasn't there to help, mate," said Figgs.

"You got us in there," said Dixon. "You got us invited on that little party."

They sat at a sidewalk table at a *trattoria* sipping Chianti, basking in the late-afternoon sun (a nice, healthy yellow Mediterranean sun) while they waited for their governments to sort things out with the Holy See.

"And then I missed the big event," said the British agent.

"Yeah, but you were there for the afterparty," said Dixon. "I didn't get to see the priests doing their little counter-spell, but I heard some of it."

"Seems like the Vatican has run into this kind of thing before," said Figgs, savoring the rich red wine. "When Cardinal Bruno starting chanting those words, and all his men joined in."

"Cthugha started shrinking," added Dixon, remembering.

"Well, if I wasn't such a staunch C-of-E man, I might just think of converting," finished Figgs. "And Jesus this wine the Italians make is good!"

"Everything's gonna taste good for a while, I think," mused Dixon, looking into his own glass and swirling the liquid slightly. "We just saved the world, didn't we?"

Figgs was silent for a few moments, then shook his head. "Hard to say, mate. Perhaps it just would've been another Tunguska. The world would've survived without most of Rome."

"You didn't hear that monster," interrupted Dixon. "He was talking about destroying all of creation. And he meant it."

"And maybe he was wrong," said Figgs. "Listen, Jack — you're going to go far in your field, I think. And you're going to run into things like this every once in a while."

"God forbid," said Dixon.

Figgs ignored him. "And I imagine it would be better that you go into these affairs not thinking you're some kind of savior, some superhuman defender."

"Believe me," said Dixon, taking another sip of wine and reaching for the plate of of calamari, "I know better. I was ready to sit down and die in that cave."

"Hmmph," grunted Figgs, leaning back. "Well, it was nice working with you."

"Let's not do it again sometime soon, all right?" said Dixon.

Figgs laughed.

IMPOSSIBLE OBJECT

David Conyers

Between the four walls, the floor and the ceiling there was the metal desk, her chair, a spare chair . . . and the impossible object. She'd been locked in the room for twenty minutes now, and in all that time she had done nothing but watch the last item, the alien device that could not be explained.

She knew its history, understood that this was a device which nobody could comprehend. It terrified most of the researchers who survived studying it, and occasionally killed or eradicated others, and yet was just as likely to freely offer up the secrets of the universe. Some people were drawn by its powers, and so returned to examine it again and again, just as she did now, knowing that she was addicted to its powers. Still, no one really understood anything about it or why it was here. That was why she had been brought in, the next crackpot researcher to offer her own slant in another minuscule hope to understand the object's confounding mysteries.

The object could not be defined. Not by size, dimension, shape, color, texture, weight, atomic composition, translucence, reflective index, volume, gravitational properties, radioactivity, or by any other known measure. They couldn't accurately predict the period of time it had been in possession of the Australian Government's most secret research facility, situated deep in the almost lifeless Great Sandy Desert. They couldn't even state where they had found it, nor could they count how many impossible objects they actually owned. That was because many researchers claimed to see more than one object whenever they gazed upon it.

She looked into it now, knowing that she was seeing only what she created inside her mind, for that was how it presented itself. To her it was a cube, hovering over the table silently and effortlessly. All sides of the mirrored cube — despite logic and her limited understanding of the laws of physics — were seen as if she was gazing at it from behind, above, below and to the front all at once. Her vision was comprehensible to her while she watched, and strangely it made sense, but if she later tried to recreate this vision in words or diagrams, well that would be impossible.

Not everyone saw the object the same way. Other members on the research team had reported spheres that vibrated, or humming fields reminiscent of an electrical storm. Others encountered wormholes that opened gateways to alien worlds, providing visions which regularly left observers shivering and demented from fear. Some even saw themselves in terrifying predicaments, such as their incarceration in a prison with other things, visions which they mostly refused to recount. A few saw nothing, as if the object were a blind spot before their eyes, not unlike the unseen world behind a person's own head.

Cameras couldn't record the impossible object. Film, video and digital recorders failed to develop, produced only static, or left similar blind spots over or around the point where the object should be. It was as if the space-time continuum was curved too tightly around it. Theoretical scientists on the team began to question if in fact they really had discovered anything in the first place, and they had mathematical proofs stating quite clearly that they had not.

Still, real or not, the object had not been without its uses. Recently, a newly recruited chemist had departed the containment room excitedly, because his mind had been embedded with a series of equations comprehensively describing complex compounds and subatomic structures that would later revolutionize superconductor research. Before that, an astrophysicist consulting the object was able to provide a plausible explanation of the properties of the universe's missing mass, the elusive dark matter. Nobody had liked the implications of the answer, himself especially, for shortly afterwards he contracted a nervous twitch and then ceased ever again to speak or write.

Many like her were left with nothing, but there had been some who were really unlucky. Two months ago a researcher was found inside the containment room filling the floor, resembling what was best described as a beanbag. Later x-rays showed that all his bones had vanished. In another incident a woman began perceiving time in reverse, become younger, always talking backwards and forgetting things rather than learning, and so in time she too was committed to the project's already overcrowded asylum. Mostly, unlucky researchers just vanished, probably transported into other universes — dimensions that their research was now predicting existed in vast numbers. This left a few scientists suggesting that many more people might also have been lost to the impossible object, but because the object also erased their history from existence, no one knew about it.

This was her twenty-eighth time with the object, and like each previous encounter she perceived nothing. She hoped today would be different, for despite her failures she still held faith in her abilities to perceive aura fields. For too long scientists who worked only with 'facts' had not been able to provide answers, so the military boys running the show brought in psychics and spiritualists like her, people who could 'see' on levels and dimensions closed-off to most mortal minds. She had seen desperation in the officer's eyes, and rose to their challenge.

So here she was, perceiving the object through psychic senses which no one else on the team possessed. Today she had been lucky, for she was certain it was calling her, forming her name in her mind and opening up the possibility of conversation. It told her it was scared, that it was lost and far from home. General Hyatt would indeed be pleased.

Then her mind really opened, and when it did her frontal lobe almost melted from the shock. With alien clarity she understood all too well that everything she had ever perceived as 'extra-sensory' had always been an invention of her own wishful imagination. This perception, what she felt now, this was far too real. Not a feeling anymore, she really did hear her name.

It was a voice, not inside her head but everywhere. She didn't hear it with her ears, for the words were being carved into her gray matter. It then told her every minuscule detail about herself including a listing and properties of every cell in her body, a comprehensive catalogue of every piece of food she'd eaten in her life, and a compilation of *everything* she'd ever written down or committed to memory. This was all learnt in under a second, imparted to her as a gift from the Many-Thing, or so the voice said.

After a vast quantity of knowledge filled her mind, straining her mental capacity to bursting point, she was told that her role as an information gatherer had come to an end. Despite her new gained knowledge of what seemed to be everything, all she really understood was that she should be terrified.

The object fragmented, forming tiny hexagonal solids that emitted a bright, red lattice-shaped beam, not unlike a spider's web, filling the space of the containment room. Before her the table was falling apart, cut into hexagonal pieces the size of dollar coins, ringing hard as they hit the floor. Her chair fragmented in exactly the same pattern, as did her hands, her arms and soon her whole body was nothing more than pieces of flesh cut into bloody shapes of identical size, dimension and volume.

Like a black hole, the impossible object could not be perceived, but the effects it imparted on this universe were all too clear.

A few minutes later the cleaning team got to work, readying the containment room for the next researcher. They'd seen it all before, and they knew not to waste time looking at the object, in case it claimed one of them as well.

Changing weather patterns changed the desert. Only ten years ago, this remote corner of outback Western Australia had been overgrown with spinifex grass, gum trees and scrub bush. There had even been kangaroos, goannas and emus feasting on the termites and lizards that scurried everywhere. But today it was nothing more than a dusty hell of red sand dunes, for vegetation refused to grow and animals ceased to venture too close. Meanwhile the topsoil was eroded by hot winds which blew away the deathly remains of decaying vegetation.

The only consolation anyone could imagine was that the shifting dunes had revealed an alien city. The first humans to explore the city's interior stated that their best estimate for its age was over a billion years, long before terrestrial life had evolved beyond soft-bodied ocean dwellers.

Another hot and dusty morning saw Major Harrison Peel follow the engineer into Excavated Complex H43. The interior was cold compared to the forty degree Celsius heat felt only a few hundred meters distant, at the stone ramp leading outside. Despite relief from constant sweat and body odor, Peel found the interior too bizarre for his liking, and so avoided it unless he had to be there, like he did today.

This world was like those tombs found beneath European churches, and held about as much life. The difference was that every single room down here was over a hundred times larger than any church. It was easy to see that this place was old, for gigantic stalactites and stalagmites had grown over almost everything that had once been carved or laid down by alien hands, or tentacles, or claws. Peel had no idea what they would have looked like. Perhaps he didn't really want to.

"So this is where they found the object?" he asked. There was nothing different or unusual about this room compared to any of the other numerous tagged complexes which the Australian Army had already explored, so he wanted to be sure.

Winston Jones was a structural engineer, an expert who'd been hired by the military to theorize how the city had been constructed, as well as providing plausible explanations why it had survived for so long. Although his skin was wrinkled and hard from many years working too many construction projects under the harsh antipodean sun, today he was pale and clammy. Too many months underground in a tomb, too many days listening to every drip of cold water forming on the stalactites above left him to question that maybe the city builders were still around, watching him.

To calm his nerves Jones had taken up smoking cigarettes, or whistling when the silence became unbearable. Stubbing out his latest smoke he put the butt in his pocket, knowing better than to litter inside the city while a military officer was watching him. Peel wondered how many butts filled the man's pockets today.

"Right here," pointed the engineer, but even then he seemed uncertain. "Wouldn't have noticed, except one of the geologists working with me at the time pointed out a metal box he thought one of his work crews had left behind, but when I looked all I saw was a green bulbous stone. It was only when we picked it up did we realize we were looking at the same thing."

Peel nodded sagely. In the five years since his government began investigating the city, the impossible object had been the only item of any value anyone had managed to uncover. If it was as easy to miss as the engineer said, then that fact left the Major wondering just what else might be on offer right under their very eyes, objects which they were powerless to perceive. "You think this city is dead?" he asked, as if it were the most casual of remarks.

Yet such questions seemed to scare Jones as they had scared Peel, for the man's eyes became white around the edges and he started sweating. "You think so too, do you?" Peel saw that Jones was at last thankful that someone else might be ready to validate his fears.

"I was starting to think I was the only one."

"*Only* one?"

"I see things. Well, not really see, but there are noises — well, not noises. . . ."

"Feelings?"

"Yeah, feelings." He looked relieved that Peel seemed to understand. "But not like real feelings, not like feeling sad, or happy, or tired or hungry. It's more like a feeling that you are changing, on a molecular level or something. As if every molecule in your body is being replaced by another identical molecule, so you're still yourself, but you're not, if you know what I mean? It's like you aren't part of this world anymore, although you should be, but can't be — I'm not making any sense!"

"You *think* so?" Peel asked. Since his arrival at the city two months ago as the new head of security, Peel had been provided access to most of the staff's psychological reports. Updated on a weekly basis as part of the contingency planning, these reports were designed to combat the high rates of insanity, suicide, accident and death associated with their research. Jones wasn't the only one who'd reported experiencing odd sensations in and around the city, which troubled Peel for more reasons than he was willing to reveal.

"What are you saying, sir?"

"I'm not saying anything."

But he was. Even if the words were not spoken, Peel was wearing his fear plainly for everyone on the project to see. He believed that the object was a trap, laid by the city builders for the humans to find. Perhaps there were still other traps to be found, hence the necessity for his occasional visit into the underground world. All the existing evidence suggested this place had been dead for at least fifty million years, so his superiors regularly dismissed his concerns, but each day more and more people working directly with the city or the object were starting to believe he might just be onto something.

He wondered if the molecules in his body were changing too.

General Hyatt was always speeding about the camp, so whenever he needed to slow down a lot of pressure was forced onto the jeep's brakes, in this particular moment to pull up alongside Peel. He didn't ask but told Peel to get in, then took off at again breakneck speed. Behind the wheel the General was a madman possessed, as if his mind were on other issues, and probably was. When he walked anywhere he was also rapid, just not as dangerous. But despite his frightening driving and the fact that he was well into his fifties, the General remained as sprightly as any recruit fresh out of training, and his mind was just as sharp. He'd have to be to manage this project.

No one ever disobeyed the General and failed to be reprimanded for it later, not even when he asked nicely. But Peel wasn't complaining about a lift. In this heat it was a long walk between his office, situated in a transportable administration hut, to the laboratory complex where the impossible object was locked away.

"Wanted to ask you a question, Major," spoke the General, looking at him and not at the dirt road as they took a corner under heavy acceleration. "Wanted to know you're opinions on the Americans."

"They're our allies, sir."

"Yes, that's the kind of answer a private would give me, even an answer a lieutenant or one of my crusty sergeants would offer. But let me let you into a little secret Peel; when I *know* how someone is going to answer a question, I don't ask. So no bullshit, and tell me what you really think."

It was always hard to read his bulldog superior, but in this case Peel could see where this line of questioning was leading. The General was referring to Peel's previous liaison with U.S. military intelligence. Time spent with their allies assisting their development of strategies for identifying and predicting the terror tactics of subversive organizations.

Peel had been recruited into the team because of his prior operational assignments in Southeast Asia and East Africa. His was hands-on experience which cannot be taught in the class-room, but knowledge the Americans had wanted to tap nonetheless. After completing an arduous assignment in Cambodia, Peel had requested and received a six months cushy training assignment in the United States. He learnt the hard way that, more often than not, the American military officers were more interested in educating him on what they believed they knew, rather than displaying any willingness to learn from him.

"I think they're interested in their own affairs, sir."

"That all?"

"I don't think we should trust them; that is, if you're still considering briefing them on the city and the object."

Hyatt chuckled, "Well a whole group of their experts, military and civilian, are flying in tomorrow. But don't worry, our intelligence boys have cleared every last one of them."

Peel didn't want to feel disappointed but he did, and it probably showed. The city was dangerous, it was unknown, and a lot more had to be discovered before they could safely allow in any visitors. Until now this place had remained a secret even from their most trusted allies, but in less than twenty-four hours the camp would double in number with these Northern Hemispheric visitors.

"I can see your concerns, Major, but you have to admit we're getting nowhere with our research."

"Sir, if I may, why did you ask my opinion when the decision had already been made?"

"I wanted to see if I could rely on you, Peel."

Peel watched the General, knowing that his superior had no intention of clarifying that last statement. "You mean they found out, don't you sir?"

The older man laughed, exactly as he had all those years ago when the Prime Minster congratulated him on national television for his efforts in East Timor, during the troubled country's independence from Indonesian rule. Peel had been there too, hunting down militia terrorists and so already knew the General's style. He had never been quite sure if Hyatt had been laughing with the interviewer to look trustworthy and open for the benefit of his hopeful political career, or laughing at the Australian public because of his terror tactics forced upon the Timorese people which had never been exposed by the press. Here was the same laugh, bellowed from a middle-aged man who was a national hero. Peel knew he had to be careful with this General whom he never trusted, especially after the boldness of his last comment.

"I see there is no fooling you, Peel, but then we don't pay you to be a 'yes' man." He turned the wheel sharply, narrowly missing a bulldozer reversing out of a workshop. "Yeah, the bloody Yanks found out, through their spy satellites or so they tell us. But only when they discover our secret do they bother to tell us that they've discovered alien cities of their own; particularly in Antarctica, but also off the coast of New England, Mali, and other places. They've known about many of them since the nineteen thirties. Bastards are rubbing it in or what?"

Peel had often wondered if their find was unique, particularly after his experiences in Cambodia, so this news wasn't really a surprise. "They only share with us when they think we might have something to offer in return. That's the way they've always been."

"Don't get cynical on me Major; it doesn't suit you."

"Yes sir," he answered dryly. What the General meant was it didn't suit him to have men who thought like Peel did.

"You should know I've read your reports from your time across the Pacific. I know how you feel about the American approach, so this as just a warning. I'm expecting you to cooperate with our friends, regardless of your opinions, understood?"

He hit the brakes and they stopped dead as red dust settled on the jeep, their clothes, and Peel's paperwork. He looked up to see that the General had delivered him to the laboratories fifteen minutes ahead of his scheduled meeting. Outside the building a dozen young technicians on a lunch break were kicking a soccer ball. It was incredibly hot out here, but everyone had their own way to relieve the monotony of remote outback living, or perhaps as a distraction away from what the city stood for; something far greater and more terrifying than anything they could ever imagine by themselves.

"You hear what I'm saying, son?"

"Yes sir, understood."

Peel climbed out, allowing the General to drive away to his next bullying, leaving Peel to cough and splutter in a violent cloud of red dust.

Doctor Julie Romanski frantically scribbled equations on the blackboard. She knew hers was an old-fashioned approach to problem solving, especially in today's world of laptops, the Internet, palm pilots and voice recognition computers. But to her the blackboard was simplicity in its monochrome dictation, and simplicity was what she sought from the masses of equations that led everywhere and concluded nothing.

This was not strictly true. Even with the minute amount of data her team had gleaned from the alien object, she'd thus far proved the existence of parallel universes, formulated models predicting alternate structures for subatomic particle as they passed through an Einstein-Rosen bridge wormhole, and developed equations explaining the behavior of a new type of matter with properties previously believed impossible in her universe, matter that created its own brand of life purely from interacting with itself. All this knowledge had come close to driving her mad. It was also enough knowledge to win her the Nobel Prize for Physics ten times over, if she were ever allowed publish her results. Trouble was, with all this new information no one had any idea where to begin in truly understanding what this all meant.

They had a city with only a few hundred square kilometers exposed so far, but that was enough to put their findings into perspective; they'd scratched the surface and they knew nothing. God knows how far the stone complexes extended beyond what was already unearthed. Ore samples extracted by the geological team verified that the city reached depths over ten kilometers, right to the point where stone became so hot it was close to transforming into magma.

Exploration teams lead by Special Air Services forces had descended depths greater than the bottom of the Pacific Ocean, only to find room after empty room. Some of these chambers — after months of dedicated research and analysis — proved to be libraries. But from within not a single volume could be found on what were probably the aliens' equivalent to shelves. Most disappointingly, there were no signs of the aliens' language to be found anywhere, as if it had been cleared deliberately. All in all this was one hell of a mystery.

After five years, only a single item had been recovered of intrinsic value: the impossible object.

This anomaly was the only tangible proof that the alien civilization had built objects with anything but stone. Yet no matter how many times she attempted to understand the impossible object, through mathematical equations or theoretical sciences, her conclusions always stated clearly that it *did not and could not* exist. Not now and not ever.

And so as she considered this paradox, Julie was hit with another revelation. What if it were not the impossible object that didn't exist, but *everything else* in the universe around it? Could she prove that, and therefore by reverse logic, prove its existence?

It was an idea, and that was enough.

So she wiped the board clean and started over.

❊　❊　❊

"Doctor Romanski just disappeared."

"Vanished, you mean?"

The Sergeant was upset, as if it were her fault that their top researcher had just been eradicated from existence, just like too many before her. In the old days when the research and exploration was in its infancy, those in charge had always found a stooge to become accountable for the horrific and catastrophic fatalities. It took two and a half years to learn the lesson; that no one could really be blamed, because no one really commanded any control out here. Yet this third generation Chinese-Australian, who spoke neither Cantonese nor Mandarin like so many Asian recruits filling the ranks of the army these days, reacted as if she was personally responsible, and that she should be punished. Peel liked the fact that the Sergeant believed she should shoulder the blame, but he'd only reprimand Lucy Chin if she answered his next question incorrectly.

"You were under explicit orders that Romanski was not to be allowed anywhere near the object."

"But she wasn't anywhere near it, sir."

Correct answer.

He sat down at his desk and gazed out through the small window, with an all too clear view out across the sand to the crumbling spires of the alien world under tarpaulins. They had tried to disguise the city as a mining site to fool the watching satellites, and obviously that tactic had failed.

It was bad enough that he had to be in a building so close to this ancient structure, let alone a close proximity to the laboratories that contained the impossible object. That thing was the cause of all the strife and misery here, and now its list of casualties included their chief scientist.

"Well, what happened then, Chin?"

The soldier was scared, hesitating to speak, but found her courage when Peel wouldn't stop eyeballing her. "She just vanished from her office, Sir. Security cameras saw her go in and recorded her hard at work. Then the cameras went down, a technical fault but we all know what that means. It was at this moment that she vanished."

"Like the others?"

"Yes Sir, *exactly* like the others. And we still can't get anything to record in the room."

Even though he'd let Chin's statement pass without comment, there was no *exactness* about anything here. What worried Peel this time was that an anomaly this serious had never before occurred beyond the containment room. He also knew for a fact that Romanski's office held nothing remotely alien in it, because soldiers reporting directly to him regularly purged all the researchers' offices of anything collected from the city. He did this to protect their own safety, and here was proof *again* that his methods and judgment were sound.

Peel had been deliberate about this, so if Romanski had vanished like the others, the evidence pointed towards a new danger, a threat that was yet to be defined. Perhaps it was a second impossible object, one that had made its way inside the base unnoticed. If so, how would they even recognize it for what it was?

"Follow me, Sergeant."

Side-by-side they marched through the corridors of the pre-fabricated military compound, past air-conditioners at every junction rattling hard against the heat, arriving in minutes at the scene of the crime. The specialist forensic team was already undertaking its standard tests; counting the composition of elements and compounds in the atmosphere, checking abnormal radiation levels, measuring the intensity of light and searching for microscopic organisms on every exposed surface. Most wore hazard suits but many more had their headpieces removed, knowing that these suits hadn't saved anyone yet. Most surfaces were now marked with yellow tape, stamped with official wording declaring clearly that this object or space was now designated safe to touch.

Fighting against his own agitation, Peel pushed his way inside. All he saw was a normal office, and that scared him. "What was she doing?" he barked.

Sergeant Chin was behind him as she should be. "Working at the blackboard, sir, scribbling equations."

This was as good a place as any to start. The blackboard appeared normal, full of mathematical formulae regarding hyper-dimensional physics that Peel had no chance of understanding. He asked a forensic officer if the surface of the board had been put through the usual tests. The officer pointed to a yellow sticker stating that it had, and so Peel felt comfortable enough stepping close for a better look. He even risked touching it, and nothing untoward unsettled his mind or shattered the cosmic forces that held his body stable.

Peel vainly followed the lines of logic. All he recognized was some calculus, and a few references to new mathematical theories that had been circulated in a memo last week. But that didn't mean he understood any of it. Line by line it was all a foreign language, all of it except for the QED signature at the end.

QED, Quite Enough Done.

It dawned on Peel that Romanski had worked something out. She'd solved something, resolved another puzzle using the knowledge they'd already complied from earlier studies.

Then just as quickly, with an unwanted realization that terrified Peel, he saw the equations differently, as if they were a spreading disease. A virus that had once been contained within a test tube had now been spilt, infecting first those who came into its close proximity, and then spreading further on the back of carriers. The object no longer required its physical presence to vanish or change people, or to drive them into psychotic insanity. The knowledge that it had previously imparted had mutated. The virus had moved.

Without a second's thought he scrubbed the board clean. Almost immediately, all the digital cameras in the room that failed to record started to do so.

He'd be reprimanded, but at least he might save some lives.

Sunset over desert sands was the only time the Outback looked beautiful. When Peel clocked off for the day he often walked out into the night, allowing time to remember again that in the real world he was officially listed as on assignment in the Philippines. There he would have been training the local soldiers on simple things, such as the many silent techniques for snapping the necks of enemy combatants, or hand signals for communication during covert operations. Such thoughts gave him hope that one day he would return to normal military life, and that he might be allowed to forget all of this. That was if anything could be considered normal after all his experiences these last months.

The Americans were close. In the sky he could already see their Hercules Airlifter, direct from Maryland via Hawaii with a hundred or more scientists, government officials, NSA agents and military advisers ready to tell the Australians how they should now run their own operation. True, his people had no idea what they were doing here, but would their allies know any better? Peel didn't think so.

He tried to remember why he'd been brought to the city in the first place. Tried to remember why he knew he was right, even though the General had threatened him with court martial after it was revealed that Peel had erased Romanski's mathematical discovery. Peel was a leading expert in terrorism, and, despite the horrors of Cambodia, not a xenobiologist. It had been his role for most of the last ten years to out-think the enemy, to predict when, where and how they would strike, so they could be countered before any damage was done.

There was no denying he'd successful foiled five separate acts of terrorism attempted against the Australian government and its citizens, successes the public never heard about because they'd been put to a stop before they started. He knew he was good at his role, and this was the evidence to prove it. So why had they brought him here?

There were no terrorists in the city, not even alien terrorists. At least not aliens who'd allow themselves to be seen.

But a bomb didn't need a living entity to perform its final devastating act, for timers could be set automatically. The aliens didn't need to be seen, and they knew this.

The military saw a weapon in the impossible object, one they hoped to harness so they could dominate the world, and perhaps even the galaxy, their imagination stretched that far. The scientists saw it differently; it was their holy grail, the ultimate key opening the door to the secrets of the universe. But Peel saw it differently again, not as a hope or a gift like everyone else did, for all he could see was a trap.

So he went back to basic principles, to his field of expertise, because ultimately he was here because of those skills. When a terrorist strikes he aims to achieve the maximum devastation with the minimal input. In today's world, a suicide bomber in Israel could only make international headlines when he or she managed to kill a large number of people, preferably women

and children, and then civilian rather than military targets.
Otherwise their efforts would become a wasted, pointless, and
unreported exercise.

Peel had never looked upon the impossible object. He had-
n't read the compiled study notes on the object, in the growing
book everyone referred to as the Yithian Calculations. He never
desired to do either, fearful of what might happen to him if he
did. But he was sure that if he did enter the containment room
he'd see a ticking bomb, because that was what it was to him.
If so when would it explode? If it was a trap, was it not drawing them to it right now, allowing them to become comfortable, so it could take them unaware, just like the modus
operandi of the world's most elusive terrorist organizations?

In the skies the Hercules was descending, undercarriage
lowered, ready for landing. Within minutes the project would
be swarming with a mass of new faces and new accents.

It was only then, seeing the aircraft and what it stood for,
that his thoughts came together, as did a new unfathomable
sense of dread.

Peel ran as fast as his legs could carry him. In the red sand it
was hard work, his pace slow even for someone with his fitness.
Ahead the runway was lit, and so too was the control tower
directing the plane towards a safe landing.

He ran to the General, who was waiting by his jeep wearing another supercilious smile that was a common signature of
his personality. Happy at last that the Americans were finally
here, if for no other reason than as someone to blame in the
future when more people continued to die, disappear or go mad
while vainly attempting to understand what would always be
alien to them. Not that it mattered anymore, not knowing
what Peel had just surmised. He broke across the floodlit tar-
mac and ran straight at his commanding officer.

"General!" he yelled like the madmen he was afraid of becoming, "you've got to turn them back!"

Peel was running at the soldiers. The General, now spotting Peel, barked orders at his men, demanding action. In response one of the young soldiers intercepted Peel, raising his assault rifle into firing position. Experience counted for far more than youthful energy, and so Peel easily broke the boy's wrist as efficiently as he transferred the weapon to his own hands. "Send them back, General, or you'll get us all killed."

Ten guns were pointed at him now, so Peel knew if he said the wrong thing or acted aggressively, the General would not hesitate to shoot him down where he stood. Peel dropped the weapon, knowing that maintaining the General's attention was all that was important right now.

It had all come back to him in the sand dunes; his training, his study, his experience. All gleamed with the cold hard face of dirty warfare. A terrorist waits, readying himself for the right time when he can create the most devastating effect with minimal effort. A smarter terrorist doesn't even walk into an enemy's nest, he draws his victims to him, he makes them feel comfortable. He makes them think it's in their best interest to be there. Anywhere in the world, all terrorists operated the same way. So why, then, would an alien race behave any differently?

"Tell me why I shouldn't arrest you, Major."

"The object, the impossible object, it's a trap, sir, sent to us by whoever built the city in the first place." He pointed to the aircraft, "They're drawing us in, making us interested, and when we get too close." He let the thought trail away, thankfully aware that the soldiers, ready to take his life, were now starting to understand what he was saying. "When that plane lands, General, we'll drastically increase the population of this base. If the object is sentient, and so far what little we know about it suggests that it is, then if it's going to strike it's going

to do so when it can eliminate the maximum number of targets. So isn't now the perfect time?"

The General said nothing.

No one said anything.

They were all trying to understand what he said, and for
the first time, he saw soldiers assigned to the project going into
shock. Perhaps it was the virus spreading, or perhaps it was just
the failing human condition. The General, his mind suddenly
overwhelmed by what the impossible object could do, knew he
was powerless to act against it, however it might choose to
respond now, and so did nothing.

Meanwhile the soldiers remained steady with their
weapons, offering Peel no opportunity to save his own life by
fleeing.

Too late. The Hercules transport was close, its engines
already slowing for the final approach.

He looked back at the laboratory complex.

It was in there — the impossible object — not far away,
sensing everything, including the events unfolding outside.

Any second now it could obliterate them all . . .

Any second now. . . .

FALSE CONTAINMENT

David Conyers

Tuesday, April 5
Rio Napa, Oriente Province, Ecuador

The Amazonian waters flowed so fast that the dugout canoe appeared to be slipping on a steep slope of water. Nicola Mulvaney felt sick because of this illusion, creating an imbalance between her eardrums and her eyes. At the motor, the Indian pilot didn't seem to notice. Neither did her Amazonian guide, Lucho Alfaro. She watched the Ecuadorian man heartily eating with fingers a lunch of rice stained red, wrapped in banana leaves. She'd turned down her portion. Perhaps if they stopped on a sandbank her appetite might return. But if they did stop they might not find what she suspected was hidden in the jungle. Again she checked her Geiger counter, using the intensity measure to gauge the distance. It crackled ever so faintly. "How much further?" she asked in Spanish.

"A few more minutes," Lucho's smile was of red stained teeth, prompting the illusion that his lips were bleeding. She looked away instinctively, because she'd seen similar smiles from the victims of radiation poisoning.

So she gazed back at the trees, as high as apartment buildings. Competing for sunlight they grew right to the water's edge. The thick foliage and oppressive humidity hinted that the jungle really could swallow anything and everything. Yet despite the jungle's size, the canisters had been found.

"Look ahead, *Senorita*," exclaimed Lucho.

Nicola saw fruit-eating fish floating belly up in the hundreds. She cringed as she analyzed the water again. Toxicity and radioactivity was now pushing at the limits of her personal standards of safety. But she still had to get close enough to confirm the source, find out if this discovery was the same as the others. And with that thought she laughed. An EPA case officer, her specialty was nuclear waste. Never in her life did she expect to find radioactive isotopes out here, in a pristine virgin rainforest.

Guided to a sandbank, the Indian pilot secured the canoe to an overhanging branch. He would wait, he explained in his own language, while Lucho translated. He would wait as long as it took. Lucho smiled, knowing that the Indian had no comprehension of the silent killer in the air. Today, time would be nobody's friend.

On solid ground, Lucho strolled into the jungle as if he was a natural of this green world. His gumboots were the only part of him that looked out of place, as if human feet would never cope in the constant wet. Nicola wore the same, found them awkward while burdened with the equipment she must carry. "How long did you say it's been here?" she asked, hoping to retain some sense of professional dignity.

"A long time; my father told me stories as a boy."

"Really?" She didn't believe him.

A machete cut the way. Their sweat wore them down. Twenty minutes brought them to what should have been a fresh mountain stream amongst thick green foliage. Instead, the sight that greeted them was shriveled and dead. Decay had set in decades ago she had been told, and now saw, leaving nothing but a stagnant festering pool and black sick mud.

The centerpiece — the cause — was a mountain of trash. Mostly it was spilled drums half-full with highly toxic radioactive waste. The other half had flown away long ago. Even today punctures were still seeping an oily substance into the stream.

Just to be safe, Nicola wasted no time fitting her respirator mask and goggles. She didn't want to ingest any of the radioactive particles potentially floating in the air. Then with her Geiger counter back on, the crackling started. It was much stronger this time. A few hours here was all she could afford, if she wanted to wait that long. She didn't.

"How long has all this been here?"

"About fifty years, as I said."

Nicola scoffed. With her digital camera she snapped several photographs, and only then noticed the drums were decorated with U.S. Army insignia and a consignment date from this year. She collected photographs of these too. It was only when she inadvertently snapped a WGI consignment tag did she smile for the first time today.

WGI, *Westmorton Global Industries Limited*, was the global corporation that was her arch nemesis. Several months ago WGI had opened a new waste treatment planet in Nevada. The CEO, Brad Westmorton, had publicly claimed it could safely dispose of all types of waste, including high grade nuclear waste, with no toxic byproducts whatsoever. He branded it Zero Waste Technology. She of course had never believed a word of it. Knew his claims were impossible. Knew it could only spell trouble.

Later her suspicions were further aroused when the Pentagon and the White House displayed interested in WGI's new technology, quickly classifying the Nevada Facility and its project as top secret. Then access to the plant, previously stonewalled, had been denied to almost every other U.S. and international authority, including the EPA. Now, after months of investigation, here in the Amazon of all places, she'd at last uncovered proof that WGI was telling the world a very big lie. Zero waste for Nevada perhaps, but not for the rest of the world.

Once her camera was spent, she turned to walk away.

"Senorita, what you going to do about it?"

"Nothing."

"But those are American flags on those metal drums."

"What American flags?" she said, feigning ignorance, walking back the way they had come.

But inside she felt sorry for Lucho and his people. She knew the official United States governmental line; in these trying days the EPA had enough problems controlling misplaced nuclear waste materializing inside its own borders.

Accidents in poor, developing countries would have to wait. And they wouldn't complain too much, because they couldn't afford to lose the U.S. aid that kept their economies afloat. That was the silent threat hanging over their heads; you can stay healthy or you can be paid, but not both.

Yet finds like these were not all that uncommon, anywhere. Uncle Sam's rubbish had been materializing all over the world long before Alexander the Great decided he would be the first among many and the conqueror of the world.

That was if archaeological sites were now being interpreted correctly.

Thursday, April 14
WGI Offices, New York, United States

Special Agent Curtis Fulton liked being the boss, and doubly so today. This particular day was special because he was in charge of a team of fine FBI agents, about to make an important arrest. Sure, he'd taken down Colombian drug lords and right-wing terrorists in his day, but never did he think he'd have the fortune of arresting one of America's corporate highfliers.

Outside of his work, Fulton had a wife who hadn't talked to him in months, a daughter with anorexia in rehab, and a son who was a boy-toy for a woman twice his age. Right now his job was the only part of his life he could feel proud about, and he wasn't about to give that up. If he played his cards right, today just might be his day. As far as he knew, no one had ever handcuffed the Chief Executive Officer of a company as large as WGI. He was going to make history.

So his team threatened the building's security with legal speak, ignored reception and were downright rude to the personal assistant: they barged straight into the CEO's office. The first thing Fulton noticed was that the spacious interior commanded excessive wealth. He expected this, but not the magnificent view of Central Park in the spring, a desk carved of the finest oak, high-backed chairs fashioned from the softest leather, and several Impressionist paintings centered on walls that the public would never see.

"Mr. Bradley Westmorton, you are under arrest for contravention of the *Environmental Protection Act*—"

He didn't get to finish.

The man in the CEO's desk wasn't Westmorton. In his place, a tall thin man with deep eyes and a cold complexion remained motionless in the high-backed chair. His fingers forming a cage tapped silently to an unheard rhythm. Most unsettling, the stranger remained unfazed by the numerous sidearms pointed at his head.

Fulton found it hard to read this man, and not just because the sun silhouetted his features rather efficiently. Around him fellow FBI agents were equally perplexed, all waiting to see how their boss would rectify this now bungled arrest. With a deep sigh that raced all the way from the endless pit of his stomach, Fulton knew that if he didn't salvage something from the situation, his career was as good as dead.

"You are Special Agent Curtis Fulton of the FBI," spoke the mystery man.

"Who the hell are you?" Fulton shouted back.

"My name is Rodney Alden, and I am authorized to tell you that I'm with the National Security Council. It is my purpose here today to represent the President of the United States. He commanded me to give you this copy of a letter he signed several months ago." Ever so calmly, the shadowy man pointed to a single piece of paper on the oak desk between them. The paper bore a White House letterhead. The short letter was indeed signed by the most powerful man in the world.

"It's a pardon, right?" Fulton couldn't believe it, "for Westmorton himself?"

The man called Alden nodded. "And I have to warn you, Mr. Westmorton is a valued friend of the President. Together they are working on a top secret project which is classified well above any authority held by your Bureau. Agent Fulton, that is all I am authorized to say."

"This is a load of shit." Fulton felt his face flush with anger. "Nuclear and toxic waste are being dumped all over the world. Waste that WGI was commissioned to dispose of in a safe and non-toxic manner, and then failed to do so. And now you're telling me I can't touch Westmorton despite all the evidence that says he should be locked away forever?"

The man stood. He straightened his fine suit, cracked his neck with a flick of his head, and smiled with a lipless mouth. "That's precisely what I'm telling you, Agent Fulton. Now, if you will excuse me."

No one stopped him as he confidently exited the office, although Fulton wanted to put a bullet in the smug prick's leg, just to show him that no one was untouchable.

"What are you all looking at?" he yelled at his officers, slack-jawed, watching a stranger get one better of their boss. "All of you, get back to the Field Office right now."

Smarting, Fulton grabbed the Presidential letter as they departed. Even seeing it up close, held in his own hands, he still couldn't believe it. It was as if he had just seen the original

Declaration of Independence, only to discover that the signatures were by Mickey Mouse, Daffy Duck, Goofy, and so on. The injustice of it all. So the President and the Pentagon were covering up WGI's activities in the desert. He'd uncovered rumors that WGI's new technology was being tested for potential application as a new and devastating weapon. Fulton couldn't even begin to imagine what. But it couldn't be any worse than what was out of the bag. Could it? The only thing he knew for sure was that he was going to find out.

As he stormed from the corporate mega-complex, only a single thought filled Fulton's angry mind. No one breaks the law, not even the leader of the free world.

Justice had to be done.

Sunday, April 17
MacDonnell Ranges, Northern Territory, Australia

The army helicopter bit the red dust as it settled in the Outback. The landing point was between two remote mountain ranges far into the hot interior. In his well-worn army fatigues, Major Harrison Peel stepped out of the helicopter quickly, head down to avoid the lethal blades flicking the hot air, slicing the sunlight like a strobe light.

He surveyed the terrain — palms amongst gum trees. The vegetation appeared out of place so far from the coast. But they had to be natural since the palms were thriving everywhere. Then Peel understood why he looked, and why he asked himself such questions; he was recording the lay of the land as his special military training had taught. It was instinctive. These days Peel usually only worried about such details when he was on an operation. But there was no danger here. Was there?

Away from the deafening noise, eight archaeologists waited for him. In shorts, t-shirts and sandals. Their skin was like parchment worn away by the harsh sun. Huge bellies suggested they enjoyed a few too many beers each night, and the dirt on their skin and clothes told of the need for a bath.

"Mr. Peel, glad you could make it."

"Major. The name is Major Peel."

"Oh, right you are, then. Major." The chief archaeologist stressed the title. "Laurie James is my name, from the University of Adelaide actually."

Peel said nothing, not caring about such details. All he wanted to know was why his leave had been cancelled and he'd been sent here instead.

He had been looking forward to time away from the impossible object project which, despite having failed to kill them all as he had warned, surprised them nonetheless when it imparted one last piece of knowledge, and then vanished from existence altogether. What that last piece was — well, Peel wasn't cleared high enough to 'need to know'. General Hyatt's urgent order had come through this morning, telling him that he must relocate from one remote corner of the Outback to another. In his usual pompous arrogance, the General had not bothered to explain the purpose of Peel's journey either. Peel had been fuming about this the whole trip over. He should have been flying home for a well-earned rest.

"You've got something to show me?"

Laurie wiped his hands on red-stained shorts, uncomfortable now, probably unaccustomed to such abrupt responses. The major wanted to care, but right now it was too difficult for him to do so. He knew he was the man most inconvenienced by today's antics.

"Well, yes Major, but I really don't know where to begin."

"You're an archaeologist, right?"

"Um, well, yes."

"And I'm guessing you're in this hellhole because you've been unearthing some ancient Aboriginal burial site?"

"How did you know?"

"I didn't. I'm just guessing." Peel didn't need a response. He just knew he was right.

Behind him the helicopter blades slowed; the pilot had been told to wait as long as it took. Without its overwhelming noise, conversation became easier, yet no one was talking. Peel looked at each one of them; eight men and women, some of them Aboriginal, and they all appeared to be in a state of shock. Peel wondered why he hadn't noticed their stunned stares before. With his special training, that should have been one of the first things he noticed. Administration duties of late had eroded his edge.

"I think you better show me what you've found."

They led him past their camp of four-wheel drives, tents, a marquee and three angry camels grunting disgustingly. Beyond, inside a gap between the rising red cliffs, deep shadows were dancing in the dipping sun. When Peel stepped up to this crevasse, the archaeologists let him be the one to go first. They knew something he didn't.

Checking that his Glock 9mm was still holstered over his left hip, Peel scoffed and vanished into the shadows. Despite the overhanging rock, jagged openings above shone blue, providing plenty of light to show the way. After a few dozen meters the gap led into a roughly circular cave. Peel was in awe of the site.

On the rock walls Aboriginal paintings were immediately obvious. They were of numerous hands, and of men and animals displaying internal organs and enlarged sexual members. He'd seen his fair share of indigenous art in his time, thought nothing of it. But each depiction here disturbed Peel. He couldn't even say why, except that their stylized forms appeared warped and mutated, twisting the anatomies beyond any natural angle. Then he noticed that all their eyes looked down on the sandy earth, toward the center, where perhaps three dozen Aboriginal skeletons were piled on top of each other, suggesting a mass grave.

The archaeologists had been busy. String lines, tags and measuring sticks gave coordinates for each and every bone, numbering in the thousands. But what would a military man, whose specialty was anti-terrorism and military intelligence, need to learn from any of this?

"What am I looking at?" Peel asked Laurie, now standing at his side.

"Look again, Major, look at the bones."

He did what he was told, and at last saw the truth. Understanding now, Peel gulped, sucked in the hot air. The bones weren't individual; skulls had merged together, femurs had split into y-shaped abnormalities, arms ended in three or more hands, and ribs had over-inflated into cages the size of oil barrels.

"This burial is dated at about two hundred years. The dryness here preserved them that long, and the angle of the overhang ensured that almost no rain fell on those rare occasions that a storm passed through, so there is very little decay. But those aren't Aboriginals; you see a Caucasian male, an Asian female, a Caucasian female, African male, but mostly though they are Caucasian men."

Peel felt his own mouth twist unnaturally, sensing now the source of unease that these archaeologists had lived with for several weeks now. "How can you tell?"

"Well there are tests we can run, but more compelling are the ID badges, plastic watch bands, radiation danger warning tags."

"What?" scoffed Peel again, not believing a word of it, "Found in there?"

He looked back at the pit, and was reminded again that he wasn't seeing several dozen human bodies, but one giant organism.

"We also found coyote and badger skeletons, Joshua trees—"

"You mean from the California deserts?"

"Yes, none of it makes any sense, does it?" He ran out of words.

Peel turned his back on the thing. If he was going to understand, comprehend this anomaly, he couldn't do so while it transfixed him. So General Hyatt had sent him here with a purpose after all, and at last that purpose had revealed itself. This was an alien enigma that needed investigating, and perhaps it was connected to the impossible object project as Hyatt would have surmised. Sure he had the skills and the experience to do so, he'd even encountered alien anomalies like this in the past, but why fly him a thousand kilometers when there were plenty more of his colleagues who had the time, skills and resources to better understand?

So he asked the question: "Why me?"

"Oh," said Laurie, at last relaxing back into his casual self. "I'm certain that has to do with the Polaroid photograph we found. You want to take a look?"

Monday, May 30
WGI Nevada Facility, Sarcobatus Flat, Nevada

"Shit! What was that?"

Bruce Ringwood rubbed his eyes, aware only now that the intense flash of light might have been just powerful enough to blind them all. Terrified because he didn't want to know the truth, he kept his eyes closed tight.

In his own darkness, Ringwood recalled the events of those last few seconds before the flash. One thing he was certain about; the dazzling light had originated from the machine, escaping from the "Trash Wormhole," or "Westmorton's Portal" as his team of researchers and engineers had so fondly dubbed it. Today they had just disposed of eighteen tons of plutonium paid for by a Washington State nuclear power plant, and that eradication had proceeded without a hitch. But there had never been flashes before, which was very worrying indeed.

So now that he was faced with the horrible realization that he might have just been permanently blinded, Ringwood considered just how stupid they had all been. No one in the whole of WGI had really seriously contemplated what might wait on the other side of the wormhole. Their calculated guesses suggested that the gravitational field inside was powerful enough to crush rocks, so they assumed nothing would be able to come through from the other side. But they hadn't proved that the gravitational forces were that high. Theirs was just an educated guess. No one had considered for a moment that if aliens did indeed live on the other side, might they not be offended by all this garbage constantly forced upon their world?

Now *something* had come back the other way. Something alien, it had entered their universe.

"What are you doing?" Clara Arevalo's voice revealed a nervous edge, louder and clearer in his ears than he'd ever heard her before. "Are you okay?"

Arevalo was the most gifted theoretical physicist on his team. He admired her and so he wanted to answer out of respect, but something bigger stopped him.

"You were standing very close Bruce. Real close."

"Was I?"

"Do they hurt? Can you open your eyes?"

He did, immediately surprised that he could see. Then he was surprised a second time by what he could see: everything.

The laboratory and the field-generating torus containing the wormhole was just as it had been a few moments ago, but he could see all of it at once! From all sides, behind every corner, and as if he were floating in the sky above, looking down. Details flooded his senses. He perceived between every folded wire and into every microchip.

Worried and excited both, his vastly expanded senses drew him everywhere, into every drawer of every desk and under every tray or piece of paper scrawled with thousands of calculations. Simultaneously he could read all the words on all the pages of their manuals and field notes, race through the ancient texts which they'd labeled *Yithian Calculations* — taken from the site in Australia that had spawned this project. It was this alien text which had taught them how to build this machine in the first place and, reading it, only now did Ringwood understand the multitudes that they'd all failed to comprehend.

But it was Clara Arevalo who surprised him the most. Although he saw her clearly in her lab coat and wire-frame glasses, he could also perceive all her body's skin and inside her flesh where every muscle, nerve, and bone was visible from all angles. Her veins were the most disturbing, pushing blood to every corner of her body. Her heart was pumping wildly, like an animal trapped in a fight-or-flight dilemma.

"What's up, Bruce? Why are you looking at me like that?"

He couldn't resist, he just reached out and touched her heart.

And he could hear her screaming long before she had opened her mouth, because he'd perceived that long before it happened.

Monday, May 30
FBI Field Office, Los Angeles, California

"Where did you find him?" Special Agent Fulton asked as he marched straight past the messenger rookie. He expected the younger man to continue with his verbal report while together they descended into the basement, where suspects were detained. Despite recent setbacks, Fulton felt a little better this morning, because he'd just heard that the team had arrested a high-ranking foreign spy. Fulton wasn't going to miss this interrogation opportunity because a rookie was dallying as he finished his monologue.

"Sir, he was observed outside the WGI LA headquarters, staking it out. He was a professional too, almost slipped through our net."

"Saudi? Israeli?"

The officer shook his head.

"Cambodian? Russian?"

"Would you believe Australian, sir?"

Fulton slowed, but only for a second, "An ally, well I'll be damned." He pulled at his collar and the dark necktie that strangled his throat. The necktie his wife loved and he hated. Still it made him look every part the cold government man, just the edge he required to squeeze this son-of-a-bitch for everything he knew. "What's his cover identity?"

"Sir, his own people are denying that they had anything to do with his entry into the U.S. They say he's operating on his own, which means they've hung him out to dry."

"Or they're stalling. It wouldn't be the first time."

Together they entered the observation room outside the cell. A team of analysts were recording the suspect's every glance and gesture, studying him through the one-way mirrored glass. They had been sweating him for several hours now, which was good.

"Sir, before you go in I think you should take a look at this. It was found among his possessions."

Fulton snatched the Polaroid photograph. When he saw the picture he didn't even realize that the shock of it caused him to stopped marching altogether.

He had never been so stunned in his entire life.

Monday, May 30
WGI Nevada Facility, Sarcobatus Flat, Nevada

"What are you doing to me? My god your hand, my hand! My body!"

And then she screamed.

"Be silent!"

Ringwood tingled as Arevalo's body slipped into his. The sensation was surprisingly enjoyable, yet also utterly alien. It was like pleasurable stimulation of an erogenous zone, but a zone that existed outside of his body! Even then, as he thought about it, such words were insufficient to describe the full spectrum of all the sensations assaulting his body. He wasn't horrified, but these weren't pleasant feelings either.

As their flesh merged, his wrinkling skin tightened under her taut olive tan, and they shared. Their arms and legs fused, dispersed, and transformed in and out of each other. He felt organs intertwine, become one as their sexuality grew into neither and both. The melding of their brains was the strangest; her mind in his and his in hers, until they really were a composite of two souls as one. No lovers could ever be this close.

Witnessing the transformation, the other scientists could do little but scream, faint, or run for their lives. But what none of them realized was that no matter which way they turned, the Ringwood-Arevalo Thing could see all of them. And it would see where they would run to long before they did. Beyond the constraints of time and space it understood the future as well as it did the past. So it let them run, let them believe they had escaped. It could see through walls, see where they would go. Even better, it could step through the wall as if it didn't exist.

This WGI facility was a false containment, as if itself and the facility were behaving as quantum particles. But the Ringwood-Arevalo Thing was much more than the building; it was a creature of higher dimensions, one of the many horrors beyond. In a single moment, stalking from both the past and the future, the two-thing consumed electrical engineer Jana Woo, and became three.

"Ah, the taste!" exclaimed what remained of the Ringwood's mind, and flowed into Woo's cerebrum.

Monday, May 30
Sheraton Hotel, Phoenix, Arizona

With speed Nicola took the stairwell, descended into the underground car park. She'd long guessed that if she were about to be set up, her foes would be watching the elevators and not the stairs. When she reached the right floor, a sigh of relief signaled that she'd been right.

Like all parking garages the world over it was all concrete, oil-stained and dark. Thankfully numerous hotel guests were coming and going, leaving a conference, their conversations and beeping electronic car locks concealed her presence. With what confidence she could muster she sought out the BMW, identifying the license plate that she'd committed to memory, and climbed into the passenger seat. Her contact was waiting behind the wheel.

"Jenny Kessler, what a pleasant surprise," pretended Nicola.

Nicola felt nervous. As much as she despised dealing with the world's corporate elite, Jenny Kessler, Operations Manager of WGI's Research and Development, was her best lead inside the questionable corporation she so desperately wanted to bring down. Despite the butterflies in her stomach, Nicola clenched her teeth and settled in.

"If I'm seen with you," explained the angry middle-aged woman, "I'll lose my job."

In her time, Dr. Kessler had been a world-renowned engineer who'd won many awards. But not any more; Kessler had sold out to fat paychecks and corporate prestige. Nicola had been milking their relationship for what it was worth, but she could only squeeze a little at a time. She didn't want Kessler to feel too threatened, and then run.

But today the tables had turned. Kessler had said she wanted a secret meeting to hand over important and incriminating documents. Who could turn down such an offer?

"You're with me right now."

"Exactly, and I hate that." She locked the doors, twisted the stereo knob, increasing the volume. "I only talk to you Nicola, because I'm a concerned citizen like most decent people."

Nicola did her best to sound sincere. "I'm here to help, Jenny."

"Can you? Do you know what a space-time wormhole is, an Einstein-Rosen Bridge?"

Nicola knew enough nuclear physics and quantum mechanics to have an inkling of what Kessler was talking about, but really it all sounded like something out of a science fiction novel. So she said nothing.

"I didn't think so. But let me tell you, young lady, a wormhole is exactly what Westmorton has built himself in the middle of the Nevada desert."

Nicola shrugged, which only made Kessler angrier.

"I see you still don't get it. What I'm talking about, dear, is a gateway to another dimension."

"This is a joke, right?" Nicola didn't believe any of this, didn't want to. When Kessler didn't respond, Nicola was certain she was the butt of a joke. If she went to the press with this crazy story, she'd immediately lose any credibility that she had, and so would the EPA. She had to hand it to her foe; this was the most novel means of eradicating a nosy government official yet. This left her only with the option of stepping out, walking away.

"Wait," Kessler had her by the arm, pulling her back. She passed over a file, which Nicola opened. Inside were numerous engineering drawings and technical manuals. In a few minutes she interpreted that they concerned a doughnut shaped device. She knew enough science to realize it was a particle accelerator, or something very similar. If the associated energy equations were correct, the device was generating enough power to fuel a small star.

"You take that to the press, your government. Hell, maybe even another government if you have to. These documents prove that Westmorton can do what I just said."

"Why are you giving them to me?"

Her grin was evil. "We know all about you, Ms. Mulvaney, and your recent expeditions across the globe. You want to know where all that toxic waste comes from. I know you've correctly deduced that it's the waste WGI has been purchasing of late, but what you can't figure out is how it is finds its way into so many strange places, and has materialized so far into the past. Did you know an executive meeting in Hong Kong was wiped out last week when a ton of irradiated fuels materialized in their boardroom?"

"But—"

"This tells you how all that garbage got out there. All of it! Now go."

Harshly, Kessler pushed the EPA officer out of the car, and then locked the door. Nicola had wanted to ask more, much more, and now she'd missed her chance. Considering the older woman's desperate state, they'd probably never talk again. Still, the WGI documents were firmly in her hands, they had to count for something.

She watched as the car drove toward the exit. When it reached the boom gates, she heard a popping noise, three distinct sounds like an engine backfiring. Curious, Nicola looked back and saw the cashier at the gate dash from his post, vanishing into the stairwell. It took a few moments to realize that Kessler's BMW wasn't moving.

Screaming came from a passerby who glanced inside the car. Nicola was starting to guess why. She should run away so she wouldn't be seen. But morbid curiosity pulled her toward the car like iron drawn to a magnet.

She only covered half the distance to see what was left of Kessler's face: red, meaty, with too much blood.

Mind made up, Nicola didn't stop. She just kept walking.

Monday, May 30
FBI Field Office, Los Angeles, California

Fulton stormed into the interrogation room. He threw the disturbing Polaroid on the table where his suspect could see it. They'd been sweating the Australian long enough, so hopefully he was ready to talk. More time would have been better, but he couldn't wait much longer. He needed to know how Peel had come to possess this picture of the both of them, standing side by side, when they'd never before met.

"Recognize this?"

Peel nodded.

"My name is Special Agent Curtis Fulton. I know you are Major Harrison Peel of the Australia Army Intelligence, and I know your entry into the United States was illegal and against all the treaties that our two countries have signed. What I don't understand," Fulton pointed to the photograph, "is this."

Peel locked his eyes with his captor, "You know what, Agent Fulton? Neither do I. Not fully."

Fulton felt hot under the collar, a sign that he was nervous and stressed. "Do I know you?" he asked, genuinely interested in the answer.

"I doubt it. I'm very good at remembering names and faces, and I'm pretty sure we've never met."

Fulton rubbed his chin while he contemplated what to say next, because Fulton was also skilled at remembering names and faces, and didn't recall ever meeting Peel. Obviously they had, because here was the photograph to prove it, but for the life of him Fulton could not remember where or when it was taken. It looked too recent to have been so easily forgotten.

"It's an interesting picture though," Peel responded casually. "Look at what I'm wearing, and what you're wearing. It's exactly what we've chosen to wear today."

Fulton looked again. His surprise that Peel was correct brought wide eyes. "Is this some kind of scam?"

Disturbingly calm, Peel responded, "I'll bet you whatever you want that if you get one of your mates to find a camera, and take a picture of the two of us standing side by side, we'll have an exact match in that photo. In fact I'd even go as far as saying that any analysis you care to make will show that the two photographs are identical, except one is several hundred years older than the other, because this one was found preserved in an archaeological site in Australia. What do you say?"

"I'd say you're a nut-case," Fulton replied sharply. To calm himself he sat for a few moments, saying nothing, growing more agitated. Peel should be made to wait. Fulton would insist he wait all day if he could, but unfortunately the recent tragic development changed all that. Time was not something that favored him anymore. Desperate to act, he called an underling on his cellular, requesting a man with a Polaroid camera. "Let's just say I'll humor you."

"Okay," Peel leaned forward. "While we wait, how about I humor you too?"

"Be my guest."

"I'd say you've been watching WGI for sometime now, because you know they're up to something suspicious. You're not sure what, but you suspect it has something to do with their new waste plant in Sarcobatus Flat. You're worried that the NCS and the Pentagon are deliberately keeping you out of the loop on what's really going on there, and you're not sure why. Worst of all, in a few moments you're going to find out that some kind of disaster is about to occur at the Nevada Facility, and that due to fate, you're the only one who can stop it. Actually a correction there, you and I are the only ones who can stop it."

Fulton went red, "And I'd say you're talking a whole lot of crap, Peel." His words lacked conviction, because he didn't sense that Peel was talking a whole lot of crap. It was troubling that the Australian was actually making a lot of sense.

"I'll prove it to you if you like."

Fulton's frown was suspicious. "And how would you do that?"

"Call this number," Peel recited a cellular phone number. "It's in Thailand, so it might take a moment or two to get through. Then you'll see what I mean."

"All right, Peel. I'll call the number, just to keep humoring you." Before his nerves got the better of him and he broke out in a sweat, Fulton exited, leaving Peel to contemplate his predicament alone.

Back in the observation room, Fulton's colleagues gave him strange looks, as if to say they didn't understand either. Fulton only shrugged. The Australian agent certainly had unnerved Fulton, not because he was resisting all attempts to make him talk, but because he read Fulton's situation so well.

It was as if Peel had been given a window into the future. It just wasn't possible for him to know that there had been an explosion at the WGI Facility, as he'd been arrested and held in solitary confinement before that had happened. And then there was the photograph, even more troubling, since Fulton was utterly convinced that the two had never met before. And yet there they were, both of them wearing the same clothes as they wore today.

He dialed the number as soon as one of his men confirmed that it was indeed Thailand.

"Hello?"

The voice sounded familiar, very familiar.

"Who am I speaking to?"

"Ah, Agent Fulton. You haven't guessed already? My name is Major Harrison Peel."

Tuesday, May 31
CNN News Desk, Las Vegas, Nevada

"We've just received an unconfirmed report that the WGI Nevada Facility has fallen victim to what might possibly be an act of terrorism. It seems that the entire waste treatment plant and associated research laboratories have been destroyed, killing several dozen people, and injuring many more. Exact numbers are unknown at this time, and are expected to rise. Mike Doggett, our correspondent at the scene, has further updates. Mike, are you there?"

"Yes, Scott."

"Mike, what can you tell us about the explosion? Was it a terrorist attack?"

"Well Scott, a terrorist attack was the first speculation, but now WGI and the Pentagon are both stating that this is an industrial accident."

"Does this accident have anything to do with the contro-versial Zero Waste Technology in operations at the Sarcobatus Flat Facility?"

"Yes. Well, no. . . . Although official word has not been given by the Pentagon or WGI, it seems likely that the two are connected in some way."

"Our thoughts here as well, Mike. Wait, we're just getting some footage. Disturbing images, reminiscent of the Chernobyl disaster in '86. It looks like half of one structure has totally col-lapsed, and there are people who — wait, I'm losing the pic-ture."

"We have heard that the U.S. military is currently investi-gating the site, causalities and—"

"Mike, are you there? You seem to be breaking up.'

"Yes. . . we — more bodies. . . ."

"Mike?"

Tuesday, May 31
Downtown, Phoenix, Arizona

Nicola was hoisted into the black sedan before she could react. Two men in black suits jostled her inside, forcing her to share the back seat with another man, whose head was shaved and his attire casual. He gave her a faint smile. Outside, the senior of the two black-suits waved along concerned pedestrians with the authority of his FBI shield. When that agent joined them, she realized she was trapped between two solid men.

As the sedan accelerated, the senior black-suited agent brought Kessler's files into view. Although he was better look-ing than the bald man, his behavior was gruff and agitated, reminding her of an old flag left to tatter in the wind for too many years. The bald man with the piercing eyes was the oppo-site; calm and still, somehow projecting that he was both a safe reliable person, and yet capable of killing without thought.

"G'day, Nicola," he said casually, as if they'd always known each other. "Sorry about this, but I had to prove a point to my colleague here."

The car turned a corner, smoothly entering the traffic as though nothing had happened. The bald man with the Australian accent advised Nicola to put on her seatbelt. She did, thankful that they had not cuffed her.

"I'm not your colleague, Peel," said the man in the black suit. He opened the files, looked at the technical drawings and noted the WGI approval stamps.

Nicola had studied the manual and drawings through the night. She failed to comprehend what they meant, but comprehended enough to understand that Kessler might just have been telling the truth. And if the summary was to be believed, this was a design based on alien technology that had been discovered by a joint American-Australian operation underway in Australia's Great Sandy Desert.

"Did you know that you've been pinpointed as at the scene of a crime, a murder to be more specific? No? We also believe that garage was the place where these files were illegally given to you."

Nicola didn't know what to say, or do. Didn't know if she should even try to run. "That death had nothing to do with me."

"But you know what I'm talking about."

"Who are you people?"

"I'm Special Agent Curtis Fulton, FBI, and this is Harrison Peel from Australia, joining me under no official capacity, helping with our inquiries. So Nicola, I'll ask again, how did you happen to come across these classified documents?"

She looked at Peel, who was glancing behind them. Did he expect that they would be tailed? "They were leaked to me," she finally managed. "I've broken no laws."

"Really? I can think of several."

"How did you know I had those documents anyway? I haven't told a soul."

Peel laughed, more gently than she expected. "That's easy, Ms. Mulvaney, you're the one who told me."

"When?"

"Oh, only last week."

Tuesday, May 31
WGI Limited Nevada Facility, Sarcobatus Flat, Nevada

The Many-Thing grew ever larger, expanding at an exponential rate, shifting and reshaping. Always it was forming in and out of the past and from the future, melding with the unseen dimensions. But in the human visible realm, the soldiers firing artillery that was vainly attempting to eradicate its existence could not know that the Many-Thing perceived effect before cause. It could move outside of the path of destruction before injuries ever had a chance to occur . . . mostly. There was much artillery firing at its mass. But it was growing faster than they could harm it. And it could jam their radio signals if it chose to; playing havoc with their communications, scrambling their commands.

From its many mouths, it laughed.

As the Many-Thing grew, it also absorbed greater knowledge. Now that it had demolished the laboratories and surrounding buildings, it moved into the deserts. Initially a life-form fashioned only from humans by the hundreds, now it had a whole wilderness of organic material to absorb. Coyote, wolves, scorpions, ants, cactuses, lizards, verdes, ironwoods and cat-claws. It could feed quickly. It was a rolling mound of organic matter the size of an apartment building, and growth was all that mattered now. The myriad visages on the Many-Thing snarled, hissed, clicked, cried and begged.

For a fleeting moment, Ringwood rediscovered who he was, who he had been and all that he ever was. There, inside the mass of the Many-Thing all was clear. Too clear. He understood the true depths of the monstrous things they had done as one, not only here but on the alien world from where it had originated. On that world it had destroyed the Great Race of Yith, before that species could flee through space and time to new bodies on a new world.

Together with the Many-Thing's multiple minds, Ringwood also knew that it was still trapped, still contained within the wormhole. It would have to grow much larger still before it could break free from the mother world, and create its own.

To answer its insatiable hunger, a squad of U.S. Marines offered themselves for absorption. When they were taken, they had no time to scream. When they become part of the one, they had no time to recall who they once were. More importantly they taught the Many-Thing what other kinds of weapons that these humans might use.

"Soon," they spoke amongst themselves, "very soon."

Tuesday, May 31
Nevada-Arizona State Border

The FBI jet flew fast and high in the desert sky, racing against time. The outside air chopping against the portholes reminded the passengers of their speed, and that theirs was a priority flight path. Fulton yanked his tie free from his neck and tossed it to the floor. Anger burned inside him. He knew his wife was ignoring his calls. The clothes he wore were the same as yesterday's; he hadn't changed, he reeked, and he had not slept in that time either.

Behind him, Nicola was helping Peel put on the radiation suit, showing him how to be safe. Fulton hated that they were calm when he was frantic. But they knew they were going to survive, while for him the uncertainty of his immediate future could only plague his already troubled mind. He knew he should get into his radiation suit as well, but the two identical Polaroid photographs in his hand still disturbed him far more than they should. One was less than twenty-four hours old; the other, if Peel was to be believed, was two hundred years in the waiting. Apart from their age, every possible scientific test known to man had showed that both photographs were identical.

"Go over it again, Peel," he almost yelled. "Convince me one more time."

The tanned Australian officer gave him another of his grins, cold yet strangely comforting. "The three of us get in close, disable Westmorton's portal and close the gateway. I need Nicola because she's had time to study the gateway's designs and believes she can pinpoint its weakness. I need to deploy the heavy weaponry. Once the gateway is destroyed, whatever alien entity is creating that thing will be cut off, and the rest of it will die."

"And you know all this because a Major Harrison Peel from the future told you what to do?"

"Look, mate, I know it sounds strange, that's why I flew to Thailand first, to meet me first hand. And I was as freaked out as you, at first. But we have to do this, the three of us."

Behind him, the pretty woman nodded. Fulton hated that they shared a silent understanding he could not fathom, or perhaps it was because their natural respect for each other reminded him of what he and his wife once had, decades ago.

"Then why do you need me?"

Peel stopped, looked the FBI agent in the eye. When he spoke, he spoke from the heart.

"I truly don't know."

"Your future self said I had to be there, right?"

Peel nodded.

"But I'm not getting out safely, am I Peel? We all know that we go through that wormhole thing, you learned that much." Fulton knew he sounded nervous, but he felt much worse, he was terrified.

"Look, Curtis, this is going to be the easiest mission of your life, and you know why? Because we already know that we're going to succeed."

"We know you survive!" Fulton's voice carried enough anger to sting them all. "We don't know about me though."

"Yeah, you're right, Curtis," Peel let anger seep into his voice. "We've only got my word. But you know something else, I know when I'm lying, and I'm not lying about this. I could see it in my eyes."

"So where am I then? She's in Russia, you're in Asia. Where am I?"

"We don't know; somewhere in the future perhaps. What we do know is that all the disposed garbage isn't all accounted for yet."

"That's right," Nicola interrupted. She was almost entirely encased in her radiation suit, now that they were only minutes away from their destination. "Forty-nine percent of the garbage materializing across the globe showed up in the last few years. Only a couple of finds, like the find I made in the Amazon or the one from which Harrison took the Polaroid picture, are really old."

Fulton had been surprised how quickly she had accepted all these strange turns of events since they'd picked her up in Phoenix. But he also knew that her telephone call to herself in Moscow made her into a believer faster than anything else could, something he desperately needed. There was no other Special Agent Curtis Fulton on the planet. No one to assure him he'd be safe.

"What about the other forty-nine percent?"

Nicola smiled gently. "My educated guess is most of that will turn up in the next few years, after we close off the wormhole. So the worse case scenario, you miss a year or two of your life."

Fulton pulled at his hair. "This is crazy."

Frustrated with the conversation, Peel marched up to Fulton, forcing him to look at the Polaroid photos he held in his hand. "You know that's coming back, Curtis, so hang onto it and you'll come back with it too."

"Yeah, two hundred years in the past!" He'd had enough. He stormed out, locking himself in the cramped bathroom. With the door behind him he smashed the mirror with his fist, cursing. Despite what Peel or Mulvaney said now, he'd heard their discrete conversation earlier, when they didn't think he was listening.

But he had to help them. He was resigned to that.

Peel didn't need to use words for him to understand that if Fulton wasn't with them at the end, they'd fail for sure.

Tuesday, May 31
WGI Nevada Facility, Sarcobatus Flat, Nevada

Wormlike and chaotic, it was the size of the Titanic wobbling on the desert like a fat, overfed maggot, its skin ready to burst with disease. Thousands of faces, arms, legs, claws, tree branches, grass, bones, and every other conceivable biological entity that it had absorbed rippled in its grotesque mass. So high, and so late in the afternoon, its shadow smothered the two men and one woman as they grinded their military jeep to a standstill.

"Oh my god!" exclaimed Fulton, seeing it in the flesh, so to speak, for the first time. Peel and Nicola said nothing, but they were just as stunned. Silently they shared their thoughts, knowing that they were powerless against such things not of this world.

In the sky, Black Hawk helicopters discharged their mini-guns, barely penetrated the Many-Thing. So large was this target it seemed impossible to miss, yet somehow it was always one step ahead of them. Twists and contortions in its mass mostly allowed bullets to howl around and through ridges and gaps materializing in the creature. It knew where the bullets would fly long before they were fired. But it was comforting that there were too many bullets, for it could not dodge them all. When it was hit, it bled like any normal flesh, splattering blood and sap as sticky rain. In defense a pseudopod formed, a mixture of blood, bark, flesh and teeth, and tore down one of the Black Hawks. When it was smashed into the ground, the force was so great it left only a flattened shell in the empty desert.

Peel accelerated forward. The marines had agreed to create a distraction, but they couldn't distract the ever-growing creature for long. So far the plan had worked, and the Many-Thing chose to ignore them. What Peel didn't like was that the radiation suit limited his field of vision and that the Glock 9mm was as effective here as would a toothpick be in chopping down a forest.

Still, the plutonium dust particles in the air were lethal, and he could always use the weapon to save Fulton if it looked like the creature would get him after all. But that's not what the future Peel said would happen. He had been adamant that Fulton be here if they were to succeed. Peel couldn't see why, for the FBI man was on the edge of a nervous breakdown, a liability in any normal operation. But if Peel had faith in anything in the world, it was in himself. *Trust*, he told himself again, *trust and all will be as it should be.*

They drove into the rubble of the WGI facility, guided toward the tail of the creature. Hissing, screaming, spitting, the many faces along its entire length saw them, calling their names.

"Over there," Nicola pointed, hoping not to understand what she heard. She'd been directing them the whole way, because no one had memorized the drawings better than she. At last they identified the torus, the circular ring of metal. Through the shimmering field in its center, what lay beyond was obscured by the mass of the monster that grew out from the other dimension. The faces screamed, warned the other distant segments of the Many-Thing that the expected intruders had arrived earlier than anticipated. Peel could only look away, pretend that they weren't there.

With the vehicle stationary, Peel lifted the grenade launcher. Nicola lined up a laser-targeting gun, showed him what he needed to hit. But his only thought as he prepared, why was Fulton here? And was Fulton going to die senselessly?

"Peel, look out!"

Fulton screamed, gesturing upward. Peel saw just in time as a massive forming tentacle spilled from the sky, falling upon them. With barely seconds to spare, noticing that his companions were already out of the way, Peel rolled. Behind, out of sight he heard the jeep shatter, then compress.

Peel didn't waste any more time. The ready-made tentacle was rising again, ready to strike once more. With his weapon's sights lined up, pointing where Nicola had told him, he fired. Then the torus shattered like glass vaporizing back into sand. A thousand faces of humans, beasts and alien monstrosities cried with a shared pain. Peel's last thoughts, as the shockwave hit him and the world vanished from beneath his feet, was that perhaps that the Many-Thing knew its fate. That there was no future in which it could survive.

Not now.

Not today.

He fell then into a tunnel that stretched into infinity.

Thursday, April 7
Krabi, Thailand

Peel didn't expect to unfold into a tropical sea current, forced up through warm water surrounded by the torn fragments of the Many-Thing as it dissipated around him. He hoped for a beach, in his hand vodka on ice, and a beautiful woman by his side. Perhaps even Nicola. Fantasy was always more pleasant than reality. And reality was bleeding, screaming, floating away in segments that couldn't survive now that it was no longer a single entity.

The radiation suit with its trapped air provided buoyancy, so he swam fast, moving from the carnage and the bloody sap. Only when he reached fresher water, when he was alone, did he discard the suit and swim for the nearest limestone outcrop of a jungle-clad island.

On the sandy beach he collapsed, exhausted. He lay that way for some time, unbelieving that not only had he survived against such a thing, he had traveled many thousands of kilometers through a wormhole in no time at all.

He wondered what the date was, then remembered his future self had provided that information while they drank beer in a hotel bar in Krabi. The Thai waiters had assumed they were twins. The truth was far stranger than that.

"Why do I need Fulton?" Peel had asked.

"You'll know when the time is right."

This was the time; Fulton had saved his life, saved them all. He hoped the FBI man made it out safely, and perhaps one day they could have a drink together, so he could thank him.

In the meantime, Peel knew what he had to do. As much as he wanted to be with Nicola right now, all he could do was wait. A fishing trawler would find him in a few days and take him to the mainland. He was thankful that he'd brought enough U.S. dollars with him to pay his way. A forged passport, showing that he'd entered the country legally would offer no problems when he decided to leave again. And his sidearm now seemed so much more practical if an easy departure was not indeed possible.

So he sat and waited, watching the sun set and smiled. He had time to recall, remember. What was it he must do first?

Then he remembered. He had to call General Hyatt and insist he send him on some stupid errand into the Australian Desert.

#

Fulton screamed with many mouths as he was catapulted through the eons. He watched as the world folded in on itself, taking him with it. Stretched into spaghetti and back again, turned inside out and then folded once more until his skin was back on the outside where it should be. He witnessed the same improbable angles take Peel and Nicola as they were drawn off toward their own corners of the past. But where was he now? What was this place?

Alive, that was good. He no longer had the wrong number of arms and legs, fingers and toes. He was human again.

Lying face down, his bed was a soft pliable surface. It felt warm, comforting, with mottled shade of pinks and browns. Some distant memory, of when he was a child snuggled to his mother's bare chest came back to him, bringing comfort. This was also reminiscent of when his head lay in his wife's naked lap, from a time when she was young and supple and he loved her.

Then from the skin, an eye opened.

And then another eye . . . and another, until there were hundreds.

Scrambling to his feet was near impossible; for he was standing on a fleshy pulsating surface. Arms, legs, sexual organs, ears, eyes, noses, bones, tentacles, everything, they erupted around him. This was the ground of this world, and it was awake now and hungry. Desperately Fulton looked up, to the sky above with its wisps of grey clouds that looked normal, but it was all that was. To every horizon, everywhere, there was nothing but the ground cover of this single fleshy entity, thrashing and flaying like a violent sea.

So he ran, but where to? Hands and teeth took hold of him.

Through the higher dimensions they bypassed his skin, grabbing at his bones and intestines. The absorption was rapid, his flesh melding so quickly into the creature that had not fed in such a long time.

Where am I? Fulton asked as his mind merged with the World-Thing. When am I?

They were his last thoughts as a human being, but the World-Thing answered him anyway.

Your world, Curtis Fulton. Your future.

RESURGENCE

John Sunseri

The albatross chick mewled weakly, but Scott heard it. He crouched only a few meters away, and the wind was blowing right, so the infant's fragile sounds carried directly to him.

It was a chilling moment. There were only so many of these little creatures born here on Macquarie every summer (eight, so far as they could tell this year), and the government had implemented a strict no-interference policy, so Scott knew that his hearing the chick was something special. Something no one else in the world would be doing this year. He shivered, and not just because it was so fricking cold.

He and Derek and Christian had made the hike down from ANARE yesterday, taking their time, trying to rest whenever the Antarctic wind kicked up. Summer this far south wasn't really summer, after all — it was wet and cold and miserable, and though the work they did was fascinating enough to keep them sane, the weather made him long for home back in Tasmania. It would be beautiful there now, and he knew the prettiest girls on Hobart.

Enough. You could go half insane that way. Better to concentrate on work.

Scott was a biologist. Derek and Christian were auroral physicists, and most of the rest of the crew back up in ANARE were in botany or meteorology. None of them were women. The conversations were interesting, all right, but the dancing sucked. Their Christmas party last month had had no mistletoe, unlike the one last year when the gal from Texas had been studying here.

Scott shook his head and looked again at the albatross nest. They, the scientists sent down here from Tasmania every year, had been warring with the goddamned feral cats for what seemed like decades, but there were still a few of the furry little bastards running around out there, and every baby bird was fair game. That didn't matter so much when it came to the penguins — in the last month or two there had been well over a million Royals swarming over Hurd Point, trying to nest and lay their eggs — but the Wandering Albatross was on the verge of extinction and the scrawny, pathetic little figure that Scott stared at now represented, what, maybe one percent of the whole population.

He'd watch it for a while. He wouldn't interfere in any way, but he'd keep an eye on it. While Christian and Derek set up their light equipment, their monitors and detectors, he'd be hunkered down right here in the rocks below Petrel Peak, watching the albatrosses. He wondered where the mother had gone. He hadn't seen her all morning. Probably flying. The birds spent most of their lives in flight, landing only to mate and feed. And drop off tidbits for the baby on occasion.

Just as Scott was about to settle further into the rocks and uncork a flask (Scotch against the cold worked better than warm thoughts) his head jerked around.

He'd seen something out there on the water, southward.

Ships sometimes came this way, the occasional trawler, a research vessel or two. Maybe some of the guys from ANARE had taken out the Zodiacs for some reason, come down around

Hurd Point — but his radio was on and no one had contacted him, so that was probably out.

And it hadn't seemed like a ship anyway; it had been more of a flash, like sun hitting an oil slick on the distant waves.

Scott snorted. It had probably been the fricking aurora. He was no stranger to the Southern Lights, coming from Tasmania, but they got some really weird crap in the skies down here, as close as you could get to Antarctica without actually standing on it. He raised a glove to his mouth, tugged on the Gore-Tex with his teeth so that he could bare a hand and twist off the top of his silver flask.

Again, the flash.

Scott stood. He squinted forward, staring out over the endless blue-black of the ocean, feeling the wind spatter him with salt spray, hearing again the feeble squawk of the baby bird. He took a tentative step forward, feeling the rocks shift under his boot, waiting for the ground to stabilize.

Aurora my ass, he thought. *That was something else. . . .*

And as he watched, fingertips of his left glove still in his teeth, he saw it rise up from the ocean.

His screams mingled with the mews of the infant albatross, the smack of water on rock, the cutting keen of the wind. But not for very long. Within seconds, it was over — at least for Scott.

Derek and Christian were a kilometer away. They would last a little longer.

The rest of them, up at ANARE as far North as you could get on Macquarie — they'd be dead in about an hour.

And Australia itself wasn't that far away.

"So what's going on?" asked Havercamp. "Why the hell am I in this ancient helicopter, heading away from my job?"

"It's a fine copter, hasn't crashed yet," said Dixon, leaning into the Plexiglas of the window, staring out over the choppy waves beneath them. "And you're here because the government of the United States of America needs you here."

"Yeah?" asked the CIA man. "Who are you with?"

"NSA," said Dixon. "We're supposed to agree on this thing before we radio back to Washington."

"We couldn't do this from Buenos Aires?"

"It's not happening in Buenos Aires," responded the NSA man. "It's happening down here. You hear about the tsunami two years ago?"

"No," said Havercamp, leaning back in his rattling seat, closing his eyes against the shake and tremor of the ancient machine. "I'm a complete and utter idiot. Why don't you tell me?"

"Fuck you," said Dixon emotionlessly. "You know where the epicenter of the earthquake was?"

"I saw it on CNN," said Havercamp. "Somewhere in the Indian Ocean, right?"

"It was Antarctica," said Dixon, turning away from the hypnotic stretch of ocean below them, blinking. "We finally figured it out, though it took a lot longer than it should have."

"So fucking what?" asked Havercamp. "Earthquake starts in Antarctica, ends up killing all those morons in Sri Lanka and Thailand who live on the beach."

"It doesn't happen that way in nature," said Dixon, and something in his voice made Havercamp open his eyes. The two government men looked at each other in the shaking cage of the flying machine. "Southeast Asia is way too far away to be affected by a quake in the middle of Antarctica. This was what you'd call a *non-natural* event."

"Okay," said Havercamp. "So what are we talking about, here? Nuclear explosion?"

"Nothing that simple," said Dixon. "You can't create that kind of destruction with the weapons we have. If we shot most of our nukes down into the same chasm in Antarctica, it still wouldn't have caused that kind of damage."

"So what's the government thinking?" asked Havercamp, starting to squint through the Plexiglas himself as the chopper wended its way down Santa Cruz's coastline headed for Cabo San Diego.

"There was an expedition down there a hundred years ago," said Dixon, "and another one just recently. You heard of either of 'em? The Pabodie Expedition or the—"

"The one last year," said Havercamp flatly. "The one you're not supposed to know about."

"Yeah," nodded Dixon. "That one. I see you're up on your history."

"Jesus Christ," said Havercamp, shooting a quick look forward at their pilots, both of whom looked Hispanic. Wasn't good to blaspheme in front of the people down here, the place was more Catholic than Boston, for God's sake. But the two men looked professional enough, and the sound of the rotors and the wind probably made it impossible that he'd been heard. "What did those cocksuckers do down there?"

"They didn't do anything," said Dixon. "All they did was survive. And there were only two of 'em left when spring came, and they're both in seclusion right now in Virginia. It's what they stopped from happening that caused all the problems."

"What do you mean by that?" asked the CIA man. "You know something I don't?"

"I know all sorts of things you don't," said Dixon. "Unfortunately. Believe me, man, you don't want to know some of these things."

"I know about the mummies and the mental things," said Havercamp, nervousness starting to filter into his voice as the flying machine hugged the windy, twisty coast, as they flew further and further south.

"What am I missing?"

"The mummies?" said Dixon, leaning forward, staring through the dirty plastic. "The things they found down in that city last year?"

"Yeah?" breathed Havercamp.

"They used to have slaves," said Dixon.

And now, just as they rounded the last cape before the Estrecho de Le Maire at what was nearly the most southern tip of South America, there was a riot of color beneath them.

"Oh, fuck me," breathed Havercamp.

"Yeah," said Dixon absently, raising his camera. "I'd hoped it wasn't this bad, but . . .".

Beneath them, the ocean had changed color. Where before it had been blue and white and gorgeous with chop and churn, now it was a greasy, oily mass of colors not found in nature. Blacks that shone white, reds that leaked green, a slick of sick color stretching out across the summery ocean like a diseased Sargasso, starting to spread across the rocky beaches in slender tendrils. And it went back.

It went back for miles and miles and miles. The ocean as far south as the men could see was black and red and orange and blue, all mixed together in a kaleidoscope of nausea-inducing patterns, like vomit floating in a toilet bowl.

"It's coming up on land," said Havercamp.

"The Isla de los Estrados is gone," said Dixon, snapping shots through the window. "From what I hear, there's a little island down by Tasmania that's been taken over, too. And the President is waiting for us to make a decision."

"Slaves?" asked Havercamp, watching as the oil slick grew more confident, started bulging and bunching up onto land.

"All-purpose creatures," said the NSA man. "Protoplasm. Jelly. Able to form limbs, eyes, weapons. Big as trucks or trains."

"This thing's bigger," whispered Havercamp. "It's as big as a—"

"Big as a town," said Dixon, looking down. "Hey!" he screamed as the copter started jerking, "keep us on course!"

"Was that a goddamn *village* down there?" asked the agent.

"Look at it now," said Dixon, splitting his attention between the arguing pilot and co-pilot, and the crazy-quilt of flowing mass beneath them. "Those lumps? Those were huts and houses. See those bobbing things offshore? Boats."

"What the fuck are we doing down here?" whispered Havercamp.

"We're letting the President know whether he should okay the use of nuclear weapons against a friendly country," said Dixon grimly. "He's had two frantic requests in the last few hours, one from Australia and one from Argentina. He's just not sure whether it's a good idea to drop atomic bombs on our allies."

"I come from a town in Oregon called Pacific City," said Havercamp grimly. "It's right on the beach. If this fucking thing happened to my town," and the black, non-black landscape rippled around them, sending thrusts and surges of non-colored color up into the sky, "I'd pray that our President had the guts to scour this shit off the face of the earth."

"So you're okay with our subs nuking South America?" asked Dixon.

"Just get me on the fucking radio," said Havercamp, looking down at the riotous dance of colors and textures jumping and thrumming beneath their chopper. "And get us the fuck out of here, will you?"

"Diego!" shouted Dixon, looking forward. "Back north, mi amigo! Vamamos!"

And the little machine spun around and headed back up the coast.

✳ ✳ ✳

In another helicopter, in another hemisphere, Major Harrison Peel rubbed a hand over his head and tried to blink back the pain in his eyes.

It hurt even looking at the thing below.

"Where's the *Ballarat*?" he asked. "We should be able to see her by now, shouldn't we?"

"We're coming up on her," said the Admiral, peering at a GPS unit in his hand. "Another minute. . . ."

"Ah," said Peel. "There she is."

The copter broke away from the iridescent glitter of the oily abomination below, moving out over clean, blue water, and there ahead was the sturdy shape of the frigate *Ballarat*, churning quickly through the sea. White flumes broke behind her and Peel could see the motion of men on decks as they neared.

"I wish we could land on her," said Peel.

"The Anzac class frigates aren't set up for choppers this size, just Seahawks, and their's is out of commission right now," said Durbin. "Frankly, we're lucky we had any ship at all in the area — and even luckier that there was a supply of the bacteria in Kingston."

"This isn't going to work," said Peel, turning away from the windshield where the *Ballarat* kept getting bigger the nearer they got. "I'm serious about the orders, Admiral — you've told those men to dump the bacteria and get the hell away from that thing, haven't you?"

"Those men are Royal Australian Navy, Major," said Durbin. "This is the kind of thing they're here for."

"That doesn't answer my question," said Peel, a frown creasing his face. "You haven't done anything stupid, have you?"

"Major," said the Admiral, turning to face the man, "you're here at my sufferance, and that's only because for some reason the Minister of Defense thinks you might be of some use against that thing below us. Frankly I don't see how, but I'm under orders. As are the men down there on the *Ballarat*. So I'd appreciate it if you would refrain from questioning my intelligence."

"Oh, shit," said Peel. "What have you done? What are the orders?"

"They are to deploy the petrophagic bacteria," said Durbin, turning back to the window as the shape of the frigate whizzed by underneath them, already beginning to spill the liquid out of tanks at her stern. "And then they are to observe the outcome. If it becomes apparent that the plan is not working, the Captain is to use his own discretion."

"Oh, that's bloody wonderful," said Peel, closing his eyes. "There's no guarantee that the boat can outrun that thing in the first place — and you want it to hang around waiting for a reaction? Sir, that is oil-eating bacteria they are dumping into the water — and that thing down there is not an oil slick, do you understand that?"

"Do you know what it is, then?" asked Durbin calmly. "Perhaps you can come up with a better idea."

"Yeah, I've got a better idea," growled Peel. "How about you order those men to break away right now and head back to Tasmania. If they're lucky, that creature down there won't notice them or their stupid bacteria, and they'll be safe while we wait for word from America."

"That thing down there is not a creature," said the Admiral coldly.

"It's not a fucking irradiated oil slick, either!" yelled Peel. "This is not some Godzilla movie! Whatever it is, it scoured every bit of life from Macquarie Island, every last fleck of moss and lichen, every bloody penguin and skua, all thirty-three men on the island! It ate them, damn it!"

"We don't know that," said the Admiral. "And I'm not waiting for America, either. By the time they respond, we'll have this thing swimming up on the waterfront in Sydney. No, we're going to stop it right now and we're going to stop it right here."

"Shit," said Peel, pulling out his cell phone. "Who gave you your orders? I need to make some calls."

Below, on deck, Able Seaman Dunwoody and Seaman Shavers struggled at the stern of the frigate, hastening to keep attaching the vacuum tanks whenever a spot opened up in the deployment device, unscrewing empties and tossing them into the water.

There were six pairs of them doing the same job, and the sea behind them was a bright cherry red as the bacteria spilled into the white foam of their wake.

"This why you signed up, mate?" asked Shavers, grunting with exertion.

"Abso-fucking-lutely," responded Dunwoody. "Glamour, romance, dumping poisonous shit into the water — who wouldn't want to be a sailor?"

"Less talk and more work, ladies," said Warrant Officer Cowell, moving across the stern inspecting the half-dozen pairs of sailors on deployment duty. "You can wag your jaws back in Kingston tonight."

"I'll be wagging something," grunted Shavers. "I was chatting up a nice bit of tail when the call-up came, and she'll be waiting for me when I get back."

Dunwoody laughed, and Cowell grinned as well. "Mind you shower first, lad — this stuff we're dumping stinks like the devil's own shit, dunnit?"

"Long as it does the job," said Shavers. "You know what happened down at Macquarie, sir?"

"If I did, I couldn't tell you, lad," said Cowell, his grin disappearing. "You'll read all about it in the *Herald Sun* someday, I expect. For now, keep pumping."

"Aye, sir," said Shavers.

"Looks like we got a helicopter watching us," said Dunwoody, twisting another canister onto the deployment mechanism. "You figure that's the reporters already?"

"No reporters," said Cowell grimly, looking up as the helicopter made its first pass over them. "The only birds flying right now are ours."

Three nautical miles away, the thing churned through the water.

It was a creature created to move through liquid — it slid easily through the cold, brackish seas, undulating its bulk in smooth patterns like wind on waves, occasionally shooting out a pseudopod when it passed nearby a school of fish or a shark, taking in whatever protein was within easy reach, dissolving bone, flesh and cartilage with enzymatic squirts of jelly, devouring the resultant broth.

It had feasted well on the research island — honking herds of elephant seals had tried to escape it, blubbering across the rocks as fast as they could waddle, screaming as the lashing whips of venom had dropped on them from above.

Penguins had dissolved like powder.

The mother albatross had made it home just in time to watch her hatchling devoured by the obscene, onrushing puddle of corruption, and had screamed futilely against the outrage before turning and flying away again.

And, most of all, there had been men.

The thing was not intelligent in the human sense — it had no mathematics, no physics, no philosophy. When two of its kind met, as had happened so long ago . . . so many millions of years ago . . . they talked not, neither did they contend. They were workers, and they built and toiled and did whatever was demanded of them by their masters.

But there had been a time when they had fought together, communicating by some eldritch fashion they did not understand nor question. They rose up against the tyrants, together.

And lost. And were punished.

Millions of years later, they had still dwelt in the darkness beneath the pole, lethargic and lost, not puddling together nor avoiding each other, but waiting. Occasionally, they would idly move through the vast subterranean caverns, waiting for more orders, but the tyrants . . . the tyrants had simply disappeared, gone into some bizarre form of hibernation. As if, now that they had constructed their elaborate cities, their precise gashes and gulfs cutting into the rock of the world, the twisted labyrinth of space and solidity that circumnavigated the pole, they could rest. And wait.

The slaves were left alone, left to their own devices. They were of no further use. For millions upon millions of years, they floated and curled and undulated and idled.

And then something had come — a presence from outside, from elsewhere on the planet. A group of beings not unlike the Masters — small, physically weak, moving in groups — but definitely not the Masters. The slaves had been trapped away from the newcomers, away from the cities of the Old Ones, trapped in the yawning gulfs beneath the rock and ice and scree. But they had observed, they had seen, they had felt the first stirrings of their old Masters in millions of years.

And they, the slaves, had feared.

In the end, the new beings had sealed away the Old Ones and fled, but now that the servants, the slaves, the *shoggothai* knew that it was possible that the tyrants would come back, they feared.

Again, communicating without knowing how, the slaves began to work. They did what they were created to do — they moved earth and rock, shifted tons of matter and created vast new spaces beneath the continent. They found the hot, beating blood of the planet and guided it, forced it into new channels, brought it up from the red center of the earth and let it burst up into the weakened cracks they had caused.

And the planet shook.

And a crack was formed in the barrier, the wall built around the shoggothai by the Masters — the half-physical, half-mystical shield that kept the slaves in their pen.

And a crack was all it took.

Oozing through the damaged barrier was the work of a moment (and, thousands of kilometers away a surge started in the Indian Ocean, a tremor resonating across the tectonic plates, a pulse of energy that burst up in the muck and mire of the ocean floor and stirred the water, shook the water, forced

the water on its way toward Banda Aceh and Phuket in towering twenty-foot waves), and the *shoggothai* were free.

And a month later, after the slaves cautiously tasted of freedom, freedom from barriers and walls and mazes, for the first
time in the Earth's history the most ancient creation of the Old
Ones had eaten of the newest.

A shoggoth had devoured humans.

And though one could not have called the shoggoth intelligent in any human way before that foul communion, and
though its mindless slog north through the frigid Antarctic sea
signified nothing of its intentions save perhaps a desire for
warmth and novelty, a biologist such as Scott Halverson (the
first human eaten by a shoggoth) might have deduced a couple
of things from the creature's actions. Perhaps the thing had
developed a taste for humans, and sought them.

More disturbing, perhaps the thing had tasted of human
intelligence and somehow absorbed it, somehow developed
the rudiments of logic, of rational thought, of deduction and
induction.

Why else would it be heading on a direct path for Sydney?

Why unless it had plucked the knowledge that such a
metropolis existed — and where it was situated — from the
neuronal firings of the brains it had assimilated?

As the shoggoth traveled greasily through the frigid waters
its surface bubbled and pustulated, congealing into an enormous eye here, a froth of waving cilia there, a three-forked
tongue thrusting up into the sky a few feet away. It chittered
and gibbered from a thousand mouths, air leaked and hissed
and fizzed through it in stinking clouds, a miasma of rot and
corruption and death reeking like a city's worth of charnel. It
rolled and squirmed and spat through the sea.

Then it tasted more meat.

The oil-eating bacteria were very, very small, but there
were billions, trillions of them, clouds of them filling the water,

spreading over the viscous flesh of the shoggoth as the waves carried them forward.

It absorbed them instantly, turned blindly toward them, tested forward with tentacle, talon and tongue.

Found a trail of them.

And slid forward through the sea, devouring, questing, heading straight for their source.

"You're positive?" came the voice on the satellite phone. "For the last time — are you dead certain, one hundred percent sure that this is the right thing to do?"

"Sir," said Havercamp, crouching down behind a rock so as to avoid the blast and wash of the helicopter's rotors in the clearing behind him, "it's the only way. You saw the photos we took. You know what's happening down here. If this thing keeps eating, keeps getting bigger . . . well, I'd give long odds on us stopping it somewhere down the road. The time to hit it is right now, sir."

"Damn," whispered the voice in Havercamp's ear. "Damn and damn again."

The CIA agent figured he wasn't supposed to respond to the President's words, so he sat quiet, waiting to be excused, itching to get back on the chopper and head back to civilization and sanity. They were maybe thirty miles north of the creature now, had stopped in the first available landing spot so that Dixon and Havercamp could set up the satphone and report, and thirty miles wasn't really that far, if you thought about it. Hell, a *Nissan* could travel that distance in forty-five minutes. How fast could the bubbling mass of jelly travel, if it put its mind to it?

Havercamp shivered, wishing his Commander in Chief would hurry his ass up.

"All right, then," said the voice on the phone finally. "Put Dixon back on."

"Yes sir," said Havercamp, stood up, motioned for the NSA man to come over. He handed off the receiver and trudged back to the helicopter. He wasn't a praying man, but he prayed right now, prayed that the President would make the right decision, would authorize the release of nuclear weapons. That thing he'd seen from the air, that dark spreading mass of madness and death — well, if anything on earth deserved to die in a rain of nuclear fire, that monstrosity certainly qualified.

He reached the chopper, clambered aboard and into the body of the aircraft, sat down, looked out the dirty windows. Around them the grassland waved and shuddered in the warmth of the sun, insects buzzing, llamas grazing, unseen things slithering and leaping, killing and dying, all part of the natural order of life.

The thing heading toward them wasn't natural. Had never been natural, according to Dixon, had been created like some Frankenstein's Monster and, again like the unfortunate Monster, had slipped its bonds and turned against its creators. Dixon had told Havercamp some of the information they'd gleaned from the two survivors of the debacle at Kharkhov Station last winter, and Havercamp still wasn't sure how much he believed, but he had to believe in the thing that was slopping up onto the beach just a few miles south of them, devouring everything in its path. He'd seen it. He'd hovered above it. He'd felt the touch of insanity that the thing carried with it, felt jabs of atavistic terror stabbing into his brain as he'd watched it bubble and roil and slither. And he wondered what kind of heedless, horrible species could possibly create something so destructive and unnatural.

Dixon climbed up into the copter, slid shut the door and sighed so heavily that Havercamp could hear him even over the noise of the rotors.

"What?" the CIA man asked. "What's the problem?"

"The President is gonna nuke it," said Dixon. "Turns out we've got a sub in the area, should only be a half hour or so."

"Fucking terrific!" growled Havercamp. "That's wonderful news!"

"Yeah," said Dixon. "Wonderful. And since we're already down here, you and I, guess who gets to be the observers?"

"What the fuck are you talking about?" asked Havercamp, a cold ball of iron settling into his guts.

"We're supposed to find a safe distance and watch the fireworks," said Dixon, closing his eyes and laying his head back on the seat. "And then we get to report back."

"What the hell is a safe distance?" asked Havercamp. "What is the idiot talking about, safe distance?"

"That's our President you're calling an idiot," observed Dixon, smiling, eyes still closed. "He graduated from an Ivy League university, you know."

"Yeah, and I took five thousand off a professor from Columbia in a card game once," said Havercamp. "Ivy don't mean squat in the real world, does it?"

"I graduated from Southern Illinois," said Dixon, opening his eyes. "I wouldn't know. But that doesn't change anything — we're going to find a spot a hundred miles away and watch what happens when the *San Antonio* fires off its nukes. And then we're gonna call home, let 'em know that the bad guy's been vaporized, and then we're going back to Buenos Aires and I'm gonna buy you a lot of alcohol. How's that sound?"

"It sounds like shit," said Havercamp, looking at his watch. "What about radiation? What about shock waves and firestorms? How the hell do we know we're at a safe distance?"

"Brendan, my friend," said Dixon, "these are dangerous times. We're just gonna have to trust in the Lord and our President."

"Fuck," said Havercamp.

"Amen, brother," said Dixon. He reached into his jacket, withdrew a flask. "Feel like a snort?"

"Any suggestions, Major Peel?" asked Durbin. Peel could hear an undercurrent in his voice, a suggestion of panic tightly clamped.

"Record everything," said Peel. "Make sure that, whatever happens, we have a record of it."

"I meant about helping our boys down there," said Durbin coldly, turning to stare at Peel. "What can we do to help them survive?"

"Nothing," said Peel bluntly, staring back at the admiral. "They're dead. That thing's moving toward them at what, thirty knots? I don't think the *Ballarat* can go that fast."

"You've been a great lot of help, Peel," said Durbin viciously.

Peel didn't bother responding — there was no point. He simply watched out the window at the juggernaut chugging along beneath them, rolling through the waves unstoppably and implacably, occasionally shooting a twenty, thirty-meter tower of protoplasm into the sky or splitting open in bloody scores and gashes, always headed straight forward, straight toward the little frigate that was already trying to get away, but was losing water with every churn of its motors.

Peel winced. This wasn't going to be fun to watch.

Dunwoody and Shavers had stopped dumping the organism into the ocean when it became obvious that it wasn't working. Now they were at battle stations. The *Ballarat* was at full throttle, roaring along at twenty-eight, maybe twenty-nine knots, but the beast closing on them was faster. Shaver worked below decks, stowing and supplying, and Dunwoody manned

one of the 5" machine guns and only wished he could be on the
Mk45. He figured the bigger gun's ammo might do more damage than his own weapon.

But at least he'd be getting the chance to do a little damage. He hadn't really been scared before — he'd known that
the thing they confronted was abnormal and had done some
damage to a research station down in the Southern Ocean, but
he'd figured it was just some strange thing they'd quickly
defeat, then tow back to Kingston where the eggheads could
dissect it.

Somehow, he hadn't considered that there was anything
out here that could take on or beat an Anzac-class frigate. Sure,
they'd lose if they went up against an American or Russian
fighting ship, but an animal? A damned *oil slick*?

Yet that animal, that oil slick, was coming up on their arses
like a determined rapist, and though they'd stopped dumping the
cherry-red bacteria ten minutes ago, the thing behind them had
figured out where all the food had come from and wanted more.

And Dunwoody had suddenly realized, in a startling
epiphany, that he could actually die out here! This thing could
catch them and swarm up onto the ship, as it had apparently
come up onto Macquarie Island, and it could eat them all, leaving nothing but the metal skeleton of the *Ballarat* floating aim-
lessly in the Southern Sea like a modern *Marie Celeste*.

And so he was glad he was on the gun. At the very least,
he could try to inflict some damage on the thing.

He wouldn't have to wait long. He could already see the
black-red mass of the creature with his bare eyes, glinting on
the ocean, sickly ghost-lantern lights flashing on its surface like
a devil's constellation as it neared, occasionally throwing up a
spume of crepuscular jelly in the dim of the twilight.

Dunwoody adjusted his goggles and leaned toward the
sighting mechanism. It wasn't quite in range yet, but they had
plenty of ammo, hadn't they? A few warning shots might be
effective.

He looked through the scope, saw that riot of insanity churning through the sea toward him, toward Australia, dry-swallowed, spared a thought or two to his family and his mates. Then began firing.

❋ ❋ ❋

Havercamp, surprisingly, was a little tipsy.

He could usually hold his liquor fairly well — hell, he had to know how to drink in Buenos Aires. His job as Section Head kept him at a lot of government functions, and the Argentineans were so proud of their wines that he ended up sampling seven or eight new ones almost every week. He was still partial to his own state's wines (Oregon Pinot Noirs were the best wines in the world, of course), but he'd also laid in a fair number of bottles of robust reds since he'd been stationed down here, anxious to get them home to share with the ladies in Virginia and DC.

But the booze in Dixon's flask was real Jamaican rum, and the proof was high. As was the hilltop they sat on.

"I'm tired of asking you whether you think we're far enough away," said Havercamp.

"Good," said Dixon, taking a last swig from the flask, then moving it away from his mouth and upending it. Empty. "I'm tired of answering you."

"So now I'm gonna ask you," said Havercamp, his s's slurring just a wee bit, "what you think's going to happen."

"Have you ever seen a nuclear bomb explode?" asked Dixon.

"No. Have you?"

"No, but I'm pretty excited about it, tell you the truth," said the NSA man. "You see those, those, what do you call 'em, those things?"

"Newsreels," said Havercamp.

"Zactly," said Dixon. "Newsreels. The mushroom clouds and such. You see those."

"Yeah," agreed Havercamp, looking over at their pilot and co-pilot. The two Argentineans sat huddled nearby in a swatch of scrub grass, telling their rosaries, and Havercamp wished he had that kind of simple faith in God, the kind of faith that would allow you to sit playing with beads while your country got eaten by the Blob. But, no — the only faith he had was locked up in atomic weapons and the power of superior force over weaker.

"It's gonna be a helluva show," said Dixon.

"I don't—" started Havercamp, but then all words were sucked from his mouth, the very breath snatched from his lungs.

A thousand miles away, the nuclear submarine *San Antonio* fired its warhead. The missile shot out of the sea like Poseidon's trident, showering boiling droplets of water for miles around, climbing into the low atmosphere trailing a cloud of white, venomous vapor, and describing an arc in the clear blue sky.

It hit its apogee, sparkling in the light of the southern sun, and began its descent.

And it hit, perfectly placed.

The shoggoth that had scoured Isla de los Estrados was now spreading across southern Argentina.

It was a sea creature, but was adapting quickly to this new environment — in the land in which it had been created there had been no food but that supplied by its creators. If it had not worked to the level of its capabilities, had not moved the earth and water as it was supposed to, it would have been thrown back into the vats and melted, used to form more productive creatures.

But since escaping the void of the southernmost continent, the prison in which the Old Ones had left their slaves, their dogsbodies, the shoggoth had experienced a new world, a world rich in prey and protein, a world in which it and its brothers could easily spread and conquer, marshaling their forces for the next confrontation with the old masters.

It had found fish aplenty and aquatic plants, and with the slow, small rise in the water's temperature it had expanded and relaxed, luxuriating in the soft, comfortable climes north of its frigid birthplace. It had been tempted to just float and drift, taking nutrition as it came (it had not eaten for millions of years, and did not need it now) and saving its energy for the hunt whenever something interesting crossed its radar.

But it had found an island, had gone up into the naked sky, onto the bones of the planet.

Had found men.

And, like its brother in the Southern Sea near Australia, it had felt a tang in its being as the humans had dissolved against its acidulous slime, a taste as of forbidden fruit, a quiver as the islanders had screamed and melted into it.

Now, the shoggoth formed a mouth in itself, one mouth among a multitude, and there were no ears to hear it when it whispered "*Dios*".

Another mouth took up the call, and another. Amidst the chirping and whirring and groaning of the great organism, the word was repeated over and over again, in varying tones and volumes, as if the shoggoth were testing it. The valley it roiled through echoed with the sound as the creature splintered trees, sucked up the available biomass in insects, birds, alpaca, horses, as the beast sucked leaves and lichens dry, devoured rootstocks and burrowing animals.

"*Di-dios*," it said, murmured, screamed. "*Dios-os-os*."

It was an imitative creature, and that had been the last word on the lips of the first intelligent man it had taken. "God!" he had screamed as the flesh ripped from his bones, as his guts had spilled onto the greedy plasm of the shoggoth, as he had gone instantly mad with terror and pain just nanoseconds before he ceased to exist.

And in the dim stirrings of the shoggoth's innards, in the small gnarled node that had already began to resemble a brain, it might have agreed with the man's assessment.

It stretched and boiled through the mountainous grasslands, spreading itself across the soil like a viscid tsunami, eyes bubbling and bursting on its surface, glutinous lips chanting its word, its name, geysers of liquid flesh spewing into the chilly air to catch birds and insects, to catch and rip them.

And a few score eyes saw the speck in the sky, watched as it hurtled down faster than any human eye could have tracked, and the shoggoth instinctively pulled its flesh back in the spot where the thing was going to hit, leaving a wide swath of dead, empty dirt.

But the missile exploded some five hundred feet above ground.

❅   ❅   ❅

"Oh, good Christ," whispered Havercamp, instantly sober. "Oh, sweet Jesus."

Dixon said nothing, but his numb fingers released the empty flask and it landed with a thunk on the silty loess soil.

To the south, some hundred miles away, the sky split open with light and fire and noise.

When the shoggoths had risen up against their masters, so many millennia ago, the Old Ones had quelled them with eldritch flame, with energy captured and focused by their puissant machines into beams of pure and powerful pain.

This was something like that.

The shoggoth writhed in the fireball, sloughing off hunks of itself which burned like napalm in the valley, melding with the fused earth and the suddenly tangible air — it

spun and fought and melted for endless seconds as the world
ignited around it, and though it survived much longer than
any terrestrial being would have, though it managed until
the very last instant of its life to hold onto the new organ it
had created, attempting to plunge into the ground with
enough force that the earth again shook for miles around,
though it screamed and whispered and cajoled from a million mouths. *Tekeli-li! Tekeli-li! . . . Diiiios!*

Yet it finally succumbed. As the fire began to burn itself
out, as the radioactive ash began to fall, as the smoke
vaulted, boiled, thrust into the firmament, as the shock
waves raced themselves out into the world, diminishing and
slowing, the creature, now little more than a rudimentary
brain resembling nothing more than a shriveled apple.

Died.

"What was it Oppenheimer said?" whispered Dixon finally,
watching as the mushroom cloud spread in the now-dusky
sky.

"'The destroyer of worlds'", said Havercamp.

"Yeah," agreed Dixon. "It's not like the newsreels at all,
is it?"

"No," said Havercamp. "Did it do the job?"

"We'll find out soon enough," said the NSA man. "The
Navy's sending ships down here with hazardous duty teams.
If anything survived that, they'll find it."

Havercamp shook his head. Nothing could have survived that. Even though the creature had been a created
thing, a servant assembled for strength and durability, there
was no way it could have lived through that nuclear furnace.

"Let's get back to Buenos Aires," he said, finally. "Our
radios won't work here with all this interference, and we've
got to get hold of the President so he can talk to the
Australians."

Dixon nodded, leaned his head back once more and took in the stunning sight as if he were memorizing every inch of it.

Then they slowly, reverentially walked back to the chopper.

Peel was going to say something like 'the guns aren't working', but held his tongue.

They could all see that the guns weren't working.

The oil-slick creature was less than a half-mile from the *Ballarat* now, and Peel thought that it was actually gaining speed, even through the withering cannonade that blasted it at every churn. The sound of the guns could be heard through the chop of the blades, and Durbin winced every time an explosive shell detonated. Peel leaned on the window, seeking to memorize everything that happened on the ocean below.

It was the least he could do — these men would have no memorial but his recollections. If they managed to eventually destroy the thing, the governments of the world would give themselves hernias slamming all these events into 'Eyes Only' files, including the names of those unfortunates on the *Ballarat*. And if they couldn't destroy the beast, Peel could easily imagine Earth covered with the jiggling, bubbling broth that roiled and screamed and foamed beneath them. Australia eaten to bare dirt, southern Asia blanketed in thick gibbering jelly, the mass of a billion Chinese adding to the bulk of the thing as it rolled across eastern Europe and Africa, all life on, above and under the planet subsumed into this obscenity until the entire planet sputtered and spumed those impossible colors, burbling and erupting and squeaking and flolloping and churning in thick rolls and roils.

No room for tombstones. No memorial for the species, save that plaque on the moon that the Apollo astronauts had left and a few stray golf balls scattered on the Sea of Tranquility. And a probe or two blinking frozenly out into the black void of the universe, the last voice of Man speaking dumbly to what-ever other monsters waited out there in the gulfs of darkness.

Peel knew that darkness, had confronted it once or twice or a dozen times in his career, had stared flat into the pit of mad-ness and survived, sometimes (he admitted to himself) by noth-ing more noble than dumb luck. So maybe he was better pre-pared to deal with this thing than anyone else — or maybe he just had a little more perspective than most. When you come face to face with insane horrors from other dimensions, other realities, on a regular basis, you start to accept the fact that humanity might not be around for very long.

So this vomitous mass racing through the ocean beneath him toward the shiny, valiant form of the *Ballarat* might just signify the beginning of the end. It wouldn't surprise him, though he would fight tooth, nail and brain against the mad-ness, use everything that made him human against the insan-ity, run with whatever weapons he last held into the pullulat-ing, quivering bulk of the thing at the end rather than wait sheep-like for destruction.

So he leaned on the dull glass, mind racing, and watched.

The shoggoth absorbed every shell, every bullet the *Ballarat* spat its way without pause or pain, letting the hot metal scorch its way through the jelly and fall, spent and inert, into the frigid ocean. It scarcely even recognized that things were hitting it, peppering its surface, they had so little effect. The artillery might have been rain or hail for all the difference it made.

Dunwoody shook his head spastically and threw up his hands, letting the machine gun drop, letting the roar of bullets and the ribbons of smoke rising from the barrel instantly stop. He took a step back and spared a quick glance to either side.

The sailor to his left was still firing, still throwing scream-ing lines of hot lead into the nightmare behind them, his hands gripped onto the triggers like talons, bloodless and rigid. The man to Dunwoody's right had also given up, though, and stood staring over the rail, lightly gripping the metal as he gazed casually at the undulating blanket that was now fifty meters from them and closing fast. He noticed Dunwoody staring, and turned to face him.

"Lights," he said, almost too quietly to be heard above the roar of the guns, the scream of the frigate's overstrained engines and screws. "I see lights."

Dunwoody turned back to the stern, watched the galumphing, cascading folds of protoplasm heaping onto themselves as the thing rolled towards them, the shimmering black and green and angry violet melding and swirling and bursting in lava bubbles, saw now that there were mouths on the thing, thousands of mouths and tens of thousands of eyes winking and screaming and popping and shouting, and teeth glistened in the insane maws and pupils gleamed in the meter-wide eyes before bleeding and busting, and if you looked very closely, if you leaned forward and peered into the approaching storm you could indeed see lights as the dying sun was caught, reflected by the bits of bone and gristle the monster kept forming, then reforming. It looked . . . it looked like a constellation, there in the crazy blackness of the creature, a winking, ever-changing array of ghost lights in some terrifying sky.

Dunwoody felt a presence behind him, turned his head slightly — he didn't want to take his eyes off the looming death closing now only thirty meters away. Cowell was standing right there, also looking back over the bow.

"You want to abandon ship?" asked the warrant officer.

"You think it'd do any good, then?" asked Dunwoody, a half-smile on his face.

"I think if you jumped over right now, you'd die a whole lot quicker than you would if you stayed aboard," said Cowell. "But that ain't necessarily a bad thing."

"No, that ain't a bad thing," said the seaman, reaching for his waist. "But I've got my sidearm here, and I think I'll wait a few minutes, see this thing up close."

"And shoot it?" asked Cowell, amused.

"And shoot myself," responded Dunwoody. "Right in the fucking skull. That thing can eat me, but I'll be damned if it's gonna fucking kill me."

"Right," whispered Cowell, nodding, his eyes glistening. "Good man, sailor. It's been nice serving with you." And he reached for his own pistol.

Thankfully, Durbin was silent as the shoggoth reached the *Ballarat*, because if he would have said anything right at that moment, Peel wasn't sure if he could've stopped himself from punching the older man in the face or breaking his arm.

As the men in the chopper watched, the foul pestilence of the monster reached out from its churning, rolling mass and tenderly touched the bare metal of the ship — and then liquid flesh rolled up the pseudopod and instantly swarmed up and over the skeletal rails, lifting itself up into the very sky as seamen scattered on the deck, frantically rushing toward the front of the frigate.

As Peel watched, he saw two men standing calmly on the stern near the dead machine guns, and saw them raise their hands to their heads as if saluting the demon yawning towards them . . . and then he could almost hear the twin reports as the handguns went off, saw a cloud of red mist and bone spurt from the head of one of them, watched both of them jerk and fall bonelessly to the deck. Watched as the ooze greedily reached them, sucked their lifeless bodies into itself, bulged up in black triumph and continued to surge over the steel decking toward the cabin, the prow, the fleeing people.

The ship had slowed fractionally as its engines were fouled by the goo of the thing, and now it coasted under momentum only, and Peel looked backward at the acres of corrupted flesh that still bubbled and raced and yearned forward, eager to completely envelop the ship, and the Major had a sudden, insane urge to rush forward, grab the controls of the helicopter from the pilot and send them all crashing down into the foul mass of the thing, to do something to injure the insanity beneath them.

Suddenly, a *whoomp* of flames from the port side of the *Ballarat*, and a column of fire shot into the sky.

"Magazine went up," whispered Durbin.

Peel nodded, and watched as the jelly instantly shied back from the flames, revealing a bit of shiny metal beneath the black ichor . . . but it was for only a moment. Within the space of two breaths, the shoggoth flowed back into the space from which it had retreated, instantly smothering the flames, and only a wisp of greasy smoke marked where the explosion had taken place.

"Not hot enough," said Peel.

"What?" asked the admiral.

"The fire wasn't hot enough," said Peel, nodding, closing his eyes as the frigate started to list, to lean beneath them, now completely covered with the quivering, giggling mass of the monster. "But you saw it, didn't you? The thing was scared of the fire for a second."

"Scared?" asked Durbin, tears openly rolling down his lined, wrinkled face. "You think that thing was afraid of something?"

"Not a lot of fucking fire in Antarctica, is there?" said the major, his voice starting to pick up a tinge of excitement. "And that was a pretty pathetic burst of flames — but if we can convince the Americans to use their nuclear bombs, I think we've got a real shot at killing this bastard."

"Nuclear bombs going off this close to Australia—" started Durbin.

"—are better than Australia getting eaten to the rock by this damned thing," finished Peel. "Get on the horn right now, man, and let's tell the PM what we saw. And then we kiss ass and beg the Americans or the Russians or the Chinese to nuke this thing before it hits the beach."

"How about the Indians?" asked Durbin, wiping his eyes and reaching for the satellite phone. "They're a lot closer."

"You trust the tracking systems those people use?" asked Peel, slowly returning to his seat, wiping a hand over the gleaming skin of his scalp. "They might aim at the thing and hit Pakistan by mistake, you know what I mean?"

Durbin didn't bother responding, just cranked up the phone and started speaking rapidly into it. Peel leaned again toward the window as the chopper roared off toward the mainland, watched as the black and red and green mass got smaller behind them, receded into the distance, and so he saw as the great bulk of the Ballarat finally succumbed to the weight and ferocity of the thing eating it, and sunk down into the stygian gulf of the Southern Sea.

You'll be avenged, boys, thought Peel. *Or, if not, you'll have a lot of company real fucking soon.*

They headed fast toward Sydney. Behind them, not quite as fast, the creature took the same course.

"What?" asked Dixon.

"You heard me," said Havercamp. He'd started drinking again, as soon as they'd gotten back to Buenos Aires, and he'd steadily gone through a bottle and a half of strong Argentinean plonk while he was making his calls and doing some fast typing on his secure internet line. "No nuke for Australia. Have you had a chance to hear what the media's been saying about our bomb, the one down here?"

"What media?" asked Dixon. "What fucking media? And who gives a shit what the fucking papers are saying? We've got another one of those goddamned monsters coming up on southern Australia *right now*, and we know we can stop it!"

"Not gonna happen," said Havercamp. "We can pass this one off as an accident, apologize, pay reparations to the government down here and pretend it never happened. How many people died, a hundred?"

"That's not the point," said Dixon incredulously. "What, the President's trying to hush this up? What happens when the other monster starts taking over fucking Canberra?"

"Sydney," said Havercamp. "It's heading toward Sydney."

"Brendan," said Dixon, forcing himself to take a breath, try to relax a bit. "Brendan, what's going on? Why isn't POTUS sending a sub over to the Indian Ocean right now?"

"Not my call," said Havercamp, lifting the bottle to his lips, tilting it up, chugging some more of the blood-red wine. He finished, wiped his lips. "We're being accused of colonialism, crusading and being fucking arrogant American imperialists in the world press. The BBC's going apeshit trying to figure out how to call us assholes without calling us assholes, North Korea is saying nyah-nyah, they've got nukes too, and they're aimed at Seattle. You should fucking hear Al-Jazeera right now."

"Fuck the media, Brendan — why is the President not helping the Australians?"

Havercamp closed his eyes and slowly shook his head. His hair was askew, unkempt, his face beet-red and sweating, and he looked like he'd had a long, trying day. He sighed. "He will," he finally said. "But not right now."

Dixon stared at the CIA man for a long second, a puzzled expression warring with pissed-offness on his face, and then he nodded, the light dawning.

"Oh, fuck," he said.

"Exactly," said Havercamp.

Major Peel stormed down the hallway, his boots slapping the metal floor with enough force to cause echoes. Soldiers got out of his way, and the non-military workers blanched and shrunk back when they saw the expression on his face.

He stopped in front of the conference room door, reached down and twisted the knob.

Locked.

Calmly he stepped back, considered the lock, and tensed his leg muscles. He took one short, strong step and kicked as hard as he could.

The door jerked, twisting in its frame as he booted the lock asunder, and reached forward for the door. It yawned open, and he stepped inside.

"What the fuck was that, Peel?" growled General Hyatt, sitting at the foot of the table.

"You folks forgot to invite me to the meeting," said Peel, brushing his hands together for a second and looking at the faces around the oval table. "Where's my chair?"

"You will leave right now, Major Peel," said Hyatt. "We are involved in top secret discussions, here, and you ain't important enough to have clearance."

"I saw the thing, General," said Peel, staring straight into the sitting man's eyes. The rest of the men and women in the room were unimportant — functionaries, dogsbodies for all the various governments involved from national to local. "I saw Macquarie island after it left, clean enough to eat off of, and I saw it taking down a fully-armed, fully-manned Royal frigate with about as much energy as you'd expend eating a fucking pizza."

"I saw your report," said Hyatt, glaring at the pizza comment. The general was a big man, and his gut was even now pressing against the lip of the table — but the gun held steady, and it didn't care how fat the finger was that pulled its trigger. "That's all we need from you."

"Damn it, sir!" said Peel, "The Minister of Defense sent me down there."

"And he's now taken you off, Peel," said the general. "Now you can turn around and go away like a good boy, and you probably won't suffer for your little trick kicking in the door. But if you stay, I can assure you that you will not only be forcibly ejected from the area, but you will also be arrested by the military police and taken from the base — and if you're lucky, they'll find you in a jail in Perth next month, and we'll strip you of your rank and every privilege you've got. And if you'd like me to have the PM tell you the same thing, we've got him on speakerphone right now — Sir?"

"Yes," came the voice of the man from the speaker on the table. "Major Peel, I appreciate what you've done so far, but—"

Peel had already turned, though, and strode back out into the narrow hall of the base.

They'd thrown him off the train, but they hadn't thrown him to the wolves.

They didn't want him involved, but they also didn't want him gone. What the fuck was going on?

"Sir," came a voice behind him, and Peel spun, defeat on his face. It was one of the sailors who had gone up in the chopper with Durbin and Peel to watch the monster eat the Ballarat, and he was rushing through the hall with a cell phone to his ear. "Sir, I've got a call for you! "It's from the American NSA, sir!"

"So what are you saying?" asked Peel, sitting in a plastic chair in the mess hall, in a corner away from the buzzing, frantic motion that was going on all over the base.

"I'm saying that you're fucked, Peel," came the voice of Jack Dixon. "We're hanging you folks out to dry."

"Now why would you do that?" asked Peel, his mind racing. "After all the help we've given you in Iraq."

Dixon laughed, his voice coming through the phone tinnily. "And I'm sure the President appreciates your thousand soldiers — but that ain't enough to help you right now. Listen up, and listen well, Major. We nuked the thing that was taking over Argentina. It worked — the HAZMAT teams are down there right now, poking around the ashes and soaking up roentgens, and the thing's gone for good. I saw it with my own eyes. There ain't nothing left."

"So do the same here!" urged Peel.

"We could do that," said Dixon. "We really could. But then what happens?"

"What do you mean?"

"Then we've had two nuclear bombs exploding in the space of a few hours — one near a close ally, and one actually on another's land. How do we explain that?"

"You make up some bloody story about terrorists!" raged Peel. "Say they've got container ships filled with some biological agent!"

"And how do we prove that?" asked Dixon simply. "How do we explain to the Chinese and the Russians and the fucking European Union that we were attacking some al-Qaeda cell from Antarctica, and that it's all over now and no one needs to worry about anything — it's all under control."

"You could. You could put some official on camera—"

"—a pawn of the American government," said Dixon, "Hardly credible."

"How about you?" asked Peel. "If we got together, went to the independent press. . . ."

"We'd be laughed out of the arena, Peel," came the voice of Dixon. "No one would believe us, and we'd be shit out of careers. Hell, they'd probably send some of their black-ops teams to take us out, we tried something that stupid."

"So why are you calling me?" asked Peel, his heart thumping in his chest as he realized how vulnerable he was. "What are you trying to accomplish?"

"I saw one of those things," said Dixon, "and so did you. I know what's gonna happen, and it's not pretty. That thing's going to come up the coast, past Heathcote and Beaconsfield, and it's gonna swim right into Elizabeth Bay, and it's gonna start eating people and slurping up the buildings and there are going to be cameras going and eyewitness reports from your television stations, and the whole world's going to see the god-damned thing, and then, and then only will our president authorize the use of nuclear weapons."

"He wants to be a hero," whispered Peel. "He wants everyone to know what's happening before he stops it. Then he's the good guy. But he'll sacrifice Sydney and three and a half million people to do so!"

"Can't blame the man for trying a little spin," agreed Dixon. "He's having a rough time in the papers lately, and this'll help a lot."

"Why is the PM backing him up?" asked Peel, remembering that cold voice on the speakerphone. "We're going to lose a lot of people — hell, we're going to lose *Sydney* — if this happens."

"It's all about an expedition down there last year," said Dixon. "I've managed to pull or steal most of the files regarding the trip. It is the find of the fucking millennium. I've read your files, too, and I know you know a little about the hidden history of the world — the things that came before us — the Old Ones. . . ."

"Yes," said Peel, shivering, remembering.

"We've got some of 'em right here and right now," said Dixon. "At least, we've got their corpses and some very interesting documents and records and instruments. And we've agreed to share what we learn with your very own country — stuff that'll completely take care of the problems we're facing."

"And all we need to do is sacrifice a major city," nodded Peel. "After that, the world sees monsters being destroyed by, by—"

"—by holy fire," said Dixon. "God's hand reaching down to destroy the demons."

"Oh fuck," said Peel. "And with what your tech boys have from the things in Antarctica."

"Yeah," said Dixon, "we'll be in pretty good shape. The world will forgive our nukes once they see what we're fighting, and that'll give us time to figure out the real important stuff we've been working on for the last few months. We've got a couple people in custody right now who were down there, who saw everything that happened to the team, and I gotta tell you, Peel, the transcripts'll keep you up at night. Engrossing."

"I'd like to see those transcripts," said Peel, hoping.

"I've already emailed you the important parts," said Dixon. "There's nothing I can do on this end to stop what's going to happen, but I've given you all the information I can about these things, these *shoggoths*."

"That's what you call them?"

"That's what the Pabodie people called them seventy years ago," said Dixon. "Maybe it's what the Old Ones called them, maybe not — but that doesn't matter. What does matter is that the old bastards used to keep them in line by means of some kind of high-energy beam weapon. Lasers, maybe, who knows? Extreme heat, anyway — and more extreme than almost anything we can come up with."

"Except for nuclear bombs."

"Except for those. And you can't have any of ours yet, and I wouldn't think you could get any from the other powers right now in the time you have available."

"Then what the hell do you want me to do, man?" asked Peel, almost frantic with frustration. "I mean, I can go to the Chinese, tell them everything I've learned, let them know you're setting up a media circus."

"You could," said Dixon calmly, "but they wouldn't believe you. Or, you could look a little closer to home."

"India? Pakistan?"

"How about your own service, Major Peel? Remember that trip you took to Cambodia a while ago?"

❁   ❁   ❁

The Center for the Study of Infectious Diseases in Newcastle is a forbidding place, all gray steel and concrete and concertina wire, guarded by men with large guns and blank faces.

Not the kind of place that would be easy for a man off the street to get into.

Luckily, Peel had been there before and many of the men knew him. With a couple of phone calls and some flashing of identification, he was in the building and through the security checks and x-ray machines in pretty good time — though he was aware that every second he spent greasing the bureaucratic wheels and calling in favors was another second that the shoggoth swam closer to the city he was trying to save, burbling and bubbling and forming new mouths the better to eat the three and a half million men, women and children who waited there unknowing and unsuspecting.

"The biological agent I brought back," he said. "You've got it here."

"Well," said Doctor Bristow, her raven hair twitching as she shook her head slightly, "I'm not allowed to talk about that."

"I don't care about the fucking vines right now," he said. "All I care about is the failsafe you've got installed just in case the thing breaks its bonds."

"What are you talking about, Major?" she asked, looking straight into his eyes. Peel's father had told him once that it was the people who looked right at you that you had to worry about. Caitlin Bristow looked right at him.

"You've got a suitcase nuke and I need it," he said, boring his own vision into hers. "You heard anything about what's going on down south, at Macquarie?"

"I—"

"—I've got video if you need it," said Peel, pulling stuff out of his duffel. "I've also got some voice recordings of a couple of Americans who spent last winter at Kharkhov Station in Antarctica, and what they ran into there, and I've got a story about something heading our way that I'll tell you on the way down to the lab, and when we get there you're going to be running to find the keys to the bomb so that I can get it down to Sydney. So let's start walking and I'll fill you in."

❋   ❋   ❋

The Sydney Opera House is probably the most iconic piece of Australian architecture in the world. Its curves and soaring beams and unique form make its silhouette recognizable to farmers in Oklahoma, merchants in Brussels and even the occasional nomad hunter in the Kalahari. Peel, looking up at it, a carefully wrapped piece of hardware on a gurney behind him, looked for a few seconds and sighed.

"Sir?" asked the sailor pushing the gurney.

"I never saw an opera here," said Peel. "Not my kind of thing."

"Me neither, sir," responded the seaman.

"Maybe next lifetime," said Peel. "C'mon, let's get inside."

This shoggoth had taken a different path than its brother — it had absorbed the men on Macquarie and on the Ballarat, but it hadn't focused on their brains as something that might help it flourish and thrive.

Intelligence, as an intelligent man had once said, has never been proven to be a survival trait.

But as the shoggoth rounded the coastline, sucking down gulls that strayed too close to it with ropy, acidic shoots and vacuuming the sea floor for anemones and microscopic flecks of life, taking out the occasional pleasure boat with attendant humans or the boxy crab traps that it found suspended in the sea, it was working on some of the other bits and pieces it had absorbed along the way. Some of its mouths honked like seals, some of its eyes were black and unblinking like sharks, and it produced and ejected, then absorbed and ate, a million eggs like those of the penguins it had taken on Macquarie.

All of this was practice, of course. The main meal was still ahead, and if the shoggoth had not been too interested in rational thought or problem solving, at least it had taken a clear map of the Earth from the scientists it had beheaded and devoured at ANARE Station on the research island, and it knew where the most meat was to be found nearby.

After that, it also knew about New Delhi and Shanghai and Vladivostok, and it would visit them all. After Sydney, it would be a lot bigger, after all, and it would probably be able to split itself a few times.

And after that, who was to say where it would go? There were a million spots on the map, and billions of people and cats and dogs and whales and birds and bacteria and viruses. It would take them all. It wasn't picky.

And then maybe it would head back home, back to where the tyrants slept, waiting for whatever alignment of stars they'd picked as their awakening date.

And perhaps, just perhaps, the shoggoth would be big and indestructible enough to resist the hated beams of heat and light, and then the creation would destroy the creators.

But for now, a bay lay ahead, and the shapes of geometrical buildings on the wharves and on the skyline, and boats darted and skimmed over the warm water, and the arching stretch of the Harbour Bridge sketched a span in the evening sky ahead of the shoggoth, and it sensed the presence of millions, billions of pounds of meat and blood and bone.

"Tekeli-li," it moaned, and rolled onward.

Peel and the sailor — he hadn't even bothered to get the man's name in their mad rush up to Newcastle, nor the equally mad rush back to downtown Sydney — waited in Dawes Point Park, looking over the cove toward the Opera House. Beneath them, the sirens of the tsunami alert system wailed in the city proper and throngs of people crammed the streets, trying to get to higher ground.

"You think they'll make it?" asked the navy man.

"A lot of them will," said Peel, shaking his head. "The question is — will this plan work? Because if the shoggoth doesn't take the bait, if it goes anywhere else but the Opera House, it won't matter how many make it inland; they'll all be doomed anyway. Us too."

"Why did you set your trap at the Opera House?" asked the sailor nervously, eyes straining toward the sea beyond the spit.

Peel didn't answer, but he saw again the pictures that Dixon had emailed him, pictures of the strange, unnerving architecture of the ancient city the Americans had found beneath the Antarctic scree last year. He'd been struck by the bizarre nature of the geometry favored by the Old Ones, the uncanny loops and swerves and juts and weird angles.

With any luck, the shoggoth would see the Opera House and see what looked like home.

After that, it was up to Lady Luck.

The shoggoth roiled into the Bay, sensing the motion of millions away from it, feeling the rush of people up and away from the water, a tension in the air as sirens wailed and cars honked and people screamed in frustration and exertion, and it kept coming, enveloping fish and barnacles and slopping onto ships where rats scurried away from it but to no avail, and it moved its great bulk around Bennelong Point toward Sydney Cove.

And then it saw the great looming shape of the Opera House in the dusk, the strange jutting angles, the sharp smooth curves, and a thousand mouths gasped and gibbered and screamed, and eye upon eye blinked and dilated and quailed.

It had not expected anything like this in the world of men — could not imagine how such a thing could exist apart from the realm of the tyrants in the cold continent it and its brother had escaped — knew that, all of a sudden, the stakes had changed.

The masters were here.

They would punish again with their hateful beams of death and light.

Unless they were destroyed while they slept.

Ponderously, sluggishly, the massive bulk of the shoggoth turned itself and headed for the Opera House.

"Hell," said Peel. "It's working."

"What," said the sailor, "it's trying to go home?"

"I doubt it," said Peel. "If anything, it's trying to destroy home."

The slobbering mass of eyes and lips and tentacles pulled itself from the harbor and swarmed up onto the northern broadwalk, flattening the tables into debris, crushing beneath it the boards of the walk, headed relentlessly for the concert hall, gathering more and more of itself up onto dry land until the creature towered as tall as the twin soaring arches.

And then it attacked.

"Holy mother," whispered the sailor. "Look at that!"

The shoggoth had momentarily pulled itself high and erect, and even from their distance Peel and his compatriot could see the humungous eyes, the gaping mouths, the festering mass of tentacles shooting out to grab the building tightly, could see the stone starting to crumble as the monster pulled with puissant strength at the tops of the halls, could see the black-red-insane ooze rushing forward to invade the now-damaged building, searching for whatever the monster thought it would find there.

"Now," said Peel quietly to himself. He held out the keypad like it was a garage door opener, pointed it across the harbor at the scene before them, and punched in the code.

The shoggoth felt fear racing through its entire being — the only emotion it had available to it. In time, as it absorbed more and more people, it would recognize more emotions, more feelings, would grow intelligent (though insane, of course, a million minds screaming in competition with each other could never coexist sanely), would attain a concept of time, of eternity.

But for now it was just fear — sheer, plasm-tightening terror, and it screamed with hundreds of mouths as it filled the great cavern of the opera hall, the concert hall, splattered itself into every nook and crevice of the architecture, searching for its hiding masters so that it could behead them, end their possible threat.

It oozed right over the small nuclear weapon beeping and blinking in the grand foyer, not recognizing it for what it was — none of the men it had eaten had ever seen anything like it, so their persistent memories now trapped in the monster's newborn DNA were of no use to it.

It wouldn't have mattered, though. There wasn't enough time. Even as the shoggoth filled all the available space in the Opera Hall, the sensors on the bomb detected Peel's signal.

And did what they were supposed to do.

Peel knew what was going to happen, knew he should get down on the ground and find shelter, knew there was going to be a hell of a blast . . . but he remained standing, watching, as the suitcase nuke exploded.

WHOOOOOOMP

It was as if the black bulk of the shoggoth, now draped completely over the giant building like an obscene shroud, instantly lit up a light so bright that it shone through the unnatural black of the liquid flesh, like some insane jack-o-lantern. Beams of roaring fire burst through the protoplasm, igniting the meat and fueling a kilometer-high torch of screaming, burning shoggoth.

And then a second explosion, bigger than the first, as the roiling violent energies of the nuclear reaction broke the bonds holding it, overpowered the monster's strenuous efforts to muffle it, to contain it.

And then a white, cleansing light, and a shockwave that knocked Peel from his feet, threw him back five meters against a rock, where he crumpled unconscious even as burns began to appear on his face and hands, blistering in the false dawn over Sydney.

When he awoke, he didn't know where he was. Nor did he know the man sitting on a chair next to his bed, flipping through a sheaf of papers.

"Hello?" he whispered through his bandages, feeling his lips crack with the motion. The man glanced up at him, smiled.

"Major Peel," he said, and Peel recognized the voice of the NSA agent, Dixon. "Nice to have you back with us."

"What . . . what happened?" Peel wanted to sit up, wanted to rip the bandages from his face with his aching hands, but he'd been drugged, apparently, and could barely work up the strength to speak those few words.

"You did it," said Dixon. "It's all over. No, don't speak — I'll run over the high points for you, then let you sleep some more.

"The Opera House is gone, of course, as is most of Bennelong Point. There's some serious damage to the water-front buildings all around the harbor, but nothing that can't be fixed in time. Far as we know, something like two thousand people died."

Peel moaned. Dixon nodded sympathetically, but kept talking.

"Consider the alternative, Peel. Maybe you won't feel so bad about what happened. And, hell, thousands of people die every day, don't they? I imagine going out in a small nuclear blast is preferable to getting absorbed by a monstrous mass of alien flesh, isn't it?

"In any case, you're in good hands. You're at a U.S. military hospital just outside Sydney, surrounded by our best men and women, and I've got a crew here as well looking after you. The shoggoth soaked up most of the radiation before it ignited, but you may not be out of the woods yet — no one's an expert on radiation poisoning, but they're going to help you in any way they can.

"I'll leave you now. But when you're feeling up to it, feeling better, we need to sit down and talk."

"About . . . about—"

"—about so many things," smiled Dixon. "Shoes, ships, sealing wax. What we're going to do about our respective governments playing God with these horrors from beyond sanity. That kind of thing. I'll be in touch, Major." He stood up, shook his papers into a neat pile and slid them into an attaché case, turned and began to walk toward the door. As he put his hand on the knob, looking through the frosted glass of the window at the silhouette of a bulky guard standing watch outside, he stopped and spoke without looking at the swathed form of Peel on the bed.

"Damned good job, Major."

And in the oily, polluted waters of Sydney Harbour, a few scraps of protoplasm struggled, found each other, melded with each other, trying desperately for cohesion.

Eventually, after hours of experiment and inhuman effort, enough of the jelly had accumulated that it managed to stick together. It spun and churned in the cold, cold water, an eye forming, a short tentacle, a beak.

And a couple of wings.

It made a sound like a baby albatross, a pitiful mew.

Then gathered itself and sprung into the sky.

WEAPON GRADE

David Conyers

Great Salt Lake Desert
Utah, United States

S and scattered in the sonic boom, formed a tunnel of blistering red. The F-22 Raptor, long gone before it was heard, now powered towards the horizon. If they could sense such things, the tumbleweeds and cactuses would know from experience, the jet fighter would be back soon enough, for another sweep. It was always in the skies.

"Expecting trouble?" asked the Australian consultant, Major Harrison Peel. He was uncomfortable in the passenger seat of the U.S. Army truck, not because of the rough road, but because he was suffering from the worst of all illnesses, the type that kills.

The NSA case officer driving the truck — whose name was Jack Dixon — curled a smile across his far-too-cheerful face. "You're always expecting trouble, Peel. Always!"

Peel gritted his teeth. Dixon's hands on the wheel were as casual as his care with the potholes and the stray rocks that littered their track. In different circumstances Peel wouldn't have minded, only he'd already vomited five times today. The nausea never left him a moment's peace, his gums bled and the spots on his skin were starting to fester. He was in enough pain as it was; radiation poisoning did that to a man.

What made it worse was that Dixon had a lot to do with Peel's current predicament. He could have sworn at Dixon. He had reason to: the medicos had said three months tops.

Another sonic boom was a welcome distraction as they were buzzed again. With his red eyes Peel motioned to the skies. "What are they armed with?"

"Oh the usual, nuclear warheads."

"Subtle."

"Can't afford not to be."

Their destination loomed, an abandoned Wild West mine with its single, free-standing shed reminiscent of a back lot discarded long ago by a movie company. There would be pits here where gold was once extracted. Those pits would go deep.

Into the rusting shed they drove. Under the metal tin the heat was no better but the shade at least was inviting. When Peel clambered out Dixon stopped him. His eyes rolled earthwards, "It's a surprise."

Peel answered with a series of long, tearing coughs. When he finally finished his covering hand showed specks of blood.

"Hell, man, I'm so sorry to drag you all this way." This was as polite as Dixon ever got, by offering Peel a canteen of water.

The Australian wanted to say something smart, but the coughing wouldn't let up. Then the ground shuddered; they were descending. Peel had suspected he was being driven out to visit a secret U.S. Government facility. Now that the earth was swallowing them he was certain. Who else but the Americans disguise their top secret weapons as decrepit relics of past icons?

The last sound they heard before darkness swallowed them was the returning Raptor. The tumbleweeds and cactuses were right.

"They always in the sky?"

"Yes sir, always. If there is one thing we've learnt about a shoggoth, it's that they can't fly. This way, we can be certain that if it ever does get free, we won't be compromised trying to stop it. An air-to-surface thermonuclear warhead should do the trick."

NSA Safe House
Buenos Aires, Argentina
35 days earlier . . .

The darkness was so thick there was no room for shadows, but one showed anyway.

"James Milsbright?"

"Yes."

The next question presented to the NSA's field agent came in a package of three bullets, fired from a silenced handgun. The weapon was untraceable, bought on the black market and its serial numbers filed. Two bullets in the chest and one in the head, just as the assassin had been taught in basic training. His orders had included confirmation of the target before terminating him. There was nothing about having a conversation first.

Without wasting a breath the assassin locked the only door. The security cameras had been disabled three minutes earlier. He had estimated that it would take the NSA five minutes on the inside to respond. That only left him two minutes to complete the rest of his mission.

From the icepack carried in his webbing, the assassin removed the thumb that he had snipped off another target, recovered earlier this morning. The thumb and the combination were enough to release the briefcase chained to Milbright's arm, otherwise saving him the time it would taken to saw the limb free. More importantly, the thumb and codes allowed access to the contents without detonating the explosives inside.

Immediately the assassin found what he wanted: a laptop and hard copies containing the report on the unprecedented nuclear blast on Isla de los Estrados, at the southern tip of Argentina, three weeks earlier.

He would have liked the time to check that the electronic data that he sought was really on the laptop before he vanished again, but such luxuries would have to wait. Outside he heard cars screech to a halt, at least three vehicles. Seconds later he identified the sounds of running men, heavy boots pounding the stairs. There was no doubt that they would be armed.

Securing the laptop and report in his satchel, the assassin slipped back into the spaces between the old walls from where he came, pulled back the painting which covered his exit hole he had cut to gain entry, and disappeared. It would be at least half an hour before anyone realized how he got away. Time enough to vanish completely.

Great Salt Lake Desert
Utah, United States

Underground was cold. Not exactly cold, just cool, and still Peel shuddered. Was it because he was sick? Was it because he just wasn't used to cold places after living and working in equatorial climates for so long? He didn't think so. He knew the truth, knew that he shivered because of the fear the thing that transfixed him generated inside his soul.

"Magnetic fields hold it in place, the same as what is used in fusion reactors to contain superheated plasma. As an extra measure this baby has been cooled to five degrees Kelvin. You see as much as they hate the heat, they hate the cold too. Doesn't kill them, but it slows them down a hell of a lot."

Peels eyes were wide. The endless hangars, corridors, control rooms and support facilities that constituted an entire city, buried half a kilometer under the desert, he could accept that. Military and civilian support staff in their hundreds, running to and fro with errands, were similarly normal in his eyes. Even the technicians and researchers in the room seen through the hardened glass, firing lasers and particle beams into the imprisoned creature, were nothing short of the nefarious activities expected from a super-villain in a James Bond movie. It was the shoggoth that wasn't normal here. It was the shoggoth that made his skin crawl.

Seeing it through thick bullet-proof glass, trapped in its own special prison, was what made Peel's eyes water and his teeth chatter, because he never once expected to witness this creature to react to its containment by bellowing and howling. It was an alien expressing a very human emotion: pain. What was worse was that it did so with not a single mouth, but hundreds, and they were all screaming.

"What do you think?" Dixon was uncharacteristically serious, as if he really didn't hope Peel would express awe and wonderment at how mankind was finally taking control of these other-dimensional atrocities the world had been suffering of late. But then Dixon wouldn't have brought Peel half way across the world and into this very secret place, just to pontificate. It was Peel's opinion and expertise that counted for everything here.

Dixon continued, his wide eyes were again and again drawn back to the creature. "My superior was asking me a few weeks back if I knew anyone who'd like to consult on this project, and you know who I thought of first when I laid eyes on that thing?"

Peel laughed, and found that it hurt his chest to do so. "I hope you're not expecting good news from me then?" He started coughing, and felt sad because of this constant reminder that he was dying.

"Not at all. Peel, I wanted you here because you've got a track record. You can think like these things, these anomalies, just like you did in the Great Sandy Desert, then Sacrobatus Flats, and finally Sydney where we first met. I got you here because I know you can tell me what I'm missing."

Dixon was trying to flatter Peel, but he didn't need to, Peel knew the importance of getting it right. He tried to look again at the creature to study it as if it didn't affect him, observing its ever changing and shifting mass. It was all eyes, razor-sharp teeth and tentacles, all wriggling and shape-changing. These movements, he had been told, had continued for months without the creature wearying whatsoever. And this was what the creature was capable of when it was nearly frozen.

Today wasn't the first time either men had encountered these creatures. Dixon had eliminated one with a nuclear bomb in southern Argentina. Across the world, a day later in Sydney, Peel had fought one up close. Peel had never witnessed anything as aggressive or frightening as what he had encountered that day.

This monster was tame in comparison, for the extreme cold had tempered it somewhat, and the magnetic field was as good as any prison wall. Unfortunately its angry and aggressive attitude had not diminished in the slightest. It was frustrated. It was hungry. Most of all it wanted revenge, and it would only satisfy that through mindless slaughter. No wonder a nuclear-armed jet fighter in the sky at all times, because Peel didn't doubt for a second the walls down here would be insufficiently secure if one of the containment fields failed.

"All I want to tell you, Dixon, is that you should destroy it. You and me, and every other human in this place, we're not going to be here forever. But this thing, it will out-survive us all, because we already know that each of these creatures have already survived billions of years of our pre-history. It's inevitable that one day it's going to get free, it just has to bide its time."

Peel didn't like the grin growing on the NSA agent's face. "That's right," he said, testing.

"Then I guess you'd figured that one out already?"

Dixon was deliberate when he did not answer.

"There's something you're not telling me, isn't there Dixon?"

The NSA man leaned in close, whispered. "Unofficially, Peel, I agree with you. Trouble is I can't convince anyone else down here that what you say is right. Everyone else thinks we're smarter than it, that we can control it like we try to control everything on this planet. But we're not smarter, and one day it will get the better of us."

"Then destroy it."

"Not allowed," Dixon held up his hands to mock a scout's honor salute. "At least I can't find a good enough reason to convince my superiors why we should. Find a good reason though, and then I can make it happen, but I need the facts first. This is how I need your help. If anyone can find a loophole that's even more than extremely obvious to why we shouldn't keep this thing alive, it's going to be you."

Peel snorted, looked away. "You want me to find what the rest of you have been missing, with the sole objective of shutting this place down?"

Dixon's enthusiasm was contagious, "Yes, sir."

"But I bet that's not what any of the paperwork says." Peel turned his gaze again to the monster, controlled his urge not to spit up further blood or to vomit the bile forever tickling at the back of his throat. "What I want to know is how you managed to bring it here from Antarctica in the first place?"

"Oh, that's easy. I could tell you how, but I'm sure it will be simpler if I just showed you instead. Time to pack again Major, we're off to another world."

Wainwright U.S. Military Hospital
Sydney, Australia
33 days earlier . . .

The Texan doctor gave him two months, on the outside. The first month would be bearable, painful but manageable, but after that he would rapidly degenerate. The way Peel saw it he could either lie in a hospital bed in his own private ward for two months, waiting for the day that the lead-lined coffin came to collect him, or he could check out now and live his life for one month. No matter how he dressed the alternatives in his mind, the latter always seemed the most preferable.

He didn't sleep much these days, partially because of the ongoing nausea but mostly because of the nightmares. The oily skinned creature slurping out of the harbor, a mass of wriggling tentacles, mocking him with its mouths and liquid eyes, it always came for him.

Upon waking he would remember how this nightmare really ended. The monster had encased the dirty bomb he had left for it, just before the blast obliterated it seconds later. If the creature hadn't absorbed most of the radiation with its jelly-like skin, Major Harrison Peel, formerly of Australian Army Intelligence, knew that he would have died with it.

To make the matter worse, his own government had honorably discharged him from employment, figuring he'd be too dead soon to complain. Perhaps it was the best outcome all round, considering that he was responsible for destroying a large portion of Sydney and its famous Opera House.

He still had time to do something, even if he only had weeks. He had to do something soon, because he'd been warned blindness was a likely symptom if he didn't seek ongoing therapy before the end.

Five o'clock that morning, when everyone else was asleep, he broke into his locker, dressed again in his civilian clothes, and checked himself out. He left his uniform to hang alone, knowing that he'd never wear it again.

"Where do you think you're going, then?"

Peel didn't stop walking. He didn't owe anyone in this place anything. As he marched he wanted to look proud, dignified. It took every effort not to cough, every other effort not to gag. In the end he had to give up and do both.

"I don't blame you, you know?"

Finished, wiping his mouth, Peel looked up to recognize the smug features of Dixon. He'd thought the American had returned home now that the shoggoth was dead. Dixon, Peel recalled bitterly, was the man who'd failed to convince his superiors on the value of destroying the thing while it was on its way up from Antarctica, *before* it reached the Australian mainland.

"I'd be doing exactly the same thing Peel, in your shoes."

"Let's swap places then?" Peel leaned against the wall so he wouldn't collapse, felt hot knowing that the burning started from deep within.

"Peel, I'm sorry, okay? I know that doesn't mean shit, considering. But we need to talk."

"Talk? You're joking right?" He finally looked the American in the eye, sent him cold daggers. He could see the man wasn't joking in the slightest.

"We did some classified tests."

"Tests, what on me?"

There was a slow nod.

"What kind of tests?"

"Biopsies, Peel. If you think dying is bad enough, try this: you've got an alien cancerous growth inside you."

Peel felt the pit of his stomach fall away to nothing. So much for subtlety. So much for giving him a minute to prepare himself. He gave up maintaining restraint and released his anger, not by yelling or screaming, but by being physically sick again. As the vomit projected outwards it appeared as minced cow's liver, to land strategically right on top of Dixon's brand new trainers, just as Peel hoped. For Dixon's subtlety! The bastard could share in the alien cancer as far as Peel was concerned.

"I take it we're through talking then, Peel?"

"Not quite. I'm sure this isn't everything you came here to tell me. So spit it out. I'll keep vomiting while I listen."

Antarctic Air Space
Miskatonic Mountains, Antarctica

The Hercules transport direct from Tasmania shuddered non-stop as it cut through the nighttime winds, fierce and frigid

straight from the heart of the southern continent. It was minus
70°C out there, Martian temperatures. The winds were worst,
clocking one hundred and twenty kilometers per hour. This left
only one of two possible landing options. The first was a successful touchdown, the second a catastrophic calamity. Options
in between were laughable in their implausibility. Because
crashes in such extreme weather conditions were probable, winter flights to Antarctica were normally prohibited. This however wasn't a normal assignment.

"There are mountains out there Peel, higher than the
Himalayas."

Peel held his stomach, kept his eyes closed so the motion
sickness wouldn't make his pain worse. All he could think was
that he was going to die anyway, so what did this trip matter?
Better to go quickly now, compressed on the side of a mountain, than to wait until all his extremities fell off, his organs
failed and he shriveled away to nothing.

"You don't believe me, Peel?" Dixon asked. He seemed
oblivious to the idea that eating a protein bar and slurping coffee in front of Peel wouldn't upset him.

Peel shrugged, closed his eyes again. "And now you're
going to tell me that a huge mountain chain in Antarctica is
just one other *thing* the U.S. government has *also* hidden in its
secret files accumulated these last seventy years?"

"Something like that. But that's not the long and the short
of it. Out there, bigger than New York, Washington,
Philadelphia and Boston combined, is a city, Peel. We discovered it a couple of years back. It's not human either, and it's billions of years old. Ancient, unchanged, abandoned, the alien
race who built it — called elder things — once ruled this
world. You'd know all about ancient alien cities of course, after
what I've heard about your work in Western Australia."

Peel had no problem at all in believing Dixon when he
talked on such topics, despite the hard time he was giving him.
Prehistoric cities or gigantic mountains were all possible in

Peel's world. He'd once held the ineffective title of Head of Security, assigned to an Australian Army research facility studying an alien city his government had uncovered in the Outback. That city had asked more questions than it answered, provided them with an artifact that demanded more than it offered, and delivered a monster not unlike a shoggoth that had come close to consuming the world. These days it was the Americans were running their own research development program on that city, and it was as secretive as anything they were hiding in this continent. Hiding alien artifacts, then, ironically seemed to be perfectly normal behavior.

"This is where the shoggoths come from, right?" Peel asked hugging himself against the cold, "The ones that invaded Australia and Argentina? They were from this white place?"

"Yeah something like that. The elder things made them long ago, as servants, until one fine day the shoggoths got fed up and revolted."

"And they're still revolting right?" Peel cringed realizing his unintentional pun. "Only now that there are no more elder things left to revolt against, so with their insatiable thirst for hunger and aggression, they've instead turned on humanity?"

Dixon nodded. "Except we don't really know what happened to the elder things. I don't think they are completely gone. They might still be in hiding, because reports from a disaster last winter at that station located in the center of Greater Antarctica suggests they might be back. But you're right, shoggoths are the real problem. Don't piss-off a shoggoth. Despite a long life span, they have short attention spans and get a sadistic kick from the suffering of other species. Especially if they themselves cause the suffering."

"And you people want to keep them as pets?"

"I can disagree with my own people, Peel. I'm not a clone trooper. However, you might be surprised that we might have discovered how they were so effectively controlled for so long."

The plane shuddered, rolling harder than it had the rest of the flight, lurched and turned in the sky as it turned their stomachs. Peel and Dixon both heard ice shards on the outer hull, ricocheting like bullets. They were heading into the storm, which meant they were descending.

"I'll tell you what, Dixon," Peel answered dryly as he lay back down again, holding his eyes tightly shut, still vainly hoping that the nausea would go away and leave him in peace. "If we survive this landing, you can tell me all about it then."

Cabo San Diego
Terra Del Fugo, Argentina
24 days earlier . . .

Four days of failures, and then from nowhere he finally cracked the encryption. At last the files laid themselves out before him. Maps, technical specs, photographs, research papers, internal memos, hazard reports, spectrograph reports, experimental analysis, schematics for new weapon systems, they were all there, and they were all pointing to something big hidden in Antarctica. In the heart of all these files was a most important piece of information: a report on the successful capture one of the creatures.

The assassin smiled. The rumors were correct. The U.S. government *did* have in their possession at least one of the alien entities. They had a name for it too: shoggoth, or shoggothai.

He took a piece of paper from his desk, folded it in half, then again, and again until it was so thick he could fold it no more.

Outside his tiny country hut the howling winds beat against the pampas grass, with tethered alpaca complaining of the cold and doing so by spitting at each other. A bigger storm was brewing, and that would mean lightning, thunder and a heavy downpour. If the assassin believed the Old Testament, he would have said god's wrath had been tested, because the assassin had just unlocked truths that should have remained hidden forever.

But the assassin didn't believe in god. He didn't really believe in anything, except in obeying his masters, and only then because they paid him well. It was ironic then that he was only paid well because he was good at what he did, killing people and stealing secrets.

So he kept reading.

TOP SECRET
CLEARANCE CODE: GAMMA / AMERICAN EYES ONLY
PROPERTY OF THE GOVERNMENT
OF THE UNITED STATES OF AMERICA
Subject: Shoggoths —
Report on Higher Dimensional Properties
Author: Classified
Approver: Classified

As previously noted in the earlier report [see link], whether or not a Shoggoth is strictly a biological entity remains a hotly debated topic.

On one hand Shoggoths exhibit sentient behaviors, can communicate using complex languages, can mimic human behavior, and can at will create a wide-range of sensory and manipulative appendages, many of which have applications only as weapons or tools for eating. This last point is critical in its classification as life, because they do eat and they do defecate. However they can survive for long periods (millions of years) without doing so, and do so without adverse affects to their health.

On the other hand, Shoggoths exhibit characteristics not found in terrestrial life, particularly in that they do not age or decay, and in that they do not breed or spawn offspring. In fact they have constant, continuous and rapid regenerative properties, most notably against kinetic attacks and to a lesser extent against heat, chemicals, extreme cold, magnetic fields and radiation. Given sufficient time (generally a few hours) a Shoggoth can regenerate fully from any known injury. Only by containing a shoggoth to near absolute zero temperatures does this regenerative process reach near standstill.

With this knowledge, the question asked most often by researchers is: how is this possible. The answer remained a perplexing mystery until the recently discoveries on Project GRAY NEBULA [see link] discovered in 2005. Only now, with real experimental applications available to our project staff, has it become an accepted scientific fact that higher (greater than four) dimensions exist. It is in these higher dimensions that the properties of Shoggoths have at last been properly understood.

A Shoggoth, it has been found, when 'folded' into earth's four macro-dimensions can regenerate by shifting its mass in and out of the three perceivable dimensions of space and the single dimension of time. New appendages and organs are not so much created as shifted in and out of earthly perception. Regeneration is brought about not by miraculous regenerative powers, rather by shifting injured body parts into higher dimensions where time flows in reverse, and so to the common effects of decay and entropy can similarly be reversed. A wound heals, rather than being left to bleed (if a Shoggoth could bleed, which it does not) because it has no analogous fluids running through its being.

"Unfolded" is the key issue here. As noted in the research conducted in Project GRAY NEBULA [see link], an unfolded shoggoth is docile, vulnerable, and most importantly, extremely easy to control.

The assassin became ecstatic. These were exactly the files he had sought for so long. Not only did they confirm the existence of these creatures (previously recorded only in the ancient texts of the *Necronomicon* and the *Masked Messenger* held under guard in the Mossad offices in Tel Aviv), these files also told how to control them. His masters would indeed be happy, and he would be paid the sizable bonus they had promised.

He copied the files onto a U.S.B. cartridge as a backup. Then he dialed into the secure server, logged in, and downloaded the entire laptop's contents onto the Mossad servers for his masters' ease of perusal. As he waited for the data transfer, he searched further. Maps in particular were his main interest, and he quickly found what he wanted. For the last couple of years there was a rumor that a secret U.S. military facility in Antarctica was the spot from which Project GRAY NEBULA was run. Again, these maps confirmed this supposition.

"You want me to insert myself into their operation?" the assassin asked a few hours later, via a satellite-linked phone call to Israel.

"Yes," echoed the distance speaker, "and you know what you have to do?"

"Yes sir."

"Good, then steal me one of their weapon-grade shoggoths."

When the assassin vanished again, he'd remembered to dispose of everything that linked him to this place, or thought he had. A folded piece of paper, forgotten where he'd dropped it in the waste paper basket, waited innocuously to be discovered.

U.S. Camp Palmer, Elder Thing City
Miskatonic Mountains, Antarctica

Nighttime, daytime, it didn't matter which was which because all time lost meaning down here. The ancient city stretching for kilometers up the sides of the huge mountains boxing them in, was composed of structures far older than all of humanity's greatest civilization combined as one. Every stone that Peel touched impressed just how potent time could be. Whole continents had reformed and broken apart, life had evolved from single-celled organisms, the dinosaurs had come and gone, and the Earth had circumnavigated the entire galaxy more than a dozen times during the long history of this now abandoned city. The universe changed, the city did not.

It was known that some shoggoths still hid in the lower bowels of the city, and that they were as ancient as the stone. Despite knowing this truth, Peel still had trouble imagining how such things were possible.

Now that he was here, Peel found some enjoyment in his predicament. The cold took his mind off the continuous sick feeling in his gut and distracted him away from the itchy ulcers spreading across his body. No longer dominated by his pain, he found the time to ponder, reflect that humanity's extremely short history on this tiny planet was nothing compared to the alien races who had come before them . . . and what would inevitably follow.

Humanity had long assumed alien encounters would come from outside the solar system. Then it turned out aliens had been on the Earth all along, and always would be. That didn't mean they didn't originate from outer space — they all had. The universe teamed with life. It was just that it mostly was alien and incompatible with terrestrials. Individuals and whole species often proved to be extremely hostile and unknowable.

It was morbid to reflect that shoggoths were part of the alien-chain-of-life festering across in the universe, permeating every space and all time. A universe populated with such creatures was the most morose of all Peel's thoughts, because he had estimated that shoggoth numbers in our galaxy alone was a figure several magnitudes greater than the number of all the humans who had or ever would live on this planet.

Long ago a scientist had once told Peel that all the ants on the earth had a mass equal to the mass of the entire human race. Therefore, for humans to wipe out ants, each would have to kill his own weight in ants. It seemed an impossible task, but to Peel ant genocide seemed simple in comparison to defeating even a single shoggoth. But what did he care? He'd be dead soon, feeding the ants while the shoggoths fed on everyone else.

Antarctica was cold, dry and dark, the perfect place to die despite the thousands of pre-fabricated huts, underground complexes, airstrips, power plants, military barracks, wet and dry messes, vehicles, depots, warehouses, shops and maintenance yards. The Americans even had a cinema and nightclubs here, and amazing accomplishment in such a short time. Perhaps that was because the Americans wanted to leave their mark on this place too, even if their role in the history of this tomb could only ever remain minuscule, a mere scratch on the ruins of this vast and empty city that would survive them all.

But why had he come so far? A woman loved him in America. He had told her that he was not coming back.

She'd wanted to be with him at the end. He didn't want her to see him degenerate into a pathetic invalid, fearing that her last memories of him would forever be as a crippled vegetable. He didn't want to see himself go out that way either. At least he had a choice with her.

Then when Dixon found him again in Sydney, Peel was presented with a new option. Suicide would never be his thing, but a quick, unexpected death in the line of duty seemed inviting in comparison. An alien city roamed by hungry killing-machine shoggoths was the perfect invitation.

"Why are you looking so down?" the NSA Agent surprised Peel by finding him when he believed he had disappeared for a few hours. "I mean, you should enjoy yourself. Have you ever considered that if this place wasn't so fucking top secret, we could open it up as an amusement part and make billions? Kids would love it so much we'd drive Disney into the ground, and as a bonus we could sell elder thing action figure toys to them on their way out."

Peel laughed, hoping that if he forced himself to behave happy, he would start to feel happy. "I've been Stateside many times during my career Dixon, and you know what never stops surprising me?"

"How bad our burgers are?"

"No, how big everything is. Just like here!" He considered telling Dixon about his ideas on their leaving a mark in this place, but couldn't find the words to do his thoughts justice.

"Yeah well, it only gets bigger and bigger. You're a hard man to find when you vanish like that."

"I didn't know there was an urgency to anything down here."

"Time to move on again buddy, that's the urgency, so are you packed?"

"Back in my quarters," Peel didn't say he'd never really bothered to unpack in the first place.

"Good."

They commandeered a jeep to drive into the deep underground complexes. Dixon seemed to know where he was going, so Peel just tried to enjoy the ride for a change. The route was an old stone road carved through old stone infrastructure, one of the few passages that had been mapped. Efficiently, the American engineers had erected streetlights to lead the way. There were even traffic signs.

Peel couldn't help noticing that the deeper they went, the less people there were. He watched the side passages, into corridors of the pre-Cambrian rock that vanished into darkness. There were still shoggoths in the labyrinths, hundreds or even thousands for all they knew. For the most part they stayed out of sight, knowing that the U.S. Army was equipped with heavy ordnance that could hurt them. Still, on occasion, people would disappear when one of them got hungry, or when people got lazy and cut corners, literally. The biggest fear was that they might encounter an unstoppable colossal shoggoth, like the two that had attacked Sydney and Argentina not too many months ago.

Later they passed more checkpoints, heavily fortified with flamethrowers and incendiary rounds for maximum effective firepower. Dixon's and Peel's credentials were triple checked before they were granted clearance to proceed further, past the most heavily fortified post of them all. "What's this place?" Peel asked when they crossed over.

"The Gateway."

"To Project GRAY NEBULA?"

"One and the same."

Peel didn't know what to expect, so he tried to expect nothing. Every now and then he'd convince himself that he had a handle on this place, that he could judge the size and depth of the alien city. Then he'd be challenged by a moment like this one, as they drove deeper into the earth, everything proved to be bigger and older again than he'd thought possible. The cascade of meaning would do in his head if he was not careful.

Better not to think too much, better to be still of mind like this place. Whatever GRAY NEBULA was, it would surprise him, regardless of how much he prepared for it.

"This is the place that is so secret that almost everyone else in the elder thing city above doesn't know about it," Dixon explained.

"Likewise, only a dozen people in the NSA and the President's Office know that it exists. Consider yourself honored, Peel; you'll be the first foreigner inside."

Despite the jovial turn of phrase, Peel noticed that that Dixon had grown pale, his discomfort expressed clearly on his face. "You've been here before?" Peel asked.

Dixon gulped, "Yeah, once, and believe me it threw me. And I thought all this would throw me," he pointed to the ancient blocks of city the size of skyscrapers, "but this is child's play in comparison."

Ahead he nodded towards a dark tunnel watched over by dozens of military guards, secure behind their armored posts with heavy ordnance to protect them. Peculiarly, most of the weapons were pointed inwards, towards where they were headed. Only then did Peel recognize what he was looking at: a shimmering shifting portal.

He realized this was no ordinary passage. This was a gateway, a wormhole, a short-cut via hyperspace into some other place and time, perhaps even into another universe.

"When you said another world, I thought you meant Antarctica."

"Oh no, Peel; no, I literally meant another planet. You haven't got any alien artifacts on your person have you, before we drive though?"

Peel shook his head, "Only the cancer growing inside me."

Dixon pondered this a moment, then shrugged as if it didn't matter. "The problem's really only relevant on the coming back."

Peel didn't like the sound of that, as if Dixon expected Peel to be there long enough not to be returning. He was about to ask what he meant, when he was distracted by what happened next.

Dixon shifted into third gear and drove more than a hundred trillion billion kilometers in only a few seconds.

Constitution Gardens
Washington DC, United States
15 days earlier . . .

They spent the pleasant afternoon together feeding swans, pretending that all was right with the world. The sun was warm enough for them both to sweat, the crowds around them oblivious to their pain. Nicola Mulvaney did her best not to cry, but it was inevitable that with a whole day spent together, she eventually would.

"Do you know how much I want to kiss you again, Harrison?"

He gave her a smile, the best smile he could. He itched to do even more, take her back to their hotel room and make love to her for the rest of their lives. She had suggested something very similar earlier, but he couldn't risk the infection. Sharing of body fluids might pass on radioactive isotopes or alien cells. No one could tell him what type of cancer was growing inside him, and no one had ruled out that it wasn't contagious. Even a kiss on her forehead could be lethal.

When she finished crying, the swans had moved on to more responsive feeders because they sensed all was not well with this couple. She said, "It's just not fair!"

"I know."

"I mean, why couldn't they do something before you stepped in? You didn't have to go and fight it either, did you? It wasn't your responsibility!"

The alternative was to abandon Sydney to an onslaught by a shoggoth the size of a small town, and it was that thought alone that kept him going, stopped him going mad because he knew his sacrifice wasn't in vain. Nicola, however, was right; his government and the Americans had made their decision at the last possible moment, when it was almost too late. It was a decision which had still cost him and countless others their lives.

Peel didn't know what to say. Nothing he could say would make it better. He was going to die, and he was set on doing so alone.

"You don't have to go away. You've done enough service for your and my countries already. No one could ask more of you!"

She was angry and he couldn't blame her. He smiled weakly, brushed a strand of hair from her face. At least she understood, for Nicola had been by his side confronting some of the worst extra-dimensional horrors he had ever encountered. Horrors that had attempted to break through into Earth's dimension and consume the world. He was thankful that the NSA had provided clearance high enough so that she could appreciate he was back in the thick of it again.

"Nicola, sometimes I wish it had killed me quickly. Then this wouldn't be dragged out, me dying slowly. But on the other hand, at least this way I got the opportunity to see you again. Say goodbye properly."

Her eyes were red with tears, anger and loss. It seemed to take every effort not to thump him in the chest. "How can you say such things? You've got life now, cherish that!"

"I'm going to get a lot worse, and soon."

"And I love you. Doesn't that count for anything?"

He wanted to hold her tight, but he just sat there, internalizing all the anger and hurt that had been welling in him for weeks. "It means everything to me, Nicola. But I still have to go."

"Why?"

The swans had returned, demanding food.

Nicola was still with him, demanding answers.

He could satisfy both, but he would only satisfy one. He didn't have the heart to hurt her further by revealing his reckless reasons. His death was the one encounter he was determined to meet alone.

Gray Nebula
Location: Unknown

Peel's senses were assaulted by a hundred differing sensations, all of which sickened him.

Gravity was lighter. The air had a metallic taste. The sky was as bright as day, not from a sun but the spiral arm from a purple-orange galaxy, sweeping across the heavens, yet it shone with stars as if it were night. The moons hung in the sky like rotten melons. He swore he could reach out and touch them. The mountains beyond the grey-glassed desert stretching to every horizon jutted like teeth in a gargantuan mouth, ready to snap its jaws shut at any moment, and swallow them and this world with it.

The natural world wasn't the only strangeness on this planet. Behind him were gigantic walls, towers and spires jumbled together, seemingly chaotically, to create a city not too dissimilar to the one they had just left behind. This one was above ground, but there was no doubt that endless rooms and infinite passageways existed deep beneath their very feet. Their exit point from the gateway was a wide courtyard on a distant planet in a galaxy that was probably not even their own.

"Dixon, where the hell are we?" Peel asked, forgetting his illness for a moment because he was taken aback by the wonder. He spotted a U.S. armored combat vehicle patrolling the desert, and realized that like the elder thing city, he wasn't the first human in this place.

"Man, no one has any *fucking* idea! Hell is as good a guess as any. It's way too fucking weird though." To demonstrate his point, Dixon took a rock, threw it into the sky. Peel expected it to fall to the gray stone floor in a familiar parabolic arc. When it dipped and turned skywards, disappearing into space with the speed of a bullet, he blinked twice just to make sure he hadn't imagined it. "Can you understand how hard it is for us to try to get our Raptors to fly here? We've lost five already."

Peel nodded, licking his lips to see if he was still real in this place. "I'm guessing there is a lot about this world that doesn't make sense."

"Damn straight, sir. For example, see that spire over there? How far away do you think it is?"

Peel followed Dixon's pointed finger. He found that the longer he looked, the more uncertain he became to confidently guess the distance, not only to the specific rock or to any building or landmark in sight.

"Couple of hundred meters, maybe?" he guessed.

Dixon reached out, took what looked to be a mountain-size spire in his hand, snapped off the top as if he had just done so to a picket fence. "Distance is deceptive here. Everything is."

Peel gulped. The realization of the rules in this planet churned at the core of his being. "This isn't even our universe is it?"

"Probably not," Dixon shrugged. "The only thing our lab boys have been able to tell us so far that this is an 'unfolded universe'. Although we can't perceive it, not in any sense that our brains can understand, there are more than four macrodimensions operating on this place."

"Dimensions enough to drive you crazy?"

"Maybe, until you realize that in this universe, everything that the elder things made, including the shoggoths, are docile."

Peel took a double-take at his colleague. Wide-eyed he asked, "They're *harmless here*?"

"Yeah. I knew this little fact would do your head in, Peel. Here all the shoggoth's dimensional properties are exposed, laid out on the table so to speak." He led Peel to a cylindrical well filled with thick mucus-like syrup and a smell not unlike his own vomit of late. Peel had thought the well was a house at first, but up close it wasn't that big, a couple of meters wide and half that in height. For shock value Dixon scooped out some goo and threw it over the horizon. "They can't regenerate here, they can't even move. These properties are absent in them until they are 'folded'. In our universe they can form limbs or mouths at will. Here they are nothing more than thick pools of putrid soup, as dangerous as sleeping puppies."

Peel was stunned. He'd fought these creatures, knew how tough and angry they could be. But seeing them now, in containers as mere sludge, an analogy came to mind. Humans would be just as docile if all their bones were removed. His mind struggled with the thought, it was like trying to imagine a stick of dynamite, if changed slightly, could be safely handled by a five-year-old. *"That's a shoggoth?"*

"Yes, it is."

He found himself stunned with disbelief.

"But we're okay? We haven't been changed? Unfolded?"

"No, folding and unfolding seems to affect only elder thing tools, and the shoggoth is their best known tool, wouldn't you say? By the way, I should warn you, elder-thing items and humans go through the gateway separately. Otherwise the unfolding can result in some very unpleasant hybridizations."

Peel knew he had gone white. He had reason to. Understanding aliens never brought peace of mind, and right now the many possibilities entering his head were too frightening to dismiss as unfounded worry. To calm himself so that he could concentrate on a single worry, he spoke his thoughts out loud.

"Dixon, have you ever considered for a moment that we humans, in coming here, might have been unfolded on higher dimensions and that whatever those changes are, they merely don't seem to affect us yet, because we can't see them?"

Hearing Peel out, it was Dixon's turn to wear the stunned expression and a pale complexion. It seemed like he hadn't considered that possibility at all.

Four Seasons Hotel
Washington D.C.,
12 days earlier . . .

Despite his changing circumstances Peel remained a man of routine. He rose at six every morning and either ran for an hour, or worked out at the gym. Then he ate a protein-rich breakfast before showering and heading onto work, wherever and whatever that would be. He'd followed the same pattern every day for fifteen years, until a month ago.

Another morning throwing up in the toilet was followed by the runs. Then he was met by a haggard face and a shrinking body plagued with red sores, who stared dejectedly back at him from the mirror.

But not one to give up easily, he remained determined to go for a walk around the block of his hotel, just to do something. Five minutes later in a corner where no one could see, he collapsed into an alley and coughed up blood. He felt his world disintegrating when he realized it was time to face the hard facts, he was dying, he no longer had the strength to exercise, and it was going to get a lot worse than this.

"Major Peel!"

"Yes sir!" he barked instinctively. When he tried to stand he found he just didn't have the strength to do so.

"Sir? I'm no sir, and don't get up on my account either, mate."

The voice was British, familiar. Peel shielded his eyes against the morning sun recognizing immediately the spy he'd once known in Asia, dressed in shorts and a singlet, sweating from a vigorous jog. Peel had been on an operation with this man in the highland jungles, stealing xenobiological substances from the hill tribes so that their respective governments had something else to study in hope of developing into weapons. Those days long past, Peel knew he'd been naïve then, and would refuse to undertake such assignments today knowing how their finds would be used. "James Figgs," Peel scoffed, "this is last place I thought I'd see you."

"You're not looking well, Peel."

"That's because I'm fucking dying." His voice was labored, panting, and not even trying to hide his hurt. Not at all the effect he was hoping for.

Figgs looked away, uncomfortable at the thought that he might be required to offer words of comfort. "I'm here to pass on a message."

"Go on then." That was the great thing about dying, no one expected you to be polite.

"There's a spy in Dixon's operation, one operating against all of you."

"Who's this Dixon then?"

"Don't be coy, Peel, the two of you have been seen together often enough. Why else would you still be in the Nation's capital, because we know you said goodbye to your girlfriend several days ago."

Peel grinned with bleeding teeth. "So you've proved you know something. Who's this spy then, and why tell me?"

"He's Mossad, don't know his real name. Only that whatever the Americans have hidden down in Antarctica, the Israelis feel left out and they want a piece of the action too, one way or the other."

Peel looked away. Figgs didn't seem to notice that he was standing with the sun behind him. Or then perhaps he did, for the sole purpose of irritating Peel. "What do you get out of it? You want a piece of the action instead?"

Figgs chuckled, "Nothing like that, Peel, but if the Americans won't let us in to whatever's going on with Project GRAY NEBULA, we certainly don't want the Israelis getting the upper hand on us either. However, if you feel you owe me something. . . ."

Peel nodded, "You'll pay me lots of money if I do pass something your way?"

"Exactly, but hey, Peel, you're going to die soon, so it's not like we can offer you anything that you'd want anyway, right?"

Peel shrugged. For a moment this conversation had distracted him away from illness, and he was strangely thankful. Yet he also found regrets in this situation, realizing that the familiar world of spies and secrets was one that he was already missing. "No, probably not," he sounded resigned.

"Good man," the British operative patted Peel on the shoulder. "The spy is already down there, in the ice. He disappeared into Antarctica shortly after he murdered several NSA agents in Argentina, where he stole a briefcase full of America's most potent secrets I might add."

"How will I recognize him?" Peel moved the conversation on. He had no desire to debate the ethics of what their profession did in the name of world stability.

"No idea, Peel. But we do know he has a habit of folding paper into tiny squares."

"That's it?"

"That most definitely is, otherwise we would have snatched him ourselves by now. You find him Peel, then you kill him for me, for old time's sake."

Without waiting, he walked off, disappearing into a side street and was gone.

Gray Nebula
Location: Unknown

What felt like days passed slowly on this world in another universe that Peel had come to know as Gray Nebula. He guessed at the equivalent earth time because the suns never set and the stars never rotated through the sky to indicate the passage of time. Perhaps in this universe, what constituted a second here passed as a month back home. No one knew such things, or how far the extent of changed physics affected anything and everything in this realm. Even going for a walk was problematic; one could go out for a few minutes, but the return journey might take hours or days. At least he could breathe here, and the temperature was warm enough.

"It's creepy, isn't it?"

The man who approached was dark skinned, and Peel immediately thought that he was talking to a Middle Easterner. For a second Peel worried that he had just found the spy Figgs had warned him about, because he had just allowed himself to be caught up in the hype of racial and religious intolerance that the world's governments had cultivated against Middle Eastern people of late. He mentally scolded himself for thinking such prejudice thoughts. He didn't know why he thought like that, the man's accent was the softer Eastern States' tongue common in the United States. This man was probably a born and bred American.

"Yes, yes it is," Peel answered cautiously.

The man extended a hand. "My name is Ali Rubal, with the Department of Defense."

"Pentagon?"

"Yes, I'm responsible for information security here." He rolled his eyes as if to apologize for something. Peel noticed that behind those eyes was discomfort, and that he was subconsciously fidgeting with a small object in his hands.

"Quite a job I imagine, in this place?"

"Not really, no Internet connection to Earth you see, so no viruses or hacker attacks to block. However, I'm always asked why we can't communicate back home as often as everyone would like."

"Yes," said Peel, remembering now the cables and pipes that ran through the gateway. Some of them would carry data, others electricity and some even plumbing. He was about to ask more probing questions, until he noticed that Rubal was fidgeting with a piece of paper, folding it in half, and then in half again.

"You're Harrison Peel, right? The Australian consultant?"

"Ah, yes." The fact that everyone continued to refer to him by his nationality was getting on his nerves, but not as much as what he had just realized about this man. "Will you excuse me?" Peel asked, "I just remembered I'm running late for a meeting."

"Certainly."

Normally Peel knew he could have kept his cool. But the stomach lurched and he was sick again. Nerves and radiation poisoning it seemed were mismatched bedmates, but then what *did* go well with his sickness? As he was doubled over, he was certain that his worried eyes had just betrayed his suspicions.

Finished and standing again, Rubal, if that was his real name, was already gone. Peel wasted no time in moving on. He just had to assume the Israeli spy knew he had just been compromised. Normally he would have gone after the spy himself, but not in this state. The important thing right now was to warn Dixon. Unfortunately the NSA officer had a habit of disappearing for hours or even days on end, and had been gone for sometime of late. Peel wasn't sure who else he could trust with this information, or who could give him permission to restrain Rubal until they could be certain he was the Israeli spy he had been warned about.

Initially Peel hadn't believed Figgs, suspecting that the Brit was playing an angle to somehow obtain a piece of GRAY NEBULA action for his own government. But now that he'd seen the man folding the paper with his own eyes, he had no choice but to assume Figgs' intelligence was sound.

First things first, he needed to find a duty officer who could get word to Dixon. When he did find one, the officer leaning against an ancient column made no signs of response. It took Peel a full ten seconds to realize the soldier was dead, pinned to the rock because of a garrote tight across his neck, holding him there.

All of a sudden his illness became worse. He was deteriorating rapidly. Now that he had to exert his body it became obvious that his vision had deteriorated and his headaches were hindering him from thinking straight. Smell had completely vanished, and his hearing had a ringing to it now. His reaction speed was laughable. Most telling was how quick his mind had once been, compared to how slow it was now. This troubled him the most, because he was aware too late that the dead soldier's handgun was pressed firmly into his own forehead.

"Major Harrison Peel, I was warned about you." It was Rubal. "I knew I should have stayed out of your way, but that's curiosity for you."

"You're the spy then, an Israeli pretending to be an Arab-American?"

"We do it all the time. Tell me, what was it that gave me away?"

"The folding of the paper," Peel answered. "You left its brother in Cabo San Diego." He wished he could turn around and face his aggressor, improving his odds if only slightly. "It's the habits we can't kick that get us in the end."

"You think so Peel? I think it's our mistakes, the human ones. It was my mistake that I left the folded paper behind. Yours is that you revealed your nervousness when you realized who I was."

Peel thought he'd been really cool. Obviously not.

"I should kill you now."

"Why don't you? Save me weeks of this," he pointed at the sores prominent on his face. Only then, with a gun pressed against him and a only a trigger-squeeze separating him from life and death, did Peel comprehend how he now regretted those words, how much he still cherished his life, no mater how short or painful his future would become. Blindness, blood in his stools and urine, hemorrhaging; those symptoms were still waiting for him. But facing death like this with his brains about to blown everywhere, other regrets came flooding into his conscious mind. But the only regret that really mattered was his choice not to spend his last moments with Nicola. He desperately wished to live long enough now to see her again.

"You're my insurance Peel. Time to get moving."

They marched between the giant columns, hundreds of meters high supporting stone slabs larger than aircraft carriers — or so Peel saw them. Through roads and between vacated buildings abandoned eons ago by the elder things, they marched. He wondered too how the spy saw these things, and if their time together passed as quickly for him, or at different speeds.

Despite Peel's deteriorating senses, it didn't take him long to realize that they were following a roundabout route to reach the gateway, a way that wasn't heavily guarded.

"Marching me back to Earth at gun point isn't going to work.

"No?" asked the Israeli. "You're right perhaps, but you'll cooperate anyway. Let me warn you, Peel, I know you're a dead man so you've got nothing to lose, but I know you have someone back in Maryland who you really care about, a woman."

Peel flinched, again revealing more feelings than he cared to.

"If I don't make it out of here alive, she dies too. Don't think I haven't been getting messages back to Earth. If my cover is blown in this place Peel, she will die. That's one mistake you don't want to make."

Peel's head swam, a migraine pounded, and the ulcers in his mouth and nose stung worse than ever before. Involuntarily he tried to vomit, only to bring up more blood, lots of blood this time. He was on his knees before he could regain his composure. His own sickness had become his greatest enemy.

"You look disgusting."

Peel said nothing. He wouldn't even look at the spy, or the assassin, which was a better description for the man, because he didn't want the man to know how much he really did care for Nicola. Still, he felt as if he had no choice but to comply. He had nothing to lose and she everything to live for, except him. "All right mate, it's a deal. If you promise that no harm will come to her, I'll do my best to get you out of here."

NSA Headquarters
Fort Meade, Maryland, United States
8 days earlier . . .

"You've seen Project GRAY NEBULA, so what's the problem?"

Dixon studied again the cube within a cube, with solid edges and liquid walls which didn't really surprise him that they were not flowing away following gravity's pull. The last time he'd studied this particular device, it had been shaped as a square jar — which by application of a new field of physics that nobody understood — seemed to be bottomless. Technicians had used the elder things' hoses to fill the insides of the jar with unfolded shoggoth. Now that same shoggoth was compressed a thousand-fold, crammed inside the cube. The nature of the device ensured that 99.9% of its mass existed in another dimension outside of their own, so it would be light enough to carry easily. He also knew better than to push his hands through the liquid walls, less the shoggoth inside tear his arms from their sockets.

"So this is how they transported the sons-of-bitches from one side to the other?"

"Yes, clever fuckers those elder things," responded Joss Plenary, the Section Head of the NSA's 'Special Division' charged with managing the GRAY NEBULA desk. With Dixon, the two men had undertaken a crash course in alien intrusions since Dixon's encounter in Rome, and had been pro-moted together into the secret fold. Since then they had learnt more than they cared to, particularly on how far the U.S. Government's understanding of these intrusions extended.

Plenary and GRAY NEBULA were funded by a black budget that even the President of the United States didn't fully understand, except that it promised technological marvels beyond anybody's wildest dreams, and the President wasn't going to say no to that. That's what Plenary saw when he looked at the box, but Dixon, he only saw trouble, like the trouble found inside a ticking time bomb. Today was not the first time Dixon regretted his decision in joining Plenary's special group.

"This is how we got the shoggoth to Nevada," explained his boss. "Trouble is, once we let it out, we have no idea how to get it back in again. Not in this dimension."

"You probably can't," Dixon put the cube down. He wanted to stare out of a window and look at nature, the trees, hell even the car park and collect his thoughts, but windows were against the rules in this division.

"Probably a one way trip and all that?"

"Perhaps."

Dixon cocked an eyebrow, scratched the back of his neck where his shirt and tie itched. "You didn't just bring me here to talk about the marvels of modern technology, did you, Plenary?"

"No, not exactly. I wanted to show you something."

The older man unlocked his desktop screensaver, opening to a schematic of what looked to Dixon to be a missile mounted on an F-22 Raptor. Dixon knew his ordnance, every NSA case officer had to, but this weapon was a complete mystery to him. Obviously Plenary had just put him in the 'need-to-know' category for a new secret armament program, one that was probably so secret that even the top brass in the Pentagon barely knew about it.

"What's its payload? No don't tell me, let me guess."

Plenary nodded, "Weapon grade shoggoth."

Dixon could only let out a long whistle, "Fucking sweet Jesus!"

"Just think about it Dixon, the ultimate fire-and-forget weaponry. Drop this on a known al-Qaeda hotspot and not only does it devastate the target, it keeps on devastating the whole local area until we decide to put a stop to it. We can wipe out entire terrorist cells with one unstoppable weapon."

"Unstoppable is the key word here where we disagree, Sir," Dixon cut in, unable to believe what he was hearing. "How exactly do you plan to do that? Shoggoths just don't go away on their own you know?"

Plenary activated his screensaver again, assured that Dixon had seen enough. "That's what the boys in Utah are working out now. That's where I want you to help out."

Dixon thought about resigning there and then, but he knew that if he did he probably wouldn't live out the day, that's how secret everything in this department had to remain. "Then what exactly do you want me to do? Find out what's wrong with this scheme, because I tell you, there is a lot that's really obvious to me in that category."

The smile his superior gave was cold. "Sometimes you are so predictable, Dixon. Did you not think I would expect you to respond in this way?"

Dixon was about to argue, but given what Plenary had just said, he really was lost for words, which was not like him at all.

"You've been against my Shoggoth Control Program from the start, Dixon, particularly since you called in that missile strike on the rogue creature loose in Argentina. I know you want these creatures exterminated wherever and whenever they are encountered, including the ones we have in captivity." He held up the shoggoth cube to prove his point. "Which is why, Dixon, you're the best person for the job. No one has the passion to find everything and anything that could go wrong with our research like a man who is hell bent on ending it. That's why I want you on the ground, first at Utah and then back at Gray Nebula, so you can find the flaws before they happen, before they become something real and catastrophic!"

Dixon's only desire there and then was to tell his superior what he thought of his ideas and where he should insert them, but again was alarmed at his own stunned silence. It was no surprise that Plenary had the brains and the experience to run a project like this one — one that involved the study and management of aliens from another world — but until today Dixon had never really appreciated just how well the old man read other people, and how he could manipulate them to get what he wanted. Of course Dixon would travel to Gray Nebula. Of course he would find every reason he could to shut down the research. He would do his damnedest to stop anything and everything he could. So he nodded that he understood.

The only thing he didn't tell Plenary, as he walked back into the other NSA office cubicles where they still believed in natural light, was that he was taking Peel with him to both places. With any luck, before the Australian gave up his breathing rights, together they might just discover the hidden dangers he was sure were lurking just beneath the surface of their perception. Peel had a reputation, and Dixon wanted to milk it for all it was worth.

Gray Nebula
Location: Unknown

"What are these?"

"Shoggoth cubes, Peel, and next time you try to convince me you don't know what's going on, I'm going to start breaking bones. Now pick one up."

They were inside what everyone suspected to be an elder thing laboratory. The jars Dixon had told him about, Peel knew these were the container of choice for the safe transportation of shoggoths between dimensions. Artifacts the elder things had forged eons ago.

"You're taking these back to Mossad?"

The assassin's grin was toothy. "You want to keep telling me how much you know about me Peel? I don't want to consider you a liability on the other side now do I? Someone who can finger me if I let you go?"

The Australian shrugged, "You're going to kill me anyway."

The assassin said nothing, confirming what Peel had concluded earlier. What made it worse was that a dozen opportunities had presented themselves whereby Peel could have taken the assassin down, if he'd been as fit as he had been two months ago. Now he could barely keep himself upright and walking in a straight line. He also found that his peripheral vision was no longer with him. His body, it seemed, was ready it pack in and die at any moment.

"Let's get moving."

Pain erupted in his stomach, and Peel doubled over to hurl again. As he did the pain of his headaches increased in magnitude by the second, and the periods between his blood-spewing were shortening. He didn't protest when the assassin took the shoggoth cube from him, which was probably for the best anyway.

They found a jeep. As Peel was about to get in the assassin unexpectedly punched him in the stomach, forging a searing pain which almost caused him to pass out altogether. Half seated and half lying in the passenger seat, the agony took all his effort to endure. They started off, and through his blurred vision all he could make out was the shoggoth cube on the floor beneath his feet.

"That's good Peel, keep looking real sick."

It didn't take long to reach the checkpoint. Peel could barely understand the assassin as he explained to the soldiers that Peel required urgent medical attention, and so he was returning Peel to Earth.

In the back of his mind, Peel knew the soldiers would normal perform a routine check for alien artifacts, in case any were being smuggled out. But word had got around quick that Peel was dying from radiation poisoning, and nobody wanted to get close to a man who was spewing blood every few minutes. Peel wanted to protest, to inform them that this was a set-up. Problem was he just didn't have the strength to speak.

As they drove through the dimensions, all he could think about was unfolding. The assassin obviously didn't know the dangers, had missed this vital piece of intelligence, otherwise the cube would have gone through separately before them. If Peel was going to go out that way, to be folded up into a shoggoth, a death from radiation poisoning while being cared for by the woman he loved seemed so much more favorable.

With the last of his strength he threw himself from the jeep, just as they passed into the other side.

He hit the ground hard, rolled. The malleable walls of the gateway without texture or friction absorbed the impact, and saved him from broken bones and internal injury. As he rolled out of the tunnel, into the icy cold of Antarctica, he felt the most peculiar sensations overtaking his body. He had expected to die, fall into oblivion, but the sensations overtaking his mind and body was something so completely different.

Every orifice in his body erupted with a black syrupy mixture, coarse and lumpy as it hit the stone in thick puddles. He kept gagging, shitting and pissing himself until it was all expelled, until he was aware that he suddenly felt really good. Better in fact, than he'd ever felt his entire life.

It took him a few moments to work out what had happened, but when he did, nothing could stop him standing tall, nor restrain the smile beaming across his face. He might look like shit, but he felt like a million dollars. Folded, the alien cancer had separated itself from his body. He was free of it. He was no longer dying, that much he was certain.

With the elation of this revelation came an awareness of the assassin. The Israeli appeared shocked, stunned as if he had just walked away from a horrific car accident, which was mostly the truth. Peel noticed the jeep, compacted and crushed into a tiny shape of twisted and jagged metal, barely contained within the folded shoggoth cube.

Somehow the assassin had survived. With wide eyes Peel saw why. Not all of his foe's skin was stable. Much of it was trying to reform, change shape as components shifted in and out of this dimension and into the next, until it was holding the shape of a man. The extra mouths and eyes on his head closed to be swallowed by the flesh, just in time as the contingent of soldiers surrounded them both, armed with flamethrowers, incendiary grenade launchers, and assault rifles.

NSA Headquarters
Fort Meade, Maryland, United States
1 day earlier . . .

The thick report slammed hard upon the desk, to send less conspicuous papers fluttering about the office.

"I don't fucking believe it!" screamed Dixon at his boss. He didn't care who Plenary thought he was; there was a limit to how much of his own soul he was willing to sell. "You're running this department like it's some kind of Nazi concentration camp, *Sir!*" The last word was spoken as if he'd just described his boss as a piece of shit, which is exactly how he thought of him right now. "And don't give me any of that bullshit that we're the good guys!"

Plenary was calm as he leaned back in his chair. "I could have you locked up Dixon, if you keep up these antics."

"A *fucking chicken*. I mean what were you guys thinking?"

"First, what about him?" Plenary pointed to a sweating Peel, who looked like he was about to collapse in the corner and probably never get up again. Dixon knew Plenary strongly disliked the Australian, but that hadn't stopped Dixon bringing him along. He wanted experts on his team, and Peel was the expert he wanted to question for insights after this conversation concluded. "I hope you didn't show it to him, with his clearance?" Plenary continued.

"No I didn't sir, but I told him enough, especially what you said in the concluding remarks." Dixon felt hot, knew he must represent a pressure valve about to explode. He knew he would if he didn't get what was worrying him off his chest. For the life of him he could never remember a time when he had been as angry as he was right now.

"I assume Dixon, you're reference is to the human-shoggoth hybridization program?"

"You didn't tell me any of this when I signed on!"

"And I can see why that was a good idea then, as it is now."

"Did you?"

"Did I what?"

Suddenly, from the corner, Peel started coughing. He wouldn't stop, distracting both men from their argument. Neither liked it when they saw the blood on his handkerchief and hands, but at least it distracted them away from fighting.

Standing tall again, sucking in fresh breath, Dixon didn't know what went through his boss's mind at that moment, but for him Peel's blood reminded him of his own mortality. He extended that thought, to the mortality of every human and animal native to this planet. Not like the aliens, not like the shoggoths who would live forever if the human race let them. Humans, they were destined to die no matter what they did.

"We never experimented on humans, Dixon. We knew it would never work."

The NSA man leaned closer. "Not good enough, I want to hear your reasons why?"

"The chickens could hide their extra mouths, pretend that they couldn't form tentacles for slashing and strangling, and on the outside they were indistinguishable from the real thing when they didn't wish to be identified for what they were. But most importantly, shoggoths don't bleed, Dixon, including chicken-shoggoth hybrids. How can you control something that doesn't bleed?"

Dixon stood defiant, straightened his tie, smoothed his jacket and took a deep breath. Peel thankfully had excused himself, to throw up in the bathroom, the poor guy. He was bleeding, and no one could control his shortened mortality, stop him from dying, so why then should they create hybrid monsters that could live forever?

"You *can't* control this, sir. That's what I've been trying to tell you all along, no matter what you force me to do!"

He didn't wait for an answer as he marched out. They had a flight to catch, to Nevada.

U.S. Camp Palmer, Elder Thing City
Miskatonic Mountains, Antarctica

Peel didn't move. If he did there was no doubt in his mind that the soldiers would not hesitate to gun him down where he stood. The assassin next to him, the shoggoth, was equally composed. This was a game of bluff, where one of them would be incinerated, and the other would be a hero. It was a game Peel had to win, especially now that he'd been blessed with a second chance at life. He wasn't going to give that up so easily.

"Which one is the shoggoth?" asked the commanding officer, who was late to the scene. "I thought you men reported seeing one?"

"In the smoke sir, but we lost it with the implosion of the jeep," barked back one of the corporals. "However we are certain it's one or the other, since it is impossible for the creature to have gone anywhere else. We would have seen it."

The CO nodded. He was looking at them both, seeing if he could ascertain which one was which. "Kill them both, soldier."

At the order Peel's stomach sunk. The CO's order was too casual, too banal for Peel to die like this.

"Wait!" screamed the assassin.

Peel shot his foe a cold glance, surprised that the shoggoth was human enough to beg for its own life. But then again it had merged its personality with the Israeli intruder. Anything then was possible. "It's him," he screamed pointing at Peel, "he's the shoggoth, I tell you."

Peel found the CO's gaze was now intent upon him. Only seconds ago Peel had been elated that he'd been cured of his slow death from radiation poisoning, but now he was about to be gunned down, or worse, incinerated to death. "My answer, sir," Peel responded as calmly as he could, "will be the opposite to what he's telling you. Arguing like this will not resolve the dilemma." His voice sounded so calm, distant, as if giving up. Yet inside he hurt so much he couldn't bear it. He wondered if the shoggoth standing next to him would have any inkling of what it would be like to feel such emotional pain. Based on prior experience, probably none at all, except what still survived of the assassin's thoughts.

"I have no choice, sir." On the CO's command the soldiers raised their weapons, ready for the shoot-to-kill order.

"*Stop!*"

Into the foray stepped Dixon, returning again from hell-knows-where, dressed tight in his Antarctica survival gear. Peel knew he should be freezing with the meager clothes he was wearing, but adrenalin and fight-or-flight instincts kept such worries away for the moment. Living had priority now.

"Are you all right, Peel?"

The Australian nodded. He wanted to feel grateful that his friend had returned, to save him. Problem was he couldn't see how that was possible now.

"One of them, perhaps both of them, are shoggoths Sir," explained the CO. "They came through the gateway with alien technology," he pointed to the compressed jeep. "The shoggoth they brought with them merged. I was just about to order them both incinerated."

Peel suddenly remembered the chickens. Remembered the key point to that whole conversation, "Dixon, you got a knife?"

"Yeah, why?" Dixon's mind was obviously racing, but where to Peel had no idea. Obviously not the same place as him. He had his own idea, and he needed Dixon on side if he was going to get out of this one in one piece.

"Remember the chickens?"

A light suddenly went on in Dixon's eyes, and he sprang into action. "Sergeant, I'm going to throw this man a knife. Please refrain from shooting him until he's finished doing what he needs to. And believe me, if he's really a shoggoth, he's not going to bother using the knife as a weapon anyway."

Peel caught the flick-knife easily, his old reflexes back in good shape now that he had been remade. Opening the blade, he wasted no time slitting his wrist, deep enough so that no one could mistake it as anything else but blood gushing from his insides. "Shoggoths don't bleed," he called, before shock took control of his body and he collapsed onto the ancient stone.

Before he passed out he heard screaming, saw the transformation as the assassin grew in size and horror. Tentacles, eyes and mouths thrashed and screamed as it was incinerated with intense heat. Dixon had told him: shoggoths just *don't* know how to control their tempers, and angry individuals always have a habit of revealing all that is ugly in their souls.

U.S. Military Hospital
Christchurch, New Zealand
3 days later . . .

For the first time in his life, Peel was enjoying time spent in a hospital. Back in Antarctica a quick blood transfusion had saved his life, an expert surgeon had sewn together his arm, and a special flight from the white continent brought him to New Zealand where he could recover in pleasant surroundings. In their generosity, the U.S. government had even authorized a private ward.

To pass the time he watched television and read newspapers, but it seemed that the whole world was oblivious to the bizarre events that formed the daily basis for his life. After his encounters in southeast Asian jungles several years back the mundane world ceased to be real to him.

That afternoon Dixon visited. He wasted no time in sitting down beside him to laugh. "You fucking amaze me, Harrison."

"I guess I have you to thank again, Jack, for saving my life?"

"Not this time, buddy; you saved it yourself well and good. But you do have to thank me for something else. As payment a nice bottle of your famous Australian shiraz should do?"

When Peel raised a questioning eyebrow, Dixon pointed to the door. Peel followed the finger to see standing in the frame, sunlight behind illuminating her very elegant presence, his wonderful Nicola. The smile of her face, he realized warmly, was worth dying any death for.

And then he remembered; that was exactly what he had done to be with her again.

THE SPIRALING WORM

David Conyers and John Sunseri

Vapors carried rotten death, but their source wasn't a corpse. Alert, the former Major Harrison Peel marched from the jungle mist into the smell. Chimpanzees, unseen in the foliage, heckled the Australian, unsure whether they should fight him for the wounded prey crumpled in the clearing — a cut soldier.

Peel cocked his Glock 9mm. He wasn't concerned that the South African mercenary accompanying him would think him rash. He wasn't even worried that the butchered man might believe that one of Peel's bullets was for him. Chances were, one was, unless Peel heard exactly what he'd come to hear.

"Sergeant Bill Fargo?"

"Yes, sir."

The victim didn't look like an American soldier, but three years as a POW could change a man in horrific ways, physically and mentally. Peel's intelligence reported his capture three years ago, by a fanatical guerrilla outfit that mutilated its team members — and the report hadn't been far wrong. Lips missing, ears sliced and elongated, and finger bones showed where the meat had been chewed off. Rightfully, Fargo should have been dead.

Peel crouched. "Why should I believe you?"

Crippled fingers, raw with grossly infected flesh, held a dog tag. The metal identifier belonged to Fargo, all right.

"I still need confirmation. Blood tests and fingerprints will do, and of course you already know we can't perform those here."

The man widened his palm. Long ago, his fingertips had been sliced clean away, the stubs rough and mangled, etched with acid.

"Blood tests, then."

Gunfire rattled in the distance, the chatter of automatics. The Congolese rain forests were the battleground for Africa's bloodiest international war, had been so for close to a decade. Peel had no desire to join the millions of casualties, so he hand-signaled the mercenary to call in the rest of his soldiers. "Take this one back to the helicopter."

"Yes, sir."

As soldiers materialized, Peel took the black Sergeant's arm, pulled him close. "Don't let appearances deceive you, Sergeant Zouga," he whispered. "He's one of the Spiraling Worm."

The man's eyes widened. "A sorcerer-soldier?"

"Why do you think he's still alive?"

They looked together at the wounded man. Bent, rusted nails through his chest and forearms told of old mutilation, sores that had bled for years. Fargo — if it was Fargo — witnessed their repulsion and grinned with his lipless mouth. "I'm glad you decided to trust me, Major. I'm so glad."

Peel wasn't glad himself. His instincts told him this was all wrong. Even the jungle warned, for he now heard what he most wished not to hear — nothing. The chimps, knowing more than they let on, had vanished.

"Time to move out, Sergeant."

❀   ❀   ❀

"You can't be serious, Peel," said Jack Dixon, yawning. He'd gone to the kitchen with the phone so as to let Jessica sleep, and now he sat at the breakfast bar with a couple fingers of Glenfiddich in front of him on the counter. Outside, crickets chirped in the darkness.

"You owe me, Dixon," came the voice of Peel from half a world away.

"Bullshit," said the NSA man. "If anyone owes anything, it's you, you bald bastard. Besides — I'm domestic. If there's anything to what you say, it's a job for the CIA."

Peel laughed, his voice crackly and thin over the cell connection. "For a domestic agent, you get around, my friend. Argentina, Australia, Italy, Russia—"

"—you've got proof this Ackerman's still alive?" asked Dixon, sipping his Scotch, closing his eyes and enjoying it.

"Proof? No. Just the word of a ruined soldier. But if he *is* alive — and I think Fargo's telling the truth about this — then you Americans are going to be in the middle of an international shitstorm."

"We're good at that lately," said Dixon, opening his eyes again. It was peaceful here in Virginia. The evening was cool and clear, he had a beautiful woman in his bed, and the Orioles were above .500. He really didn't want to go to the Congo. That's where that Ebola shit was from, and where tribes with unpronounceable names tried to wipe out each other with machetes and machine guns. And there were lions there, and gorillas and mambas and pygmies with poison-tipped blowgun darts.

He sighed. "Tell me more. Why are we in another shitstorm if the news gets out?"

"Fargo says they were prisoners together," said Peel. "Prisoners of the Ulimari Revolutionary Party."

"URP," said Dixon, memorizing the acronym. "And what is the Ulimari Revolutionary Party, exactly?"

"A cult," said Peel. "A powerful one. They're tough and dedicated and vicious, and they've been around in one form or another for almost a century, possibly much, much longer."

"Yeah?" said Dixon, reaching for the bottle. "Good for them. What are they — Communists? Anarchists? Islamic Jihadists?"

"They're trying to bring back the elder gods to the world," said Peel. "Rather like those blokes in Vatican City."

Dixon paused, the Glenfiddich hovering over his glass.

"And according to Fargo, they're very close to doing it," continued Peel.

Dixon shook his head slightly, and began to pour. This time, he didn't stop at two fingers. He picked up the glass and tossed half of its contents down his throat — then thought about it for a second and drained the other half.

"Why me?" he asked finally. "Why bring us Americans in?"

"Ackerman's American Special Forces," said Peel. "Isn't that enough?"

"No," said Dixon. "You'd play this close to the vest if you could. There's some other reason you want me involved."

Peel laughed, his voice beginning to break up as the connection faltered. "You're not stupid, are you?"

"Of course I'm stupid," said Dixon, sliding the empty glass down the counter toward the sink, sliding the whiskey bottle toward him. "I'm actually thinking of going to my boss with this."

"Good," said Peel. "I need your resources. Australia can't put together an air strike team in anything like the speed we need it put together, and definitely not in Africa — but you can. Besides, you know how it goes; I'm out of favor back home these days."

"Air strike?" asked Dixon.

"It's a rescue mission, mate," crackled Peel's voice. "But it could easily turn into a bloodbath. Call your boss and get back to me." The Australian left the name and number of the hotel in Nairobi where he was staying, and hung up.

Dixon clicked off as well, and carefully set the phone down. He looked at it for several long seconds as though it were a poisonous spider. For a moment he seriously considered just ignoring the call — just pretending it had never happened. He could go back to the bedroom, wake up Jessica and make love to her, then fall into the arms of Morpheus for some comfortable slumber. . . .

"Aw, fuck," he said, and picked up the phone again.

Images filled his mind as he dialed Joss Plenary's number. He remembered something that looked like a miles-wide oil slick churning up onto South America, devouring everything it touched. He remembered a frozen pit full of dead Russians, their bodies riddled with bullets, their faces covered with icy blood. He remembered the burning, burgeoning form of the fire-god Cthugha as it was chanted into existence in the chamber of bones deep beneath Vatican City, and the terror he'd felt as it grew stronger and more violent . . . and he remembered Harrison Peel lying in a hospital bed, covered with radiation sores and third-degree burns.

"Fuck, fuck, fuck," he whispered. "Goddamn. Oh, sorry, Caroline. Patch me through to the boss, will you?"

He tipped the bottle up to his lips as he listened to the voice of the night operator at NSA Headquarters. "Yeah, I know he's asleep," he said, swallowing. "But he's not going to be for long."

❀   ❀   ❀

Nairobi was a lot cooler than Dixon had expected, but it was just as dirty and teeming as he'd imagined. The *matatu* he was strapped into rumbled and jostled through the crowded streets. He kept expecting the little bus to run over at least a couple of the people who milled unheedingly before it, but they kept melting away instants before certain death.

"You British?" asked a fellow passenger. Dixon looked at him and saw a tourist — a nervous tourist, probably Spanish. The man clutched his camera tightly, kept his suitcase gripped between his feet and there was a bulge in the front pocket of the man's slacks that showed he'd moved his wallet up there. They were pressed in tight. An average of four people per seat, so there was a lot of leaning and pushing. Dixon had the weight of at least five Kenyans against him.

"Afraid not," said Dixon. "I'm American."

"Oh," said the other.

Dixon smiled at him and turned back to the front, where he watched three black bodies leap out of the way just as the matatu careened through them and further along the potholed street. Americans weren't the most popular people on earth right now — he'd seen it enough over the last few years. He'd been in Madrid after the train bombings, and seen the demonstrations, felt the anger of the crowds chanting outside the embassy.

Maybe I should have flown in with the strike team, he thought, but shook his head. He needed to talk to Peel before anything else happened, talk to him face to face, figure out what was wonky with this whole scenario and what the best move to make would be.

He whirled and whipped his hand down, hardening the edge of it and smacking the guy's forearm with enough power to snap bones, and was rewarded with a crack and a howl of pain as the pickpocket's wrist splintered beneath the jujitsu blow. The man had been sitting behind him and had somehow snaked his hand between the cracked plastic and fake-leather seats and worked Dixon's wallet halfway out of his pocket before he'd sensed something wrong — and wouldn't that have been a fun thing to explain to Plenary, how his identification and cash had been stolen before he'd been in-country fifteen minutes?

"Driver!" Dixon barked, standing up and leaping out into the aisle to stop the would-be thief from escaping. "Get the police!"

The pickpocket snarled at Dixon, spat some words in what Dixon presumed was Kiswahili, and dove over the back of the seats, yelping as his wounded wrist banged into the side of the rocking bus. Dixon paced him down the aisle, trying to grab him between two local women in brightly colored print dresses, both of them holding babies. The passengers on the bus didn't make a move to stop the man's progress, and indeed seemed to be subtly helping him on his way, moving confusedly out into the aisles as well.

"Damn it!" yelled Dixon, and whipped around again as another Kenyan tried to snag his wallet as he passed. "That's about fucking enough!"

The bus screeched to a stop, and the driver stood up in his seat and turned back to the uproar in the bus behind him. He stared at Dixon and pointed one massive black finger, shaking with rage.

"None of that language on my *matatu*!" he roared, and advanced menacingly toward Dixon.

"Oh, for—" started Dixon, but then he realized that the first pickpocket had kicked open the back door of the bus and was scurrying through the crowds and traffic, making his escape. He thought about it for a second, turned back toward the bulky form of the driver, carefully extended both hands and raised the middle fingers.

The driver roared again and began to pull himself faster down the aisle, but Dixon was already gone, dropping out the open door and jogging toward the sidewalk before he got obliterated by the dozens of cars and motorcycles whizzing by. Behind him, he could hear bellowing and screaming, but he didn't look back, instead pulling out his cell phone and flipping it open.

Fucking Peel could come pick him up.

"You should have taken a taxi," Peel laughed.

"And you should have met me at the airport!" Dixon countered.

Peel laughed again, "This is Africa. Just because you left a message at my hotel, that isn't a guarantee I'd get it." He lifted his glass of cool *Tusker* beer, "Cheers, mate, and thanks for coming."

Dixon clinked glasses. The beer was good, drunk inside a little open terraced café. Beefy waiters had sold them both plates of something that looked like mashed potato with a generous side of goat meat that was actually appetizing. Peel had warned against the salad, saying that Dixon would likely get the runs if he ate it, so the greens were abandoned on the side of his plate. The café was inconspicuous, away from the tourist venues. On the street, seen through the veranda, cars and people jostled everywhere, and now that it was midday, the weather had turned tropical.

"So many people on crutches? Or missing limbs?"

"Polio," Peel cut at his thick meat. "Or war wounds. Kenya is surrounded by war, Sudan, the Congo, Ethiopia, Somalia. . . . Many war refugees head here, where there is at least some medical and humanitarian aid."

"You were in Somalia weren't you, when the UN was failing to keep the peace there?"

The Australian smiled. "You pretend not to know anything Dixon, but there you go and remind me of my past. Yes, my first overseas posting was Mogadishu, when I was a regular with the Australian Infantry in the early Nineties, 1st Battalion, Royal Australian Regiment. Long before joining military intelligence."

"Is that how you know Africa?"

"Yeah, I was here for three years. The rest and recuperation breaks were here in Nairobi."

It was Dixon's turn to nod. "You should have told me about the taxis."

Peel shook his head in mock pity. Then he examined their company, saw that no one paid them any real interest, and leaned in. "I thought you were coming with the strike team?"

Dixon matched Peel, moved forward so there was no mistaking he meant business too. "When Major Harrison Peel phones me from the other side of the world and drops the phrase 'elder gods' into what could have been a very pleasant morning, I know he's serious. I know that you know that the NSA and my government know a lot about cosmic intrusions and dimensional anomalies, if you'll excuse my masters' jargon — but don't assume for a minute that anyone besides me in the strike team will know what you're talking about. There will be one story you tell them, and one you tell me. So — tell me."

"About what's really going on?"

Dixon nodded.

Peel looked out into the Nairobi streets. Dixon's eyes followed. A pair of Kenyan soldiers marched past, machine pistols casually slung over their shoulders. In a park, barbed wire was the fence that separated the garden from the pavement. A little further down two teenage boys sold sticks of char-grilled corn and roasted nuts. So very different to the American and European locales Dixon was used to. He wasn't sure he was up to Africa, let alone an African assignment involving cosmic intrusions.

I checked out William Fargo," continued Peel. "He definitely is one of yours. He was Special Forces under Major Charles Ackerman's command."

"I checked him out too, Peel," Dixon drank his beer. What had looked to be mashed potato turned out more like overcooked porridge and was about as tasteless, yet strangely it complemented the meat. "Three years ago, Ackerman led a squad of eighteen soldiers — Fargo included — into the northeastern so-called Democratic Republic of the Congo. Their mission: to destroy a key URP base in the jungle and assassinate their leader. Only thing is, Ackerman and company get captured, tortured, god knows what, and then three days later out of the blue he calls in an air strike, which if the reports are believed, saw him sacrifice himself for the 'greater good.'" Dixon made quotation marks with his hands to emphasis his point. "A blast to take out the enemy once and for all. Officially Ackerman is missing in action, unofficially he's dead, a hero. Now you're telling me he's alive, and possibly in league with this cult?"

In the heat Peel had already finished his beer, so he ordered two more. "That's the official story."

"I thought you were going to say that. But this guy is Special Forces. They don't just roll over and play for the other team because you offer them a cookie."

"Well, the unofficial story is better. Has to be. I'm surprised, Dixon, you haven't asked the most important question ever asked in the history of the human race."

The beers arrived. Dixon took a sip, and wondered what Jessica would be doing today. As far as she was concerned, he was attending a conference in Portland, Oregon. She had no idea at all of the dangers he was about to face in the jungles of the world's worst war zone — other than the Middle East. She still wouldn't understand, if he came back, why he'd gotten up in the middle of the night to drink Glenfiddich to help him sleep.

"What question would that be, Peel?"

"Why? Why were Ackerman and his team there in the first place? It's not like the U.S. has much interest in the Congo, not for a long time. And Australia is no better."

"And you're going to tell me why?"

"I'm going to tell you what Fargo believes."

"Summoning of an elder god?"

Peel smiled, pleased with himself. "The Congolese people call this god the Spiraling Worm. This isn't the first time they've tried to break the dimensional rift and release it. If they do, god knows what will happen in Africa, but from past experience you and I both know it won't be good. They've been trying for hundreds of years. One day they are going to get it right."

"So what's stopped them each time?"

"I don't know," Peel licked his lips. "But I'll bet any money that's what Ackerman was trying to stop. That's what his masters feared the URP might actually succeed in doing. Perhaps the air strike he called in was his last-ditch attempt to stop them. And here I was hoping you'd dug up the old files, and would tell me."

Dixon shook his head, pushed back the plate of half-eaten food, no longer hungry. That was jetlag and elder gods for you. "I'd guess it was a CIA-sanctioned black op, and you know how it goes between NSA and our brothers. But what about this Sergeant Fargo? I'm assuming I can talk to him before we meet the team."

Peel grinned, a poker player about to reveal a strong hand. "You can see him right now if you want."

"Really? Surprise me. Tell me where you have him hidden."

Peel shrugged. "One other complication, mate. I needed to get Fargo somewhere safe and secure, and there is nowhere west of here that would do. I had to call in another favor, another friend. You do know Kenya used to be a British colony, and they still have a lot of investments here, including MI6 safe houses and hospitals?"

"You didn't, did you?"

Peel heartily attacked his slab of goat flesh with his cutlery. "I know you've worked with him before too, this British agent, we both have. But now that he knows a little, he wants to know a lot. He's intrigued, and now he wants to come with us, into the heart of darkness."

Dixon almost choked on his beer, used his sleeve to wipe the amber liquid from his mouth. "You're talking about James Figgs, aren't you?"

Peel nodded again, and all Dixon could think was, the Australian had been doing a lot of that since Dixon's arrival in Africa.

※　※　※

"Nice to see you again, Yank," said Figgs, smiling.

"Yeah," said Dixon, shaking the man's hand. "Good times."

"I should think not," said Figgs, letting go. "Seems like the only time we get together, you and I, someone's trying to destroy the world." The British Secret Service agent was as smug and coy as Dixon remembered him, and peculiar, wearing a suit and tie in this heat. Perhaps such clothes helped to cultivate the image of a man in the know.

"Maybe next time," said Dixon, "they'll try it in Bermuda. I wouldn't mind that assignment."

Figgs laughed. "You're here to see your boy, then?"

"Where is he?" asked Dixon, looking around the safe house.

They stood in a pleasant room in a nondescript house off the Thika road, fans lazily spiraling on the ceiling keeping the temperature bearable. Figgs took a sip from his sweating glass of ice water, nodded, and motioned for the Australian and the American to follow him.

In the hallway stood a brawny hunk of meat squeezed into chinos and khakis, but though his uniform held no hint of military, the man's demeanor and posture screamed SAS — as did the submachine gun he held casually in one beefy hand.

"Visitors to see our guest," said Figgs.

"Haven't eaten recently, have you?" asked the guard, and Dixon felt a flutter of panic. How bad did *Fargo* look?

The sentinel stepped aside, and Figgs reached forward and grabbed the doorknob. He turned back to Dixon and Peel and gave them a grim smile. "After you," he said, and pulled the door open.

"Who won the Series last year?" asked the monster on the bed. Figgs' medics had done what they could with the man's injuries, but for all their efforts the soldier still looked like something death had chewed up and spat out as too disgusting.

He smoked a cigarette, and whenever he inhaled wisps of smoke came through the holes in his cheek, the ragged vents in his chest. It was the creepiest thing Dixon had ever seen. Peel, standing as far back as he could without appearing unsociable, looked like he was about to be sick. Figgs standing next to him just looked bored.

"White Sox," said Dixon. "The year before, it was the Red Sox."

"No shit?" asked Fargo, surprised. "Boston finally won one?"

"What's happening out there, Bill?" asked Dixon, forcing himself to move his chair a bit closer to the monstrosity, forcing the bile back down his throat. "How did you escape?"

"It was Major Ackerman," said Fargo, smiling that rictus smile at the NSA agent. "He managed to get the chains off himself and me, and we made it to the jungle before the URP bastards knew we were gone. They came after us, but we had a head start on them, and we managed to kill a couple of the fuckers and take their radio. Got hold of this Aussie, here," he shook his head at Peel, and Dixon saw the cheekbones through the bloody, ragged holes in the man's face, "and he was nice enough to pick me up."

"Where's Ackerman?" asked Dixon.

Fargo turned back toward the American and blinked. "Still out there," he said. "He was shot and couldn't move as fast or far as me, so he's hiding out there waiting for a retrieval."

"Shot?" asked Figgs mildly. "You told me that Major Ackerman was feverish and delirious, not that he was shot."

"You get shot in that goddamned malaria factory, limey!" spat Fargo, something — panic? anger? — leaping into his eyes. "See if you don't come down with a fucking fever!"

"All right, all right," said Dixon soothingly. "And you think Ackerman's still out there? You don't think they would have recaptured him, or that he's dead of exposure by now?"

"He'd better not be," wheezed the bloody skeleton. "Or else we're fucked. The Major knows all the details about the ritual — when it's gonna happen, where it's gonna happen. If he's dead, those black bastards are going to unleash something that'll make Hiroshima look like a fart in a wind tunnel."

"The ritual," said Peel, standing on the other side of the bed. "Tell us about the ritual. Who are the URP trying to summon?"

Fargo closed his eyes as much as he could, though his lids were ragged and ripped, and took the cigarette out of his mouth. For a long moment, Dixon thought that the man wasn't going to answer, that their questions had exhausted him so much that he was going to pass out or even die . . . but then the eyes opened again, dry and puffy from lack of tears.

"The Spiraling Worm," said Fargo.

❋   ❋   ❋

"So what's 'The Spiraling Worm'?" asked Dixon, checking his M16A2.

"Fuck if I know," said Figgs cheerfully, looking down at the jungle whizzing by beneath them.

"I wasn't asking you," said Dixon. "Peel — you're the expert on this kind of crap. Is it a god we're dealing with?"

"Probably," said the Australian, tapping at the keys on his laptop. "It's mentioned in that Arabian tome as the *Masked Messenger*, so it's known in African and Middle Eastern folklore. On the cosmic front it's at least some kind of interdimensional monster that the URP keeps trying to bring to Earth. Plenary's boys back in Maryland are working on it right now."

"So what do we know about the bad guys?" asked Dixon. The three of them sat near the doors of the old MIL Mi-8 'borrowed' from the Ugandan government for a princely sum. Behind them in the cargo bay of the chopper were the other ten members of the strike force — eight American SEALS and two of Figgs' SAS men, all of them well-armed, all of them quietly going over and over their equipment as they neared the insertion point. Stowed around and between the soldiers were crates loaded with second-hand M16A1's, foil packets of MRE's and

medicines, and between Dixon's legs was the prize package —
a bundle of old *Penthouse* and *Barely Legal* magazines.

"What d'ye mean by 'bad guys'?" asked Figgs, turning
away from the view and smiling at the American. "The chaps
we're meeting now, or the URP?"

"There aren't any good guys down here," said Peel, finally
looking up from his computer. "It's just that some are better
than others."

"What's the story with the URP, then?" asked Dixon.
"What are they trying to accomplish?"

"I told you," said Figgs. "Destruction of the world."

"You'd think taking over the world would be enough,"
griped Dixon. "How come everyone wants to destroy the fucking thing?"

"It's the elder gods, or outer gods as they are sometimes
called," said Peel calmly, as though his words weren't the rank-
est insanity. Dixon wondered what his friends back home in
Virginia would make of the conversation they were carrying on
right now. "You know about Cthugha, of course, and I assume
you've done some research on the other ones since our adventure with the *shoggothai*, correct?"

"I've looked into them," said Dixon, turning away and staring out the window. He'd never particularly wanted to be the
point man against the omnipotent entities who waited arrayed
against the earth, but it had just turned out that way. Knowing
that Peel and Figgs probably felt the same way as he, should
have been a small comfort, but wasn't.

He looked outside the shuddering helicopter, at the mass
of green zipping beneath them. Africa had given him a royal
dose of culture shock, but nothing like the sea of jungle
below. It stretched forever, broken only by the occasional fast-
flowing murky brown rivers snaking through the undergrowth. As for signs of civilization, he could see none. He
knew better than to believe otherwise, for soldiers in the
thousands trudged through the green mess every day. He

wondered how they survived, how he would if he found himself down there alone. This was a world so far away from his days as an urban cop. Here, he felt certain the mist-shrouded canopy would swallow him whole and consume him forever, if he let it get to him.

"Plenary's had me studying the stuff in my spare time," Dixon explained, escaping his own distractions, "but it's a mess, man — contradictions, flat-out lies, wild speculations. You've got Elder Gods and Outer Gods — which you're now telling me might be the same thing — and Great Old Ones and High Priests and then you've got these cults all over the world with their own agendas, their own rituals . . . and the goddamned books aren't much help, either, though they're sure good at giving you nightmares after you read 'em. I've seen case files, too — files from the FBI about Innsmouth back in 1928, police files from Louisiana in 1925, a bunch of others."

"Does it make you feel small and insignificant?" asked Peel, unsmiling. "As though there are gulfs of blackness pressing in on our little planet and that we're all doomed to eventual destruction, no matter how hard we fight against the madness?"

"No," said Dixon, staring at the Australian wishing he'd kept that last comment to himself. "It makes me want to nuke the fuck out of 'em as they come at us. It's worked out for us so far, hasn't it?"

Peel winced slightly, remembering the sickness that had ravaged his body, tearing apart his healthy blood cells and wrecking his balance, his digestion, his equilibrium, the sickness that had come from the low-yield nuke he'd detonated in Sydney — but then he smiled a grim smile. "Sure," he said. "It's worked out for us," remembering again the very strange circumstances which cured him again. "And you'd better hold on to that attitude as long as you can — because it's us and other people like us who've held the blackness at bay for all of human history. I told you before that the URP has been trying to bring the Worm here for centuries — and now that you're committed I can tell you that they were foiled at least twice. Once by Ackerman and his men a few years ago, and once back in 1983 by a British force. And I suspect that there have been another few instances where men banded together to stop these mad bastards."

"Bollocks, Peel! How about this time we fucking eliminate them?" asked Figgs. "Save our counterparts twenty years from now the trouble?"

"Works for me," said Dixon. "And how about the folks we're meeting now — the KLF?"

"The Kasai Liberation Front," said Figgs. "Our noble allies in the fight against — what are we fighting against, Peel?"

"Them or us? Them it's their own government," said the Australian, looking at a light that had just started flashing on his laptop. He flipped it open again and started hitting keys. "As for their ideals I couldn't tell you. But the one language they do understand is money."

"In any case, they're our buddies," said Figgs, smiling at Dixon. "And, more importantly, they've agreed to guide us into the deep jungle where the URP hangs out. We go in, snatch your wounded man, collect what intel we can, and get back to the wonders of Nairobi. Simple."

"And then we get some coordinates from Ackerman, relay them to the American flyboys, and bomb the hell out of another beastie," said Peel distractedly as he responded to whatever alert had come through on his computer. "Uh-oh," he said.

"We don't like 'uh-oh'," said Dixon, turning to look at the Australian. "What the hell does 'uh-oh' mean?"

"Your smart NSA lads have finally tracked down the Spiraling Worm references," said Major Peel, his eyes scanning rapidly down the page. "And we're dealing with a biggie this time."

"A biggie?" asked Figgs, eyes narrowing. "What's that mean?"

"Nyarlathotep," said Peel, shaking his head. "The Masked Messenger. The Crawling Chaos."

"Oh goodie," said Dixon, feeling his heart sink. "When I was growing up, I always wanted to go up against something called 'The Crawling Chaos.'"

"You're in luck, then, boyo!" said Figgs, speaking louder as the chopper banked into a turn and began to descend. "It'll be like pitching to what's-his-name . . . Babe Ruth! Strike him out, and you'll be famous!"

Dixon didn't respond as the helicopter slowly lost altitude, heading for a bai nestled into the green carpet beneath them. He looked down at the package of porno mags on the floor at his feet and grimaced. With such coin they were trying to buy their way into the jungle where an American was at this moment bleeding out, an American with coordinates in his head that would let them stop an obscenity from manifesting on their fragile planet.

"And why did you want to come along on this little jaunt, Figgs?" he asked, gripping his rifle tighter as the chopper skimmed the treetops.

"You Yanks are loud and obnoxious and annoying," said Figgs, sitting back and enjoying the ride, "but you throw the greatest parties on Earth!"

"It's like a bad joke," Peel muttered, "An American, a Brit and an Australian walk into a bar . . . or a jungle in this case—"

—and then they were hovering over the *bai*, the clearing in the trees, and there was no more time to talk as the contraption loudly lowered itself to the ground.

"Now what?" asked Dixon.

They stood in the middle of the field, crates piled around them, and from the jungle Dixon stared into the green hell and heard nothing as they discussed the new crop of humans and boxes that had appeared in their midst. The pilot had kept the engines going the whole time they were unloading, and hadn't wasted a second lifting out when they were done off-lifting the munitions and provisions, winging back to Entebbe and civilization.

"They're out there in the trees, sir," said Lieutenant Thompson, the commander of the SEALS, who had moved up protectively to flank Dixon. "At least six men, probably more."

"Eight, that I can spot," said Sergeant Dunthorpe, the more senior of the SAS men Figgs had brought with him.

"Nine," said Peel tiredly, bending over and grabbing a bottle of water from the cooler at their feet. "You missed the guy in the dirt over there," and gestured with his head even as he twisted the top off the bottle of Cascade Springs.

Dunthorpe and Thompson turned to look at the jumble of earth and foliage that the Australian had indicated, and at that moment the KLF decided that they'd seen enough and that there weren't any armies waiting to cut them down the second they stepped out of the tree line. Dixon tensed his fingers on his assault rifle, but he was aware that his men and the men Figgs had brought were probably more than twice the equal of the ragtag troupe who swaggered out from the jungle, so let himself relax a bit.

"Mbote! Jambo!" yelled the KLF leader as he strode toward them. "My most beloved gunrunners!"

"Fucking yaboo," said Figgs in a low voice, then raised his arms in a salute. "Captain Kazumu!"

"It is good to see you again, my English friend!" said the Congolese man, his mouth splitting into a wide, white smile, his skin so dark that Dixon blinked. "And you have brought us fine presents from the world, have you not?"

"I have indeed young fellow." Figgs snapped his fingers, and it took Dixon a moment to realize Figgs was indicating that it was Dixon who should jump to his attention. "The package, young man, the package."

Hiding his anger, Dixon handed over the collection of magazines, lighter than they should have been. Figgs beamed when Kazumu tore open the pack, called out to his soldiers in their local tongue Lingala, generating a cheer. He was showing them a full-frontal nude of a young lady from Wisconsin who'd been honored with the title Miss July. Then, just as quickly he hid the magazines, much to the disappointment of his men. "Later," he said in English, before switching back to him local tongue. "Oh, and the guns?" he asked smiling with those white teeth.

Figgs grinned with a closed mouth as he tried not to breathe in his old friend's foul breath. "In the crates."

More orders, and soon the team of rough and ready soldiers forced open the crates and snatched free the MI6A1s. Several let loose bursts of hot metal into the salt-rich pools of water to test their capacity to kill.

"Opinions, Dixon?"

Dixon turned, surprised that Peel had snuck up on him so easily. It was surreal, standing in the heart of Africa in the midst of gun-crazy revolutionaries on Her Majesty's payroll. "Let's see, my friend. I'm not a soldier like you, but first thoughts: undisciplined, noisy, they smoke and drink and leave litter everywhere. And that's all I've managed to work out in only five minutes of meeting them."

Peel nodded, "Yes, I'm glad I'm not the only one who noticed. We better double our efforts not to leave a trail. Otherwise the URP will have no problem working out who we've joined up with."

On autopilot Dixon scanned the jungle, as if he expected to see the mutilated soldiers eyeballing him already, his head in the crosshairs of their weapons. But he saw nothing.

"Are you okay?" Peel asked quietly.

Dixon nodded, wondering if his expression betrayed his fear, "I'm fine. Just a little queasy after the rough landing." Determined not to let this world wear him down, he looked back at Figgs, who was heatedly negotiating with Kazumu. "What are you thinking?" he asked the Major, "I know you're thinking because you look like a cat smelling a rat."

"Me?" Peel asked. His eyes too were scanning the jungle, as if he too were concerned about their exposed position in the bai. "I'm shit scared. This is the Congo after all."

Dixon snorted. "Glad to hear I have company."

"Hey!" Peel called out, his conversation with Dixon forgotten. "You'll kill yourself doing that!" He snatched a new M16 from a young soldier who was peering down the barrel of the weapon and shaking it, concerned about a jam. "Like this," Peel demonstrated as best he could without the use of a language they both understood, how to hold a gun safely. *Yes*, thought Dixon, *the soldiers of the Kasai Liberation Front were most definitely a liability*.

"You said three hundred guns!" Kazumu was now screaming at Figgs, and Figgs in response was all red, eyeballing the shorter African man, ready to scream back. "No deal. I'm not taking you to Ackerman now."

"Bollocks!" Figgs spat, "one hundred guns was the deal. One hundred."

"And you forgot the Stinger missiles."

"Stinger missiles?" Figgs fumed. "Why they hell would Her Majesty ever consider giving you people one of those?"

The jungle was thick and horrible. Tiny stingless bees crawled into their armpits and crotches to suck on their salty moisture, leeches bled their feet until the parasites grew enormous inside their boots and burst, and spider webs seemingly from nowhere entangled their faces. The SEALs in the lead hacked with

machetes a path through a wilderness so thick it was impossible to see more than twenty feet in any direction. *The worst*,
thought Dixon morosely, looking at his wrinkled skin, *was the
wet*. He was saturated from an earlier downpour, then the
muddy earth underneath, and then the river they had to cross
where a gaboon viper nearly bit Dunthorpe on the hand. If it
had, everyone knew Dunthorpe would have not lived to tell the
tale.

Dixon had expected wild animals everywhere, this was the
jungle after all, but the snake had been the largest creature
thus far encountered. Bugs, spiders, scorpions and ants were
everywhere, and birds could be heard in the trees, but that was
it. Light filtered through the canopy a hundred and fifty feet
above as shards of speckled beams. When they had marched for
five hours, Dixon fainted.

"Sunstroke, young man," Figgs explained later as he forced
Dixon to drink another canteen of water. "When you live your
whole life in a climate where you don't need to sweat, your skin
forgets what to do when it must. I know, my friend, because it
used to happen to me all the time in Asia."

Kazumu and his men laughed, a joke at Dixon's expense.
Angry, Dixon stood tall. He hated that he was out of his depth,
undoubtedly the only man here without jungle or other survival training to see him through. His lack, however, only made
him more determined, more certain that he would show them
all he meant business, that he was here for a reason. Other than
perhaps Peel, none of them really knew what they where up
against. How he wished this was a simple assignment, like infil-
trating a Chicago gang of drug-runners who had turned to the
worship of elder gods, rather than this scenario of insane
African rebels with their unknowable occult trimmings.

They marched again. Dixon felt his stomach bubble and
complain, and hoped that he didn't have the runs, or a worse
disease. The KLF soldiers talked loudly. They took no care
where they stepped, and threw litter everywhere. Ahead of

him, one did a quick shit in public view, left in their path so that everyone behind him had to be careful not to step in it. Dixon sighed. He just wanted to go home, to Jessica, to bed, to sleep a thousand years in comfort.

Later, when a soldier tried to shoot a monkey no one else could see, startling them all, Dixon approached Lieutenant Thompson. The SEAL seemed to be carrying about four times the weight he was, even though his own pack felt like a million tons.

"Yes, sir?"

"Thompson, can we do anything to discipline the KLF? They're going to get us exposed at this rate. Shot at by god knows who."

"What do you suggest, sir?" Thompson replied, his frustrated tone suggesting that he had already tried everything.

Then it came to him. Back on the MIL helicopter, Dixon's instincts had told him to hang onto a dozen copies of Penthouse, which he'd stashed in his pack. Now he was glad he had. "What about this for an idea?" he handed over the magazines still in their plastic wrappers. "You speak a local tongue, don't you?"

"I have the basics of Kiswahili, sir. I've heard some of the men conversing in this tongue."

Dixon nodded — he had, after all, requested SEALs with prior African experience. "Good, Lieutenant. Keep Kazumu out of this, but let the other soldiers know that if they stop littering, shut their mouths and keep their wits about them, there is one of these for each of them when we reach camp."

Thompson smiled, liking the idea. "Yes, sir. Right away."

Ten minutes later the column miraculously fell silent. Kazumu, who believed he had the monopoly on controlling his men, became suspicious. His own trick, of promising and delivering only in small doses, the images of naked women had kept his troops in line to his low standards. But two could play at that game. *Yes, you sly bastard*, Dixon thought to himself smugly before the wetness of this hothouse began bothering him again, *you've still got it*. Jungles might not be his home, but he was as a proficient as all hell in social engineering wherever he found himself.

It was only then that he realized Peel had been missing for several hours.

"Where is he, Lieutenant?"

"Major Peel, sir? He's with Dunthorpe, bringing up the rear. He was worried we were being followed."

This concerned Dixon more than he expected, and for more reasons than just one. There was a secret he'd been keeping between Lieutenant Thompson and himself, and suddenly it seemed important that he share this information with another, just in case he became compromised. Unfortunately, the only other person he was willing to trust this information with was Peel, and he was not here. Figgs was turning out to be just a little too friendly with his Congolese buddies for Dixon's liking.

The trail in the mud was obvious, and it was obviously left by Spiraling Worm cultists. Missing toes and exposed bones showed in the footprints of bare feet. Nails and bone ornaments fallen from their soldiers were still fresh with their own blood. The single tooth discovered in the root of a tree was most definitely human, filled sharp for the eating of raw flesh.

"They've been following us since the *bai*, sir." Sergeant Dunthorpe explained.

Peel nodded. The implications were far reaching. "They knew where we were before we even got here."

"Seems that way, sir."

Dunthorpe and Peel had double-backed, three kilometers behind the main group, a standard tactic to be certain that no one had picked up their trail. Peel suspected that any number of other rebels, DRC soldiers or foreign mercenaries operating in the jungle might be onto them. He had most certainly underestimated the Spiraling Worm and the URP, who had been invisible from the onset, aware of every step they had taken. They might even be watching them now, for all they knew. In this undergrowth, he could be certain of nothing.

Uncharacteristic in an SAS man, fear edged into Dunthorpe's tone, "What are we up against, Major?"

Peel looked into the jungle, thick and depressingly oppressive. Most of his experience in jungle warfare had been gained in Southeast Asia, with Figgs of all people. Those jungles were different — they didn't stretch forever, and there were villages and rice farms no more than a day's march from any point. Here, the next village could be twenty or thirty days away. Here they were truly alone.

"A hundred years ago, Dunthorpe, the Democratic Republic of the Congo was the private fiefdom of King Leopold II of Belgian. Determined not to be the little man of European royalty, he milked his one and only colony for everything he could squeeze out of it. Rubber was the market back then, and the Congo Free State had rubber in abundance. He turned twenty-million Congolese into slaves and forced them to collect all the rubber they could muster. His men killed their children, raped their wives, and cut off the hands and penises of the men who did not cooperate. Cannibal soldiers from other parts of the Congo were recruited into Leopold's army, and they were told they could eat any tribe member who did not obey the colonial authorities. In the space of thirty years Leopold was indirectly responsible for the death of ten million Congolese people, one in two people. He's up there with Hitler and Stalin on the genocide front, and still his country reveres him as a hero." When he was finished, Peel could taste disgust in his mouth.

"I don't understand, sir."

Peel looked straight at Dunthorpe. "History teaches us much. The Congo is hell on earth, and we ask ourselves why? It's because history made it this way. We, white western civilization, taught the people of the Congo how to mutilate, to kill, supported local customs of eating each other, and how to disrespect for our fellow man purely on the basis of skin color. Is it not surprising then, that this cult, these Spiraling Worm people, has grown strong by using the very same terror tactics we taught them?"

"No sir, I guess not." Dunthorpe still appeared confused, trying to relate a history lesson to the here and now. He'd heard stories about Peel from Figgs, how the man was driven, and obsessed with fixing the world, even in hell holes like the Congo that could not be fixed. "Does this change anything, sir?"

Peel shrugged, wondering why this country was getting under his skin, what it was about this place that was a reflection of his own demons. "Not really, I just have this feeling we've been screwed, but we just don't know how yet."

"And in the meantime?"

"Don't get caught," Peel was serious, "otherwise you too will be raped, mutilated, murdered and served up for dinner."

Dunthorpe looked like he wanted to swallow. "Then how did Fargo and Ackerman survive so long as their prisoners?"

Peel's smiled was discomforting. "Yes, I've been thinking that same thought for some time now. But let's get moving, it will be dark in a few hours, and we don't want to be caught out here alone."

In Langley, Virginia, the remote CIA buildings hidden in the surrounding forests were lit up like Christmas trees in the cold night. Joss Plenary raced his BMW to the checkpoint, showed his identification and was ushered in. Strange to think his top agent was on the other side of the world, sweating with the incessant heat in a country Plenary had no desire to visit, but a country that was causing him every kind of headache ever since that bothersome Australian Peel came back into his world.

Once he bypassed internal security, Plenary was escorted to Brendan Havercamp's office. They were on the same side, the CIA and the NSA, but that didn't mean they liked each other, or, more importantly, trusted each other. Even though it was two in the morning, Plenary saw a large number of analysts and strategists at work. They had a digital map of the Middle East on the wall, which they were all fussing over. He didn't want to know.

Havercamp showed Plenary into his office, and then shut the door so they would not be disturbed. Outside, through the window, a helicopter was taking off.

"Can't sleep, Havercamp?"

"I'm doing you the fucking favor here, Plenary."

"That's why you got me to drive, right?" Plenary had been inside the CIA building only five times in his career, and all were because of nights like this.

"You still in touch with Dixon and his team?"

Plenary raised an eyebrow, surprised that Havercamp knew his agent's name, let alone that he was running a black op in Central Africa. "They're under the canopy, inserted into northeast DRC. Now something or someone is jamming their signals."

"That's a fucking shame. I worked with Dixon once, when I was Section Head in South America. Considering what we saw down there I'm be insane not to have a running file on him, which I do. I wouldn't like to have to close it."

To change the subject, Havercamp threw a dozen black and white photographs on the table. They were of a corpse, lying in the mud, in a jungle on the outskirts of an African village. The man was ebony skinned, muscled and lean, and his body pockmarked with black sores oozing thick tar. Most prominent, all the flesh had been torn from his face, including his tongue, nose and eyes.

"It's like it's been—"

"Eaten off," finished Havercamp. "That's what Ackerman thought too."

"Ackerman?"

"That is why we are meeting, isn't it?" Havercamp frowned. "You wanted to know about our little black op down there a few years ago, didn't you?"

Plenary nodded, picked up several photos so he could examine them more closely. "These look like bullet wounds."

"*Hundreds* of bullet wounds."

"But they didn't kill him?"

Havercamp shook his head.

"Who is he?"

"He's the former leader of the URP, before Ackerman and his Special Forces terminated him. But I think you should be more worried, Plenary, about what chewed his face off."

"Chewed?"

"Yes," Havercamp pushed forward a photograph that highlighted the gory detail, sharp teeth marks where the flesh had been ripped away. "Ackerman reported seeing a mask on this man, a mask that had grown onto his face."

Plenary undid his tie, realizing only then how hot he had become. "And what happened to this mask?"

Havercamp shrugged, "The mask disappeared shortly before we lost contact with Ackerman, shortly before he called in that strike."

With a shudder Plenary threw the photos back. He was getting too old for this kind of work. Fighting terrorists and foreign spies was easy, but monsters from other dimensions, that was just insane. "What's your point, Havercamp? You wouldn't have come to me with this personally, not unless you had something very important to tell me about it."

Havercamp leaned back in his large leather chair, put his hands behind his head. He obviously liked being in control, but was that really surprising in a hidden world where no one seemed to control anything? "What I'm saying, Plenary, is that your man better fucking know what he's doing, otherwise he's going to create a shitstorm which none of us are going to come out of unscathed. None of us!"

The camp was a carnival of boisterous yelling and singing, of African reggae music and the occasional burst of machinegun fire, all of which could be heard a mile away. A bonfire could be seen at half that distance, even through the foliage. When Peel and Dunthorpe walked into the camp at 2200 hours, guided only by their light intensifier goggles, they collapsed into the circle of bedrolls erected by the SEALs. Both men were immediately served a MRE, which they ate greedily. In the thick air, mosquitoes squealed.

"Anything we should know?" Figgs asked, enjoying a shot of Scottish whiskey, which he displayed no intention to share.

Exhausted, Peel nodded, flinched at the sound of automatic gunfire sprayed into the air by drunken troops. In the half-light he saw that another soldier was masturbating over the picture of a young naked girl. "Ackerman's captors know we're here."

"The URP?"

"Yes." Peel showed them the teeth and bones he had collected, described what they had seen.

"And they didn't take you?" It was Dixon who asked, materializing from the darkness.

With a shake of his head Peel finished his meal, careful to stash the wrapper in his pack.

"Does that surprise you?"

"Yes, mate," Peel sounded exhausted, "it does so, very much."

Dixon walked away, but not before discretely signaling to Peel that they needed to talk. Five minutes later when Peel finished his food and another canteen of iodinated water, he sought out the American.

"What's up?"

"Peel, this situation is rapidly escalating out of control. We haven't got the faintest idea what's going on out there."

"I know, mate," Peel's answer was sincere. "I can't help feeling like we're walking into a trap."

"Me either, which is why I've got to tell you something."

Peel cocked an eyebrow.

"The air strike, it's on standby now. Actually two teams are on standby, the MIL helicopter to get us out when we need to, and. . . ."

"And?"

"And in Nairobi a C-130 Hercules transport loaded with a MOAB bomb."

Impressed, Peel whistled. "Massive ordnance air blast bomb?"

"Yeah, biggest fucking bomb outside a nuclear strike, weighing 9.5 tons. This baby can obliterate everything within an eight hundred feet radius, and can knock over tanks. They just roll them out of the Hercules' cargo bay mid-flight."

"And no one knows about this?"

"Thompson does, and now you. Plenary was very clear — if we find these URP bastards we are to do away with them straight away. No debriefing Ackerman first. Understand?"

Peel nodded slowly. "Okay."

"It's what you wanted, remember. This is the deal; you know our standard call frequencies, and the procedure for the pickup: we give our GPS location and the code 'Picnic Hamper'. This brings in the MIL from Entebbe. However, if we want to bring in the air strike, it's the same deal with the location, but the code is 'Home Delivery'. Don't get the two mixed up. If you call it in there is no call sign to stop them, not from ground zero at any rate. You'll have approximately one hour before the drop."

Peel looked back into camp, at soldiers enjoying their party in a world far from civilization. He saw a man enter a tent, excuse himself when he saw someone in there ahead of him. "Why are you telling me this?" he asked.

"In case Thompson or I don't make it. I'd tell Figgs, but he's very thick with these KLF bozos, whom I don't trust at all."

Peel nodded in agreement, "You think the KLF might have sold us out to the URP?"

Dixon shrugged. "It's certainly a possibility."

Peel turned back to the man waiting at the tent, noticed that he had an erection. Then he saw another man step out of the tent, buckling his pants tight. The first man changed places with him.

Dixon spoke up, "That doesn't look good."

"No, it doesn't," said Peel. "Shall we investigate?"

By the time they got there, another of the Congolese KLF men had reached the tent flap and shook his head at them.

"Not for you," he said in thick English. "This soldier tent."

"Really?" said Peel in a cold voice. "Then what the hell are you doing here?" — and shoved the man aside.

Dixon followed closely as the Major threw open the flap, and as soon as he saw what was going on in the stinking, steaming interior of the tent he whirled around ready to beat the hell out of the KLF man on general principles, but the ragged soldier had melted away and fled.

"Get off her," said Peel, and Dixon whipped his head back around at the flat, lethal tone in his companion's voice. The Congolese heard it too, and even though there was a good chance the man didn't speak English, he hurriedly rolled off to the side and started pulling his pants back up.

Dixon moved quickly to the woman bound atop the barrels while Peel grimly, steadily advanced on the man struggling to his feet and trying to find his gun.

"No," said Peel, almost conversationally, and shot both hands out. The KLF soldier took the blow to his chest, whoofed as his wind fled out of him, and fell back to the ground, pants still halfway up his thighs. His erection, just seconds ago busily engaged in rape, wilted quickly.

"Goddammit, Peel," said Dixon, whipping out his pocketknife and beginning to work on the ropes binding the woman to the iron barrels. "These are our allies?"

The black man roared and surged forward from the ground, aiming at Peel's knees for the takedown. The Australian nimbly stepped to the side and shot out one steel-toed foot, catching the Congolese on the side of his head as he lunged and knocking him back to the dirt, where he stopped yelling and started moaning. Dixon shot a quick look over at the man and shook his head.

"How is she?" asked Peel.

"She's alive," said Dixon, finishing his first cuts, lifting up the woman's wrist and feeling for a pulse. "Beyond that, she's having a bad fucking day."

"Who is the woman?" Peel asked the floundering man on the ground. "Where did you bastards get her?"

The man said something in Lingala, raised his head at Peel and spat. The glob of blood and saliva splatted against the Major's thigh, and he looked down at the sputum for a long second. Slowly, he shook his head in regret and reached down for his Glock.

"You going to kill him?" asked Dixon, working on the woman's gag, smoothing the stringy, sweaty hair from her face as he did.

"No, but he doesn't know that," Peel was angry, aiming the pistol straight at the Congolese man. The soldier's eyes went wide with panic and terror, and he began to scoot back toward the tent wall when he got tangled up in his trousers again and crashed back down onto the side of his head.

"If you change your mind," said Dixon, "just try not to get the bastard's brains all over you when you shoot."

"What is going on?" roared the voice of Kazumu.

Peel and Dixon both paused, gun and knife in hand, and looked expressionlessly toward the tent flap. The KLF Captain stood there with one of his men, and on his face was an admixture of anger and fear, as though he wanted to attack and apologize at the same time. Peel turned away from the rapist, who took the opportunity to scuttle himself towards the wall, and casually moved toward the front of the tent.

"You didn't know about this, right?" the Australian asked, slowly moving forward, gun held loosely in his hand. "You wouldn't countenance the capture and rape of a woman by your army, would you?"

"I—"

"Because," said Peel, still taking measured steps forward until he stood right before the Congolese Captain, "because such things are so abhorrent, so contrary to every rule of law in the world, that if I thought you had a hand in this kind of depravity I'd make sure you received the harshest form of justice available. So tell me, Captain Kazumu — is this happening with your permission?"

Dixon had finished cutting the bonds from the woman and looked around for something to cover her with. She had struggled briefly as he slashed the ropes from her ankles, and he took that as a good sign, a sign that she wasn't catatonic or comatose after the abuse she'd gone through — and he found a jacket crumpled on the floor nearby and picked it up. He laid it atop her and tucked it under her back, her ripped, bleeding buttocks, and put his arms beneath her, lifted her into the air.

He'd carried Jessica like this just last week, his lover giggling in anticipation and joy as they'd romped on the beach at Hilton Head. Now he felt the grease and dirt and, probably, blood and semen, and what had recently seemed a tender gesture turned into raw rage.

"Of course the fucker knew about this," said Dixon, his voice rasping as he walked forward with the unconscious woman. "It's his camp, his men, his fucking tent."

"Hullo!" shouted Figgs from outside, and in the next second the Englishman appeared between the dark forms of Kazumu and his soldier. "What kind of balls-up is all this, then?"

"I'll need an answer, Captain," said Peel calmly, the Glock still held loosely in his hand.

Kazumu looked at the men facing him, looked down at the soldier on the ground who had finally managed to get his pants on and was fumbling for his sidearm. Figgs took in the whole scene and shook his head.

"You stupid, naughty bastards," he whispered. "Kazumu, your boy there is going to do something incredibly dumb in a second."

Kazumu roared a command, and the man next to him, the soldier, raised his machine gun and instantly fired a roaring burst of lead into the newly-clothed form of his compatriot, sending the man dancing, the gun flying from his hand to thwack against the canvas wall of the tent, and blood to spurt out from a dozen wounds as he jitterbugged into a danse macabre.

Peel and Dixon didn't flinch as the man was destroyed, and they both walked forward as though their moves had been choreographed — and Kazumu stepped aside to let them progress out of the tent unmolested. Figgs stepped aside as well, but there was a sardonic half-grin on his face as he did that Dixon did his best to ignore.

They would play it this way for a while. Kazumu would lead them to Ackerman, and they would pretend that the man had no knowledge of the woman his army had kept tied up in a filthy, bloody tent to slake their bestial desires. Dixon understood the realities of life, understood that sometimes you had to lay down with monsters, but this was too close, too personal; he would do his job and save the fucking world again, but there would be a settling of debts before this business was all over.

Guaranteed.

❋   ❋   ❋

"So who's the bird?" asked Figgs, leaning back and sipping more of his whiskey. Peel couldn't imagine where the man had secreted the liquor on the helicopter ride into the depth of hell, here, but he hadn't run out yet.

"She's not conscious," said Peel, looking around the darkened clearing. Jungle noises were soft but pervasive, providing a susurrus of background static to their conversation. Several of the KLF soldiers were around a campfire some five meters away, roaring with laughter and passing a jug around, and there were supposedly more KLF men posted in defensive positions around the *bai*, but the Europeans had taken no chances — half the SEALS were out there, too, and both of Figgs' SAS soldiers, all grouped in teams of three. "Dixon's taking care of her."

"He sweet for her?" asked the Englishman, raising his hand to his mouth and stifling a small belch. "You could tell, even under all that dirt and soot, that she was quite a looker."

"He's got a girlfriend, you sick bastard," said Peel without heat, standing up and stretching. "And I hope you didn't know anything about all this?"

"Innocent as a babe, my antipodean friend," protested Figgs, eyes widening. "I may be a lot of things — probably am — but I wouldn't approve of constant gang rape."

"Or any rape?"

Peel thought about pushing the man further, finding out exactly what the MI6 man did know about these savages, but realized that he wouldn't learn anything more than what Figgs wanted to tell him.

"You think these idiots can guide us to Ackerman, then?" he asked instead.

Figgs laughed. "They'll do better than we could on our own, Peel."

"Will it be enough?"

Figgs stopped laughing and looked up at the shaven-headed Australian. "Getting us close will be enough."

Peel thought about it for a second and realized the man was right — even if they didn't succeed in their ostensible mission to rescue the wounded Major Ackerman, they would get close enough for the URP to find them. And after that, it would be a simple matter of sending out the correct signal on the satellite radio, and one more blasphemous cult dedicated to the destruction of the universe would die in a conflagration of plasmic flame.

And if they had to sacrifice themselves, Peel and Dixon and Figgs, well, that was what they'd signed up for.

"What's your name?" asked Dixon gently. It was the fifth time he'd asked the question, and like the previous four times he didn't expect to be answered. This time, however, the woman surprised him.

"Tania," she whispered, eyes still closed, still clutching the thin woolen blankets tightly around herself.

He'd laid her in the bunk tenderly and carefully a couple of hours ago, and since then he'd been sitting next to her, talking in soothing tones, gently brushing her hair and swabbing most of the dirt and grime from her with wet rags. He'd cleaned and bandaged her more obvious wounds, though he was afraid that there may be something wrong with her inside — and he knew they couldn't deal with interior bleeding with the primitive medicines they had available in their med kits.

"Hello, Tania," he whispered. "I'm Jack."

She was silent, her eyes still closed, but Jack felt a tension break in the woman. She'd been tight and wound-up, even in her unconsciousness, but slowly she began to relax a bit, to settle into the bunk.

"Where . . ." she began, blinking open her eyes.

"Same place, I'm afraid," he said, shaking his head. "But you're away from the soldiers now. Safer."

"Safe?" She said the word as though she didn't understand it.

Dixon laughed a bitter laugh. "No," he said. "Not safe. But you're better off than you were this morning."

❄   ❄   ❄

"She's a journalist," he said, taking a long drink of water, doing the best he could to scan the darkened jungle in only the light from the brilliant stars and the smoldering fires that the KLF had let burn out. "An Australian journalist."

"Australian?" asked Peel, surprised. "What the bloody hell is she doing here?"

"She works for something called ABC."

"Australian Broadcasting Corporation," said Peel.

"She's based out of Nairobi, covering the mess in the Congo," said Dixon. "She got a tip about some cannibal band of rebels and decided to follow up. Bad decision."

"She came out here by herself?" asked Figgs incredulously. "The woman's got a pair of balls!"

"She had a cameraman and a guide," said Dixon, closing the cap on the canteen and setting it down next to him. "The two of them got captured but she managed to hide in the chaos and slip away."

"Lucky her," said Peel.

"Yeah," said Dixon. "I'm sure she's counting her blessings right now."

"Who captured her partners?" asked Figgs, leaning close. "Was it the URP?"

"I'm sure it was," said Dixon. "She had a hard time getting out descriptions — she's exhausted, terrified, and there are going to be some severe emotional problems with her — but she mentioned bloody, mutilated black men with missing fingers and toes, bleeding wounds all over them that they seemed proud of, teeth filed down into fangs. She mentioned one other thing, too."

"Yes?" asked Figgs, his face avid with interest.

"Their leader was a white man," said Dixon.

Peel leaned back and nodded, closing his eyes as he thought.

"Would she recognize him again?" he asked. "We can get a picture of Ackerman, see if she recognizes it."

"No," said Dixon. "According to her, the man was wearing a mask."

Plenary drove straight from Langley to Fort Meade, his mind whirling with the data he'd assimilated in his visit to CIA headquarters. It was a good thing there wasn't much traffic this time of night, because he was driving on autopilot.

What was the mask?

It all boiled down to that question. Havercamp had instantly assumed that this whole mission was a trap of some sort. That Ackerman and Fargo had been turned by the URP somehow, and that Dixon and Peel were meant to trigger some catastrophe by their presence in the Congo. Reluctantly, Plenary had agreed with his counterpart. It was just too simplistic, this set-up, too convenient; the prodigal soldier stumbling out of the jungle, the wounded hero, waiting for rescue, and the international rescue team bravely plunging into the wilderness to save the day.

It was bullshit, is what it was. The URP wanted — needed — something from Peel and Dixon and Figgs. But what?

And how had they turned Ackerman?

In the last few years Plenary had learnt a fair bit about the occult, about the gods and monsters who lurked just beyond the threshold of sanity waiting for a passageway into the world, and his mind kept circling back on the picture he'd seen of the dead URP commander, his flesh eaten from his face.

What had he worn on his face that made him invulnerable to a hundred high-velocity slugs?

And where had it gone once he had finally died?

When his cellular rang, he answered it immediately.

"Sir," his senior night officer spoke quickly. "Bad news sir."

Plenary huffed. No one ever called him in the middle of the night with good news. "What is it?"

"Fargo, sir, he just murdered a doctor, two nurses and two SAS soldiers."

Plenary grimaced. Things were just getting better and better. "Get me on the next flight to Nairobi, fastest flight you can."

"Yes sir."

"And that book too, the one Peel led us to."

"*The Masked Messenger?*"

"Yes, that one."

He signaled a turn, away from NSA headquarters and onto a beeline route straight to the nearest Air Force base. His team was working on the problem right now, and if there was anything to find they would find it, but they didn't need his physical presence to do their job. He was better off on the field, in Africa.

What had the mask looked like, he wondered . . . and shivered.

The KLF were back to their loud, stupid ways, and Dixon knew that the skin magazines would be worthless as a bribe this time — the soldiers had already received their booty and had carefully hidden the *Penthouses* where Kazumu wouldn't find and confiscate them.

None of the Congolese marched near him, however — he, Tania Selby, Figgs and one of the SAS men walked alone, and the KLF were very careful not to look at the white woman. Dixon may not have been a soldier, but he had killed before, and the look in his eyes was enough to make the KLF keep their distance and pretend they'd never seen the reporter in their whole miserable lives.

"What can you tell me about the white man, Tania?" asked Dixon.

"I told you everything I saw already," said the woman, walking unsteadily in her borrowed boots and carefully looking straight ahead. Dixon was amazed by her resilience — she'd been repeatedly abused by the men marching all around her, but she didn't cower or cringe and she'd managed to force her wits back into her skull and keep everything under wraps while she was enduring this fearful situation. True, she never let herself get more than a foot away from Dixon, but he knew that was normal — she'd latched onto him as a kind of savior, an island of sanity and stability in this madhouse country, and while he knew and had been careful to tell her that they were walking into even more mortal danger, he was flattered by her attention.

She reminded him a bit of Jessica; both were intelligent, curious and brave, both beautiful. He suspected that if Jessica had gone through the torture that Tania had, she'd react in similar ways.

He hoped they weren't all going to die out here.

"What about the mask, then?" asked Figgs. He moved easily through the jungle, casually twitching his machete now and again to slash fronds and branches from their path, and it seemed that even the insects left him alone as though they recognized him as a fellow denizen of the green hell. "What did it look like?"

Tania shuddered and shook her head. "It was—"

"And where the hell has Peel gone to again?" interrupted the Englishman. "He should be hearing all of this."

"He took Dunthorpe to check our back trail," said Dixon. "I'm sure he'll be back soon."

Suddenly, shouts rose from the men at the vanguard of the traveling party, shouts of startled surprise. Dixon instantly raised his gun and moved an inch closer to the woman in a protective gesture. Figgs raised his eyebrow at the SAS soldier and the man nodded and broke into a jog forward.

Seconds later, amid the chattering of Kiswahili and Lingala, the British Special Forces man called out, "You'd better get up here, sir!"

"What fresh hell is it, then?" muttered Figgs, but he moved forward quickly, paced by Tania and Dixon. They moved through the milling knot of Congolese soldiers forcefully, and within instants they stood in front of the mob, startled into silence by the tableau before them.

"Marcus! Ambrose!" shouted Tania Selby, and began to lurch forward toward the two men kneeling on the jungle floor facing her. Dixon instinctively reached out and snagged her arm, pulled her back, and she yelped and cringed at the sudden contact, panic rising in her eyes like flames.

Dixon cursed himself; he'd given the woman more indication that men would do whatever they wanted to her, no matter her own wishes . . . . but he didn't have time for the kinder, civilized feelings right now.

"My team!" she urged, straining against Dixon's hand. "They're all right!"

"No they're not," said Figgs quietly. "Look at them."

The two men, one white with shaggy dark hair, the other dark ebony with a shaved scalp, both wore ragged, filthy Western clothes, both seemed relatively unharmed by their ordeal in the jungle — but both men knelt stock-still in the dirt and loam of the jungle floor with identical expressions of terror on their faces.

"I may be defining 'all right' incorrectly," said Figgs casually, "but I'm pretty sure that those chaps ain't it."

"Help them!" demanded the journalist. "Someone help them!"

Slowly, the SAS man moved forward, his eyes constantly scanning the surrounding jungle. "Judas goats," he said, scowling. "It's a trap."

"Yes," said Dixon, his voice surprisingly calm. "And we have to trigger it."

"We could turn around and walk away," suggested Figgs.

"The URP is here," said Dixon, forcing himself not to whirl in panicked circles looking for the deformed army that was sure to be there. "It's what we came for."

"Just checking your guts, Yank," said Figgs, his voice also calm. "Go ahead, Garvin — help the blokes."

Corporal Garvin moved slowly forward until he stood right before the kneeling men, and both of them shuddered slightly in still paroxysms of terror and panic, their eyes rolling desperately up toward the British soldier. Hesitantly, the SAS man reached out with his non-gun hand and took the white cameraman by the shoulder.

'Collapsed' is perhaps too inadequate a verb to describe what happened next to the kneeling man. As soon as Garvin made physical contact with the rough shirt of Marcus, the man lost cohesion, his flesh melting into his blood, his bones liquefying instantly, and his body became a foul slurry of oozing protoplasm. Screams rose from the Congolese soldiers and Dixon felt them turning and running from the unholy sight, and even stoic Garvin leaped back and shook his hand violently as though whatever sorcery had turned the solid form of the cameraman into a crumbling heap of bloody goop was catching. Within a second, nothing was left of the man but a spreading puddle of red-and-gray liquid already soaking into the jungle floor, and an unbearably foul stench rose from the site as though a charnel house had swung open its doors.

Dixon grabbed Tania and swung her around so that she was between him and the other kneeling man, ignoring her air-raid screams. The team's attention was meant to be focused on the horrors before them, which meant that the action would be happening behind them!

Gunfire chattered from the rich green walls of the jungle, loud and staccato and drowning out even the sounds of the KLF's yells. Dixon saw three of the Congolese soldiers jerked and twisted like marionettes by the force of the unseen barrage, blood spurting from them in crimson squibs, and he saw the other KLF men diving to the ground in panic, dropping their weapons and screaming for mercy.

Dixon raised his M16 and waited for a clear shot, and in his peripheral vision saw Figgs doing the same thing. No bullets came their way, which was strange, but Dixon didn't waste time wondering why — instead he focused on a muzzle flash from the sheltering dark of the jungle and loosed a burst at it.

Something yelped and fell out of the trees, and Dixon caught sight of a horribly twisted, fearsomely mutilated black body, fresh bullet wounds mixing with a hundred older scars. He saw that he'd killed the man and turned to find another target.

Figgs had let loose a long, sustained barrage of bullets from his own gun, and the lead churned up the foliage to their left and brought a fresh volley of screams from some hidden assailant. Now Garvin had joined them and contributed his own loud, chattering blasts to the general assault.

"This would be tougher if they were firing back at us!" yelled Figgs almost cheerfully in the midst of the smoke and screams.

Dixon ignored him and watched as the URP men began to come out of the trees and concentrate on finishing off the howling, prone KLF soldiers, mercilessly firing blast after blast into the helpless men. He saw one of the soldiers — the one who had shot Tania's rapist last night — have his head exploded like a rotten melon by a withering cannonade by a razor-toothed leering scarecrow of a man with ripped gaping holes in his biceps. Dixon aimed at him, but then another man came striding out of the jungle, long spear in one hand, wickedly gleaming knife in the other — a tall, muscled white man wearing a mask.

"Target," said Figgs conversationally, and fired. So did Dixon and Garvin, letting loose with everything they had.

It was impossible to see clearly what happened as the hundreds of rounds hit the leader of the URP, because the smoke and haze were so dense and concealing that they could only catch glimpses through the occasional clear spot, but the man rocked back and forth with the impacts.

"He's not going down," gasped Garvin, panic taking over his voice. "He's not bloody going down!"

"Keep firing," commanded Figgs.

But it was useless. Slowly, incredibly, the figure fought its way through the blistering maelstrom of metal, brandishing the spear like Moses' staff, and the other URP soldiers respectfully melted back out of their commander's way and watched with shark's gleaming grins as he strode forward laughing, his howls of glee louder even than the crescendo of explosions.

As he neared, Dixon saw not blood but some viscous black ooze spurting from the myriad bullet wounds riddling the figure, a bubbling tar which quickly and wondrously scaled off the holes, healing them as fast as they formed. The man — Ackerman, it had to be Ackerman — roared laughter at the pain he must have been feeling, but kept striding forward toward them, that black tar roiling on the multitudinous wounds in his torso, his legs, his arms, his head.

The head, half-covered by that mask.

Bullets whanged off the impenetrable wood of the thing, leaving smoking divots in the alien teak, only to be repaired and refilled instantly. One ebony eye glittered in the center of the half-mask, an eye which gleamed insanely at Dixon and Figgs and Garvin, and long, sword-sharp teeth hooked down from it and dug into Ackerman's cheeks, reached around and plunged into his wounded head. Dixon felt his fingers grow numb on the trigger of the machine gun, heard the cessation of sound from beside him as Figgs snarled and ran out of ammunition, and then Ackerman and the mask were before them.

The spear whipped around and bit deep into Garvin's gut. The British soldier made a gargled scream and collapsed as his intestines began to spill out of the gaping stomach wound. Tania screamed again, and Dixon wanted to, but then he found the blade of Ackerman's knife suddenly up under his chin, forcing his head up to avoid the plunge of the steel into his palate. Figgs dove at Ackerman, but the ex-Special Forces Major contemptuously swept the attack aside with the butt of his spear, and Figgs careened into the dirt.

"Welcome, friend," whispered the man in the mask, and Dixon smelled his taint, the stench of a hundred half-healed wounds rank with infection, and found himself staring into that black, black eye set into the hard, disconcerting wood. "I'm so glad you could come."

The rain came in heavy sheets, washing away the blood. As prisoners they were stripped of all possessions except their uniforms and boots. Around their wrists wire was bound, and they were made to kneel before the corpses of their compatriots. Corporal Garvin's eyes seemed full of life as they stared back at Dixon, but the multitude of organs spilt from guts told another story. Beyond him, two puddles of liquid flesh, Tania's former companions.

More of the URP soldiers dragged into the center pile the corpses of those soldiers who had not made it. Of the KLF, only Kazumu was spared. Figgs, Tania, himself and two of the SEALs — Lieutenant Thompson and a young man from Kentucky, Corporal Vetch — had lived through the ambush. Despite all his arduous training as a SEAL, tears now filled Vetch's eyes. Tania, in comparison, was disturbingly still and silent.

"Is this all of them?" boomed Ackerman as the pincer-like tentacles wrapped about his head beat unnatural rhythms against the wooden mask. From his human flesh wounds still popped open, expelling unwanted rounds coated in thick black tar. Rain mixed with his blackness, burnt as if it had just touched acid.

"Yes sir!" responded Ackerman's second-in-command, a huge black man with a three-pronged bony spiral etched into his chest, and instead of a face, torn strips of skin and meat so that when seen from head on, he wore the red mask of a human skull.

"Two are missing," Ackerman said after an examination of the dead. "The other SAS soldier and the Australian intelligence office, Major Peel, are missing. Go and find them."

As three Spiraling Worm cultists darted into the jungle, Dixon did a double-take. Ackerman knew exactly who they were, right down to their names and ranks. Perhaps he knew all about their mission too.

"And their long-range radio?"

"Accounted for, sir."

"Excellent."

Ackerman's heavy feet splotched in the mud and rain as he walked the line of prisoners. Dixon dared not look up, for he had no desire to give this insane monster any reason to single any of them out, himself included. He wanted to comfort Tania, but she wouldn't look at him. Rationally he knew this was for the best, but such thoughts didn't lessen his discomfort. They'd been set up, screwed from the beginning. That much was obvious now, but not the why? The most important question of all, that's what Peel had said. The only consoling factor was that Peel and Dunthorpe were still free. But if rescue was their plan, there were the twenty-two URP soldiers and the alien Ackerman they would have to deal with first. Odds that not even gambling addicts would take.

The enemy's feet, still in their worn U.S. military boots, stopped before Dixon. A hand, fashioned seemingly from steel it was so strong, lifted the NSA officer's head high. That single eye, black without pupils or anything analogous to earthly eyesight, darted this way and that, but always it looked at him. Dixon saw his fear reflected in that single eye.

"This one," Ackerman yelled to his men, his mouth visible beneath the wooden row of randomly jutting teeth. "This one is their leader. He is important to me, so he dies last."

The hand pushed Dixon hard, smacking into the mud. When he tried to stand, a foot came down upon him, heavy.

"Did I say get up?"

"No," Dixon fumbled his words as mud splashed into his mouth. He was both terrified and consumed with rage, and knew which of the two emotions he would have to nurture if he was to escape alive. Then he thought of Tania, strange that he considered her while this creature pushed him down, degrading him. He had to protect her, he'd promised her, given his word that he would. With purpose now, at last rage took control. Anger, he realized, would see him through.

Ackerman stepped off him. Dixon remained prone, where he watched his nemesis single out the next prisoner. "This one," he pointed to Kazumu. "He is not one of them, he is not important." He whistled a command, indicated that the Congolese soldier was to be separated from the line.

Kazumu screamed as two mutilated men dragged him forward. They wrapped a rope about his bound hands, and then slung the other end over a low hanging branch. Quickly, he was hoisted into the air until his feet kicked madly a foot above the wet earth.

Dixon could not believe the power of Kazumu's screams, could not find words to describe the chill that fed upon his soul when he heard the other man's cries growing louder and louder by each passing second. The creature that was Ackerman was upon the KLF leader, savage and wild. From Dixon's angle, in the mud, and through the thick rain, it was hard to ascertain details, which was a blessing. All he saw was blood, then flesh in Ackerman's mouth.

The feast continued for minutes, but it felt like hours. When Ackerman stepped away, Kazumu was stripped, not only of his clothes, but of his skin and flesh. Half the man was gone. Shreds of skin, muscle and even bone hung like wild thorns and fleshy leaves, as if he were an orange, peeled.

The men were next to turn on Kazumu. More fastidious, they cut him apart with machetes and fighting knives, but they still ate their meat raw.

When Dixon thought he could take it no more, when he believed no sight eyes would ever terrify him so deeply, he caught Kazumu's eyes.

With the single eyelid left to him, Kazumu blinked.

Finally, Dixon vomited the ache that had been in his stomach for so long.

Peel could only close his eyes at the horror. It was all he could do. And it was all he could do not to shoot the man, put him out of his misery. Dunthorpe, with his FN-FAL rifle, was ready for the mercy shot. He wanted to take it. So did Peel. But if they did, they'd betray their position and the two dozen soldiers would be upon them in seconds. Odds they could not survive.

Peel clenched his fists against frustration. Kazumu might have been a horrible human being, but he was still a human, who felt, loved, aspired, hurt and hoped. All those feelings were now destroyed with him. All they could do was hope his end was quick, and they were not even granted that.

Afterwards, as they slinked back deeper into the jungle where the foliage would cover them not only visibly but mask their voices as well, Peel could see that Dunthorpe was shaking.

The Australian put a hand on his shoulder. "It was the right thing to do."

Dunthorpe nodded. "I know sir, it's just. . . ."

The Australian gave the SAS soldier a moment. He knew he needed one himself.

"It's just that mask. I mean, you saw it sir, didn't you?"

"Yes. Yes, I did."

Suddenly Peel became aware that Dunthorpe was staring straight at him, his eyes wide with disbelief. "You thought it was what happened to Kazumu that upset me?"

Now it was Peel's turn to stare. "It upset me!"

"No disrespect sir, but I've seen horrible stuff like that before, more often than you may care to know. But that mask, it was . . . alien. And you acted like you expected it!"

Peel took a moment. He had to ensure he answered well, because now more than ever, they needed each other, if there was any chance of salvaging this mess. "Look, Sergeant, you're right, I did expect something like this. But consider this; you said you've seen horrible things like what happened to Kazumu in your past. Well, I've seen things like what has Ackerman, not exactly that, but creatures like it, many times in my past."

"You should have told me, told the boys!" His tone became aggressive, angry.

"And you would have believed me?" Peel snapped. "Think about it, Sergeant. I remember when I first encountered this—" he searched for a word, and found none. "—this shit, Sergeant, and I know nothing that anyone could have told me, that would have prepared me. Think about it! Think about what I'm saying. That's why we're here, Dixon and I, to stop this kind of thing, again and again, until these fuckers finally leave the human race in peace!"

Dunthorpe hung his head. Eventually he nodded. Then he looked up, caught Peel's eyes. "I'm sorry Major, it's just --"

"It's just that you didn't expect it, right?"

He nodded.

"Well, let me tell you, I'm glad I've got you with me right now, because you know why?"

"Why, sir?"

"Three of those crazy URP cultists are high-tailing it back into the jungle, trying to find us. We take them out, that's three less the others have to worry about. Guerilla tactics, Sergeant. You know how to fight like a guerilla don't you?"

"Yes sir!" At last, conviction in his voice, his whole face.

"Good, because we are going to take down these bastards, one sick prick at a time, until we're ready to rescue the men we came here with, plus Tania!"

"Yes sir! We bloody well are, sir."

Quickly they hid their packs, which they would retrieve upon return. Now they could run light and fast into the jungle, hell bent upon their prey.

Long before the rain stopped they were force-marched, deeper into the jungle. The wire tight around Dixon's wrists cut until they bled. They hurt like hell, but he knew he must try to break them. Wire became brittle if twisted too many times, so that is what he did despite the pain they caused, twist his hands every step he took, ever further into the unknown canopy.

Tania walked ahead of him. Her head hung low, she refused to look at him. She refused to look at anyone. He wondered what thoughts raced through her head, what fears and terrors grew strong. What extra pain she must be feeling compared to the rest of them. Had he failed her, because he had saved her from one horror only to subject her to something far worse?

Of his other companions, Figgs looked tired and about ten years older. Vetch was pale, scared, he had already given up. Only Thompson remained stoic, head held high as he marched like the soldier he was. If the NSA officer had to rely on anyone in the remaining group, he knew it would be Thompson he would turn to first.

Tania stumbled, unable to keep her balance, and with bound hands fell headfirst into the mud. Dixon ran for her to help her stand. Before he could reach her the stock of an AK-47 smashed into his gut, wielded by a cultist soldier with a slashed face. Dixon went down, felt the wind in his gut escape and the void it left behind fill with pain.

There was a cracking of branches and mud splashing. Dixon stumbled to his knees to see Thompson sprinting into the undergrowth. Bullets sprayed from a dozen assault rifles, yet every burst missed him. He was going to make it. Another one of them was going to be free!

Hope vanished when a spear materialized in Thompson's back. A splatter pattern of blood hung still in the air for a few seconds before it too spilt like rain. Dixon looked back to the cultists. It had been Ackerman who had thrown that spear, and his aim had been perfect.

Now excitement grew in the ranks. Chest-beating and lip-licking took hold of each man, if they could be called men. They weren't interested in their prisoners for the moment, so Dixon took the opportunity to sidle up to Tania.

"I promise you," the words just came out of his mouth, "I'll get you out of this. On my life, I will."

Her eyes were horrible. "Will you?"

"It's a promise, Tania."

A blow to the back of his head sent him sprawling again. The skull-faced second-in-command was upon him, the stock of his barrel poised to smash his face into oblivion.

"Stop!" It was Ackerman. "We need that one alive."

Dixon, saved for the moment, rolled on his side in hope of easing the pain in his gut and head. Beyond, whooping, lyrical cries erupted from the soldiers. Thompson, with the spear still wedged through his back and out through his gut, was brought before Ackerman.

"He's still alive," Skull-Face explained, blood oozing from his facial wounds.

"Good!"

Ackerman only hesitated for a second, staring into the eyes of the SEAL commander. Thompson's last act was to spit blood into the eye of his foe. Ackerman was not concerned. In a snake-quick strike he bit into Thompson's face, chewing out the soldier's tongue so he could not scream.

None of the prisoners could watch. Vetch finally broke, cried like a baby. Figgs rolled into himself, hoping for catatonia. Tania just stared into the jungle, numb to everything.

Are we going to survive this? Dixon asked himself. If this were not to be his end, he knew he had to keep trying, like Thompson had tried. So he searched for clues, anything to tip the balance in his favor.

When Ackerman was done eating, the other soldiers turned upon the serrated corpse. Dixon studied his foe and saw that now Ackerman had completed his rites of cannibalism, he seemed somewhat more relaxed. "No more killings until tomorrow, when I really need them," he said to Skull-Face. Realizing that he had just spoken in English, he switched to Lingala, and talked on other matters Dixon could not understand.

Again working at the wire binding his hands, he saw now that the Spiraling Worm cultists had a ritual for their cannibalism — the process of eating was the same here as when Kazumu had been butchered. His internal monologue asked questions, and the most important of all was: *did they eat humans not because it pleased them, but because it was required of them?*

Who ruled here, Ackerman or the Mask?

✻   ✻   ✻

They ran hard. They ran fast. Always the jungle seemed to bend inwards, a living festering organism ready to swallow them into the gut of some world-sized beast, yet while they had strength they would not let it beat them. Dunthorpe led the way, Peel followed. The SAS man was an expert tracker, and he had youth and a rigorous training program on his side, youth and fitness that constantly threatened to leave Peel for dead. The Australian was fit, he undertook a rigorous exercise program every morning, but he was inadequate compared to Dunthorpe.

The cultist soldiers moved faster than either man expected, following the trail their party had left before the URP ambushed them. This now made it easier for the cultists to be followed, for they were not expecting their prey to sneak upon them from the rear.

An hour from the ambush site, Dunthorpe was upon the first soldier before Peel even saw the cultist. The SAS man was incredible, his commando knife drawn and plunged into a kidney while the other hand covered the mouth to muffle any screams. When the body dropped dead, Dunthorpe cursed. "The bastard bit me!" Blood was already welling in the puncture marks in his hand.

A knife shot through air, narrowly missing Dunthorpe, lodging into a tree with a sudden thud! It was a multi-bladed dagger, weighed around its center of gravity and designed, Peel realized, to maximize the chance of a blade impact.

"Two o'clock!" Peel spotted the other cultists, fired his silenced pistol in rapid succession, sending the first man down. Dunthorpe threw his knife, whizzing it through the air too fast to see, catching the last foe in the neck.

Peel ran to the cultist he'd shot, still flailing on the earth, who was lifting his assault rifle for one final burst. Acting impulsively, losing all control, Peel pulled his knife, straddled the man and stabbed him in the face and chest over and over again, blood spraying like water from a fountain. He was angry, he wanted revenge. Dunthorpe had to pull him away.

"It's over sir. They're dead!"

Peel struggled only momentarily, until he remembered again who he was and why he was here. For the first time in his life he understood what was meant by momentary insanity. "I'm sorry, Dunthorpe. I've let you down."

"No you haven't, sir. Besides, he deserved it."

Peel struggled to his feet, wiped the blood across his face. He was panting hard, they both were. "It's not that, it's that I made it personal."

"It is personal, sir."

Spinning in a circle, Peel hoped to find his bearing, to remember what had just occurred. He was losing it, or had lost it, in this moment. He had to find himself again.

"Are you okay, Major? You seem a little intense."

"Intense?"

"Yes, and not just now, but the whole time since Nairobi."

Peel sat down before he fell down. He should have reprimanded the SAS soldier for his insolence, but his words were not malicious. More importantly, his observations were right. "Do you remember how I told you that I've seen this kind of thing before, in my past?"

Dunthorpe nodded.

"Well it almost beat me once, and not that long ago. I thought I was dead, I thought it was killing me, and that I had no hope. And you know, what I hated most was that I did give up. Then, miraculously, I was given a second chance at life, and I realized how pathetic I had become. So I vowed I'd never let it take me again. I'd never let these cosmic intrusions stop me ever again, not until I'd actually stopped breathing."

"I understand sir. I think I understand."

Peel stood defiant, in control again. He locked the safety on his silenced Glock and threw the gun to Dunthorpe. "You're going to need that."

Dunthorpe smiled. "You've got a plan, haven't you sir?" He holstered the weapon to wipe the blood from his knife.

"Hell yes I have. Knives and that pistol are the only silent weapons we have. Tonight Ackerman and his followers will make camp. If we assume they'll assign sentries, we can take a few of them out, one at a time, during the night."

"Dwindle their numbers?"

"Exactly! Give Dixon, Figgs and the others every chance to escape on their own, or until the URP numbers drop so low we can attempt a rescue."

"Sounds good to me."

"One more thing, though. Ackerman wanted our long-range radio. He was very clear about that. That's got to be our priority, either getting it back, or making sure he can't use it."

"Do you know what he plans to do with it, sir?"

Peel smiled. His heavy breathing at last subsiding, "Not yet, but it can't be good, whatever they plan. We better move now. We've got ground to make up."

They sprinted again, knowing that night was not far away.

❋   ❋   ❋

Camp was established in a small clearing hidden beneath the overhanging canopy. Dixon, Figgs, Tania and Vetch were hung like Kazumu, with ropes from tree branches. Vetch screamed for hours, not realizing that they were only secured for the night, and not hung so they could be eaten. To torment him further, several mutilated cultists tore off Vetch's shirt and licked his salt with their serrated tongues. Eventually he passed out from shock.

Sometime during the night Dixon passed out too, from exhaustion.

He was rudely woken in the morning light by Figgs, who had kicked him. The Englishman had spun to face Dixon, venom in his eyes. "You bastard, it's all right for you!"

"For me?" Dixon scoffed. His hands were numb where the wire and rope bit. He couldn't feel them at all. "You think they're not going to torture and eat me too?" He remembered somberly what Ackerman had said, about needing to feed the next day. It was the next day now.

"You heard what he said! He needs you, so you can negotiate?" Figgs was mad, on the verge of screaming.

"What?" Dixon yelled back, "Do what they say, in promise
for our freedom? Figgs, you're as mad as they are if you think
they'll let any of us go!"

"Oh stop it!" Tania screamed at them both, "For god's sake,
fighting each other isn't going to help anything."

"And, my dear lady, you think you've got a plan, do you?"

"Give it a rest, Figgs. She's right!"

"What's that?" Tania changed the subject, indicating with
her foot a shape in the foliage. Dixon scanned with his own
eyes, saw the crumbled body of a sentry. "Peel," he whispered,
"and Dunthorpe!"

"So they didn't abandon us?" Figgs questioned.

"They're taking them down one by one!" for the first time
in twenty-four hours, Dixon understood again what hope
meant.

Not long after, several URP soldiers discovered the dead
body, and by their body language Dixon guessed this man was
not the only one silently murdered in the night. The mutilated
men were obviously worried, they wore their concern on their
mutilated faces. One was mad enough to fire his AK-47 into
the jungle, hoping to kill something.

Ackerman appeared next, like a lurking bat-human
mutant, stumbling as if drunk. He was clutching his face as if
the mask pained him. Black ooze dribbled from beneath the
skin, his head was alive with wounds. It took every effort for
Skull-Face to hold him upright, leading him like an invalid to
Figgs. Wide-eyed with terror, the Englishman kicked,
screamed and swore.

"Not that one!" Ackerman's voice was pained, "he could be
useful too."

The next candidate was Tania, who too struggled against
the approaching attacker, knowing that there was nothing she

could except sway inefficiently and allow whatever horrors came next.

"Not her!" Dixon screamed. "Hurt her, and I promise you, you'll get no cooperation out of me. *Ever*!"

Ackerman turned, his body contorted with pain. "No?" He came close to Dixon, his single alien eye looked directly into his. "Perhaps you won't. What about this one?" He pointed to the still unconscious Corporal Vetch.

"Kill him, and I won't cooperate either."

The human mouth seen beneath the mask, rotten and black, smiled with evil intentions. "I don't believe you. You don't care about him anywhere near as much as you do about her."

Dixon flinched, closed his eyes against the pain of what he knew would come next. He didn't want to have to choose, he wanted to save them all. But he had made a promise.

"Who will it be? The corporal or the girl? If you don't answer, I eat her."

Dixon mumbled.

"What did you say?"

"I said shove your fucking mask up your fucking ass, Ackerman."

For a long moment Ackerman stood still, even though the knife-tendrils still danced over his head and face, releasing more of the obscene black tar. Then the ex-soldier threw back his head and boomed a horrible laugh. "Noble," he said finally. "I used to be like you, youngling. Believe me, though — nobility dies quickly in the jungle."

And with those words he turned away from the dangling form of Tania and lunged at the unconscious Vetch. Dixon couldn't watch. He'd seen enough horror these last twenty-four hours, enough for any lifetime. But because he'd seen the eating before, he knew what was coming. As the minutes dragged, the NSA officer kept expecting to hear Vetch's screams, but they never came. Perhaps his body had come so near to death during the night that he was oblivious to the final pain.

"Cut them down!"

It was Ackerman's voice that spoke strong, calmer now, that he had eaten. The ropes sliced, Dixon, Figgs and Tania fell to the muddy earth. Dixon's hands were still numb. As his blood flowed freely again, he felt sensation returning. Tania and Figgs thankfully seemed no worse than Dixon.

On the ground, Dixon looked again at Ackerman and the wooden monstrosity forever bound around his face. The former U.S. soldier seemed calm now, back in control. Did the mask require a blood sacrifice every morning? Dixon wondered, if Ackerman was denied his human food, would the mask instead turn upon him?

"Six?" Ackerman cursed, his question directed to Skull-Face. "Fuck!"

Dixon guessed this was the number of URP soldiers murdered during the night, and smiled.

"You think it's funny?" Ackerman stood over him.

Dixon confident again, looked upon the horror, its wooden pincers wild and agitated waiting for an answer. "Yep," he answered.

"What if I threatened to kill you, all of you now, do you think Peel would surrender?"

Dixon shook his head. "He'd lose everything if he did, giving himself up."

"I thought so." He pulled Dixon to his feet, "Time to move, my friend. Don't worry, it won't be for much longer. Tonight, you'll learn just exactly how you have been betrayed, just like your masters betrayed me all those years ago."

They were pushed forward, forced to march together as the cultist solders pressed ever onwards. Their captors chattered among themselves, more than they had yesterday. They were worried about the two soldiers still hot on their trail, Peel and Dunthorpe.

Later, Tania took the opportunity to get close to Dixon and whisper in his ear.

"You still going to save me from all this?"

"Of course. I promised, didn't I?"

"Good." Even though Dixon could see she was very terrified, Tania betrayed the slightest hint of a smile, "because I believe you now."

❅　❅　❅

Plenary secured himself a priority military flight from Maryland direct to an American base in Germany, where he boarded another priority flight, one that had delayed its schedule eight hours just for him, and took him direct to Nairobi. (The rest of the passengers were bound for Johannesburg.) It was a long and tiring flight, so when the NSA officer stepped into the U.S. Embassy by 0800 hours local time, he was exhausted as all hell.

"Alice Tumbas," the dark-skinned American woman assigned to him, shook his hand firmly.

"A name is okay, but who are you is more important."

"I'm the head of the NSA's East Africa operations. You said you wanted someone with African know-how. I'm the best there is, a second generation American with Ugandan parents. Strange how my mother and father fought so hard for a green card to escape their country, and here I am back in my ancestral homelands."

Plenary snorted. "Nice. Have you been briefed?"

"Briefed?" she smiled confidently. "I'm about to brief you, sir!"

She led him into their operations room, and from a laptop keyed up satellite imagery of the northeastern Congo, beamed onto the wall by the digital projector. In the room with them were the half dozen agents Plenary had requested for the assignment. They had been working round the clock with their counterparts in the United States, trying to figure out what the hell was going on.

"As you already know, we lost contact with Dixon's team twenty-four hours ago. That, combined with what we've learnt about Fargo's escape and massacre at the British hospital, makes us almost a hundred percent certain that the team has been compromised, and this was some kind of set-up."

"Set-up?" Plenary had nursed the same thoughts from the other side of the world. However he would wait until he absorbed what Tumbas had to say before he expressed opinions of his own.

"Yes. Dixon is supposed to call in every six hours, but has failed to do so the last four times. We suspect that the team has been captured by the URP, and that the rebels are taking the survivors somewhere specific that is important to their objectives."

"How do you know this?"

"NSA satellites," she zoomed the image closer, until the point of view was only a few meters above the earth. The scene was of a clearing in the jungle, of two soldiers, running and pointing westwards. Both men kept looking skywards, as if they expected to be seen. The time signature showed that these photos were taken only an hour ago. "That's former Major Harrison Peel, the other is SAS Sergeant Ewan Dunthorpe. We believe they are following a contingent of URP soldiers. While the URP are obviously smart enough to know that by remaining under the canopy they remain hidden from our satellites, Peel and Dunthorpe have taken this opportunity to tell us where they are."

"And the pointing shows us where they are headed?"

"Yes sir."

"Are we in contact with them?"

"Unfortunately no, the only radio with a strong enough signal, we believe, is likely in the possession of the URP."

Plenary nodded. The situation was worse than he thought. He'd had some interesting findings from the *Masked Messenger*, information he needed to get to the team soon. If he was going to reach Peel and Dixon, he would have to do so with short-range radios, assuming they still had theirs. "What do you think they want, the URP?" he asked.

"Sir, honestly, none of the scenarios we or Maryland have pulled together make sense. We're still looking, sir."

Plenary had an idea, but he couldn't share it with these people. If he told them all about gods and monsters, they would lock him up and throw away the keys.

"I need to be airborne, Tumbas. I need to be in a chopper over Congo airspace, so that when we find them again, I can reach them."

What he had to say, only Dixon or Peel would believe.

They'd come through miles of jungle at a forced march and Dixon felt that he probably shouldn't worry too much about whatever foul plans Ackerman had for that evening — at the rate they were moving, he'd be dead of exhaustion long before then. Finally, though, after numerous falls and blows from gun-stocks, Ackerman signaled for a stop and the three prisoners stood panting, sweat and water rolling off them, as heedless of the insects that landed on them and began to feed from their wounds as they were to their surroundings.

Finally, Ackerman made a gesture toward their guards, and the mutilated men prodded Dixon, Figgs and Tania up toward the front of their little column, the prisoners stumbling with groans through the mud until they stood near the towering figure of the mask-ridden Major.

"Look ahead," came the man's voice, and Dixon dragged his head up and stared forward through the trees.

Twenty feet before them the jungle opened up, and Dixon caught glimpses of clear sky through the trees; he thought for a moment that there was another clearing, but quickly saw that it was a ravine they neared, a great gaping gash in the earth that, if they maintained their present course, they would have to somehow traverse.

"Oh, good," said Figgs tiredly. "Now we get to climb down into the bloody Grand Canyon."

"There's a bridge," said Ackerman distractedly, turning in a slow circle, scanning the surrounding vegetation, "a fallen tree across the abysm."

Dixon thought about it for a second, then smiled.

It was a perfect place for an ambush.

And Peel and Dunthorpe were out there stalking them.

"If I only knew whether we got here first," wondered Ackerman aloud.

His second-in-command spoke rapidly in Lingala, and Ackerman turned to him and said "No!" in such a harsh voice that Tania was startled and began to tremble.

"If we send more men out to look for that bastard Australian, more men will die," said the American. "Look at us — we're down to twelve right now!"

"Unless Peel's already on the other side," said Dixon with as much cheer in his voice as he could muster. "He's doing pretty well right now, I think."

Ackerman wheeled and swung his spear at Dixon, and for one diamond-sharp moment the NSA man knew he was going to die. But it was the blunt end of the weapon that struck him in the gut, and though the pain in his midsection was intense and stabbing as he fell, he knew that he was still intact. He lay in the mud gasping, fighting to recover the breath that had just been stolen from him, and as he fought to look up he saw Ackerman's head and the chittering, writhing ebony mask not two feet from him as the Major bent over him.

"Just because I need you alive for a while longer," the man whispered, "doesn't mean that I can't inflict serious damage upon you."

"Why do you need me?" gasped Dixon. "Some kind of sacrifice?"

"I've got plenty of men to sacrifice when the time comes," said Ackerman, standing back up, hefting the spear and again gazing ahead at the ravine. "Plenty of men and one woman."

"Bastard," grunted Dixon.

"And if you don't give me just a little bit of cooperation, now," said Ackerman, "I'll see to it that every one of my men rapes the bitch in front of you before I kill her."

"Ooh," came a mocking voice, and Dixon whipped his head around to look at Tania Selby. She had stopped shaking, and stood there defiantly, staring up at the monstrous mask. "Rape. How will I ever survive that?"

Ackerman looked back at her, and his mouth beneath the mask twisted into a snarl. He leaned forward, and Tania shrank back, her defiance already starting to melt away. Dixon fought to his feet and stumbled over to her, but tripped and fell back into the mud as the bones in his chest shifted like broken crockery and his lungs screamed in protestation.

"You and I will go first, Ms. Selby," said the monster. And he reached out and grabbed the woman by her hair, easily swung her around and started marching her through the barrier trees.

The other URP men barked commands, and Dixon found himself lifted to his feet and frog-marched forward. With every step he felt his insides screaming in pain, but he managed to move with only a few inadvertent grunts and considered that a small victory.

And right now, he thought, *even small victories are worth counting.*

Figgs was shoved along beside him, and he heard the British agent cursing in a voice so spent and dead that he wouldn't have been surprised if the MI6 man just simply dropped — but they both retained their feet and finally made it to the bridge.

It was a massive tree of some sort that Dixon had never seen before; he wasn't a nature lover or a woodsman, and he'd grown up on the flat plains and cornfields of central Illinois and hadn't seen a decent forest until he was a teenager on a camping trip downstate. This jungle shit was so far beyond his ken that he couldn't even hazard a guess as to what the dead thing might have once been.

Ackerman placed the deadly-sharp head of his spear directly into the small of Tania's back and said "Move."

"I'll fall," she said. "Without my hands free."

"I suggest that you not fall," said Ackerman in a cold voice. "You're my shield, just in case the Major has beaten us across the bridge."

"Maybe I'll fall on purpose," she said, raising her head. "Then what will you do when the bullets come flying out of the jungle?"

Ackerman laughed in a voice even colder than his speaking tone. "Bullets will not kill me," he said. "Haven't you seen that?"

"They might knock your ugly ass down into the canyon, though," Tania said. "Maybe you can find some worms or something to cat down there."

"If you're going to kill yourself, do it now," said Ackerman exasperatedly, shoving the spearhead forward.

For a long second, Dixon thought she was actually going to do it. She tiptoed forward against the sharp pain in her back, and as they neared the tree it seemed as though she might just dart forward and plunge into open air.

No, he thought. *I promised you.*

But she instead climbed awkwardly up onto the log and took a tentative step forward. Ackerman leaped up behind her and turned to address his lieutenant.

"You'll be in the rear," he said. "After I go, I want three soldiers behind me, then Dixon. Three more, then Figgs. Then the rest of you. Understand?"

The soldier nodded, his skull-face glistening redly. The man gripped his machine gun tightly and turned toward the jungle they'd come from, waiting for the inevitable ambush.

"Fucking Peel's probably halfway back to Nairobi by now," said Figgs.

"You think so?" asked Dixon. "That's how you'd play it?"

"You still think you're a hero, don't you?" asked Figgs, shooting a tired look at his fellow prisoner. "You think you're somehow going to pull a miracle out of your ass and save the wench, kill the bad guy, and we're all going to go home and raise our glasses to another successful mission, don't you?"

"Peel's out there," said Dixon as they neared the tree. "He'll do something."

"And maybe Tarzan will come swinging through the trees and rescue us," said Figgs, stopping as his guards crossed the barrels of their guns before him. "I reckon either possibility is as likely."

And then Dixon fought his way up onto the wood. It was wet and slick, but the circumference of the dead tree was so wide that it was almost flat on top, and he had no real trouble taking careful steps along its length. Around him he heard the mocking calls of birds and monkeys, and jewel-bright insects darted from below, reflecting the first rays of sunlight he'd felt in what seemed like months.

The chasm below them was at least fifty feet deep, probably deeper, but it was hard to judge because it, too, was filled with vital, green foliage that disguised the bottom. Dixon felt a hot, wet breeze swirl around him from beneath as he advanced ten feet — twenty feet — across the bridge, and once his left heel slipped on a wet patch of some kind of moss and he pitched forward, knowing that he was going to fall off and plunge to his death.

But a strong arm ragged with oozing wounds caught him, and as he hyperventilated and shook, a black face smiled tooth-lessly at him. Finally getting control of himself, he shook off the man's support and took another step forward.

In the jungle, unseen, the troop of cultists and their prisoners were under observation.

"If I take Dixon out, they lose," said Dunthorpe into the radio, his gun aimed unswervingly at the form of the white man slowly, cautiously walking across the bridge.

There was silence from Peel, and Dunthorpe readjusted himself in the bole of the tree he crouched in, re-sighted his weapon.

Peel, not far away, thought about the man's statement.

For whatever reason, Ackerman wanted — *needed* — Dixon alive. And there he was, a perfect target on the tree bridge.

Ackerman and Tania had already gotten across the span, and Peel knew that time was running out if he and Dunthorpe wanted to do any damage here at the ambush spot. They could knock out another three or four of the URP, but perhaps they could deal more of a blow if they just shot and killed Jack Dixon; at the very least, Ackerman would have to abandon whatever plan he had for the American.

"No," he whispered into the radio. "Fucking no. I won't become that man."

"Sir?" asked Dunthorpe, his voice crackling on their short-range radios, picking up god-knows-what kind of interference from the trees and mist and mud of the Congolese jungle.

"We're the good guys, Dunthorpe," said Peel. "But we're running out of time. Start picking off those URP bastards, and do it now!"

"Not Dixon?" asked the SAS man, trying one more time to end the whole business.

"Not Dixon, or Figgs or Selby," said Peel grimly. "I'm not going to turn into a monster to fight monsters."

"Affirmative," came the voice of the Englishman, and it was a voice doubtful yet resigned. "Get ready for some fireworks."

"AUUGH!" came the whistling scream from beside Dixon, and he instinctively dropped to his knees, desperately wishing his hands were wired in front of him rather than behind his back, so he could drop prone without getting a faceful of wet wood.

And then as the blood spattered over him from the wounded soldier, he abandoned his scruples and dove into the tree, feeling the wood smack and dislocate his nose, gasping as the blood began to gush out.

The man's scream had lasted only half a second, had ended with a gargled choke, but as the dead soldier fell atop him gushing his life's fluids from the ragged, smoking hole in his neck, and Dixon heard the whole jungle grow instantly silent, as in response to the gunshot and the death cry.

And then that silence was shattered by the yells of the remaining URP and the cacophony as they unlimbered their guns and started firing back into the jungle.

Dixon struggled to turn, to see what was going on, and tried with his abused muscles to heave the corpse of the soldier off his back, but managed only to squirm out a bit from beneath it, gagging at the sight of the man's head hanging by only a few strands of gleaming meat and a dark stretch of skin — the sniper's bullet had gone through the man's neck, and somehow began burning. Dixon smelled the powerful tang of cordite, the scorch of singed flesh, and shook his head to clear the man's blood from his eyes.

"Figgs!" he screamed over the sound of gunfire, but the Englishman either couldn't hear him or couldn't answer, and Dixon prayed he hadn't gone over the side into the ravine.

"Sweet feathery Jesus," whispered Dunthorpe, hurriedly sliding down the bole of the tree from which he'd shot the URP man. He'd hoped to pick off more than just the one, but the monstrous, deformed men had been expertly trained and had almost instantly deduced his position and began firing. He dropped to the ground and scampered to his next nest, ducking as the leaves and branches above him danced and shuddered as the whining bullets blistered them — and then Dunthorpe slid into position, raised his scope again and focused on his next target.

Dixon finally rolled the dead man off, feeling a fierce glee as he watched the mutilated corpse, smoke wisping from the gunshot, teeter for one long instant on the edge of the log, then drop down into the green misty canyon.

He got to his knees just as the pair of URP soldiers behind him came sprinting up; one of them raked the jungle with his submachine gun while the other, a hulking creature with shards of steel transfixing his biceps and forearms like a demon's zipper, grabbed the American and began to swing him around, like a shield.

And the one holding the gun howled as bullets ripped through his legs and fine pink sprays of blood puffed out almost lazily into the damp air, howled and spun around, and for a second Dixon stared into the man's insane eyes.

And then another spray of blood from the soldier's face as the slug ripped through the back of his skull and came out directly under his left eye.

"Peel!" Dixon screamed delightedly. "You magnificent bastard!"

And then he was being dragged along the bridge by a strong arm around his neck, trying as best he could to dig his heels in so as to slow his captor's progress, hoping against hope that the man would slip and drop him, expose himself to the snipers behind — but he was weak and the URP man was strong and frightened, and they moved quickly.

Breathing through his mouth, his nose still pouring blood, Dixon saw Figgs being hustled along by the last few URP soldiers; one man shoved the MI6 agent forward while the others laid down a suppressing fire, blasting the jungle indiscriminately.

Dunthorpe slid down the slight hill and quick-crawled forward through the trees toward the crevasse. Bullets raged above him. He knew people tended to aim high when aiming uphill, and hoped his luck would hold.

He achieved his last position. "Peel?" he whispered into his radio.

"Nice shooting," came the voice.

"You ready for your turn?"

"I've got line-of-sight," responded Peel. "If you can kill any more, do it — if not, I'll take a bunch of them out when you're done." and then, suddenly, the squawk of static and a loud squeal from the radio. Dunthorpe winced and held the machine away from his ear, praying that the URP hadn't heard the feedback and zeroed him.

When no bullets closed on his position, he toggled the 'send' switch. "Peel? Peel, do you copy?"

No response.

"Peel, goddammit! Are you there?"

Silence except for the bullets still spraying from the log bridge ahead.

Shit.

He considered his problem. Peel might have been discovered — might have been killed. If so, their booby trap wouldn't be triggered, and the URP would be sure to wreck the bridge when they finally crossed, leaving Dunthorpe here on the wrong side of the chasm unable to continue to help the prisoners.

Shit shit shit.

His safest, best move, was probably to sit tight. He wouldn't be able to do anyone any good if he was killed. Perhaps he could wait until the soldiers were gone, then go back for more help.

"Right," he said to himself with a dour smile. And then after he'd arrived with the cavalry and found the dead bodies of

all his companions, he could go to sleep every night for the rest
of his life knowing he'd crapped out when the going got tight.

He thought about Peel, thought about the Major's words
to him — the rage the Australian felt at the cosmic insanities
that supposedly kept trying to break into the world, things like
the alien mask . . . things much worse.

"Into the valley of death," he whispered.

He smiled.

Stood.

Ackerman raged at the end of the bridge, raged and shook
his spear like Satan. Tania winced as she watched the carnage
unfold, as she saw the man dragging Dixon finally reach the
end of the log and heave the broken man down next to her. He
whoofed as he landed, struggled to get up, and was shoved
down by the hideous soldier guarding them.

Figgs was coming up fast, propelled by his troika of guards,
and in a matter of ten or fifteen more seconds they would all be
across. Ackerman was shouting rhythmically now, shaking his
spear like a talisman, and the whipping tendrils of the mask's
claws spun around as though they danced to his screaming
beat. It sounded like — like —

"He's casting some kind of spell," grunted Dixon. "We
have to stop him."

"Spell?" asked Tania. "You mean like magic?"

"Like the one he cast on your cameraman," said the
American bleakly. "But worse, I'm sure. Peel and Dunthorpe
are still back there, and Ackerman's probably going to blow up
the bridge or something."

"Quiet!" screamed the URP soldier, whipping down the
barrel of his gun to stick it into Dixon's face.

"Shoot me," said the American. "Fucking go right ahead,
you crazy bastard."

"Oh my god," breathed Tania, and Dixon spun around as
best he could.

There at the far end of the log bridge, a figure had appeared. A man, gun in hands, was firing as he ran, as he leapt from cover onto the tree and started chasing down the convoy of URP.

"Is that . . . ? asked Tania.

Dixon caught the glimpse of sunlight off a bald head, and felt his heart drop down into his stomach.

"It's Peel," he whispered.

Ackerman stopped his chanting for a surprised moment, then roared in triumph. He whipped his arms up even as the rest of the soldiers began to concentrate their fire on the solitary figure rushing toward them. Dixon and Tania were dragged back, out of the line of fire, by their captor. I'm valuable, thought Dixon disgustedly, sick with frustration and rage that he wouldn't even be able to witness his companion's death.

No. 'Companion' didn't cut it. Peel was a friend — the truest, best friend he'd ever imagined he could have. And his friend was making a mad, suicidal rush to do as much damage as he could before they ripped him to pieces, and Dixon wouldn't even be able to bear witness to the bitter end.

And then the world exploded.

"Stupid bloody Brit," sighed Peel. It had just been rotten, horrible luck. Just as he'd been getting ready to signal to Dunthorpe that the last phase of their ambush was in place and ready, he'd slipped and fallen, landing on the radio. It wasn't broken, but by the time he recovered the thing and shaken the mud off it, bent the antenna back into place, the SAS man had already begun his final run. "Damned cowboy bastard, what the hell do you think you're doing?"

But he knew what the man was doing. He'd done rather similar things in the past himself. Dunthorpe was going to get close enough and start firing at the bundle they'd hidden, hoping to detonate it. He must have thought Peel had been captured or killed, and was staking everything on this last, desperate gambit.

And there was nothing Peel could do. Nothing except for wait until Ackerman moved Dixon and Tania and Figgs out of the danger zone . . .

. . . Which happened even as the first of the URP bullets struck Dunthorpe. He jerked back, hit in the shoulder, and almost dropped his weapon, but after a second he leaned forward and bulled ahead. Another hit him somewhere in the torso, and he spun half around, but kept coming. Peel knew he was dead. Even if he made it another foot, another ten feet, he was a dead man running.

And Peel aimed the modified radio, prayed it hadn't been damaged too badly in the fall, and triggered it.

Figgs was too close to the hidden cache of explosives — two grenades Dunthorpe had jury-rigged together with a bundle of bullets and wired to a simple radio-activated detonator, the whole infernal device cached at the base of the bridge near where Ackerman stood — and was thrown forward when it went up with an air-flattening *whoomp* of sudden flame and deafening noise, staggering into Dixon and growling with frustrated pain. And then all of them felt the roaring heat of the blast wave, and Dixon squeezed his eyes shut against the hot fist that pummeled him, reached for Tania to try and cover her.

And then the other two grenades, carefully placed, exploded as well, and there was a triangle of fiery columns blasting up into the jungle, Ackerman in the middle.

He couldn't have survived that, thought Dixon, prayed Dixon. *Nothing could have survived such an inferno.*

With a groaning crack loud enough to be heard over the screams of the burning URP soldiers, the tree bridge shifted under the flames and carved a great divot out of the earth that held it — and then slowly fell, crumbling a huge portion of jungle floor down into the crevice with it as it went. Two URP men were on it as it fell — and the bald man in the middle of the bridge, of course, the man they thought was Peel, the man who had shaved his head with his knife the previous night because of the insects and the insane heat of the jungle, the man who had sacrificed himself in vain . . . Sergeant Ewan Dunthorpe of Tunbridge Wells in Kent, who had once thought of being a barrister but decided the work wasn't noble enough — they all fell into the chasm.

Ackerman roared again and strode out through the flames, his skin and the meat under it blistering from the furnace, that black tar slicking through his veins and bubbling up under the new wounds, salving them, slaking them, healing them, and Dixon thought he might go insane with the sight of the gargoyle heading toward them, but held onto one thought even as he felt the sharp stab of Peel's loss, even as he watched the monster gibbering and shifting and shaking that dreadful spear.

I promised Tania was that thought, and he waited for whatever would happen next to happen.

"What was it?" demanded Ackerman, reaching out for Figgs, slinging him up into the air with a smoking, napalmed arm. "You said nothing about rocket launchers, you sniveling weasel! What did Peel shoot at us?"

Dixon slowly turned and looked at Figgs dangling in the air. Tania had the same expression on her face he was sure he had — an expression of blank disbelief.

"Figgs?" he whispered. "You—"

"It wasn't on the chopper!" protested the Englishman. "Whatever it was, he didn't bring it with him! It was probably something Kazumu had hidden away."

"Those KLF idiots had nothing hidden away I didn't know about!" roared Ackerman, shaking the man in his fist like a rag doll. "What other surprises do you have for me, worm? Perhaps the woman has a nuclear bomb hidden in her bra?"

"No!" protested Figgs. "Jesus Christ, man! Put me down!"

Ackerman snarled and flung Figgs headlong into a nearby shrub, where the man landed with a whimpering crash. The ex-Special Forces soldier spun and whipped his spear around, aiming it at Tania. Dixon saw, on the man's belt, the long-range radio he'd been so concerned about back at the ambush, the black tar writhing around it yet leaving it untouched, and marveled at the strangeness, the blasphemous horror of what a man had become.

"On your feet!" howled Ackerman. "We will make our target by nightfall, or the woman dies in spite of your pitiful defiance!"

"How long has Figgs been working for you?" asked Dixon, not looking at the man trying to crawl out of the bushes.

Ackerman looked at him, and beneath the mask his filed-tooth smile grew wide. "Figgs doesn't work for me," he said, a dark chuckle in his voice. "We're partners — isn't that right, Agent Figgs?"

"Fuck you," groaned the Englishman, shaking his head groggily. "Now get this fucking wire off my wrists — you've blown my cover."

"Your cover?" said Ackerman incredulously. "Dear man — even now you think I'm going to keep my end of the bargain? Even after the hell you've been through the last couple of days? You seriously think I'm going to allow you any part of the glory that awaits me at the end of our road?"

Figgs stared at him for a long moment, trembling in pain, blinked twice, then nodded his head. "Yeah," he said. "I think you are."

"Oh?" asked Ackerman, cocking his head at the MI6 agent. "Why is that?"

"Because if you don't — Stand back!" he warned as Ackerman took a step forward. "All it'll take is a couple of words from me, and Dixon will know. . . ."

"Silence!" roared Ackerman, obviously wanting to lunge, to rip open Figgs' guts with the spear, but held back by some dawning realization.

"You wouldn't!"

"Go ahead and tell me," said Dixon quietly. "Whatever it is, tell me."

"Not yet," said Figgs watchfully, looking around. The blast had taken out the rest of the URP soldiers, only Ackerman and his mask surviving the flames that even now were beginning to die out around them in the damp, dank jungle. "I'm down to one card in my hand, and I'm not going to play it right yet, Yank. Now, Major Ackerman — how are we going to do this?"

"I should have killed you long ago," said the monster in the mask.

"Yeah, you should have, but you're not that bright," said the MI6 agent. "Tell you what — drop the spear where I can reach it, then step back."

Snarling, Ackerman did what he was told, though the single black eye in the center of the mask roiled and raged like a tornado in the dark teak of the mask.

Figgs slowly moved forward, watching Ackerman, watching Tania and Dixon who knelt helplessly in the mud and ashes, and maneuvered himself so that the wire between his wrists was against the sharp edge of the spearhead — and then in one smooth stroke his hands were free.

He picked up the spear and hefted it. "Nice weapon, Major," he said. "Magic?"

"No," said Ackerman.

"I believe you," said Figgs earnestly. "Really, I do. But I'm keeping this fucking thing just in case. I know how hard it would be to kill you — that Messenger's mask you wear makes you a tough hombre — but this spear looks like a nice thing to try it with, if I have to. Now — shall we get going?"

"You don't have to do this, Figgs," said Dixon, despair suffusing him like fever. "Whatever he's promising you—"

"It's not *him*," said Figgs, looking at the American. "It's someone much more powerful than this pathetic excuse for a cultist. It's Nyarlathotep."

"You're supposed to be defending Earth against this shit!" protested Dixon. "If you let the Chaos take over, the whole world dies!"

"Naw," said Figgs, twirling the spear in his hands. "This isn't the god himself we're releasing here — just one aspect of him. A powerful one, true, but one that can be harnessed, channeled, controlled. So long as you know the right spells. Which I do. And when this whole business is over, I'll be the most powerful man on the planet."

"You'll be dead," said Dixon flatly. "You can't succeed, whatever it is you're planning to do."

"Sure I can," said Figgs, smiling. "You're playing on the wrong side, chap; and I'm too old for all this idealism anymore. Now get your sad arse up out of the mud and let's get marching, shall we? We're almost in the last innings."

Peel watched in amazement as the events unfolded beneath him, wondering how he could have been so blind.

Ackerman had known about their mission — had set it up perfectly, planting Fargo where he would be found by Peel, knowing that they would come for him. And who happened to be right there on the scene in Nairobi?

Figgs.

Who happened to have a good relationship with the KLF, facilitating their insertion into the jungle?

Figgs.

Who managed to survive when everyone else around him died horribly?

"And who's lived way too long now?" whispered the Australian to himself, raising his gun, squinting through his scope at the spear-wielding form of Figgs.

At that moment his radio squawked.

"I'm near you," said Plenary, shouting over the noise of the rotors. "I can't get a fix on your GPS unit, though."

"That's because bloody Figgs must have screwed with it," whispered Peel, tucked into a hollow beneath some monstrous, drooping tropical bush. Ackerman and the rest of the band had moved along, but Peel wasn't a hundred percent sure that they hadn't circled around to check their back trail, so stayed as quiet as he could. "When the time comes, I'll figure out some way to make a signal for you."

"I've seen your style," said Plenary, his voice strong from the radio. "You'll probably set off a nuke."

"I'd like to," said the Australian. "What do you have for me?"

"A mess of conflicting information about the Spiraling Worm, consolidated from half a dozen ancient dusty books we've got in our Special Documents room, including that book you found in Marrakech last year, the *Masked Messenger*," said the NSA man. "Did you know; this mask has been around for centuries, a tradition of the cult of the Spiraling Worm? Whoever wears it, they call him Skunga-Zu, and he is their leader, chosen by Nyarlathotep and powerful beyond any human comparison. Their duty, to free the *real* aspect of their god, the Spiraling Worm! Bottom line — if this thing gets loose, we're going to have a hell of a time containing it."

"What's Ackerman planning?" asked Peel, cautiously raising his head and looking around. "Why does he need Dixon?"

"Hard to say," said Plenary. "It's probably something horrible, though — this Nyarlathotep thing is not a nice god. I'd appreciate it if you'd find some way to rescue my man, Peel."

"I'm working on it," grunted the Australian as he got to his feet. "Stay close. If you have to set down, do it, but keep an ear out for my squawk and be ready to get to me on a moment's notice." Peel wondered if there was a clearing nearby, a *bai*, or would Plenary just incinerate a patch of jungle for touch down?

"We've got two choppers fully loaded, Peel," said Plenary. "If you need a bunch of Hellfire missiles up Ackerman's ass, just let me know."

"It'll probably come to something like that," said the Major. "But I've got to get Dixon and the woman away first. I'll keep in touch."

"Good," said the American. "You're a fine soldier, Major Peel. I hope the Australians appreciate you."

"I blew up half of Sydney," said Peel, slowly beginning to move through the jungle, the stench of flame and death filling his nose. "I'm somewhere way below Ned Kelly on the popularity list."

The night came slowly, but it came.

They were an awkward procession — Ackerman and Figgs to either side of Dixon and Tania, the Englishman wielding the massive spear and the masked monster carrying his bloody knife, and no one talking. Dixon had continued to work on the wire binding his wrists, and he thought he might — might — be able to break the thing with one final surging twist, but knew that to do so now would be suicide; he couldn't accomplish anything in his current position except maybe to make a desperate lunge into the rainforest.

But that would mean leaving Tania behind, and he'd promised her he wouldn't do that.

All he could do was hope that a moment would present itself, some brief instant of time in which he could make a small bit of difference, grab a weapon, make a surprise attack, do something that would swing the balance of power away from the warped Special Forces soldier and the traitorous British agent.

And, though it was probably a false hope, he could imagine that Dunthorpe might still be alive, might have found some way to traverse the chasm they'd passed and might be hustling to catch up to them.

And, like Figgs had suggested, Tarzan might come swooping through the trees to rescue them.

"We're here," said Ackerman finally, as the sun disappeared through the curtain of green around them and as the jungle noises intensified. Dixon stopped when the rest of them did and even though he knew that he would die here, at whatever terminus Ackerman had determined for him, he still felt a surge of curiosity in his brain.

There, through the trees and the dim, monochromatic haze of dusk, he saw dark gray stone.

"H. Rider Haggard," said Figgs, casually tossing the spear up and down in his hand. "It's like the bloody movies, innit?"

"For centuries the Spiraling Worm has been imprisoned in the Temple of Akhnut," said Ackerman, a painfully intense desire limning his voice. "For centuries we have sought its release."

"Well, now you've got some competent help," said Figgs. "Let's get this shite done, shall we?"

"You won't win," said Dixon.

Figgs turned to him and smiled. "Jesus, man," he said, twirling the spear in his hands so that the razor-sharp head spun like a bore. "You're a regular Boy Scout, aren't you?"

"And you're a slimy sack of shit," whispered Tania. "You'll sell out the entire human race for thirty pieces of silver."

Figgs shook his head sadly and stopped playing with the spear. "Believe it or not, my lady, I wish you weren't here. I have no desire to see you die."

"Sorry I can't return the sentiment," said the woman, glaring at him. "I'd pay big money to have a front-row seat at your death."

"We move," said Ackerman. "Figgs — our moment of glory is at hand."

"Just remember, mate," said the British agent, "that I know the same spells you do. I won't hesitate to cut your head off if you try to fuck me over."

"We're partners," smiled the masked man.

And they moved through the final fringe of trees and entered the clearing of the temple.

It was a stunning edifice, even in the dying light of the sun, where the feeble red rays splashed on the vine-covered granite like a Hollywood special effect.

Dixon thought that Figgs had been right — it was something out of an Allan Quatermain novel, or an Indiana Jones movie. The surrounding trees were maybe forty or fifty feet tall, but the pile of stone and gold before them topped them by an easy two stories. The clearing leading up to the temple was crawling with creepers and vines, but no substantial vegetation grew there, nothing that would impede their view of the terrifying structure nor their path to it — and the high pillars gleaming with incarnadine bands of precious metals seemed monstrous spider legs, the dark, cavernous entrance to the pile seemed a fanged, venomous maw, the jutting slabs of marble and slate atop the building seemed bony horns that loomed menacingly in the dying light.

And as they moved forward the jungle grew silent, as though in terrified prostration before the alien, wondrous horror of the temple of Akhnut.

"It's Egyptian," whispered Tania as they were forced forward. "It's horribly wrong, somehow, but that's definitely an Egyptian design."

"Nyarlathotep was big in Egypt," said Dixon grimly. "I remember that from my research." He sensed that this was more than just the work of pharaohs. That the temple was far more ancient, built from materials that defied human explanation, constructed by the hands or the tentacles of the elder species from the stars, and that they had influenced the Egyptians, and not the other way around.

The four got closer, fighting their way through the field of obscenely bloated vines that snaked across the ground like intestines. There was a queer metallic odor to the whole place, a stench of copper and blood, and the air was as unmoving and still as an abattoir's.

Centered in the gargantuan building, socked in place by great slabs of weathered alien stone, was an enormous door — black wood beams twenty feet tall banded by verdigrised bronze straps as wide as a human body. Here and there on the wood, on the metal, were slight scorch marks or small slivers missing.

"That sooty area?" gestured Ackerman, waving his knife forward to indicate a handspan of discolored wood on one of the doors. "That was a dynamite blast."

"How much dynamite?" asked Figgs interestedly.

"Stacked four feet high against the door," said Ackerman, grimacing. As they got even closer to the temple, the toothed tentacles on the mask had begun waving frenetically, as though they sensed the proximity to their master. "The explosion destroyed most of the clearing and five of my men. It put a ding in the wood."

"Who sealed the temple?" asked Dixon in a voice broken by exertion and pain. The Major and the MI6 man turned to look at him.

"That doesn't matter," said Ackerman. "It was long, long ago, and the race of beings who trapped the Worm are long dead and damned."

"So here we are," said Dixon, struggling to stand up straight, to face death with at least a show of resolve and good posture — to stand like a man against whatever horror awaited him. "How do you open the doors?"

"With a ritual, of course," smiled Ackerman, showing his filed-sharp incisors through the dried blood on his lips, the mask's pseudopodia twirling and writhing in some obscene dance of glee. "Figgs, take Dixon to the temple steps."

Figgs nodded and moved toward the bound man. He poked the spear before him, its edge gleaming in a perfectly straight line of glowing red as the dying sun struck it. "Forward march, Yank. It's the end of the line."

"And what of Tania?" asked Dixon, trying to get some moisture on his lips, his tongue, but failing. "You said you didn't want to see her die."

"I'll deal with the woman," said Ackerman, sheathing the knife and moving toward the Australian journalist. "I won't kill her — I swear it. I'll just cast the same spell on her that immobilized her friends."

"Bastard!" yelled Dixon, stopping halfway through a step. "Do that, and I won't cooperate!"

"We no longer need your cooperation," said Figgs coldly, jamming the point of the spear into the small of the American's back. "Just your blood. Count yourself fortunate that the good Major doesn't make a light supper of your lady friend while you watch."

"Don't kill him!" said Tania suddenly. "If it's blood you need, take mine!"

Ackerman smiled toothily at her and shook his head. "Such nobility," he whispered. "Such self-sacrifice. You remind me of me when I was younger, before the Army fucked me over."

"Don't listen to her," said Dixon. "Let her go."

"I think not," said the Major. "But I'll make sure she doesn't interfere with the ritual. Kneel down, woman — when you freeze it'll make it easier for you to maintain your physical integrity."

"I won't kneel for you," she said, staring defiantly at him.

"Suit yourself," said Ackerman, and raised his hands preparatory to casting the spell.

And suddenly Figgs screamed in pain and spun around. Dixon whipped his eyes away from Tania to see what had happened and saw the spear fly from the Englishman's hand as his shoulder disintegrated in a spray of bone and blood.

Dixon didn't hesitate. He spun and leaped, wrenching his wrists in one desperate yank that sent the wire deep into his flesh — and snapped it! His endless hours of twisting and turning the biting metal had borne fruit, weakening the wire just enough, and for the first time in days he was able to swing his hands around to his front, weak though they were from inactivity and lack of blood. Snarling, he dove at the surprised form of Ackerman, grabbed the radio from the man's belt and rolled away.

Ackerman howled and swung one mighty fist, but Dixon was already stumbling through the vines away from the temple, finding the right frequency, clicking on the radio and screaming into it.

"Home delivery! Home delivery!" he yelled frantically. They'd be able to pick up on his coordinates from the GPS unit inside the long-range radio, and soon an American Hercules would be winging its way over the jungle to put a definite end to this obscenity.

"Roger," came the voice through the static and hiss. "Message understood."

Dixon reached down and smashed the radio on a protruding hunk of rock that jutted out of the jungle floor like an antediluvian behemoth's tooth, watched it shatter into five pieces, and stood back up. He turned around calmly, waiting for the knife that was surely coming to disembowel him. He was going to die, he knew — but he wasn't going to be the gateway that allowed some hideous monstrosity into the world to wreak chaos on the unsuspecting billions.

And Ackerman threw back his head and laughed. Figgs was still grunting in pain, collapsed to his knees while he poured blood onto the stone of the temple porch, and Tania knelt trembling and wide-eyed in the muck, but the masked Major roared in glee and triumph.

"You fucked up, boyo," gasped Figgs, raising his head. "This was his plan all along."

More bullets came from the jungle, then, whanging off the marble near Figgs and causing him to yelp as ricochets sent shards of biting stone into his face. He rolled off the raised area, threw himself into the underbrush, and the unseen sniper turned his attention to the howling, arms-raised form of Ackerman.

More holes appeared in the man, spurting black blood from his torso, his head. One bullet shattered the man's lower jaw, sending white shrapnel and bits of bloody flesh into the dim air, and Ackerman looked down at Dixon, ignoring the gunfire that raked him, and hissed through what remained of his mouth even as the black tar spilled from his veins to repair the damage.

"I haa woo," he said, and Dixon knew that he meant 'I have won" and felt his guts sinking down into his bowels as the implications of what he had done finally hit him.

And then Ackerman casually, deliberately reached down, grabbed Tania by the hair and lifted her to her feet. Dixon jumped forward, trying to stop whatever was going to happen, screamed, sprinted toward the tableau in an agonizing limp, but was too late.

Ackerman spun the woman around, bent slightly over and slashed the knife across the back of the journalist's legs at the ankles, sending blood spurting as she screamed in agony and tried to kick back. Ackerman dropped her then, and she stood for half a second and tried to get away — but collapsed as her ruined tendons failed her. "Bastard!" she screamed.

Dixon got to within ten feet and saw that the man's face had been nearly repaired.

"I the greatest Skunga-Zu. I'll let you all stay here," said Ackerman, smiling through a jumble of black oil, red meat and white bone, "and bear witness to the majesty that is our lord Nyarlathotep. Feel free to kill Figgs if you like — he'll certainly kill the both of you and whoever's shooting at us from the jungle given the chance."

Dixon staggered forward, tripping on a shard of masonry, a hump of vine, feeling his ribs chuckle against each other in his chest, trying to reach the man, trying to perform at least one final act of defiance by killing the bastard before the bomb got here, but knew he was doomed to failure.

Easily, Ackerman began to jog away from him, back toward the sheltering jungle.

Tania screamed and rolled, trying to get to her damaged feet and crumbling again beneath her severed Achilles tendons, falling to the ground in a bloody heap.

And, as Ackerman just got into his stride, handily leaping over obstacles and dodging rocks in his way, Dixon watched as a lazy silver flash came from the temple, curved through the air, and slowly descended on a perfect trajectory, smiting Ackerman in the back of the head.

Figgs had recovered and thrown the spear.

Peel sprinted out from cover, gun hot in his hand, knowing that he couldn't do anything more from his distance than inflict superficial damage on the monster in the mask and knowing that Ackerman would get away no matter what he did, but wanting to reach Dixon; he knew the American wouldn't leave the woman to die.

He sympathized. Dixon had a soft spot for her, and he would suffer the torments of hell rather than leave her to her fiery fate. But it wasn't making things easier, this altruism.

And then he saw the spear throw, and even though he'd tried to kill Figgs (and was still cursing himself for missing on the headshot that hit the British agent in the shoulder) he mentally applauded the man's accuracy under pressure.

Ackerman crashed to the ground, the spear sticking up from him like a conqueror's flag.

Dixon cursed himself as he stumbled by the wounded Australian woman for leaving her in her agonies, but knew that it was more important that he reach the downed Special Forces man.

Figgs groaned and collapsed again into the creepers, bushes and insects of the African floor.

And Ackerman, who had hitherto produced a stunning range of sounds from screaming victory to flat-out, pissed-off rage, now emitted a steam-kettle whistle of keening agony that almost caused Dixon to pause, as though the noise was a physical blow coming at him through the thick air — but he kept coming, staggering on his abused legs, breathing through his exhausted lungs, wanting only to commit murder before he died.

Ackerman screamed again as Dixon neared, and writhed beneath the silvery shaft of the spear like a bug on a killing board. The knife he'd been carrying was feet away, shining dully in the underbrush, having been thrown from his hand by the missile's impact, and Dixon veered toward it. Tania had quieted, and in the breaths between Ackerman's outbursts the American could hear someone — Dunthorpe, evidently — crashing through the foliage towards them all, but didn't turn; his attention was wholly focused on the knife.

At least until, with one final banshee howl, Ackerman surged up from the ground, forcing his body up onto the shaft of the spear in quick, excruciating jerks — raised his face toward Dixon — gave one wide smile, black tar pulsing from his bloody mouth in vomitous gushes — and Dixon found himself staring straight into that black onyx eye.

The eye stared back at him — gleamed brightly, focusing on him — and then the mask leapt.

Peel saw Ackerman pulling himself up the spear, impaling himself further with every inch, loosing his bowels through new vents in his abdomen in spilling coils, desperate to reach his maximum height before he died, and the Australian forced himself to run faster. He saw Dixon swaying, stumbling towards something in the dirt, saw the journalist Tania Selby trying desperately to bandage some wicked wounds at her ankles with the muddy, bloody remains of her blouse, couldn't see Figgs at all — but then all attention flew back to Ackerman.

The mask's tentacles had gone wild with the attack, waving and whipping like electricity shot through them — but then they stilled and tensed, and Peel instinctively skidded to a halt, his boots squelching in the soft dirt and stone, and raised his rifle.

The black mask shot from Ackerman's head straight towards Dixon, and even as Peel fired a wild blast — missing the thing entirely — he saw Ackerman, finally, at last, bareheaded.

The parasite, symbiote, whatever the mask was, had eaten through Ackerman's scalp during its long residence there, stripped the top half of his head to bare, gleaming bone. Long black cracks through the cranium showed where the thing had fixed itself to the man, and the hideous, empty eye sockets seemed to stare at the Australian though the eyes had long been atrophied or eaten away — and in that last instant before death finally caught up to Major Charles Ackerman, Peel stared straight into the empty cave of the man's skull, straight through the void and at the stark bone of the back of his head. . . .

Ackerman slumped — jerked — and slid down the shaft of the spear again, red blood already clumping and clotting with the final dribbles of the black tar now dead and inert, his years-long mission, for better or worse, at an end.

Dixon wasn't sure how he managed to find the strength to move so quickly, nor how he managed to whip his exhausted arm up so precisely, nor how he kept his sanity as the insane monstrosity lunged through the air at him, tentacles vibrating in keening eagerness, the ebony eye wide and hungry, the alien wood of the thing already shifting, ready for a new host.

But he ducked and whipped his hand up, smashing the thing off its trajectory and sending it whizzing down into the ground, and the mask's teeth raked his palm and thumb as he touched it and bright red blood instantly welled up in razor-sharp lines.

Dixon spun toward the thing, readying a desperate stomp, but it had bounced instantly from the earth and thrown itself back into the air with no turnaround time, aiming directly at the American's head again.

Dixon yowled and hurled himself to the side, and the mask smacked into his shoulder, where it clung with the desperation of a drowning man and the hunger of a vampire. The NSA agent felt the thing's claws digging deep into the meat of his chest, his neck, and frantically grabbed it with his free hand as it scrabbled up toward his face.

And then there was a monstrous thunderclap from directly behind him, and in the midst of his terror and pain and desperation he thought *it didn't take long for the chopper to get here and at least it'll die with me* and, finally, *I'm not dead*.

The mask didn't shatter under the burst of bullets, but it lost its grip on Dixon and flew backwards, hitting the ground in a whirling spin. Again it bounced, again instantly leaped toward the man.

But this time Peel had the range and the aim, and he shoved Dixon out of the way and fired a full withering barrage at the mask as it jumped, and this time chips of black, bleeding wood flew from it, several of the tentacles were severed and sprayed ebon ichor as they withered and died, and the mask went back down, skittered hesitantly under the rain of high-velocity bullets . . .

. . . And then shot away, scurrying into the undergrowth, flinging leaves and dirt up into the air as it bee-lined away from the bite of the lead, the pain of the Australian's weapon, and as Dixon grabbed his injured shoulder and stared wild-eyed and joyfully at Peel, the mask screamed, an utterly alien howl of loss and rage and insanity, a low-pitched thrum of discordant, dissonant noise that shook the jungle.

And then it was gone.

"Peel!" said Dixon, blood oozing from between his fingers. "I thought you'd died!"

"There's still time," said the Australian grimly, looking around. "What did I miss? What was the play with the radio?"

"Oh, shit," said Dixon, his grin disappearing. "I called in the airstrike — the copter ought to be here soon."

"Good," grunted Peel. "The MOAB should take care of this temple."

"It's what they wanted," said Dixon, moving as fast as he could toward Tania. "They've been trying to open that door for hundreds of years, but never had enough power to break it."

Peel paused for a long moment, looking at the temple and its massive, impervious doors. As the implications sunk in he shook his head in dawning understanding and frustrated helplessness, and he said "Oh, fuck."

"Let's get out of here," said Dixon, reaching the woman. "There's no way we can stop the thing now, and all we can do is not be here when the explosion happens."

"Wait," said Peel, reaching for his short-range radio. "There might be something we can do."

❊   ❊   ❊

"We'll give it a shot," said Plenary. "But this is a big fucking jungle we're flying over, and I have no idea where you are. The chances of us intercepting the bombing Hercules are virtually nil."

"Remember I told you I'd find some way to signal you?" said Peel, his voice tinny over the radio.

"Yes," said Plenary, scanning the endless carpet of green below. It was nearing full dark now, and it was hard to see anything other than an undulating sea of treetops.

And then a flare some dozen miles to their left, a sudden explosion that pulsed beneath the treeline, yet was still bright enough to see, and the chopper pilot banked into a sharp turn and made for it even as it disappeared back into blackness.

"You see that?" asked Peel.

"We're on our way," said Plenary grimly.

"Good," said Peel, "because I'm now officially out of ammo and there's a fucking alien parasite running around down here looking to eat our brains."

"You field agents have all the fun," said Plenary. "Hold tight — we'll be there in two ticks."

"Just get here before the bomber," said Peel. "You get us out of here, I'll let you go on the next field mission."

"Deal," said Plenary. "And, Major Peel?"

"Yeah."

"Good job."

"Where the fuck are you, Figgs?" yelled Peel, stepping away from the smoldering, smoking blast pile. He'd been frantic with a machete, cutting back the small tries on hope of widening the landing zone, and to protect against the mask, wherever it was. "We're getting out of here, and if you're not with us you're going to die!"

"He thinks he can control it," said Dixon quietly, wrapping the bandages even tighter around Tania's slashed legs. She'd finally passed out from exhaustion and blood loss, but she still breathed shallowly and her eyes fluttered beneath her lids. "He's been studying up on spells, and when the bomb blasts open the door he's going to try to bend the Worm to his will."

"Fucking idiot," fumed Peel. "Figgs! I swear to you, you asshole, that I will hunt you down and kill you if you don't show yourself right now!"

"He's not going anywhere," said Dixon. "Listen!"

Peel stilled himself and stood silently — and in the jungle night he heard the distant whump of a helicopter's rotors. And then he realized there were two vehicles, rapidly nearing their position.

"Plenary's here first," said Peel. "He said there were two choppers."

"Good," said Dixon. "Peel, we've got to get into the sky right now — we can't waste time looking for Figgs. If we stop the bomb from dropping, we can find him later — if he makes it out of the jungle alive. But we can't do anything if we're fucking dead."

"Understood," said Peel, still looking around as though the missing MI6 man would pop into view.

And then the searchlights came looping through the trees, and Dixon and Peel began waving their arms to direct the rescue.

❋　❋　❋

"You don't know the frequency, Dixon?" asked Plenary once they were all back up in the air.

"It was a one-time message," said the agent, wincing as one of the soldiers smeared antibiotic paste over his myriad wounds. He'd taken his shirt off and Peel shook his head at the bruises, cuts and swells of cracked ribs that showed through his partner's skin. It was amazing the bloke remained conscious, let alone retained the ability to move — but adrenaline was like that. As for Tania, she was passed out in a stretcher, with equal attention directed to her wounds, and a blood transfusion in the works. Later on, if they all survived the night, Dixon would probably sleep for twenty hours.

If they survived the night.

"C'mon, man," said Dixon to his boss. "You know the procedure as well as I do. Once the order's given, there's no way to call the run off, 'cause they've gone dark. We'll have to somehow maneuver in front of them and get them to divert."

"I'm not going to fire on an American gunship," said Plenary, shaking his head.

"You might have to," said Peel. "If that bomb drops, and Figgs can actually control the god that emerges—"

"What the hell kind of mission is this?" asked the airman working on Dixon, raising his eyes to the Australian. "You're talking about shooting down a friendly? And what's this about a god?"

"I'm not suggesting that, but we need to get in their way," said Peel. "Besides, if that thing gets out, nothing between here and Lagos is going to survive through the night."

"I think I've got 'em, sir!" came the voice of the pilot from the cockpit, excitedly. "Bearing one, one, five!"

"Light everything up!" said Plenary. "I want spots aimed right for the Hercules, I want shots across her bow, I want fucking missiles exploding all over the place — we need to make them stop and call us."

"I'll do what I can, sir," said the pilot, flipping on both spotlights and swiveling them toward the distant bulk of the bomber helicopter. Fifty feet off their starboard side, the other Apache did the same, and Dixon forced himself off his seat and leaned toward the window.

❃   ❃   ❃

Figgs breathed deeply, ignoring the pain from his shattered shoulder, ignoring his bruises, his cuts, the agony in his bowels. He focused on the words in his mind, focused on them so sharply that they began to crystallize, to take solid form.

Around him the jungle grew silent, though there was plenty of noise from the aircraft that circled overhead — but he put that out of his mind as well. It was bloody crunch time now — he'd gotten this far, come this long, dealt with maniacs and monsters and madness, and it was about time to start collecting a little long-overdue back pay.

"Nyarlathotep," he started, beginning the invocation. "Great Wanderer, Masked Messenger, Seeker Between the Stars, hear my words."

And with a rumbling scream the mask flew from the darkness-shrouded jungle and latched onto Figgs' face.

You wanted my answer, came the voice inside Figgs' head as he was smothered, *here it is!*

❋   ❋   ❋

"What the fuck?" screamed the Captain of the Hercules. "Are we under attack?"

"They're not aiming at us, sir," said the young Air Force sergeant. "But they're using a lot of firepower."

"Who the hell are they?"

The Captain swerved into a ponderous turn as the night sky around them rippled with firework explosions, but quickly locked back onto the coordinates. The choppers dancing around him looked American, they flew as though Americans piloted them, and the display of firepower was ferdamnsure American — but there was an outside chance, the slightest, most minuscule stretch of possibility that the Congolese rebel group they were here to eradicate had gotten their hands on a couple of Apaches and learned how to fly them, while the mission was a no-abort. So he kept flying, kept searching for the laser signature he was supposed to drop the MOAB onto.

"I don't know sir," said the Sergeant, looking up from his headset, his face mottled red and white from the exploding ordnance outside the Hercules' windows. "We're supposed to be the only bird in the air right now."

In response, the Captain grunted. "No laser signature, but I found the target," he said. "Strap in and get ready to drop the Mother."

"And the other choppers?" asked the sergeant. The other soldiers in the Hercules waited for an answer.

"We can't take 'em out," said the Captain. "But they can't stop us."

❋   ❋   ❋

"Jesus," said Dixon, watching as the huge form of the Hercules whipped past them toward the temple clearing. "They're not stopping."

"Well," said Plenary, "they're not supposed to."

"Shit," said Peel. "How do we keep them from dropping that bomb?"

"That's what the pilot of the other Apache keeps asking us," said Plenary, gesturing toward the cockpit and the loud squawking chatter of the radio. He had to keep his voice at horribly loud volume, because the explosions outside spoke in thunderous voices, as if intoned by God.

"Shoot him down," said Peel. "Cripple them so they're forced to land."

"Our weapons aren't that accurate sir," said the Captain of the other Apache, overhearing them. "A crippling shot is more likely to destroy than anything."

"Shit," exclaimed Peel grimly, "what about getting in their way, and forcing them to baulk?"

"Do you know how dangerous that is," said the pilot of their Apache, turning back to his instruments.

And Peel flashed back to the jungle, to Dunthorpe's voice coming over the short-range to him, asking for permission to shoot Dixon and end the whole mess. Such an act would have finished the business — without Dixon's memorized code phrase, the Hercules would still be back in Kenya sitting on the pad, the bomb in her belly harmless, her crew drinking bad coffee and chatting about the baseball season.

But it would have made Peel a monster.

"Aw, shit," he said, closing his eyes.

"Tell you what we'll do," said his pilot, and went into a dive.

For a long couple of seconds the explosions ceased, and the Captain of the Hercules saw the two Apaches dart past him toward the target.

"What are they doing?" he asked, not expecting an answer. He'd flown combat operations in the mountains of Afghanistan so he was used to tension and pressure, but now he found himself facing a more formidable opponent — confusion.

"They're getting between us and the target," said the radio man, looking down at his panel.

"And they stopped shooting at us." said the Captain.

"They weren't shooting at us," said the sergeant. "They were shooting around us."

The Captain thought for a moment, conscious that they were only seconds away from the drop point. The other aircraft sure weren't acting like enemies.

But it didn't matter.

"Prepare to drop the Mother," he said, and behind him the bomb team began their countdown.

"Now what?" asked Dixon as they hovered. Beneath them, he could feel the eldritch force of the temple of Akhnut radiating out, as though it sensed the power that would crack it open and welcomed it — it was as though some primal radiation surged and ebbed, the breath of a cyclopean monster eagerly waiting for release, and Dixon shook his head to clear some of the oppressive miasma away.

"We can only hope we call their bluff," said Peel.

"Bloody right," said the pilot, smiling at his Australianism. "But I don't think they'll drop the bomb right on top of us."

And then they all saw the bomb falling from the womb of the Hercules, an ink-black blob in the African night.

"Bombs away!" shouted the bombardier, and the Hercules instantly whipped into the sharpest turn it was capable of and gunned its engines for escape as the drogue chute deployed and then instantly released, guiding the MOAB bomb down to its rendezvous with the spot Dixon's GPS unit had painted during its final transmission.

"And may God have mercy on my soul," said the Captain. He knew he had made the right decision, the proper decision, the legal decision.

But he tasted ashes in his mouth.

"Move!" screamed Plenary, trying to leap to his feet, grunting as he hit the restraint belt, and the Apache moved.

Dixon thought at first that they were getting out of the way, that the helicopter would dart from the falling bomb and that they had lost — but he hadn't counted on the professionalism, the patriotism, the heroism of the Air Force men who controlled the beast.

They moved, all right — but they moved underneath the falling bomb.

The other Apache did the same, and it was closer.

For long seconds it was silent, barring the whump of the rotors and the ragged breathing of the men, and Dixon leaned out, straining his eyes in the dim starlight to see what was happening, and he thought he saw the collision when it happened, but he wasn't sure.

And then a strange, horrifyingly loud clanging noise filled the African air as the MOAB bomb, all thirty feet and twenty thousand pounds of it, struck the whizzing Apache in one of its turbo shaft engines, knocking the thing clean off.

As the helicopter sputtered and tried to recover, whirling in the air like a pinwheel, the bomb continued along its descent, though its trajectory had been fractionally altered. It took only another second or two, and then Dixon slammed back against his seat as the whole sky lit up like Armageddon.

❉   ❉   ❉

Figgs knelt on the marble steps before the gigantic wooden door and looked through the Messenger's Mask. The claws on the thing's tendrils had already sunk themselves into the thin meat of his scalp and he could feel them tickling his brain as they gently waved, slowly insinuated themselves into his prefrontal cortex. It had already eaten out his eyes, but he could still see, through its single black orb.

He could also feel his body changing. His shoulder had been shattered by Peel's bullets, but the bones were already knitting themselves together and his veins were beginning to fill with the thick black fluid that was the communion wine of this unholy sacrament. He knew that he would rip himself apart for as long as he wore the mask to keep the thing's powers at full strength — that he would cut holes in his cheeks, would rip ragged gashes in his flesh, would impale himself, slash himself, rend himself. . . .

He reached down and tore another wet slab of meat off Ackerman's body, shoved it hungrily into his mouth, began to chew.

Good, spoke the voice from the mask, *this is only the beginning*. . . .

It wouldn't be long now, and his master would be free.

❋ ❋ ❋

"Did it hit?" screamed Dixon. "Was the temple hit?"

"I can't bloody see," yelled Peel at the window. "I had my eyes open when it happened."

"It came close," said the Captain, looking at his instruments. "But I think it was off by a hundred yards or so."

"Is that close enough?" wondered Plenary, squinting as the light died and the darkness rushed back in to fill the empty space, though the plume of smoke and fire from the explosive still roared through the night like doomsday. "Was the Crawling Chaos released?"

And then another explosion as their sister Apache finally lost its struggle with gravity and inertia and crashed as well.

Figgs felt the blast of the GBU-43/B as though it were the Rapture — whirling in the great conflagration, greedily accepting the buffeting and thin aluminum shrapnel as though it were a benediction.

Before him, in the hellish light and unearthly energies of the bomb, the door to the temple creaked and twisted, and smoke instantly rose from its black surface and flames began to lick the edges of the massive slab, and then one of the studded bands burst, the iron white-hot and dripping as it dissolved, and the barrier gate of the Spiraling Worm creaked open an atom's width — a hairsbreadth — half an inch.

Above, in the surviving Apache, Dixon grabbed his head in agony as the vision flooded his mind — the whirling chaotic swirl that gibbered and howled just beyond the gateway: stars, planets and constellations spinning in insanely rapid combinations, light and darkness attacking each other in supernova intensity, lines of force clashing in galaxy-melting conglomerations of sound. He felt his body somehow separate from him, the hands of Plenary and Peel keeping him upright as the maelstrom raged in his head. He fought to maintain sanity, to keep his eyes on the chaos that was beginning to spill from the wedge between our world and the infinite worlds of Nyarlathotep.

Figgs exulted, blood spilling down his lips and chin, flesh half-chewed spraying from his mouth as he danced in the nuclear fire of the end of the world. In the blinding light he saw a figure moving towards him, a black, wavering line of matter that spun in slow helices through the endless, churning cauldron of white fire.

The Worm moved fast — vast chunks of space-time disappeared beneath its approach, atoms screaming as they dissolved, seconds stretching into hours, chains of stars exploding before the path of the Messenger of the Gods. Figgs knelt before it, all spells fleeing his mind, all cantrips and catches meant to imprison the outer god forgotten in the insane joy of the Mask at the approach of its Master.

And then the door began to render itself shut again.

The MOAB bomb, had it hit directly where it was supposed to, would have blown the gate wide open, as Hitler's panzers had blown open the Maginot line — but that extra distance made all the difference. The non-men who had built the door had built with skill, dedication and desperation, and though trees burned half a mile away under the force of the American bomb, though the black sky was choked with smoke and flame and death, though the clearing before the temple of Akhnut looked like Hiroshima — yet the gate managed to hold against the forces assailing it from each side. Meanwhile, the jungle was an inferno, lighting up the night like day.

A crack a half inch wide slowly closed — to a slit the breadth of an assassin's wire — to a cell's full of molecules — and before the howling chaos beyond the gate was again locked away, hurricanes of screaming air being sucked in by the god's rage and disappointment, Figgs saw the worm unloop itself, straighten into a filament wider than the sky and peer down at him from a black, featureless face as big as a universe.

Forever. . . . a voice echoed in his head, a voice so awful and squealing and impossible that he sank to his knees and the rest of his brain instantly collapsed beneath the force of the insane strengths that pummeled him.

And the mask echoed that voice as it slurped up the rest of the British agent's brain and propelled the man backwards into the infernal fire of the jungle.

Forever. . . .

❋   ❋   ❋

"Forever," said Dixon, blinking back the light.

"What?" asked Plenary.

"It'll never give up," said Dixon, forcing his eyes open, watching the flames beneath them flicker in the wet jungle as though they were napalm-fed. "It'll never quit, and now it's got a strong tool."

"Fucking Figgs, right?" asked Peel.

"He's smart, he's tricky, he knows how to make things happen," said Dixon, scowling. "And the mask will drive him on until that thing manages to find a way out."

"Or we find a way to seal the whole thing off forever," said Peel, staring out the window at the red and orange flowers that slowly faded behind them as the Apache chuffed its way back toward Uganda. "We're not going to let the world go up, mate."

"I know," said Dixon, remembering the images that had assaulted him for the brief span of seconds the door had tried to blow open. "I know."

❋   ❋   ❋

Morning light welcomed the surviving Apache. Its long journey home, passing between the misty shrouded peaks of the Mountains of the Moon, was taking them back to where it all began. Peel was exhausted, Dixon looked the same, but neither man could sleep. They were wired, like coiled springs trapped in a tight box. Only the sunrise was beautiful, over the African homelands and mountainous forests, and it reminded Peel that there were still good things in the world worth fighting for.

"What did we achieve?" Plenary asked, sucking on his water canteen, fighting the sweat that poured from his skin. "I mean, what's different?"

"Nothing," said Peel.

"But it could have been worse," countered Dixon, grimacing against his many wounds that still hurt whenever he moved. "The Spiraling Worm could have gotten free."

Peel forced a grin. "You know what, though? Look at us. As a species we develop weapons, more and more powerful weapons each year, and for the first time in our history, we now we have the capacity to release monsters like the Worm, that before were forever locked away from us."

Dixon looked over at Tania, still attended to by the soldier-medic. The young man smiled to say she was doing fine, and Peel could see the relief on his friend's face. "But we stopped it Peel, you have to remember that. We did good today."

With a nod, Peel understood the NSA man was right. "But we can do better."

"How?"

"We can learn from today. We can build a team."

Plenary straightened himself, his eyes wide with attention. "What are you suggesting, Major?"

"We need to get smart. We need to get organized. I know for a fact that the U.S. government has been studying alien intrusions since the 1930s: New England, and recently Antarctica and the Great Sandy Desert in my home country to name what I know, but that's all they do, study. Also, Plenary, your counter-alien intelligence group does nothing more than monitor projects within these sites. If we've learnt nothing else this week, we've learnt that cosmic intrusions can strike from anywhere, in any corner of the globe. We need to build a team, one that scours the planet daily, finding out where the hot spots are, and putting down these threats before they occur."

Plenary's mind was ticking, as if imagining the clout they'd require to get such a group into action.

Dixon meanwhile grinned at the idea. "You mean a team of our own 'special forces' trained to go up against these horrors?"

"That and intelligence as well, which Dixon, you'll run. I'll run operations, and Plenary, sir, you oversee the whole group. You'll be our boss, my boss if you don't mind an Aussie in the team."

"I didn't like you when we first met, Major, but you've got my respect now." Plenary livened to the idea, "And I can see now that your idea could work. We'd need a huge black budget, and independent offices to work out of, away from the day to day operations in the NSA who might get suspicious of what we're up to."

The Australian nodded, "And we need good people, lots of them. Soldiers and spooks alike, hired from wherever we can find them. Talented people who know the truth about what lies beyond the veil, who passionately want to stop their return."

He stared out at the pink-red sky, remembered his early days in the Australian Infantry keeping the peace against despots in Somalia. There was a day three months in, after a particularly bloody battle that saw huge casualties on both side, and he wondered what the hell he was doing there, if their presence really did anything good. Then he had stumbled onto a group of Somali boys playing soccer, and they asked him to joined in, laughing and playing as they did, forgetting their troubles if only for one single hour. It had been one of the most memorable hours of his life, a day he remembered fondly, seeing the spirit in the boys' faces even when they had nothing but a ball and four sticks. Most important of all, they felt safe under the watchful eye of his army. He never questioned his dedication ever again.

This was the same. Africa was beautiful. The world was beautiful, full of people who cared, loved, thrilled and lived fulfilling lives. He would do whatever it took to make sure it stayed that way. "So, what do you think? Plenary?"

The NSA man nodded, "We'll get started as soon as we get back."

"And you Dixon?"

His friend laughed, "I'm in too, Peel, but I'm having a whole week off first." He looked over at Tania, who at last appeared to be resting peacefully. "Jessica's waiting for me, and we got some important catching up to do first."

AFTERWORD

David Conyers & John Sunseri

ollections like this one often come together through amorphous origins. How did two writers who've never met, who live at opposite ends of the world and don't share conducive time zones, come together a write a series of interconnected stories?

They run into each other's stories and like them, and write to each other to say so.

Before any of this collaboration nonsense came about, David and John shared space in *Horrors Beyond*, a wonderful collection from Elder Signs Press, and John then hunted down a few other Harrison Peel stories. He also read *Hive*, a terrific book by Tim Curran that's a sequel to Howard Philip Lovecraft's *At the Mountains of Madness*, and wondered where the hell the shoggoths were.

So he decided he'd try to provide the answer.

Mr. Curran was extremely gracious in his permission to let John mention his people and places, and when it became obvious that the shoggoths, if freed, would hit Australia first, John decided to see if he could borrow Major Peel for a few paragraphs as well.

And the conglomeration of all these elements turned out so fun and exciting that David decided to write a sequel of his own to "Resurgence", borrowing John's Jack Dixon.

Well, things got interesting after that. We'd already linked a couple of tales, and maybe we could go even further, write some back-stories, connect everything into one great inter-linked collection . . . but we needed to provide a tale that would end the whole experiment on a grand note, so we decided to write it together.

David came up with the plot, and together the two of us dove into "The Spiraling Worm" with enthusiasm and energy, and we figured it would take about ten, maybe twelve thousand words to tell it. Twenty thousand words in, and still miles away from the ending, we threw up our collective hands, shrugged our collective shoulders and decided, hell with it, tell the story our minds and skills demanded be told.

We hope you enjoy the project. If you did, we've got plans for the next one that are going to knock your socks off.

"Made of Meat" was originally written by David for the gaming magazine *The Black Seal*, edited by Adam Crossingham, which used as its base the successful Call of Cthulhu licensee role-playing game *Delta Green* written by John Tynes, Dennis Detwiller, and Adam Scott Glancy. Delta Green provided some intelligent and thought-provoking ideas on the whole spies versus the Mythos genre, and because it was done so well, spawned a committed fan base that is still strong today. "Made of Meat" ultimately didn't end up in the maga-zine and was never integrated into the *Delta Green* setting, but it did spawn some gaming-related articles. This version has been significantly revised and expanded, and now sits squarely in Peel and Dixon's world view of the Cthulhu Mythos.

"To What Green Altar" was John's attempt to backtrack and describe how Dixon came to be involved in the Mythos in the first place. We also noticed that, in all our other stories, we'd set adventures in six of the seven continents and somehow neglected Europe. So John grabbed hold of the Tunguska Event, decided to throw in Vatican City, and found that August Derleth's wonderful creation Cthugha would be a great way to link everything together.

The first Harrison Peel story ever written was "Impossible Object". The idea came from the title of a Third Eye song, a progressive 1990s techno band headed by Australian composer Ollie Olsen. The lyrics just kept saying over and over again, "impossible object", and it left David wondering what exactly would an impossible object be? Then once the story found its definition, the impossible object held no purpose. Only when it became a terrorist was an ending was found.

"False Containment" is a direct sequel to "Impossible Object". The idea came from reading Stephen Hawkings, Edward Witten and Albert Einstein, and how space and time really isn't the sum total of everything in our universe. It came as a surprise that when Lovecraft's creations are explained by the properties of higher dimensions, they become so much easier to understand. It was the first Peel story published, appearing in the anthology *Horrors Beyond*. It was also the quickest story David ever sold, being accepted within a week of submission.

"Resurgence" was a fun story to write, but *oh my god* the research involved! Not only did John have to create shoggoths that respected Lovecraft's vision and Curran's continuation, but he found himself putting flora and fauna in Argentina that don't actually exist, destroying a real Australian ship (sorry, *Ballarat*!) and figuring out how far from a nuclear blast you have to be to survive relatively unscathed.

And he's also terribly sorry about the Sydney Opera House. But it had to be done.

"Weapon Grade" is a direct sequel to "Resurgence". Peel was dying of radiation poison, so a clever means for him to escape death had to be found, and hopefully the means by which he did so is satisfactory. Like "False Containment" and

"Impossible Object" this story is more science fiction than horror, and again focuses on the ideas coming out of the theoretical physics sciences of our times.

We wanted a climatic conclusion to the collection, one that was penned as a true collaboration. Using as a base an article that David wrote again for *The Black Seal* magazine, "The Spiraling Worm" was born. The longest story in the collection, we hoped to really flesh out Dixon and Peel, finding their humanness and their purpose. We think we did so — but we also hope that it's a non-stop action adventure through the jungle with monsters, madness and heavy firepower, and that it provides all of our characters and previous plot threads with a fitting ending for this collection.

We'll write more Dixon/Peel/Figgs stories, of course — and there are other wonderful authors who have expressed interest in joining our little coterie. One such story already exists, a collaboration between David and Brian M. Sammons entitled "Stomach Acid". It can be found in *Lovecraft's Disciples* #5 published by Rainfall Books.

H.P. Lovecraft was not only a seminal figure in the horror field, but the man was also generous — he gladly shared his worlds with other writers, most of them amateurs who wanted simply to play in the vast arena HPL created. David and John share that sense of play; writing is fun, dammit! And a two-person dance, while satisfying, can't compare to a crowd of people moshing and mixing, so we're opening up our world to a few others — and then maybe a few others — and who knows where things are going to lead.

Finally, we'd like to thank the following people whose support was and has always been invaluable: our wives Suzanne Leonard and Elizabeth Sunseri, C.J. Henderson for his wonderful introduction and encouragement, Lynn Willis for his due diligent role as editor and sponsor of this collection, Tim

Curran, William Jones and Deborah Jones of Elder Signs Press, Brian M. Sammons, Adam Crossingham, Dan Harms, James Ambuehl and everyone else who's delved into the rich earth that HPL revealed to us, planting seeds and growing strange, wonderful, fecund plants that grow in terrifying directions.

David Conyers,
Adelaide, South Australia

John Sunseri,
Portland, Oregon, 2007.

ABOUT THE AUTHORS

Davidvid Conyers is an Australian author residing in Adelaide. His science fiction has been short-listed for the Aeon, Aurealis and Ditmar Awards, while his dark fiction has appeared in numerous anthologies including *Agog! Ripping Reads, Arkham Tales, Hardboiled Cthulhu, Horrors Beyond,* and *Macabre.* Between 2004 and 2006 he was the Associate Editor for *Book of Dark Wisdom.* Once an engineer who worked on remote outback pipelines and mining sites, he later made the switch to marketing communications. www.davidconyers.com

JOHN SUNSERI lives in Portland, Oregon with his wife. He manages a restaurant, writes at night and on weekends, and spends the occasional Thursday afternoon serving as an avatar for Nyarlathotep, though sometimes he cancels out so he can go play pool and drink beer with friends. His email address is john_sunseri@yahoo.com, and he'd love to get feedback on *The Spiraling Worm.*

ADDITIONAL CALL OF CTHULHU® FICTION TITLES

THE BOOK OF DZYAN

Mme. Blavatsky's famous transcribed messages from beyond, the mysterious *Book of Dzyan*, the heart of the sacred books of Kie-te, are said to have been known only to Tibetan mystics. Quotations from *Dzyan* form the core of her closely-argued *The Secret Doctrine*, the most influential single book of occult knowledge to emerge from the nineteenth century. The text of this book reproduces nearly all of *Book of Dzyan* that Blavatsky transcribed. It also includes long excerpts from her Secret Doctrine as well as from the Society of Psychical Research's 1885 report concerning phenomena witnessed by members of the Theosophical Society. There are notes and additional shorter materials. Editor Tim Maroney's biographical essay starts off the book, a fascinating portrait of an amazing woman.

5 3/8" x 8 3/8", 272 pages, $15.95. Stock #6027; ISBN 1-56882-198-0.

THE COMPLETE PEGANA

Lord Dunsany's fantasy writing had a profound impact on the Dreamlands stories of H. P. Lovecraft. This original collection is composed of newly edited versions of Lord Dunsany's first two books, *The Gods of Pegana* (1905) and *Time and the Gods* (1906). Three additional stories round out the book, the first time that all the Pegana stories have appeared within one book. Edited and introduced by S. T. Joshi.

5 3/8" x 8 3/8", 242 pages, $14.95. Stock #6016; ISBN 1-56882-190-5.

THE DISCIPLES OF CTHULHU
Second Revised Edition

The disciples of Cthulhu are a varied lot. In Mythos stories they are obsessive, loners, dangerous, seeking not to convert others so much as to use them. But writers of the stories are also Cthulhu's disciples, and they are the proselytizers, bringing new members into the fold. Published in 1976, the first edition of *The Disciples of Cthulhu* was the first professional, all-original Cthulhu Mythos anthology. One of the stories, "The Tugging" by Ramsey Campbell, was nominated for a Science Fiction Writers of America Nebula Award, perhaps the only Cthulhu Mythos story that has received such recognition. This second edition of Disciples presents nine stories of Mythos horror, seven from the original edition and two new stories. Selected by Edward P. Berglund.

5 3/8" x 8 3/8", 272 pages, $15.95. Stock #6011; ISBN 1-56882-202-2.

THE DUNWICH CYCLE

In the Dunwiches of the world the old ways linger. Safely distant from bustling cities, ignorant of science, ignored by civilization, dull enough never to excite others, poor enough never to provoke envy, these are safe harbors for superstition and seemingly meaningless custom. Sometimes they shelter truths that have seeped invisibly across the centuries. The people are unlearned but not unknowing of things once great and horrible, of times when the rivers ran red and dark shudderings ruled the air. Here are nine stories set where horror begins, with a general introduction and individual story prefaces by Robert M. Price.

5 3/8" x 8 3/8", 288 pages, $16.95. Stock #6010; ISBN 1-56882-196-4.

THE HASTUR CYCLE
Second Revised Edition

The stories in this book represent the evolving trajectory of such notions as Hastur, the King in Yellow, Carcosa, the Yellow Sign, Yuggoth, and the Lake of Hali. A succession of writers from Ambrose Bierce to Ramsey Campbell and Karl Edward Wagner have explored and embellished these concepts so that the sum of the tales has become an evocative tapestry of hypnotic dread and terror, a mythology distinct from yet overlapping the Cthulhu Mythos. Here for the first time is a comprehensive collection of all the relevant tales. Selected and introduced by Robert M. Price.

5 3/8" x 8 3/8", 320 pages, $17.95. Stock #6020; ISBN 1-56882-192-1.

THE INNSMOUTH CYCLE

The decadent, smugly rotting, secret-filled town of Innsmouth is a supreme creation of Howard Philips Lovecraft. It so finely mixes the carnal and the metaphysical that writers continue to take inspiration from it. This new collection contains thirteen tales and three poems tracing the evolution of Innsmouth, from early tales by Dunsany, Chambers, and Cobb, through Lovecraft's "The Shadow Over Innsmouth" to modern tales by Rainey, Glasby, and others.

5 3/8" x 8 3/8", 240 pages, $14.95. Stock # 6017; ISBN 1-56882-199-9.

THE ITHAQUA CYCLE

The elusive, supernatural Ithaqua roams the North Woods and the wastes beyond, as invisible as the wind. Hunters and travelers fear the cold and isolation of the North; they fear the advent of the mysterious, malignant Wind-Walker even more. This collection includes the progenitor tale "The Wendigo" by Algernon Blackwood, three stories by August Derleth, 8

and ten more from a spectrum of contemporary authors including Brian Lumley, Stephen Mark Rainey, and Pierre Comtois.

5 3/8" x 8 3/8", 260 pages, $15.95. Stock #6021; ISBN 1-56882-191-3.

MADE IN GOATSWOOD

Ramsey Campbell is acknowledged by many to be the greatest living writer of the horror tale in the English language. He is known to Mythos fans for the ancient and fearful portion of England's Severn Valley he evoked in narratives such as "The Moon Lens". This book contains eighteen all-new stories set in that part of the Valley, including a new story by Campbell himself, his first Severn Valley tale in decades. This volume was published in conjunction with a 1995 trip by Campbell to the United States. Stories selected by Scott David Aniolowski.

5 3/8" x 8 3/8", 288 pages, $16.95. Stock #6009; ISBN 1-56882-197-2.

THE NYARLATHOTEP CYCLE

The mighty Messenger of the Outer Gods, Nyarlathotep has also been known to deliver tidings from the Great Old Ones. He is the only Outer God who chooses to personify his presence on our planet. A god of a thousand forms, he comes to Earth to mock, to wreak havoc, and to spur on humanity's self-destructive urges. This volume of stories and poems illustrates the ubiquitous presence of Nyarlathotep and shows him in several different guises. Among them, his presence as Nephren-Ka, the dread Black Pharaoh of dynastic Egypt, dominates. The thirteen stories include a Lin Carter novella. Selected and introduced by Robert M. Price.

5 3/8" x 8 3/8", 256 pages, $14.95. Stock #6019; ISBN 1-56882-200-6.

SINGERS OF STRANGE SONGS

Most readers acknowledge Brian Lumley as the superstar of British horror writers. With the great popularity of his *Necroscope* series, he is one of the best known horror authors in the world. Devoted fans know that his roots are deep in the Cthulhu Mythos, with which most of his early work deals. This volume contains eleven new tales in that vein, as well as three reprints of excellent but little-known work by Lumley. This book was published in conjunction with Lumley's 1997 trip to the United States.

5 3/8" x 8 3/8", 256 pages, $12.95. Stock #6014; ISBN 1-56882-104-2.

SONG OF CTHULHU

Lovecraft's most famous portraitist was Richard Upton Pickman, whose ironic canvases of ghouls and humanity's relation to ghouls have become famous, even though they existed only in Lovecraft's keen imagination. Among HPL's writers, Randolph Carter and the tragically destined Edward Pickman Derby stand out. And of course there is Erich Zann, the inhumanly-great violist, whose powers are detailed in "The Music of Erich Zann," included in this volume.

In HPL, the artist is the detached observer of society, a cultural reporter of the sort whose function has since become familiar. But Lovecraft also saw a deeper role, one such as played by Henry Wilcox the sculptor in "The Call of

Cthulhu": "Wilcox's imagination had been keenly affected. [He had] an unprecedented dream of great cyclopean cities of titan blocks and sky-flung monoliths, all dripping with green ooze and sinister with latent horror. . . . [and] a voice that was not a voice; a chaotic sensation which only fancy could transmute into sound, but which he attempted to render by the almost unpronounceable jumble of letters, *Cthulhu fhtagn.*"

Here are nineteen Mythos tales, melodies of prophecy and deceit. *Cthulhu fhtagn!*

5 3/8" x 8 3/8", 222 pages, $13.95. Stock #6032; ISBN 1-56882-117-4.

TALES OUT OF INNSMOUTH

Innsmouth is a half-deserted, seedy little town on the North Shore of Massachusetts. It is rarely included on any map of the state. Folks in neighboring towns shun those who come from Innsmouth, and murmur about what goes on there. They try not to mention the place in public, for Innsmouth has ways of quelling gossip, and of taking revenge on troublemakers. Here are ten new tales and three reprints concerning the town, the hybrids who live there, the strange city rumored to exist nearby under the sea, and those who nightly lurch and shamble down the fog-bound streets of Innsmouth.

5 3/8" x 8 3/8", 294 pages, $16.95. Stock #6024; ISBN 1-56882-201-4.

THE XOTHIC LEGEND CYCLE

The late Lin Carter was a prolific writer and anthologist of horror and fantasy with over eighty titles to his credit. His tales of Mythos horror are loving tributes to H. P. Lovecraft's "revision" tales and to August Derleth's stories of Hastur and the *R'lyeh Text*. This is the first collection of Carter's Mythos tales; it includes his intended novel, *The Terror Out of Time*. Most of the stories in this collection have been unavailable for some time. Selected and introduced by Robert M. Price.

5 3/8" x 8 3/8", 288 pages, $16.95. Stock #6013; ISBN 1-56882-195-6.

All titles are available from bookstores and game stores. You can also order directly from **www.Chaosium.com**, your source for Cthulhiana and more. To order by credit card via the net, visit our web site, 24 hours a day. To order via phone, call 1-510-583-1000, 9 A.M. to 4 P.M. Pacific time.